The Little Red Book

by

D B Minter

ISBN: 978-1-918038-83-5

The book is dedicated to Deirdre with love and gratitude.

"Remember tonight, for it is the beginning of always"

Dante Alighieri

The Gramophone Club members:

Greg Witton

Florence Witton

Tobias (Toby) Elden

Verity Elden

Ronald Henrow

Dulcie Henrow

Benjamin Tiller

Hildegard Tiller

Alexander (Alex) Sutton

Violet Smithson

Dorothy Bateman

Hannah Longsmith

Bettina Emberton

The cast of Le Nozze di Figaro:

Figaro   Finley Reason

Susanna   Susie Lattern

The Count   Sebastian Moran

The Countess   Lydia Moran

Cherubino   Dominic Rivers

Barbarina   Barbara Fenlon

Antonio   Tony Lattern

Featuring Ricky Wenger

The Cast of Don Giovanni;

Don Giovanni   Ricky Wenger

Leporello   Dominic Wegner

Donna Anna   Anna Kimber-Smythe

Don Ottavio   Archibald Horatio-Irvine

Zerlina   Zoe Billing

Masetto   Matt Foster

The Commendatore   Lord Smythe

Featuring Finley and Susie Reason – Sebastian and Lydia
Moran

The cast of Cosi Fan Tutte

Don Alfonso   Sebastian Moran

Fiordiligi   Bridget Kennedy

Dorabella   Niamh Kennedy

Ferrando   Connor Clarkson and Roberto De Luca

Guglielmo   Sandor (Sandy) Kovacs and Luigi Conti

Featuring Ricky Wenger – Dominic Rivers – Lydia Moran –
Finley and Susie Reason

As 'The Little Red Book' is the second novel in the authors
proposed trilogy of novels with an operatic connection, several
of the characters from the first novel of the series, 'The
Incidental Legacy of Carlo Negrini' (2024) make guest
appearances in 'The Little Red Book.'

PART ONE...

THE GRAMOPHONE CLUB

CHAPTER 1

A small commuter town in Hertfordshire, England

1992

I lived a quiet life in a very pleasant part of the county – thirty odd miles from Central London, which enjoyed a reliable fast train service into the capital, serving many residents of the town, who worked in London but preferred to reside in a greener environment.

My name was Alexander Sutton – known to everyone as Alex. I was a single man, aged forty-nine. Being tall, I was considered a good looking young man, but I now felt that my age was catching up with me. I was one of those commuters who took the train to London every morning, as I was an administrator for the UK's Labour Party, working at their Central London headquarters. I would be taking early retirement next year, when I reached fifty with a decent enough pension to be able to continue to enjoy a reasonable standard of living.

My residence was a 1960s two bedroom purpose built maisonette. I owned the first floor of the building, my neighbour owning the ground floor, with both owners having separate entrances. I entered via the back of the building, which had a mature, decent size garden, which contained an old oak tree. The back garden was exclusively mine, with my neighbour having to make do with the small front garden. A short staircase led up to the living quarters. The main living area consisted of a large high ceiling spacious living room, a self-contained dining room and a smallish kitchen. The master bedroom was again a large airy room overlooking the garden, with a lovely country outlook beyond the garden. A small second bedroom and bathroom completed the living quarters. I loved my home, which possessed a special cosiness, suiting my quiet lifestyle.

I was a classical music lover, being particularly passionate about opera. I regularly attended concerts and opera in London after work, taking the train back home following performances. I had been thinking of late of extending my social circle locally and with retirement creeping up, I would have more time to meet like-minded people with similar interests. I'm also considering writing a novel – something with an opera connection to the plot.

With that in mind, when I was next in our local library, I studied the notice board, and amongst requests for dog walkers and coffee morning groups, I noticed a small notice tucked away in the bottom corner of the board advertising for new members of a gramophone club. My interest was immediately piqued and I made a note of the telephone number of a Greg Witton, who was the individual I needed to contact.

Greg was delighted to hear from me and he gave me the background to the club. It was founded ten years ago by Greg and a few local friends, and the members met every fortnight and took turns to host an evening in their respective residences. The host chose what records to play – mostly vinyl LPs, but more and more CDs were beginning to replace member's collections. It wasn't as random as it seemed. A *little red book* listed every piece of music that had been played over the ten years. Each host then added their choice of records to the book, which was handed over to the next host in line for the honours to list their own upcoming programme, ensuring a variety of repertoire and not too much repetition of popular pieces.

Generally, the evenings were themed around a particular enthusiasm of the host, and this made for interesting debates on the different musical tastes and dislikes of the various members – which could get heated at times, but was always in good humour. Tea, coffee and cake, was served by the host during the interval, when the social aspect of the evening took shape, as the only rule of the club was that the music itself was to be listened to in absolute silence. A programme note was printed, or handwritten and distributed, with the more confident members adding a few spoken words about the theme of the evening, and about the individual pieces of music chosen. It was an absolutely excellent arrangement, a simple concept but highly effective and no membership fees were ever involved.

Greg, whose house was a few streets away, was the host for my initiation evening to the group. Greg's wife, Florence, stayed out of the living room during the performance, as she wasn't a musical enthusiast, but joined the group at the interval as she served the refreshments. Florence was unfortunately, mildly asthmatic, which made her seem older than her husband, who was in his mid-forties. Greg was rather nondescript in the looks department, but was slim and fit, being a keen cyclist. He worked at the county's pharmaceutical company, cycling to work every day. Greg and Florence had one teenage daughter. Greg was highly respected by the rest of the group, as he was the founder of the club, but in all honesty, he came over to me as a bit of a dull dog. His musical tastes were strictly on the mainstream side, and he had an aversion to solo piano music. Any member who programmed it during their hosting evening got short shrift from Greg. To be fair to Greg, his main gripe with piano music was more to do with the way the instrument was recorded than the music itself. His argument was that recording engineers hadn't really mastered how to get the best sound from the piano on disc and were in some cases doing a disservice to the pianist, and to the composer – in this, he possibly had a point.

Two couples attending were there as a sort of foursome, as the couples were evidently very close friends, knowing each other for a long time. The four were near neighbours, living about five miles away from our village-feel town. What was interesting to me was how different the two men were from each other, both in personalities, and in musical tastes. Tobias Elden, who was originally from Wales, and his wife Verity, loved the nineteenth-century Romantic composers, and were also keen on opera, whilst their friends, Ronald Henrow, and his wife Dulcie, were averse to Romantic music, especially composers such as Bruckner and Mahler, as well as having no time for opera. Their musical tastes lay more in the baroque and renaissance periods, and certain English twentieth-century figures, such a Benjamin Britten and Michael Tippett. Tobias was a jolly chap in his mid-fifties, recently retired from a successful career in the media. He possessed a ready wit and his cultural interests were wide ranging, including literature and poetry. I took a liking to him immediately. Tobias's wife Verity, a retired hospital administrator, was a pretty looking woman. The pair seemed to be a most devoted couple, and although were long term married, remained childless.

Ronald Henrow, from a small town in the county of Gloucestershire, was also in his mid-forties and was exceptionally tall, with a slightly awkward gait. His speaking voice contained a certain preciousness, almost camp in its delivery, but as I found out later, his wife, Dulcie, ten years older than Ronald, had arranged elocution lessons for him, to rid him of his country accent, but the lessons hadn't quite worked out, leaving Ronald with a strange 'no-man's land' accent. Back in Gloucestershire, Ronald had been the manager of a record store, whilst Dulcie, came from a posh, fairly wealthy and well connected family, with members of the Tory government being family friends.

Ronald had been on a visit to the small cathedral city of St Albans, in the county of Hertfordshire, and had suffered a minor car accident whilst there. It was at the accident and emergency department of the local hospital following the accident, that he'd met Dulcie, who'd been a nursing Sister at the hospital. Dulcie used her family connections to arrange employment for Ronald at the Ministry of Defence, in an administrative role at their Central London office. Ronald sang in a choir and had taken several musical examinations, and although music was an amateur pastime for him, he took his studies very seriously. The pair, despite their very different backgrounds, eventually married, Ronald moving to St. Albans. They'd been married for a much shorter period than their friends, the Eldens, and like them, remained childless. Verity and Dulcie have been best friends for many years; both had had long-term careers with the English National Health Service.

Hildegard and Benjamin Tiller, another couple who were founder members of the club, were older than the Eldens and the Henrows – more mid-sixties than mid-forties. The Tiller's lived in a small pretty village about nine miles away. I immediately felt a warmth and kindness about them when we were first introduced. Benjamin was a retired engineer, originally from Yorkshire, as tall as Ronald, but chunkier, without Ronald's preciousness – he was what one would describe as a man's man. I understood that they were the first couple to introduce CDs to the club. Benjamin, with his engineering background, was perhaps more interested in recording technique than the music itself, but evidently, he'd never bored the group with science. Hildegard had a European background and seemed to be the real music lover of the couple, with absolute concentration on whatever piece that was on the turntable or in the CD machine. They were a long-term married couple with adult children and grandchildren. Hildegard and Benjamin were devoted to each other.

Violet Smithson, an elderly local widow, was also a founding member of the club, her musical tastes being on the old fashioned side, which consisted mainly of English composers from the turn of the century, such as Hubert Parry, Charles Villiers Stanford, who was actually Irish, and the younger, Albert Coates, who'd written music of a popular style. On the rare occasion when Violet hosted an evening, I'm told that the music was played on a small vintage 'Dansette' record player that would hardly do justice to the pieces she'd chosen. The group, being a polite lot, would never have embarrassed her with negative comments, either about her choice of music, or about the less than acceptable reproduction sound of her record player.

Dorothy Bateman was another local widow, but younger than violet, and attended regularly, but never hosted an evening herself. She generally caught up with her knitting whilst the music was being played.

Besides the core members of the group, new couples and singles attended gramophone evenings as a curiosity event, and in most cases they'd never attended again. Although the regular members were always most welcoming to new attendees, the newbie's probably felt that they'd be outsiders to the main clique, and, if their musical knowledge was less than up to scratch, they'd gone home feeling that the forum wasn't for them. I, on the hand, despite some initial scepticism towards me from the founder members, decided from the very first evening, that this was a group that I very much wanted to be part of. During the playing of a Beethoven symphony recording, chosen by the evening's host, Greg Witton, I was beginning to think about the sort of programme I'd put together for my first hosting evening.

Three months later, having attended six gramophone evening, it became my turn to host an event. I'd noticed that looking through *the little red book* of previous programmes, opera had been neglected. Popular arias, choruses, overtures and orchestral intermezzos from well-known operas appeared from time to time in mixed recital programmes, but whole acts of opera had never been done in the ten years existence of the gramophone club.

My plan was to play complete acts, of the three Da *Ponte/ Mozart* operas, over several hosting evenings. I would start with *Le Nozze di Figaro,* which was the first opera in the series – continue with *Don Giovanni,* and, conclude with *Così fan tutte.* For my first evening, I decided to play the first two acts of *Figaro,* which would take up the second half of the evening. For a shorter first half, I chose Mozart's final symphony, No. 41, known as the *Jupiter.*

I picked a brand new recording of the *Jupiter* symphony, which I had recently purchased. The orchestra was the Chamber Orchestra of Europe, conducted by Nikolaus Harnoncourt. For the opera however, I went for a 1959 cherished recording from my collection, conducted by Carlo Maria Giulini, with an all star cast on the EMI label.

I printed out copies of the Italian text with an English translation, so that everyone would be able to follow the drama, the opera being a perfect combination of words and music. I also provided a brief summary of the plot at the top of the page.

I thought to say a few words about the librettist, Lorenzo Da Ponte, before the start of the second part of the evening, as an introduction to the opera. So much has been written about Mozart and everyone had seen Peter Schaffer's *Amadeus*, either the original play or the film version, but not so much was known about Da Ponte, who lived a most colourful life.

All the regulars turned up at my home for the gramophone evening, and were most curious as to what sort of programme I would present. A few new potential members, had also attended, including an attractive woman, who immediately caused a bit of a stir as she had the sort of looks that turned heads of both genders. Her name was Bettina Emberton. She'd been living in the area for three years, and like me, had seen the advert for the club in the local library. So what was so striking about Bettina? It seemed to me to be a combination of a winning smile, lovely dark brown hair and eyes, a slim but shapely figure and a friendly but not gushing manner. I couldn't quite detect her accent, but it wasn't a London or home-counties one, more like a refined northern accent. Chatting to Bettina during the interval, whilst everyone was tucking into my pre-prepared smoked salmon on savoury biscuits, fruit cake, with tea or coffee, Bettina told me that she was the owner of a dating agency based in the West End of London, and like me, commuted every day to her office.

I cleared the table of the interval snack, the chattering eventually died down, and everyone took to their seats. I put the first side of the recording of Mozart's *Le Nozze di Figaro* on the turntable and stood facing our little group of music lovers.

'Thanks everyone for attending my very first gramophone evening that I've been honoured to host, and to be able to indulge myself by choosing whatever music I wish to play, and foist upon you all – whether my choices are to your musical taste or not. Most importantly, I have made my first written contribution tc the club's little red book. *But of course, that's the beauty of our club... we listen to music that we wouldn't necessarily put on our own turntables. That way, each of us widens our own musical knowledge and experiences, which is an absolute brilliant concept – so my thanks go out to our founding members who devised the workings of the original idea, and have kept it going for the past ten years.*

I wish to say a few words about the librettist of the opera we are about to listen to, Lorenzo Da Ponte. Da Ponte was born in 1749 in Ceneda, now known as Vittorio Veneto, in The Republic of Venice. His birth name was Emmanuele Conegliano and he adopted the name of Da Ponte in 1763, when his father converted from Judaism to Christianity. Da Ponte trained for the priesthood and was ordained in 1773. Having moved to Venice, teaching Latin, Italian and French, Da Ponte also started to write poetry. But he was then banished from Venice for fifteen years for taking a mistress, and consorting with the infamous libertine, Casanova. He managed to obtain an introduction to the composer, Antonio Salieri, known to us today mostly from the play Amadeus, *and with his help, became the librettist to the Italian Theatre in Vienna. Besides the three opera libretto's he wrote for Mozart, Da Ponte was the librettist for twenty-eight opera's by eleven different composers. Due to debt and bankruptcy, Da Ponte emigrated to New York, after spending time in Paris and London. In New York, Da Ponte dabbled in teaching, distillery, grocery and opening a book shop. He became the first Catholic/ Jewish professor of Italian literature, at New York's Columbia College. He also introduced opera to the city with performances of Mozart's* Don Giovanni, *as well as performances of the music of Rossini. At the age of seventy-nine, he became a US citizen, and at the age of eighty-four, he founded the New York Opera Company. He died in New York in 1838, aged eighty-nine...*

Phew...what a man!

Let's now hear the first two acts of Le Nozze di Figaro.

I carefully held the arm of the turntable, moving the stylus onto the vinyl, and the overture commenced.

At the end of act two, following the amazing ensemble that concludes the act, the small audience clapped and smiled, despite the time overrunning its normal scheduled finish.

As the group were leaving to go home, thanking me for a lovely evening of music listening and the interval repast, Bettina took me aside, handing me her business card, and saying quietly that I should give her a call, if I felt that her dating services could be of any interest to me. I was rather taken aback at being propositioned, business wise, by Bettina, as one of the unwritten rules of the gramophone club was that commercial discussions or sales promotions of any description was taboo at musical evenings. Once everyone had left, I put the business card away in my bureau with the thought, as to whether Bettina only attended the event looking for potential clients, and that we would probably not see her again at a gramophone club evening. On reflection, I would be disappointed if that indeed was the case, as I found Bettina to be an extremely attractive woman and she looked vaguely familiar; had I met her somewhere before?

Starting a series of gramophone evenings, devoted to the three Mozart/Da Ponte operatic masterpieces, had given me food for thought about my promise to myself, to write a novel.

Over the following few days, with nervous trepidation, I started
to put pen to paper.

11

CHAPTER 2

I didn't yet have a title for my novel but due to immersing myself in the Da Ponte-Mozart trilogy of operas for the gramophone club events that I was hosting, I wanted my text to contain reference points to the operas *Le Nozze di Figaro*, *Don Giovanni* and *Cosi Fan Tutte*.

ALEX'S NOVEL

OPERA (1)

Brighton
1960

'Where will we stay, Ricky, when we arrive at Brighton station?'

 Dominic turned to his friend whilst the two of them were sitting on the train, travelling from London to Brighton.

'I spoke to my old friend Finley on the blower the other day, and he said we'd have no problem finding a bed and breakfast guest house down West Street – there are loads of them in the street leading from the station to the sea front.'

 'That's great Rick and I'm looking forward to meeting Finley, you've told me so much about him – he sounds like a *brill* character.'

'Fin's alright mate – he was the best barber in the *Big Smoke,* and I can tell you that Brighton's lucky to have had him.'

'If he had been doing so well in London Rick, why did he move to Brighton?'

'*Bird,* mate; Susie, his girl, lived in Brighton – they were planning to get married.'

'Blimey that's a big step – he must be mad about the girl' said Dominic with a thoughtful look and a furrowed brow.

'The problem being is that Susie works for her ladyship, Lydia Moran, and the lady's other half, Lord Sebastian Moran, had the *hot's* for Fin's Susie, and he was determined to have his wicked way with her.'

'But surely Fin would sort out the posh git, His Lordship?'

'Well yes, but it's complicated cause Fin owed his lordship loads of dosh, and had threatened to go to the old fuzz if Fin didn't pay up. Besides, from what I heard, Seb was a nasty old bugger, despite being able to turn the charm on with the birds.'

Fin had been absolutely right – it took the boys no time at all to find accommodation in Brighton's West Street, having passed several houses with a 'no vacancy' sign on their front window. It was a rather dilapidated tall old house, with a grumpy, scruffily dressed owner, who signed them in and carefully counted the cash payments taken from the boys. He offered the key to the room, which was situated on the third floor, without the usual courtesy of showing them the room before taking their money. The small room with two single beds was in poor condition, looking as if it hadn't seen a duster in a month of Sundays. The bathroom and one separate toilet were along a dark corridor – to be shared with all the other guests with rooms on the second and third floors. A ground floor bathroom and toilet serviced the rooms on the first floor.

'Let's get something to eat Dom,' said Ricky once the boys had unpacked their rucksacks, using the bathroom and changed into clean clothes.

As far as Ricky was concerned he was in Brighton for one reason only...to pick up as much crumpet as he could, chat them up on the seafront, then have his way with them on the beaches after dusk.

If that didn't work, his friend, Fin, knew all the local pubs in Brighton where the dolly birds tended to congregate. The birds that frequented the pubs were usually up for some hot action.

Dominic, aged seventeen, was four years younger than Ricky, still inexperienced with the opposite sex, and shocked at his friend's casual approach to picking up girls for sex. Dom was used to watching romantic films and following the pop music of the day, with their lyrics of falling in love, and fantasised about attending the local clubs. He'd envisaged dancing to the music of Elvis Presley, looked to meeting someone special whom he could fall in love with, and hopefully, the love would be reciprocated.

As well as having had different attitudes towards the opposite sex, Ricky and Dominic's food tastes were also poles apart. Ricky thought of food as fuel to consume as quickly as possible – so the nearest Wimpy Bar would be his perfect destination for a bite to eat, before going on the prowl to attempt to satisfy his lust. On the other hand, Dominic enjoyed good food, his mother being a fabulous cook, so he was looking for a budget bistro around the town to tuck into some decent food. After much discussion the boys decided to each go their own way for the rest of the day and evening, and meet back at the boarding house later that night.

The trip to Brighton was the first time Dominic Rivers had travelled away from home without his parents... but why did he choose to go with Ricky Wenger, who wasn't a close friend, being four years older? Ricky and Dominic were neighbours in the North London suburb of Southgate, but Dominic best friend had been Ricky's younger brother, Melvyn. The two boys, Melvyn and Dominic, had been inseparable, both at school, where they'd sat next to each other, and, out of school, spending most of their free time in each other's houses. They were like twin brothers and very much alike – well behaved, polite and both keen on their studies.

Melvyn's older brother, Ricky, was the exact opposite – wild and mischievous, with little interest in school work. At the age of thirteen, Melvyn was stuck down with leukaemia, and died.

Dominic was totally bereaved and in denial – still turned up at the Wengers' house, expecting to see his great friend. During that period, Ricky, who was also grieving for his younger brother, felt sorry for Dominic, and befriended him, despite the age difference and not having much in common with each other. So over the following years, the two lads hung out together, which enabled Dominic to keep close to the Wenger family, as being in the house where he and Melvyn had spent so much time with each other.

Dominic and Melvyn had shared good and bad experiences together, in their few short years as boyhood friends. One of the highlights was their Saturday morning trips to the cinema, where they'd watched all the latest cowboy films. Later, when they were a bit older, they'd visited the cinema on a Saturday afternoon and became fans of musicals. They'd watched films such as *Seven Brides for Seven Brothers, Carmen Jones* and *Kiss Me Kate*. The boys had been entranced and had sung the hit tunes together when they'd be back in one or the other's houses. There was a school trip to the West End, to see a production of Shakespeare's play, *Hamlet*. Being Shakespeare's longest play – it was just too much for ten year old boys to absorb – the play had gone well their heads. However, the boys loved being in the West End with all their bright lights and so many people mingling around – it all seemed so exciting, and they'd couldn't wait to be grown up, to be able to spend regular time uptown.

The boys' class teacher was Mrs Lunger. Her slim attractive looks were deceptive as she was ferociously strict. Although it was not particularly unusual for the early 1950s to be a supporter of communism in general and of the Soviet Union in particular, Mrs Lunger's absolute adoration for its leader, Joseph Stalin, was total. She would speak about Stalin with love in her eyes, and on 5 March 1953, when it was announced that the great father of the nation had died, Mrs Lunger was in floods of tears all day long.

Dominic found maths extremely difficult and instead of trying to help him understand the subject, Mrs Lunger mocked him, and in front of the whole class, announced that the young Rivers would end up selling matchboxes on Petticoat Lane Market if his maths work did not improve. Melvyn, who was good at maths, told Dominic to ignore Mrs Lunger's stupid remarks and that he would help his friend with the subject – which he did, but Dominic still failed his 11-plus exam.

Mrs Lunger had strange ideas about what current news events should be debated in class with ten year old boys. The sordid details of two controversial state execution cases that occurred during 1953 were endlessly explained to the boys, despite some of the them finding gruesome aspects of both cases extremely upsetting. In January of that year, the nineteen year old Derek Bentley suffered death by hanging, in London, as punishment for the murder of a policeman. Mrs Lunger spent a whole morning explaining to her pupils the full facts of the case. A planned burglary by two lads, sixteen-year old Christopher Craig, and nineteen-year old Derek Bailey, had gone wrong, and in the melee, a policeman was shot dead. What made the case so scandalous was that it was Craig who shot the policeman, with Bentley, supposedly, shouting 'Let him have it.' Legally, Craig was too young to be executed, so Bentley paid the ultimate price.

In June of the same year, 1953, in the US, a married couple, Ethel and Julius Rosenberg, were put to death in the electric chair – their crime being passing secrets to the Russians. Mrs Lunger was beside herself, being a strong supporter of the Soviets and communism in general. She wrote letters to the British government, requesting them to petition their American counterparts, for a reprieve. In any case, the whole case against the couple had been extremely controversial, as a lot of commentators expressed doubt of the couple's guilt, especially, Ethel Rosenberg. The death of Stalin and then the Rosenberg case, unhinged Mrs Lunger. She started to act in a strange way in the classroom. In the middle of a lesson, she would suddenly stop teaching, sit down and cry. The boys had been embarrassed and didn't know what to do; they'd just shuffle around on their chairs, looking at each other, shrugging their shoulders, with some of the boys putting a finger to the side of their heads and turning the finger around, indicating that poor Mrs Lunger had a screw loose. Then suddenly, Mrs Lunger would pull herself together, stand up straight and had continued teaching in her familiar emphatic way, as if nothing had happened. Eventually, the head master got to hear of Mrs Unger's strange behaviour, and she was asked to take long term sickness leave. She never came back to teach at the school.

One of the final acts Mrs Lunger performed, before her mental collapse, was to take the boys in her class to visit the law courts in London. For some reason, it was the divorce courts she was particularly keen for them to experience in session. On the other hand, perhaps she had already started her mental breakdown, as why would one take a class of ten year old boys to the divorce courts? Dominic and Melvyn, sitting on an uncomfortable bench in the public area, had to listen to a very distressed middle-aged woman explaining to the court, how abusive her husband had been to her, insisting on unnatural sexual practices. When the judge asked the woman to clarify what she meant by unnatural, she whispered the word 'anal' and then burst into tears. The two friends, and the other boys in the group, were totally confused by the woman's narration, not yet being of an age of sexual awakening. The more sensitive of the group, which included Dominic and Melvyn, wondered, why the woman, who had not done anything wrong herself, had to endure such public humiliation, to obtain a divorce from a man, who seemed to be an absolute rotten husband.

CHAPTER 3

Along the sea front, Brighton morphed into Hove. Hove was a more genteel part of the seaside resort. A night club, called Downtown, situated just off the main road on the corner of a residential street, nightly attracted a full house of teenagers, who jigged along to the top ten records of the hit parade. But of course, the youngsters were also there to meet members of the opposite sex, and many holiday romances had been conceived during a visit to the club.

Dominic felt nervous as he made his way along the sea front on his way to the club, as he'd never been to a club on his own before. He had tagged along with Ricky, to a couple of clubs in London's West End, but whilst Ricky was in his element, chatting up the girls, Dominic had felt out of his depth. He'd not been old enough to have made any headway with girls that he considered too sophisticated for him, or to even attempt to flirt with them.

Being the height of the summer season in the middle of August, Downtown was packed, with Dominic joining the queue to gain entry, as well as showing ID, to confirm that he was over the age of sixteen, which was the youngest age the club allowed attendees to be. Dominic was sure that some of the girls were younger than sixteen, but the doorman turned a blind eye to them, if they were pretty! They were much stricter with the boys – many were turned away if they seemed young, and their ID was deemed inauthentic. As well as, some boys got turned away just because the doorman didn't like the look of them.

Dominic had bought a coke from the non-alcoholic bar and stood at the side of the dance floor, watching couples jiving and doing the twist, to the music of Chubby Checker, Bobby Darin, The Everly Brothers, Connie Francis, Paul Anka, Roy Orbison and of course, Elvis Presley.

'Are you in Brighton on holiday?'

Dominic asked the girl standing on her own by the edge of the dance floor, whilst the disc jockey was playing a quieter Elvis number.

'Yes, I'm in Brighton with my parents... having travelled down from Manchester for a week's holiday. My name is Rosalind, what's yours?'

'Dominic.'

'That's a nice name... Let's dance.'

She grabbed his hand leading him onto the dance area. They just caught the final verse of the Elvis romantic song, as they leaned into each other, Dominic putting his hand around Rosalind's waist, getting a whiff of her lovely smelling perfume, whilst shuffling around the floor. The music changed to Chubby Checker's new dance craze, the twist, and as both of them wanted to show the other that they were up with the latest; they got straight into the groove, each showing off their moves.

Dominic couldn't believe his luck – never before in the London clubs had he had the courage to approach girls; here, the first girl he'd chatted to immediately reciprocated, and they spent the rest of the evening together, breaking sweat with the fast numbers and snuggling up together for the slow ones. Dominic was in seventh heaven.

Rosalind Gerstein, aged sixteen, had been looking forward to spending a week in Brighton. Her school friend, Denise, who had holidayed there during the previous summer, had said how lively the resort was and that it was a great place to meet boys. Rosalind was in Brighton with her mum and dad, staying in the famous upmarket Grand Hotel on the seafront, her dad being a successful business man in Manchester. Although Rosalind had an older brother, he had gone off on holiday with his mates, so it was just the three of them in Brighton.

Dominic walked Rosalind back to the Grand Hotel, hand in hand, along the sea front, stopping to kiss several times along the way. They'd arranged to spend time together the following day. Dominic skipped his way back to West Street, feeling lightheaded and very happy having spent the evening with a beautiful girl, who he couldn't wait to see again.

Ricky was back at the guest house, also in a chipper mood as he'd scored with a local girl that he'd picked up on the beach. Dominic related the story of his evening, his meeting with Rosalind, but Ricky showed little interest in a boy-meets-girl romance, holding hands and passionless kisses. He had grown out of all that and was interested only in real sexual conquests – the more variety the better.

'Rosalind and I are spending the day together tomorrow.'

'Hang about mate – not so fast, Dom. We're meeting Finley tomorrow and I told him you'd be coming along.'

 Dominic, in his excitement of meeting Rosalind, had totally forgotten about the arrangement to meet with Finley.

 'Can I bring Rosalind along?'

'Don't be daft mate – no way; Fin wouldn't want a sixteen-year old teeny bopper bird to cramp his style. He's got serious crap to sort out with Lord Sebastian and needs my help.'

'But why did I need to go? After all, I'm only a seventeen-year old boy and don't understand financial matters'

 Ricky, grabbed Dominic's lapels and getting into his face made things clear, brooking no argument.

'Listen my friend – I agreed to go on holiday with you because Fin asked for my help, and he said to bring a mate with me for back-up to help intimidate his Lordship if he'd didn't get the message to lay-off trying to get his Susie into bed – *cap ire!'*

Early the next morning, Dominic telephoned the Grand Hotel and asked to speak with Miss Gerstein, who'd been a guest at the hotel with her parents, Mr and Mrs Gerstein.

'I'm sorry, sir. there's no responses from their respective bedrooms. They could be in the breakfast dining room. Would you like me to Tannoy for Miss Gerstein to come to reception to take your call?'

'That would be kind of you'.

Dominic heard the Tannoy in the background, requesting Miss Gerstein to please go to the reception.

'Hello Rosalind, Dominic here. So sorry to disturb you whilst at breakfast.'

'That's OK – I had finished my breakfast anyway. What time to you want to meet and will you pick me up at the hotel?'

Dominic feeling quite awkward spoke hesitantly.

'Rosalind, I'm so sorry but I can't see you today. I forgot last night that I had promised the friend I'm on holiday with, that we'd visit an old mate of his today, and my friend insisted that I accompany him.'

'Ah, that's alright Dom. I'll spend the day with my mum and dad, which will please them no end.'

Although Rosalind was putting a brave face on the situation, Dominic could tell by her voice that she was more than disappointed at the turn of events. She had been thinking about him all night in bed. Dominic could be her first proper boyfriend, although living so far from one another – she in Manchester and he in London would make things difficult. At least it could a fabulous holiday romance, something to boast about to Denise when back in school.

Rosalind thought that perhaps Dominic was making an excuse – that he'd hadn't really fancied her after all; maybe her kissing had been too tame last night; maybe she'd needed to have shown more passion. But she'd been conscious at the time of not appearing too forward, or too easy to seduce.

Dominic promised to phone her the next day and make arrangements to spend time together, but Rosalind wasn't entirely convinced of his truthfulness.

However, fate had conspired against further meetings between the two of them in Brighton. Rosalind's grandfather, who had been in poor health, died suddenly during the following night in Manchester, with the consequence that the Gersteins immediately cancelled the remainder of their holiday week in Brighton and travelled back home within hours of receiving the sad news.

When Dominic telephoned the Grand Hotel the Gersteins had already left, but the receptionist informed him that there was an envelope for a Mr Dominic, to be collected at the hotel's reception. Dominic went immediately to the hotel, picked up the envelope, opened it and found a note from Rosalind.

The short note explained the reason why she and her parents had gone home to Manchester. She'd requested him to keep in touch. The note concluded with her home telephone number only – but it didn't include an address.

CHAPTER 4

On the previous day Dominic and Ricky visited the Morans house, and had been introduced to Lord and Lady Moran. They'd spotted Finley Roreson and his girlfriend, Susie Lattern, working together in the garden, picking herbs, that Susie would be using later to cook the lunch. Finley hugged his old friend Ricky and told him how great it was to see him.

'And this presumably is your young friend you promised to bring along.'

Dominic stepped forward, shaking Finley's hand. 'I'm pleased to meet you. Ricky told me so much about you – being the best barber in the world!'

Finley burst out laughing. 'Steady on old chap, that's a bit of an exaggeration. Maybe the best barber in Brighton, or even London, but the world? I don't think so!'

Susie, carrying a tray of herbs, came over to greet them on her way to the kitchen – apologising for not stopping to chat, as she was running late for lunch preparation.

'Catch you guys later.'

Susie sauntered off back into the house.

Dominic could see why Finley was besotted with Susie. She was gorgeous looking – a pert slim blonde with a flirtatious smile. Finley was short and stocky with thick dark hair falling down almost to his shoulders – perhaps not a good advertisement for a professional barber!

The large house, located in Rottingdean, further along the coast from Brighton, was an old Edwardian building, with many bedrooms, specious living areas and several rooms used as staff quarters.

The Morans, both in their mid-thirties, had been married for five years, and although it was originally a love match, the passion had since receded and Sebastian was constantly on the lookout for sexual adventures.

Susie Lattern, a local Brighton girl – was employed by the Morans as a cook and as general helper to Lady Lydia. His Lordship, Sebastian, was arrogant enough to believe that as Susie's employer, he had seduction rights with her. He flirted shamelessly with Susie around the house, even with his wife present. Lydia was fond of Susie and the two of them were more like friends than mistress and staff.

Dominic felt the various tensions in the house. He noticed that the Morans were at odds with each other bickering over trivial domestic matters. Dominic's first impression of Finley was positive, thinking him to be a lively personality with a quick thinking intelligence.

Finley was up against a ferocious adversary in Sebastian Moran. Money was no problem for Moran as he had inherited a fortune from his late father. He had invested in Finley's barber shop for a bit of fun, as he liked to go drinking in Brighton with his barber friend and be introduced to all the girls that Finley knew in the town. Finley was in love with Susie and had no interest in flirting with other girls, but he indulged Moran, to keep in his good books, so not to be troubled by having to pay back his loan from His Lordship.

The problem started when the relationship between Susie and Finley became serious, with plans to marry. Sebastian Moran became intensely jealous and his attitude to Finley changed. He demanded his loan back from Finley with full interest. Finley was in no position to pay back the loan, so he closed his barber shop and started looking for work around town. To keep Finley close so he didn't disappear, Moran offered him a job as a general manservant in his house. Every month when Moran paid Finley, he took off a chunk of his wages towards paying down the loan.

The positive feature of this outcome was that Susie and Finley worked in the same house, and were able to spend much time together. The negative aspect was that Finley and Moran nearly came to blows over Susie. Every time Finley left Susie's side, Moran seemed to appear and had some domestic task or other for Susie to undertake.

'I want you to accompany me to London for a few days, to help with the organisation of the networking event, being held at the prestigious Carlton Club,' Moran suddenly announced to Susie, as she was in the kitchen, finishing off the washing up of the lunch dishes.

'I don't think Finley would be very pleased with me going to London with you.' Susie replied with a cheeky grin on her face.'

'It's not Findley's concern' Moran responded sharply – then turned on his charm with a big smile as he put his arm around Susie's waist.

'Please do not touch me, Sebastian; I'm in love with Finley and we'll be getting married soon. Besides, your wife, Lydia, as well as being my boss, is a dear friend, and I wouldn't want to do anything to cause her any upset.'

'Let me worry about Lydia – we have an arrangement to do our own thing. And I'm sorry to give you the bad news – they'll be no wedding until your young man pays me back what he owes.'

'You can't stop us getting married'

'Well... let me make clear,' continued Moran with a smirk on his face and pointing his finger at Susie. 'I just have to pick up the phone to Brighton's chief constable, and with one word from me you'll see your lover boy carted away in handcuffs and marriage would be the last thing on his mind.'

He changed the tune and tried to turn on the charm, whispering in Susie's ear. 'I'd give you a fabulous time in London.'

Susie was disgusted. She turned her back on Sebastian and walked out of the kitchen.

Finley, hiding behind the kitchen store cupboard, heard the whole exchange between Susie and His Lordship; he became seriously alarmed.

Rounding up Ricky and Dominic, Finley asked them to stay-on in the house for a few days, so that they could devise a plan to outwit Moran – show-him-up for the cad that he was.

'We'd booked our guest house for three nights, so we'll have to go back there tonight, Fin, but once we've checked out in the morning, we can come back here...can't we Dom?'

Dominic, although feeling ready to go home the next day, especially as Rosalind had gone back to Manchester, saw the look in Ricky's eyes and nodded in ascent.

'Good,' said a relieved Finley. 'I'll arrange for you both to stay in our guest bedroom for a couple of nights and we'll get one over His Lordship.'

The following morning, before returning to the Morans,' Dominic put a phone call through to Manchester. 'Mrs Gerstein speaking – whom am I speaking to?'

'Oh...hello, Mrs Gerstein – Dominic here, a friend of Rosalind's from Brighton. I'm sorry for your loss.'

'Thank you young man, but I won't waste your time. You can't speak to Rosalind and please don't telephone here again.'

'Oh Right, sorry. Did I do, or say something, to upset her?'

'No, no... It's not that at all. The fact is that we're a Jewish family and my understanding is that you're not Jewish. We didn't mind Rosalind having a short holiday friendship with you, but as far more serious dating with our daughter goes, it's totally out of the question, so goodbye, Dominic.'

Mrs Gerstein put down the phone before Dominic had had a chance to say another word.

'You alright mate?'

Ricky saw that Dominic looked down-in-the-mouth, and despite his rough and ready ways, he felt protective towards his younger friend.

Dominic explained to Ricky about the phone conversation to Rosalind's mother, and, how disappointed he'd been, thinking that Rosalind could have been his first proper girlfriend – despite the geographical distance between them.

'It's only a bird, Dom... There are plenty more fish in the sea!'

'You don't understand Ricky. I'm not like you, I want a steady girlfriend.'

'No... My friend, what you need is sex with lots of different girls. You're far too young to even think about a relationship. Let me teach you a seduction technique. Believe me, once you've experienced sex with a variety of girls, you'll forget about your Jewish princess. Actually...what you need is an older woman to teach you how it's done.'

'Do you fancy Lydia – Lady Moran?'

'Well, she's certainly very beautiful, Ricky, but what would she see in a young boy like me?'

'Maybe nothing at all... but I'll tell you what. Lydia is desperate to get her own back on His Lordship and you just maybe the answer.'

Dominic thought about the gorgeous Lydia Moran and suddenly felt sexually aroused.

CHAPTER 5

'I've a plan for you, Fin, which will enrage His Lordship but will distract him enough for you and Susie to quietly get hitched.'

Fin was all ears. 'What are the plans then, Ricky?'

'We're going to get young Dominic to flirt outrageously with Lydia, which will make Sebastian mad with jealousy. Perhaps he would start to think about his own behaviour and lay off trying to bed your lovely Susie.'

Ricky and Dominic had moved into one of the guest rooms of the Moran's house, which was at the back of the house near to the staff quarters.

'We have three days to pull this off, boys, whilst we're staying here.' Ricky said, taking charge of the plot to embarrass Finley's boss and tormentor.

The three boys were sitting on the bed in Ricky and Dominic's small bedroom.

'OK... this is how it goes. Fin... You get on well with Lydia, yes?' Finley nodded with a smile on his face. 'Pay special attention to her tonight over dinner. Be your most charming self. After dinner, when Sebastian heads to the snug for his after-dinner port, take Lydia aside and explain to her about your young handsome friend, Dominic, and how, when he first saw you, he was completely smitten, and couldn't stop talking about you all night.

Finley was rather dubious about his friend's plan, but thought it was worth a try.

'You were especially flirtatious with Her Ladyship this evening,' said Susie, with her arm around her man and looking lovingly into his eyes.

They were in the staff quarters after completing all the chores of the day and were relaxing in front of the television. Finley started to explain about his friend's plan, with Susie looking at him in total disbelieve. She immediately disentangled from him, stood up and shook her head. 'No, Fin... My darling, that's a bad and dangerous plan, as you know what His Lordship, is like. He can seduce as many women as he wishes, but if his wife even dared to look at another man, he would be so furious he might even kill her!'

'I know it's a risk Susie, but Ricky and I would restrain him if he got violent.'

'I've got a better idea. Why not disguise Ricky's young friend as a woman? He's young and pretty enough to get away with it, with a smooth and beardless face. Then if Sebastian catches them together, he would think only that his wife is entertaining a new female friend from Brighton.'

'Ha ha... I knew that I was marrying not just a pretty face but a delicious cunning minx.' Finley laughed raucously, adding, 'That's capital Susie sweetheart. This escapade could turn out to be loads of fun as well as an embarrassment for His Lordship.'

'C'mon, lover boy, let's go to bed.' Susie held her hand out for Finley to grab it, as she led him into the bedroom and started to kiss him passionately. As he responded to her ardour, his thoughts turned to what a lucky fellow he was. Susie was his and his alone – he wasn't going to let some arrogant lordship near his beloved and he was determined to get the better of Sebastian Moran.

During that night, Dominic had an erotic dream. *The woman in the dream was definitely Lydia, Lady Moran. Lydia was wearing a see-through night dress, which showed the contours of her voluptuous figure. She had led him to a darkened room and they'd embraced. Lydia smelt delicious. Her perfume had overwhelmed Dom, a combination of sweetness and sexiness. He explained that he was inexperienced in sexual matters and she'd laughed in his face. 'That's why I want to seduce you. I lust after adolescence boys who are just past the legal age for sex.' He felt scared and thrilled at the same time as Lydia undressed him and touched his penis, which grew big and stiff in her hands.* He woke up with an erection and a huge disappointment that after all that, it was just a dream.

'Your husband wanted me to accompany him to London, and I know exactly what he had in mind when there!'

Susie was with her boss, who was also her friend, in Lydia's bedroom suite the following morning. The suite consisted of two separate bedrooms, a lounge area and two bathrooms. The main bedroom contained a large double bed where Lydia and Sebastian slept together when His Lordship was behaving himself and being loving to his wife. But more often than not in recent times, Sebastian had been banished to the spare bedroom, which also had a double bed, but a smaller one. The naughty lordship tried a couple of times, to convince Susie to join him in the spare room once Lydia was asleep. Susie was appalled with the suggestion and told him so in no uncertain terms. Unfortunately, Sebastian was insensitive and would not take no for an answer – in fact, Susie's forthrightness was a turn-on for him, and the more she fought his ardour, the more determined he'd become to seduce her.

Susie explained the dressing up plan to Lydia but stressed that Dominic was besotted with her Ladyship – the dressing-up idea was a safety net in case Sebastian caught them together. Lydia felt that it was a rather silly idea to dress-up the young man as a woman, but she was amused at the idea. However, knowing how her husband's fury was quickly unleashed if thwarted in any way, she suspected that Sebastian would blow his top if he'd caught his wife flirting with either a man or a woman.

Dominic, feeling rather sheepish, quietly knocked on her Ladyship's door, which was opened by Susie with Lydia standing immediately behind her. 'I'll leave you two to get to know one another.' Susie said, as she disappeared into the second bedroom.

'Please sit down next to me and tell me all about yourself.' Lydia ushered Dominic towards the sofa as he was looking awkward standing around the room. 'Come a little closer – don't be shy.'

'There's not much to tell. I'm very inexperienced, but I don't want to be disguised as a girl.'

Lydia laughed. 'No, that's fine. I thought it was a crazy idea anyway. But tell me, do you fancy me?'

'Well'... Dominic blushed. 'I had a sexy dream about you last night.'

Lydia looked closely at the young man for the first time, with thoughts that he was nice looking but totally innocent. The idea of corrupting his innocence had given her an erotic charge. As Dominic related his dream to Lydia she grabbed him and started to kiss him passionately.

Just then there was a loud knock on the door with Sebastian shouting, 'Open up immediately or I'll smash down the door!'

What had alarmed Sebastian so much that made him threaten to break down the door?

It was Ricky, who'd had the daft idea to stir the pot, by sending an anonymous note to His Lordship suggesting that his wife had agreed to a secret assignation with a lover in the garden that evening. Ricky then sent a further note to Sebastian with a message from Susie that she would be happy to see him privately in the garden at dusk.

Dominic panicked as he jumped up and ran towards the room that Susie had gone into. Susie was sitting at a desk and writing a letter. 'What's the matter Dominic?'

'His Lordship is in high-dudgeon and is banging down the door! Where's the window?

'Don't be crazy. Why do you need to run away? He won't attack you. His bark is louder than his bite. You'll hurt yourself jumping out of the window.'

'It's only the first floor and I'll be careful.'

Dominic opened the window, went over to Susie and gave her a hug. Before she could stop him, he jumped out of the window. Susie went over to look. He seemed fine. He quickly picked himself up, landing on some shrubs and running as fast as he could towards the garden gate and completely out and away from His Lordship's estate.

In the rush to get away from the estate, Dominic dropped his wallet on his run to the garden gate.

Susie, happy to see that Dominic escaped without incident, locked the second bedroom door from the inside and went back to her desk to continue writing her letters.

Lydia opened the door to her husband who rudely pushed passed his wife looking around the room, under the bed and in the cupboards. 'Where is he?' he shouted.

'Who are you looking for, Sebastian?'

'The lover you're meeting in the garden tonight Lydia'

Lydia, not having had knowledge of Ricky's bold plan for the garden various rendezvous arrangements, was totally flummoxed as to what her husband was talking about.

'Don't play the innocent with me, my lady. I know your sexual taste for young men, and that snotty twerp who turned up with Finley's roguish friend, Ricky Wenger, had caught your eye and you'd had plans to seduce him in the garden tonight. But the boy's not around the house this morning and our bedroom door was locked. You obviously couldn't wait until this evening and had invited him to your room this morning.'

Although Lydia was confused by her husband rattling on about garden meetings, she was aware that she had been kissing Dominic when Sebastian tried to open the bedroom door and that the young man was hiding in the second bedroom.

Sebastian tried to open the door to the second bedroom, but it was locked.

'I'll be back with one of my men who will be able to unpick the lock. If that young man is there in the room I'll kill him!' Locking the main bedroom door from the outside and posting one of his servants to stand guard at the door, he departed at haste.

Whilst all this was going on, Finley had slipped quietly into the bedroom and hid in the corner.

Susie unlocked her door announcing that Dominic, being so scared of Sebastian, had jumped out of the window and had fled from the estate.

'Oh my god...' Lydia, her hands flying up in the air, shouted at Susie, 'Was he hurt in any way?'

Susie laughed. 'No, he was fine and dandy. He ran like-the-clappers to get away from here.

'What's going on Fin?' Findlay emerged from his hiding place, and explained about Ricky's idea of sending anonymous notes to Sebastian alerting him to plans being hatched for the evening in the garden. Susie and Lydia looked at each other in amazement wondering what the hell was being plotted!

Before Finley could elaborate they heard voices at the door. Sebastian was back with his locksmith. Susie ran back to the second bedroom and locked the door. Sebastian stormed into the room with his man following behind. 'Right... would whoever is in there unlock the door and come out or shall I ask my man, Jimmy, to unpick the lock.'

Lydia, now knowing that Dominic had made his escape thought to have a bit of sport with her hypocritical husband. Going on her knees, she looks up to Sebastian and implored him to forgive her as they were only having a bit of sport with young Dominic, by dressing him up as a girl.

'No matter if the little squirt is a male or female I'll have his guts for garters when I open that door. He will be so disabled he won't be able to walk to the garden tonight for his assignation with you!'

'Please be merciful, my dear lord and master!'

'Jimmy, unpick the lock!'

Just as Jimmy took his tools out of his bag and went towards the lock, the door opened and Susie walked slowly out of the room, asking, 'What's all the commotion about?'

'Susie,' gasped Sebastian.

'Susie,' uttered Lydia with a half smile on her face.

'I was just teasing you, my dear; I know how jealous you get and all that garden stuff was just a joke at your expense.' Lydia now had a big smile on her face.

Sebastian asked his wife for forgiveness, but at the same time he winked at Susie. Despite being told that the evening's shenanigans were all nothing but a joke, he'd been still determined to get Susie out into the garden that evening. As well as not be entirely convinced of his wife's innocence.

Just as everything was settling down, in walks the gardener, Tony, in a dishevelled state carrying a broken pot of carnations.

'Somebody jumped out of the window and smashed this pot!'

Sebastian frowned, 'So the rascal was here after all.'

'No, sir, it was me who jumped out of the window' Finley suddenly feigned a leg injury with a limp.' 'I panicked when you entered the room in such an angry state as I was involved, with my friend Ricky, in the make-believe garden arrangements.'

Tony came forward and handed a wallet to Finley. 'This wallet must be yours then as I found it amongst the bushes.'

Finley was about to pocket the wallet when Sebastian grabbed it. Examining the item, he noticed that the wallet had a photo of Dominic inside.

'Ha ha,' exploded Sebastian. 'It was that young man after all who had jumped out of the window!'

'No, no,' said Finley. 'Dominic asked me to look after his wallet whilst he was in the house, as he told me that he was very careless and tended to misplace things.'

Everyone looked at each other with the same thought – that this was a score draw and that all would be resolved one way or another in the garden that very evening.

CHAPTER 6

Dominic, once he was well away from the Morans' estate, slowed down to catch his breath from all the running and thought about what to do next. Ideally, he would like to get back home to London as quickly as possible, having had enough of Brighton to last a lifetime. He would like to make his way to the railway station, then telephone the house and ask to speak to Ricky, updating him on what had occurred earlier in Lydia's bedrooms, and ask him to collect his luggage when his own time at the house was up and he was returning to London.

Whilst mulling his plan over in his head, he suddenly realised that his wallet was missing – it must have dropped out of his pocket whilst jumping out of the window. Without his wallet he could go nowhere. Reluctantly, he'd have to return to the house, and hopefully, someone would have picked it up from the garden.

Dominic was very scared of Lord Moran following that morning's incident and he was determined to keep out of his way when he returned to the house. He slipped in by the back door and went to the kitchen where Susie and Finley were sitting drinking coffee. Sitting with them was a beautiful-looking young girl who looked about the same age as Dominic.

Susie rose from her seat and went over to Dominic, followed closely behind by Finley. They both gave him a hug, being hugely concerned that he hadn't suffered any injuries during his jump and run from the house.

'I'm fine thanks but I had to return because I mislaid my wallet.'

Finley quickly interjected. 'No problem mate, I have your wallet, which the gardener, Tony Lattern, Susie's uncle, found in the bushes.' He handed the wallet back to its owner.

Susie turned to the girl sitting at the table and introduced the two youngsters to each other.

'This is Barbara Fenlon, my cousin from Devon, who's visiting us for a few days. Let me introduce you to Dominic Rivers, a friend of Finley's buddy. Ricky Wenger. Dominic – please meet Barbara...Barbara, please meet Dominic.'

The two youngsters shook hands, both staring into each other's eyes. There was an instant attraction between the two of them.

At dusk, Susie and Lydia swapped clothes, hairstyles and make-up – then masked their faces before making their way into the garden.

In the darkness, with the only light coming from the pavilion, it was hard to see anyone, let alone two masked women.

Barbara and Dominic had started to chat together earlier, and once Susie and Finley had noticed the immediate attraction between the young pair, they thoughtfully indicated that chores were awaiting them – making their exit from the kitchen.

Dominic was excited but confused about his frequent changes of whom he was sexually attracted to! He'd met Rosalind at the disco club and he'd thought that she was the girl that he wanted to spend the rest of his life with. Things not working out with Rosalind upset him greatly. But in the house he experienced something different to what he felt with Rosalind. He couldn't believe that he would have had feelings for a woman nearly twenty years his senior. But Lydia had awoken something in him he hadn't know he possessed, which was an erotic charge. No, he'd had no romantic inclinations towards Lydia – it was purely sexual. Perhaps Ricky had been right all along in telling him to forget romance and to enjoy a host of multiple sexual encounters. However, the sequence of events in Lydia's bedroom had not only frightened him, but had also totally cooled his ardour for her.

His initial attraction for Barbara, fell somewhere between Rosalind and Lydia. Barbara was very pretty looking, as was Rosalind, but following his erotic encounter with Lydia, Dominic's sexuality had started to obsess him and he saw Barbara as a potential sexual partner, and well as a future romantic girlfriend.

Barbara, an eighteen-year-old confident art student, had fancied Dominic from the moment she saw him and was keen to spend time with him.

Dominic and Barbara were in the gardens pavilion, tucked away in a dark corner, passionately kissing. Hearing someone else entering, the pair broke apart and saw that it was Her Ladyship.

'That's Lydia Moran,' Dominic whispered to Barbara, who hadn't yet been introduced to the Morans.

'What's she doing in here?'

'She must be secretly meeting somebody!'

Finley walked in, looking a bit sheepish.

Finley knew that the masked figure was Susie disguised as Lydia, but he thought to have a bit of sport with his fiancée.

'Lydia, my darling, I, I... secretly desire you – I'm desperate to make love to you!'

Susie smacked Finley on the face. 'You're a total scumbag, wanting to be unfaithful with Lydia.'

'Ha ha, ha... I knew all along, who you were. I thought we should have a bit of fun with the garden shenanigans!'

'I knew too that you knew who I was; the smack on the face was just a warning in case you ever thought of cheating on me.'

Barbara and Dominic saw and heard this hilarious exchange and were highly amused – but by keeping still and quiet, they were not spotted in the dark corner.

Sebastian walked towards the pavilion and was shocked to see Finley in an embrace with his wife. He was furious and wanted to confront them, but remembered his arrangement to meet with Susie. He found Susie by the fountain, but he was so annoyed at what was going on in the pavilion that he was no mood to make love to her.

'Did you know that your fiancé is making love to my wife in the pavilion?' Sebastian blurted out.

'Well, you better go and sort them out.'

Entering the pavilion, Sebastian shouted. 'You're a *blaggard,* Finley. I will have your guts for garters!'

Susie, Imitating Lydia's voice, started to plead with Sebastian. 'Please, husband, don't hurt him as I truly love him.'

Just then, Lydia, who had quickly discarded her disguise, stepped into the pavilion and asked in a quiet authoritative voice. 'What's exactly going on in here?'

Sebastian turned around, with his tongue hanging out of his mouth. 'Lydia... it's you – but, but...but – I thought...'

Susie – now using her own voice...' Are you objecting, Sebastian, to me making love with my husband to be?'

Sebastian... turned this way and that, slowly realised that he had been made an utter fool of.

Barbara and Dominic emerged from their dark corner of the Pavilion, others realising that the young couple had seen and heard the whole absurd theatre happening in front of them.

Everyone stared at Sebastian awaiting a response from him – Susie and Finley, Lydia, Barbara and Dominic and entering the pavilion, Tony, the gardener. Other members of the staff also started to make their way to the pavilion, all curious to witness the humiliation of their boss, who most of them hated.

'Please forgive me, Lydia, I've been a stupid fool.'

'No Sebastian, you're not sorry for the pain you've caused. You're just sorry that you've been found out!'

Sebastian dropped to his knees, begging his wife to accept his sincere contrition.

Not look directly at him, Lydia responded with a harsh tone in her voice.

'Three things you must agree to for me to accept your apology. One: Never ever bother Susie again. Two; Write off 100% of Finley's debt to you. Three: Give your blessing to the marriage of Susie and Finley, and arrange and pay for the wedding party here in our house.'

Sebastian looked absolutely shattered and totally beaten. 'Yes Lydia, I agree to all of your three requests.'

Everyone started to clap their hands, including the staff members who were crowded around the pavilion's entrance. Susie and Finley both looked ecstatic and were hugging and kissing each other.

Sebastian went towards Lydia, but she rejected any advance from her wayward husband, turning around and walking out of the pavilion towards the house.

The wedding was a joyous occasion, Barbara staying on in the house to be Susie's bridesmaid, and Ricky was Finley's best man. Lydia and Sebastian had a sort of reconciliation, with Sebastian promising to turnover a new leaf and be a loving faithful husband, and Lydia promising not to flirt with any more young men.

Ricky and Dominic eventually decided that it was time to head home to London. Finley couldn't thank Ricky enough for his help in sorting out his problems and Dominic professed his love for Barbara, which was reciprocated. The young couple planned to meet up again as soon as they possibly could.

CHAPTER 7

Hertfordshire 1992

'So, Alex... What's your book all about?'

Tobias Eden and I were enjoying a drink together in a Soho wine bar. The two of us had formed a friendship following my joining the membership of the gramophone club. We'd started to meet up regularly in London after work. I was in my final year in full-time employment with the Labour Party. Tobias was a few years older than me, and having officially retired from his main career, he still did an amount of freelance work with various media outlets. We would enjoy a few glasses of wine and travel back together to Hertfordshire, by train. Or occasionally, we would go to a concert or an opera and catch a late train home.

'Well... As I was featuring the Da Ponte/ Mozart operas at my host evenings at the gramophone club, I thought to loosely base the novel on their three great operas, but dressed in twentieth century garb. So far, I've only tackled *Le Nozze di Figaro*.'

'That makes sense Alex, as that's the opera you're currently playing for us. I'm intrigued to know how you've adapted all the various characters that populate the opera.'

'I've set the plot in Brighton during the year 1960, concentrating on Acts Two and Four of the opera only — specifically, the bedroom and garden scenes. I've dispensed with a number of the characters in the opera. There is no equivalent of a Doctor Bartolo, Marcellina, Don Basilio or Don Curzio. My Figaro is called Finley and his Susanna is Susie. Count Almaviva is Lord Sebastian Moran and the countess is Lydia, Lady Moran. Cherubino is Dominic and Barbarina is Barbara. The small role of Antonio, the gardener, is Tony. I've also added one other character to the plot, that doesn't appear in the opera. His name is Ricky – Dominic's best friend.'

'Sounds fascinating; At least we'll know you're not writing an autobiographical novel by linking your story to existing opera plots.'

'Hmmm... There would be no chance of that, Toby, as my backstory would make a totally boring novel!'

Toby realised that he knew very little about Alex's background – he had just made an assumption that his friend had come from a typical middle-class, north London family. He also sensed reluctance by Alex to talk about his personal life. Their recent friendship was very much based on their mutual love of music and the arts in general.

The silence between the two men started to become a tad uncomfortable... Toby quickly continued the conversation by asking Alex if he could have a sneak preview at what he had written so far.

'Sorry, Toby, Nobody will get to see the book until it's finished, edited and hopefully, published.'

'That's OK. I'd be the same if I was writing a book. I must say that I really enjoyed your *Figaro* opera night at the club and I'm looking forward to hearing the last two acts at your next hosting event.'

'Well, you won't have to wait long. The next hosts are Ronald and Dulcie, and my turn follows their evening.'

Having ordered and enjoyed another glass of wine, the two friends made their way to Kings Cross station to catch a train back to their respective homes in Hertfordshire.

CHAPTER 8

The following week, I made my way to the Henrows' residence with much anticipation. Although I hadn't established a friendship with Ronald, in the same way as I'd done with Tobias, I admired his dedication to the music he was into, despite his perceived lack of any emotional attachment to his favoured composers. As a personality, Ronald didn't do *emotion,* period, but I respected him nevertheless, and Dulcie, was an excellent foil to her husband, a vibrant friendly woman who got on with everybody.

All the regular members turned up for the Henrows' hosting evening. Tobias and Verity Elden were both looking very comfortable, relaxing in their friends house. Benjamin and Hildergard Tiller displayed their natural warmth and well-being showing genuine interest in everyone's welfare. Violet Smithson had been her usual rather stiff and old-fashioned self, but she'd never missed an event. Dorothy Bateman, with a big smile on her face, had her knitting with her. Greg Witton attended on his own without his wife, Florence, whom we only saw on the evenings the Wittons' were hosting.

Hannah Longsmith, who had been away on a long sabbatical holiday for the first few events that I had attended, including my own, finally returned to the fold. Everyone was delighted to see her back in the group and Dulcie immediately grabbed my hand to introduce me to Hannah. My initial impression was that she was a rather handsome forty-something confident woman. Hannah wore her medium-brown hair in a short crop and was dressed in an impressive tailored suit. The look was one that implied 'I may be a female, but don't mess with me!' I had heard, through the others, that she was a high-flyer in the world of city finance, but she'd been a genuine music lover and when she'd hosted an event, her choices of music had always been interesting and stimulating. Hannah was a single woman and I had been informed by Toby that her private life was a closed book.

Two new couples attended, who seemed a good deal younger than the long-standing members, and were both, evidently, new to the area. They were checking to see if our little group were people they would want as new friends, as well as sussing out if our collective musical tastes appealed to them, or not.

I had actually forgotten about Bettina Emberton, when just as Ronald was getting ready to introduce the evening's programme, in she walked, full of apologies, blaming a delay on the train whilst making her journey home from her London office. She hadn't attended an event since she'd shown up unexpectedly at my hosting evening. We were all surprised to see her as we had thought that her attendance at my event was solely to promote her matchmaking business.

Ronald stood by his hi-fi system and put his hand up for everyone's attention. Silence prevailed as he welcomed the guests, especially the two new couples, the Harrisons and the Digbys, and the return of the group's dear friend, Hannah Longsmith.

As Ronald was speaking, I noticed that Bettina had squeezed herself tightly into a chair next to Toby. His wife, Verity, gave Bettina a non-too friendly quizzical stare.

Ronald had always insisted on being called by his proper name, disapproving of Ronnie. He was explaining some technical aspects of his choice of music and was losing everybody's attention, until Dulcie gave him a sharp nudge from her elbow and he stopped showing off his recent musical diploma expertise.

I was expecting Ronald to programme music from the sixteenth century, composers he had spoken about enthusiastically at previous gramophone events. Composers such as, Giovanni Pier luigi da Palestrina, Thomas Tallis, William Byrd and Tomas Luis de Victoria were some of the names Ronald had studied for his diploma, and he was eager to promote music from that particular era. But he hadn't chosen to programme them for that evening's event, but rather twentieth-century composers, concentrating on two of the great names of English music: Benjamin Britten and Michael Tippett.

I was familiar with a lot of Britten's music, being especially keen on his opera, *Peter Grimes,* and I had visited Aldeburgh, Britten's home town, for their annual festival several times, but I knew very little of Tippett's musical output, who was the grand old man of England's living composers.

Ronald started the programme with a recording of Britten's solo cello suite No 1, recorded by the artist Britten wrote the suite for; Mstislav Rostropovitch, the great Russian cellist and friend of the composer. It was recorded at Snape Maltings in 1968.

The next piece Ronald programmed was Britten's violin concerto. The recording, dating from 1970, was performed by Mark Lubotsky, as the violin soloist, with the English Chamber Orchestra, conducted by the composer, which was also recorded at Snape Maltings, the concert hall Britten, and his partner, the tenor, Peter Pears, had built for Aldeburgh Festival performances.

The violin concerto was an early work by Britten, written in 1938/9, composed whilst Britten was living in New York, and premiered there in 1940, by the Spanish violinist, Antonio Brosa. Not having previously heard the concerto, I thought it was a fabulous piece – a mixture of lyricism and virtuosity.

During the interval, Dulcie served a selection of delicious homemade cakes with tea or coffee. I spent the interval chatting with Roland about the music he'd just played and about Britten in particular. I realised how much he knew about the composer and I was highly impressed with his knowledge and understanding of this important English musician.

I noticed whilst chatting with Ronald, that Bettina was monopolising Toby – they were chatting very intensely together in the corner of the room. His wife, Verity, and her friend, Dulcie, were also deep in discussion, but Verity kept looking over to the corner of the room – her facial expression and body language showed a woman in some distress.

The second half of the programme was devoted to one work: Tippett's oratorio, *A Child of Our Time.*

I hadn't previously heard the piece either in concert or on record, but I knew that it was the composer's most famous work and I was keen to listen to Ronald's chosen recorded version. He chose a classic version from 1975, conducted by Colin Davis – a great champion of Tippett. The orchestra was the BBC Symphony Orchestra with the BBC Singers and a stellar line-up of soloists. They were: Jessye Norman, Janet Baker, Richard Cassilly, and John Shirley-Quirk.

What I wasn't prepared for was to be totally moved by the work and Ronald's chosen recording of it. By the end I was trying, without success, to hold back the tears. The irony, being, that it was the non-sentimental Ronald, who had chosen to play a piece that left me an emotional wreck.

Tippett wrote both the words and the music of *A Child of our Time*, between 1939 and 1941. It was first performed in London during 1944. He had been deeply affected by events that occurred in Germany during 1938. The assassination of a German diplomat in Paris by a seventeen-year old Jewish refugee precipitated violent pogroms all over Germany. The infamous event was known as Kristallnacht. For a number of days, violence ensued – synagogues burned down, business premises were smashed, homes were destroyed and some Jews were stoned to death, with thousands arrested.

Tippett wished to capture a universality of outrage at those particular horrific events. He had the inspired idea to add five American spirituals, which were integrated into the score. He chose: *Steal away;Nobody Knows the Trouble I See, Lord; Go Down Moses; O, By and By;* and *Deep River.*

The group were quiet and thoughtful at the conclusion of the oratorio, and the usual bonhomie one experienced at the end of a gramophone evening was absent. I noticed that even Bettina was less than her effervescent self, looking as if she had been crying. The Tippett piece must have affected her deeply.

On the way home my thoughts were, might had I misjudged Ronald? Not everyone wore their hearts on their sleeves.

CHAPTER 9

The Eldens and the Henrows, being long standing friends, held regular dinner parties in each other's houses. Because as well the couples being music lovers they also enjoyed cooking, especially the men, who were competitive with each other in both musical tastes and in their respective cooking skills.

My telephone rang. It was Toby.

'Hello, Alex, how are you?

'Well thanks, and you?'

'We're all good.'

'What did you think of Ronald's evening?

'I was very impressed with his programme, especially the marvellous Tippet oratorio, which left me in bits.

Toby chuckled. 'Yes, Ronald's a dark horse. He protests too much about his stiff-upper-lip cold English persona. His Tippett recording the other night affected him emotionally as much as it did for the rest of us.'

'Look, Alex, I'm sorry for the short notice, but we're having a dinner party on Saturday, and we'd love to have you join us. Besides Ronald and Dulcie, we had invited Hannah Longsmith and her mysterious partner, whom none of us have ever met, even when she'd hosted a gramophone evening. But he's unavailable, so we thought that you'd like to join us.'

I responded jokily, but unfortunately, Toby picked it up as me being sarcastic. 'Oh, you just want me as a substitute for Hannah's mysterious *copain,* to even up the numbers.'

'Oh no... Alex. That's not the case at all. Verity and I had spoken about our desire to invite you to one of our dinner parties, from the time we'd first met you at Greg Witton's gramophone event. We'd thought for a while that our regular foursome dinners with the Henrows could do with a bit of shaking up, so when we first met you, both of us knew instinctively that we wanted you at our parties.'

'Stop digging, Toby, you don't have to explain anything. I would be delighted to accept your invitation, and I look forward to it. Just don't try to do any matchmaking for me with Hannah. I'm just joking!'

When I had put down the receiver at the end of the telephone call, I thought of Bettina, the actual professional matchmaker, who'd seemed to be all over Toby at the gramophone event the other evening; Verity hadn't been impressed.

CHAPTER 10

As is typical in a long marriage, there are times when an established relationship hits a roadblock, and that was the current case with Toby and Verity. Toby had always possessed a wild streak in his character. His background was lower middle class, from a coal mining small town in south Wales. Toby grew up during the period that Wales still had grammar schools and being a bright boy, he'd won a place at a leading school. He'd sung in the school choir and had taken an interest in the arts at a young age. He'd read literature and politics at university, where he'd met Verity. With his degree under his belt, he moved to London, securing a place at TNB (The Nations Broadcaster) as an apprentice in the news department. Spending his whole career at the TNB, he rose to become an editor of the corporation's nightly news magazine programme, which was aired on television following the main evening news. Verity was a dedicated nurse with the NHS. Like her husband, Verity steadily moved upwards in her career progression, eventually becoming a senior administrator, responsible for several large London hospitals. The pair were certainly an upwardly mobile couple during the 1970s and 1980s.

Amongst friends, Toby liked to hold court on a variety of subjects, from politics to the arts, with music being his special subject. He took great pleasure in debating with his old friend, Ronald Henrow, as they had differing opinions about certain composers. If Toby was in a provocative mood, he would bring up the name of the nineteenth-century Austrian composer, Anton Bruckner, whom he adored, which was like a red rag to a bull to Ronald, who detested Bruckner's music, and a fierce argument would ensue. Toby, who was incredibly articulate, would always get the better of poor Ronald, who became tongue-tied, when the metaphoric heat was turned up during the discussion. Toby, who enjoyed a malt whisky or two, which mellowed his personality, and at that stage he liked to show-off and recite romantic poetry by heart. Verity, who was a much quieter individual, actually had more operatic knowledge than her husband and always made the decisions on which operas they'd book. The couple regularly attended performances at Covent Garden and being members of the Glyndehurst Opera Festival, they'd visited the Sussex festival at least once a season and sometimes twice, attending at least two different operas at each visit. However, Toby usually decided on which orchestral or chamber concerts they wished to attend.

What Verity didn't know was that there had been no flirting going on between Toby and Bettina. Bettina, whose matchmaking business was faltering, due to the fact that men were reluctant to come forward for a consultation, whereas, women were much less shy to do so. Consequently, the numbers hadn't added up; too many female, and not enough male clients. Bettina had commissioned a management consultant firm for advice on how to attract more men to her scheme. The problem with a management consultant was that the only thing they were good at was to charge a large fee!

In their wisdom, they'd advised Bettina to target the affairs market. More and more married men and women were seeking discreet love affairs that wouldn't destroy their marriages. But it was wise for the married to look outside of their own social circle. The answer to the business problem was to segue from introducing singles to each other, to facilitating infidelities. The consultant suggested that men would pour forward in numbers with such a scheme in place. Of course, what the highly paid consultant did not divulge was that the same problem would occur, but in reverse. They'd have many more men apply than women, who'd be far more cautious in seeking professional help to indulge in an affair.

'What a surprise Bettina, to meet you on the train.'

'Hello, Tobias, it's good to see you.'

'My friends call me Toby, and I would like to consider you a friend.'

'Of course Toby, but I'm afraid that my name, Bettina, has no shortcuts.'

'Well, there's no reason to shorten such a nice name, but my parents had a lot to answer for, naming me Tobias.'

'I'm sorry that I haven't been back to the gramophone club since attending the event where the music played was from the wonderful Mozart opera, *The Marriage of Figaro.*'

'Well, I hope we'll see you again soon at an event'

'I'm planning to attend the Henrows' evening next week.'

'That's great, and I look forward to seeing you there.'

The chance encounter on the train, travelling from London to Hertfordshire, occurred one evening, just a week before the Henrows' gramophone event. They'd been on their way home from a day's work in the capital. It was one of those awkward occasions where the conversation was a bit stilted, both being conscious of other passengers eavesdropping on the chat, the passengers passing their journey time making up all sorts of absurd scenarios in their heads about the true nature of the relationship intentions of the couple sitting near to them.

A few days later, they met up unexpectedly again on the same train home, but that time it was much later in the evening, being almost the last train out of London. Bettina was working late, seeing clients who were unable to attend a daytime consultation, due to their own working schedule. Tobias and Verity had tickets for a concert at the Royal Festival Hall, but they'd got into an awful row during the day about some trivial matter, that by the evening, Tobias had forgotten what the row had been all about.

Verity had got herself into a serious strop and refused to go to the concert. Tobias did not wish to miss a concert of Bruckner's great eighth symphony, with Sir Georg Solti conducting the

London Philharmonic Orchestra. It was a very rare occasion for Tobias to attend a concert on his own. Either his wife was by his side, or he had attended with his new friend, Alex, if a particular programme did not appeal to Verity. When Verity refused to go, he thought of telephoning Alex, but being in a foul mood, he thought it best to go alone and indulge himself with several glasses of whisky as his sole companion.

Hearing Bruckner's wonderful cathedral sounds of music, mellowed his mood somewhat, but he had had one too many whiskies before and after the concert without eating anything, so he was half-cut when he alighted the train to take him back home.

'We mustn't keep meeting like this.' Chuckled Bettina – when taking the seat next to Tobias on the train. This time they'd had no other passengers near them, so they were able to chat without being overheard.

'You're a matchmaker, Bettina. I hope you advice your clients about the perils of a long-term relationship.'

'You OK, Toby?'

'Yes – I'm fine but I've had a few drinks at the concert hall, and my wife's not talking to me, but otherwise I'm good...'

'Why is your wife not talking to you?'

'We had a silly argument but I can't even remember what caused the row.'

'How long have you been married?'

'Oh...forever – we met at university and we've been together ever since. I love Verity, but sometimes I feel that I would just love to touch another woman's body, just to make me feel young again.'

'Look, Toby, it's not unnatural in what you desire. It happens to a lot of people in a long marriage. The key is; not to throw the baby out with the bathwater – if you get my meaning.'

Bettina gave Toby a saucy wink.

Toby looked confused and embarrassed.

'Are you suggesting...you and me?'

'No...No... Toby – you're a good looking man, but that's not it at all... I'm suggesting professional advice that I'm able to offer you.'

Toby furrowed his brow, not understanding what exactly Bettina had in mind.

'Excuse me, Sir, could I see your ticket, please?'

Both Toby and Bettina suddenly became aware that the ticket collector was standing by their seats and the chat stopped in its tracks. Tickets were produced promptly and the official moved away.

'Look, Toby, this is an inappropriate conversation on a public train. This is my office phone number – give me a call and I'll explain what I have in mind.'

Bettina handed her business card to Toby. The conversation died and both were left with their own thoughts for the rest of the journey.

Toby phoned Bettina the next day, as soon as Verity left the house to go to her yoga class. Bettina explained about her new matchmaking scheme for those that were married or in a relationship.

That wasn't what Toby had expected. He'd thought that what Bettina was promoting on the train the previous night was something more akin to couples' therapy. However, Toby was intrigued and he made an appointment to meet with Bettina in London for a consultation the following week.

The phone call occurred just a few days before Ronald Henrow's gramophone evening, where Toby and Bettina met up again, but in a totally different environment. The two of them had been extremely curious about each other in a social context and there was much small talk quietly going on between them, before the concert, and during the interval.

Verity had been right to be concerned about what was going on between her husband and the newish attendee, but it was not what she had thought, but potentially, very much worse!

CHAPTER 11

The first thing I noticed when arriving at the Eldens' house for the dinner party, was the difference between the Henrows' and the Eldens' houses. Well, actually, the exteriors of both properties were exactly the same, just being a couple of streets away from each other's. The houses dated from the 1960s, when properties, in particular ones built in larger town's suburban streets, had an architectural style that was uniform in design. Both houses were pebble dash semi-detached, three bedrooms, a separate living and dining room, smallish kitchen and garden, upstairs bathroom, with an extra toilet downstairs.

As both couples were professionally successful, I would have thought that they would be living in larger detached houses in a more upmarket part of the town. But on reflection, as neither couple needed bigger houses to accommodate children, they were able to indulge in their specific lifestyle priorities that could have been stymied by servicing expensive mortgages. Toby and Verity spent a lot of their money on expensive seats at the opera and Michelin starred restaurants. Ronald and Dulcie, on the other hand, did not go to the opera but loved to travel long-haul, which was pricey. Ronald was also a wine collector, buying Premier Cru Bordeaux from the Hertfordshire wine society.

The Eldens' living room had a warm and inviting feel to it, paintings by contemporary British artists on the walls, bookcases full of hardback fiction and non-fiction, plus a large collection of long-playing records and opera programmes. The furniture was comfortable and the lighting subtle; altogether, a room made for stimulating conversation and relaxation. The Henrows', on the other hand, with the same size room had coolness about it. They favoured a minimalist look, with bare white walls, and only a few chosen ornaments on display, with the centre of the room dominated by a harpsichord, which Ronald was learning to play. Their books, records, music scores and wine collection, were tucked away somewhere in the house, but not for guests to look at and admire.

'Come in, Alex, it's good to see you.' Toby answered the door with a warm smile on his face and gave Toby a friendly hug.

'Thanks for inviting me.' Alex handed a bottle of champagne to his friend.

'How did you know that we always started our dinner parties with a glass or two of champagne?'

'Well, I reckoned a bottle of champagne would always be a safe bet!'

The others were already relaxing in the living room, Ronald and Dulcie, both with a glass of bubbly in their hands.

Verity popped in from the kitchen to say hello, and by her side was Hannah Longsmith. I greeted Verity with a kiss and I shook hands with Hannah, whom I had only previously briefly met at the Henrows' gramophone evening.

'I may have been in the kitchen chatting with Hannah, but Toby was the actual chef for the evening,' Verity was chuckling, as she handed me a glass of champagne.

The conversation during drinks was friendly and civil, without anything remotely controversial cropping up.

Following a champagne refill, we were asked to follow the hosts through to the dining room. A large table, beautifully set, dominated the room. I was seated next to Hannah, with Ronald and Verity opposite us. At the far end of the table, nearest to the kitchen, was Toby, seated next to Dulcie.

Toby poured a lovely white burgundy wine for the guests, whilst he went off to the kitchen to get the starters and to check the oven for how the main course was doing.

A prawn cocktail was served with fresh homemade brown bread. The prawns, plump and juicy, was served on a bed of crispy iceberg lettuce, accompanied by Toby's special cocktail sauce – his own version of the traditional Marie-Rose.

My initial disappointment that Toby, whom I believed was a creative amateur chef, had decided on a conventional prawn cocktail, for the starter, had completely disarmed me. It made me realise that one doesn't have to produce original recipes to prepare and serve good delicious food.

The same applied to the main course. Toby chose a traditional, but a tricky dish to get right. It was Beef Wellington, beautifully cooked, medium-rare Aberdeen Angus, cased in pastry, with sauté mushrooms. Onion gravy finished off the dish. It was served with dauphinoise potatoes and green beans.

The room was quiet whilst we all devoured our food with mumblings of appreciative mms' around the table. Compliments to Toby morphed into a round of applause. A flushed host graciously responded.

'Thanks for your appreciation, folks, but if you think my cooking is satisfactory, wait until Verity wow's you with her amazing chocolate cake and her homemade ice-cream.'

Verity looked a bit embarrassed. 'Let our guests decide about the chocolate cake.'

Toby added. 'We have a real treat to accompany Verity's fabulous dessert, a glorious *chateau d'Yquem*.' More spontaneous applause ensued!

During the gap between the main course and dessert, the chat turned to music. 'I can't tell you how much I missed the gramophone evenings during the time I was away', piped-up Hannah to the room in general.

'I'm not sure how much you're into opera, Hannah, but Alex, our newest committed member, has started a whole series of events, playing the complete Mozart/Da Ponte operas.'

'Yes Toby, I've seen the red book, and although I'm not a massive opera fan, I love Mozart, and besides, it was about time we had complete operas as part of the club's repertoire. It was something missing from our programmes.'

Verity, accompanied by Dulcie, disappeared to the kitchen to sort out the dessert and perhaps indulge in a little gossip between close friends.

Meanwhile, Ronald and Toby changed places, so that Toby was now sitting next to Hannah.

Ronald, who had been fairly subdued during the dinner, maybe with thoughts on how he could trump Toby's cooking when it was his turn to host a dinner party.

'Hannah, You didn't miss much at Alex's event – eighteenth-and-nineteenth-century operas are boring. I may take a book to read for the next instalment of *The Marriage of Figaro*.'

My face became red with the shock of Ronald's remark; I was unsure on how to respond. Then I noticed a half-smile on Ronald face and realised that his ungainly approach was just his way of opening up a musical debate. So I smiled back and replied.

'So, Ronald, what operas do you like? Or should I say which operas do you approve of?'

I then noticed that Toby had moved closer to Hannah and they were facing each other, quietly conversing. He had also slightly dimmed the lights. So it was left to me to fight it out with Ronald; Toby had heard it all before and perhaps thought that a heated debate with Ronald would be a good initiating ceremony for me, to earn the right to be a regular at the dinner parties.

'The only operas worthwhile bothering with are seventeenth and twentieth-century ones.' To be more specific, the operas composed by Monteverdi and Cavalli, and from the twentieth century, Janacek, Britten and Tippett'

'Crikey, Ronald, you only chose five composers from over four hundred years of opera performances and goodness knows how many thousands of composers?'

'I would make an exception for some of Handel's operas. But even with him, all those never-ending *da capo* arias are so blooming tiring. The composers I appreciate are the ones that the music doesn't get in the way of a real-life dramatic setting.'

'Ronald, I don't mean to be rude, but do you know what? I really feel sorry for you. I don't know why you even call yourself a music-lover.'

'My musical hero is the composer, Igor Stravinsky, who stated that music had no emotional content whatsoever or contained extra meaning in the notes, other than the music itself; music was about music – nothing more, nothing less.'

'It's interesting, Ronald – that you had quoted Stravinsky: Other than his early ballets. I consider his later music cold and unfeeling. It lacks emotional content!'

'Well, that's where our respective forks separate in the road. I've studied music theory and my interest is in the music only, historically and architecturally, not becoming tearful, listening to over-ripe Romanticism.'

'I fear you protest too much. I had noticed an emotional response from you when you played Tippett's "A Child of our Time" at your own gramophone event!'

Before the exchange morphed into personal insults, the ladies announced, 'dessert is now served.' Toby poured the dessert wine and we all settled down to enjoy Verity's chocolate cake.

Coffee and liquors followed, with us gathered back in the living room. Again I noticed that Toby was sitting quite close to Hannah. I was confused. I already had the suspicion that Toby, despite frequently telling me that he and Verity were exceptionally happy, had a roving eye. Seeing him monopolising Bettina at Ronald's event, I assumed that she was his interest, which wasn't surprising, as Bettina was a gorgeous-looking feminine woman. Hannah, though, whom I found slightly masculine in appearance and manner, and unlike Bettina, not at all flirtatious, seemed an odd choice for Toby's attention.

Meanwhile, Verity and Dulcie, were loading the dishwasher and generally tidying up in the kitchen.

'I'm worried about Toby.'

'Snap, Verity, I'm concerned about Ronald.'

'OK Dulcie...you go first'

'We haven't been married as long as you and Toby have – and maybe we still have adjustments to make in getting along together on an everyday basis – and I hate to admit it but that I find his company boring. He's so stuck in his ways, like an old man, but he's actually younger than me. Look, I know ours wasn't a love match and I never expected unbridled passion from Ronald – he's not made that way – but I thought our common interests and respect for each other, would see us through. I've done so much for him – got him out of managing a record shop with a cushy civil service desk job at the Ministry of Defence. And I helped him to change his regional accent to an acceptable establishment one – but everything is about him. All his leisure time is taken up with his musical studies – his choral singing and his wine collecting. Not that he even drinks the wine – for him it's all about collecting. I appreciate his cooking, but even then, his ambition is to follow a recipe in even the smallest detail. Where is the joy, the fun, the inspiration to all his activities?'

'Oh, Dulcie, you must have known what to expect when the two of you got together?

'Listen, I was getting to a certain age that I had given up on the idea of marriage. I knew I couldn't have children and did not really want any, but I thought I could encourage him to adapt from his bachelor ways and see life more in the way that I do, more light-hearted, more fun, less of taking life so seriously. Look, financially we are very secure and we've both got our health – what the hell was our problem! During my long career in nursing, I'd come across so many very sick patients, who'd tried so hard to be well again and get back to a normal life that they felt so grateful for. Observing their spouses on visits, I saw the love for each other in their eyes. Ronald and I had been so lucky in the stack of cards we'd be given, that, although I'm non-religious, I believed it was a sin not to enjoy life more!'

Verity had listened very carefully to Dulcie's stream-of-conscience narrative. She had suspected that all was not right with their relationship, but hadn't realised how unhappy her dear friend had been.

'But what about all the travelling you did together?'

'Well, yes, the travelling was good, up to a point; but again, Ronald being Ronald, the locations were always his choice, and when we were there, wherever that happened to be, it was always his decision as to which museums, art galleries and concerts we were going to attend. Anyway, I've rattled on for much too long – tell me about your problem with Toby?'

'Hmmm, I'm absorbing all you've said, so let's leave my marital issues for another day. In any case, I think we go should go back and join the others. But let me ask you just one question: What would you ideally like to do?'

Dulcie looked into Verity eyes and said, very quietly. 'I'm at my happiest when I'm with you.'

Verity took Dulcie's arm as they marched back into the living room, with big smiles on their faces without a trace of Dulcie's recent angst visible to any of the others.

CHAPTER 12

As it happened, I caught the flu, so I was indisposed and unable to host the next gramophone event. The rules of the club stated that if a designated host had to pull out for one reason or another, they would have to wait until their turn came around again, so no disruption of the hosting sequence was disturbed.

In the circumstances, when I started to recover from sickness, I decided that for my next gramophone evening, I would skip playing Acts 3 and 4 of *Le Nozze di Figaro* and move on to play the Da Ponte/ Mozart second opera, *Don Giovanni*. But my plan was to play the complete opera in one evening. That would mean starting earlier than usual and finishing a bit later.

To compensate for the inconvenience, I bought a complete recorded set of *Le Nozze di Figaro* for each of our regular members. The performance I chose was a different one from the one I had played at my event, which was an LP-only version. I had yet to invest in a CD player, but planned to do so for my fiftieth birthday the following year. As far as I was aware, all the regulars had already starting using CD's, except Violet Smithson, but that may encourage her to invest in a CD player. The performance I decided on was a classic Decca recording dating from 1955, with a stellar cast. Eric Kleiber was conducting the Vienna Philharmonic Orchestra. This recording had just become available on CD and I bought nine copies of the opera set. That would include: Toby and Verity; Ronald and Dulcie; Greg and Florence; Hildergard and Benjamin; Violet; Dorothy; Hannah; and I also thought to include Bettina, in case she attended the event. Additionally, I bought a copy of the recording for myself, in preparation for my CD player purchase.

I thought to include a full synopsis of the opera with each CD set, which I printed out, using my office printer.

Act 1

Susanna tries on a wedding bonnet, whilst her fiancé Figaro measures the room in the castle given to them by the count, reminding Figaro of the 'droit de seigneur,' the ancient feudal right of masters to dally with their maiden servants. Figaro vows to thwart him

Figaro's old enemy Bartolo and Bartolo's former servant Marcellina enter with a marriage contract between Marcellina and Figaro, which they intend to enforce.

The page Cherubino enters, protesting about being sent away to the army because the count found him dallying with the gardener's daughter Barbarina. When the count comes out of hiding, he discovers the hidden Cherubino.

Figaro arrives with a group of peasants praising the count for abolishing 'droit de seigneur.' The count sends Cherubino off to join his regiment.

Act 2

The countess laments her husband's neglect, Susanna tells her of his designs on her, and of Figaro's plan to send a cross-dressed Cherubino to meet the count instead of her. Cherubino arrives to prepare for his 'tryst' with the countess, but the counts arrival forces him to hide in the closet. Susanna returns unobserved and hides.

The count told that Susanna is hiding in the closet, demands that she emerge. He goes to fetch tools to open the door, taking the countess with him. Susanna releases Cherubino, who escapes through the window while she enters the closet. Returning with her husband, the countess confesses that Cherubino is inside. Both are nonplussed when Susanna emerges. Figaro arrives. The gardener Antonio enters complaining about someone jumping from the window; Figaro claims it was him. The count is relieved when Bartolo, Marcellina and Basilio enter demanding that Figaro marry Marcellina or repay his debt.

Act 3

The Count pursues Susanna. She agrees to a rendezvous, but the count then overhears her plotting with Figaro. Alone, the countess ponders her unhappy marriage. Figaro confesses that he was born into a respectable family and requires his parents' consent. In his description of his history, Marcellina recognises Figaro as her long-lost son; Bartolo is his father. Susanna and the countess write to the count inviting him to the rendezvous; a pin must be returned as acknowledgement. A group of peasant girls arrive offering flowers to the countess, with the disguised Cherubino among them. Barbarina forces the count to let her marry Cherubino. The wedding celebrations begin. Susanna passes the letter to the count.

Act 4

That night in the garden, Barbarina laments losing the pin she was to return to Susanna. Figaro resolves to interrupt the tryst between Susanna and the count. Marcellina goes forward to forewarn Susanna.

Barbarina, Figaro, Bartolo and Basilio hide. Disguised in each other's clothes, Susanna and countess enter to ensnare the count.

Cherubino arrives seeking Barbarina, but sees (as he thinks) Susanna, and flirts with her. The count takes Cherubino's place wooing 'Susanna.' Figaro, seeing through Susanna's disguise, feigns seducing 'the countess,' and is caught by the count, who refuses to forgive his wife for her apparent infidelity. The truth is revealed and all is set right.

As it was Toby who was taking over my hosting slot, I requested the record shop to send the package of the recordings directly to Toby's residence, where he could distribute copies to each member at the event evening. Separately, I posted the printed copies of the operas synopsis to his friend.

Once I was feeling better and more human again, I decided to get back to writing my novel, which I had recently neglected.

CHAPTER 13

London
1970

'Let me buy you a drink.'

'Oh, thanks Sebastian, it's great to see you again after all this time.'

Ricky and Dominic had fallen out badly with each other following a blazing row regarding the travails of Dominic's love life. The rupture of their friendship occurred a few years after their crazy escapades in Brighton during the year of 1960.

In 1970, Dominic, a university graduate, had been working as an administrator in a London insurance company – a typical nine-to-five job with an average salary. He'd managed to buy, with a hefty mortgage, a small flat in London's Kings Cross area.

Ricky, on the other hand, went into sales, as soon as the two of them had returned to London from Brighton, and he'd flourished in all sorts of different occupations. By chance, he'd met up again with Sebastian Moran, who'd used the art of persuasion to recruit Ricky to work for him as a life-insurance-cum-financial adviser salesman.

Ricky knew that his old friend, Dominic, also worked in insurance. He'd twisted Dominic's arm, to agree to join him and his new boss, Sebastian, for a drink at the popular wine bar, Shirreffs, on Great Castle Street, a small street just off Regent Street North.

Raymond Hartman, who'd recently, founded the retail fashion store, Pop Shop, the store that was the number one destination for the young fashion conscience Londoner, had been a regular at Shirreffs, which was located almost next door the Pop Shop store. It being Raymond's local, the bar attracted many of the fashion industry hot-shots and their followers, mixed with a coterie of fashion models, fashion designers and those, perhaps, who were still lower down the food chain, but possessing upwardly-mobile aspirations. The modern newly established sector of financial adviser executives had also chosen Shirreffs, as their drinking-hole of choice in London's West End. The combination of executives from the two different industries, that had both morphed from a traditional public image, to being very much of-the-moment, created an electric buzz around the bar. Sebastian also used the location as a sales recruitment centre, ending many a wine-soaked night with a few new recruits filched from various fashion companies who had worked in showrooms that were dotted around the area.

The staid life-insurance industry had been rapidly changing, building their own sales teams that were starting to encroach on city stockbrokers trading territory, moving into the financial advice arena as well as marketing traditional insurance products. The newly expanded industry attracted a different type of entrepreneur – flashy, get-rich-quick types – who were building sales forces and linking them up to respectable long-established recognised life-insurance brands
.

Lord Sebastian Moran had quietly dropped the moniker Lord, and he'd become discreet about his aristocratic background, which wouldn't have sat well with the self-made business people he'd began to mix with. Moran had bought a small moribund insurance company to tie-up with the rapid-growing sales force he'd been building. Sebastian and Lydia had divorced in 1965 and sold their Rotingdean, Brighton, estate; Sebastian had moved back to Central London, where he'd started cultivating friendships with all the movers and shakers in the newly developing businesses that were created during the social revolution of the 1960s.

Ricky and Dominic's trip to Brighton during the summer of 1960, turned out to be longer and more adventures than they could have ever envisaged. Dominic had been really excited to have met Rosalind Gerstein at a Hove night club, and when they'd started getting intimate walking back together to her hotel along the sea front, Dominic thought that he'd found his first girlfriend. But that prospect, unfortunately, did not survive for more than that one evening. With Lydia Moran, he was quite confused, feeling a physical frisson that a mature sophisticated woman would have fancied him. But then he'd had the amazing good fortune of meeting Barbara, and it clicked for both of them, with Dominic thinking that it was third-time-lucky!

Barbara, being a student at the time she had met Dominic, influenced him to continue with his education. He'd gone back to school to do A-levels, which led to him being offered a place at a London University, to read philosophy and politics. Barbara's college was located in Bristol and her family home was in the county of Devon. The geographical distance between the young couple conspired for intermittent meetings only, but when they'd managed to get-together, with Barbara spending a weekend in London, or Dominic visiting Barbara, either in Bristol, or when he had occasionally been invited to stay with her and her family in Devon, they professed, sincerely, their love for each other. The problem had been that Barbara was, by nature, flirtatious. She'd become involved with a mixed gender crowd of art students at college, who'd prided themselves on being unconventional in their general behaviour, especially mocking the idea of sexual monogamy. They'd thought that society had been brainwashed by religious leaders and right-wing politicians into believing in the concept of one-man-one-woman relationship for the whole of their lives. Why only a man and a woman? What about sex between a man and a man or a woman with a woman – what would be wrong with that?

One Friday afternoon, when Dominic had arranged to travel down to Bristol, to spend the weekend with Barbara, he caught an earlier train than he'd originally planned and thought to surprise her by arriving before the scheduled time. He'd been excited and looking forward to seeing Barbara, as they'd not seen each other for while. He'd bought a lovely bunch of flowers, in vibrant colours, to brighten up her rather dull campus bedroom. No response came from his knocking on her door. As the door was unlocked, he quietly entered and was confronted with Barbara lying on her bed stark naked, entangled sexually with a big hairy brute of a young man who was straddling the girl Dominic had thought was the love of his life.

At that moment, Dominic lost his innocence – he felt extremely foolish and utterly betrayed. He threw the flowers down onto the floor and stormed out of the room, walked back to the station in a complete daze and caught the next train back to London.

Sebastian and Lydia were divorced; Dominic and Barbara's young love crashed and burnt; but what about Finley and Susie? They'd remained ecstatically happy with each other – the marriage had been a complete harmonious coupling.

With extra money he'd received from Sebastian, which was well over and above the amount Lydia had made him promise to pay Finley, the couple left Moran's employment. They'd moved to London, where Finley had opened a barber shop in the Soho area, which became hugely successful. Susie also worked in the shop having trained as a manicurist. The couple lived above the shop in a beautifully furnished flat.

What about Ricky Wenger's love life? Ricky being Ricky, he'd not changed. He'd always had a voracious sexual appetite and loved to play the field. Becoming a successful salesman he was able to splash the cash on seducing classier girls than the one's he'd chased during the time in Brighton. His luxury pad in Marylebone saw a succession of beautiful girls coming and going – the doorman of the block of flats found it all very amusing; but the doorman did not complain, as Ricky made sure that he was generously tipped.

Ricky and Finley were still good mates, but at times Finley despaired at his friend's cavalier attitude to woman, and worried, that Ricky would one day get himself into trouble if he didn't control his sexual addiction.

CHAPTER 14

'So, tell me, Dominic – how much does the Fenston Insurance Company pay you?'

'Sorry, Sebastian, but that's too personal a question.'

Dominic blushed. He was beginning to feel uncomfortable with Moran's constant inquisition about his current employment situation.

Sebastian, Ricky and Dominic, were propping up the bar at Shirreffs, smoking and sharing a good bottle of Bordeaux wine.

'Let me top you up, my friend.' Sebastian filled up Dominic's glass and put a friendly arm around the younger man's shoulder.

It's OK – I understand that you're embarrassed to divulge your salary because it's pathetically small. Ricky told me that you had bought a flat in Kings Cross. Why would you want to live in Kings Cross? It's such a run-down part of London – full of prostitutes and drug addicts.'

'Oh, come-on, Sebastian, Kings Cross isn't that bad; it's a great central London location, both for the city and for West End.'

'Hmmm...Have you been to Ricky's flat recently?'

'Yes, I was there recently and it's a most impressive pad.'

Ricky smiled and looked very pleased with himself, whilst giving Dominic an affectionate elbow shove.

'Seriously though, you stayed at my estate in Rottingdean ten years ago so you'll know the lifestyle that's possible if one had the wherewithal to fund it. Come and join my fast-growing sales team, and who knows, in a few years' time, you might be able to afford an estate similar to the one I'd owned.'

'Sebastian, I'm not being facetious, but your wealth was inherited. It had nothing to do with commercial acumen; you were just born lucky!'

Now the shoe was on the other foot, and Moran was looking a bit sheepish.

'Fair enough...' Sebastian put his hands up, indicating acceptance of Dominic's point.

'But that's why I've given up the aristocratic way of life and gone into business. I realised that we're 1970 not 1870, and that aristocratically swanning around town, with everyone bowing and scraping, wouldn't cut it.'

Ricky had been quietly listening to the exchange between the two and suddenly intervened.

'Dom, Please understand that Sebastian is a changed man from the person that had caused us such grief back in those Brighton days. His divorce from Lydia cut him up hugely and he'd started to examine himself and his behaviour.'

Ricky looked at Sebastian, seeking an affirmation from his boss that he could continue. Sebastian gave Ricky a knowing nod of the head.

They obviously had a well-rehearsed routine. Sebastian playing the big I am, showing off about his money and his lifestyle, with Ricky describing Moran's epiphany, taking part in a Dale Carnegie motivational course, which changed him from a posh playboy into a serious business entrepreneur.

'Dom, Sebastian's the best boss I've ever had. I'm making more money than I'd ever earned elsewhere. Besides he's great fun to work with and we're having a ball!'

'Fair enough, Ricky, but I know nothing about sales.'

Sebastian intervened. 'We'll teach you all you need to know. Actually, it would be Ricky teaching you, as you'd be working directly for him.'

Over another bottle of wine and numerous cigarettes Sebastian and Ricky explained to Dominic how he could make a lot of money.

It was known as the pyramid system. Sebastian was the owner of the company – and following the purchase of Lucas Life – immediately re-naming it 'Intermezzo.' His position in the organisation was at the very top of the pyramid. He'd coached and motivated six lieutenants that he'd personally recruited – Ricky being one of them – who'd reported directly to the boss. Sebastian would take a percentage cut of all the sales earnings of Ricky and his five colleagues. They'd called the payment, 'override.' Ricky recruited his own team, which was the team that Dominic would subsequently join, and a percentage of Dominic's sales earnings would be added to Ricky's salary, with another tranche of the sales paid to Sebastian. Dominic would not only market the company's products to clients, but even more importantly, and potentially more lucrative, Dominic would recruit his own team and earn a percentage of that team's sales. Dominic's team would set out to find their own recruits, potentially adding to Dominic's commission as well as the colleagues above him – right to the top of the pyramid, which naturally... was Sebastian!

Within the following twelve months, Intermezzo's sales force personnel had grown from a team of fifty to an impressive fifteen hundred. Offices had been opened up and down the country, with five separate offices within the square mile around Oxford Circus. They'd opened two offices in Oxford Street, two in Regents Street, and one in Haymarket.

The original six of Sebastian's recruits, were regional managers, each responsible for a multitude of sales offices working with the various branch managers. Ricky Wenger, being one from the first tier of the original recruits was the regional manager for London, and one of his recruits, Dominic Rivers, had become the branch manager of one of the Oxford Street offices.

Dominic reported directly to Ricky, who reported to Sebastian. As the sales organisation grew, with so many layers of managers, the three who'd had the personal connection dating from their Brighton/Rottingdean days, remained extremely close and were friends as well as colleagues.

Sebastian had started to attend the Glyndehurst Opera Festival in Sussex, during the summer months, and his favourite opera was Mozart's *Don Giovanni*. An invitation to Glyndehurst from Sebastian was something his managers prized, whether they liked opera or not. What they appreciated was the sheer glamour of the venue. Their wives or girlfriends would be able to show-off their finest evening dresses, and the best vintage champagne would be consumed with a luxury picnic in Glyndehurst's exquisite gardens.

Having done some research on the librettist of *Don Giovanni,* Sebastian became fascinated with Lorenzo da Ponte; in particular the poets association with perhaps, the greatest rake of all time, the libertine, Giacomo Girolamo Casanova. Sebastian saw himself as a modern-day Da Ponte – a man with a divergence of many different talents, who was irresistible to women.

In Sebastian's mind, his friend and colleague, Ricky Wegner, was the Don Giovanni of today and Dominic Rivers was his manservant, Leporello.

The 1960s saw a big change in British society; young people began to gain their voices, moving-on from the stratified 1950s, where everyone knew their place. Although Sebastian was in his mid-thirties during the early 60s, he couldn't help but be affected by the opening up of the class system, in which the British Empire had been built.

The aristocratic Morans had been part of the British establishment for hundreds of years. When Sebastian inherited the title following his father's early death, he was cock of the walk, thinking that the world was his oyster – and for him it truly was!

He'd married Lydia Williams, the daughter of a rich middle class Sussex business man, in 1955. Being a single woman at the age of thirty during the 50s was considered being left on the shelf. Lydia, had been a beautiful, well educated young lady, who'd had many young men vying with each other to date her, but had been prepared to wait for 'the-one' that would sweep her off her feet. Sebastian had known how to do that – and having a title, certainly hadn't harmed his chances! The huge wedding was a society occasion with a guest list that included many Lords and Ladies and some minor royals.

The pair had been deliriously happy during the first few years, but Sebastian, being true to his aristocratic background, was anxious for a male heir. Unfortunately, Lydia failed to become pregnant and although, following tests, it was Sebastian's sperm that was the problem, he still, very unfairly, blamed his wife for the lack of an offspring.

From the disappointment of being childless was quickly followed by Sebastian looking to quench his thirst-full lust with other women. And any woman who'd worked on their Sussex estate in any capacity was fair game for seduction.

Following all the shenanigans with Finley's fiancée, Susie Lattern, which ended up with Sebastian being really contrite about his behaviour, Lydia gave her husband the benefit of the doubt.

But it didn't take long for the Lord to revert to his old ways. Once Finley and Susie left the their estate and new staff had been recruited, Sebastian cast his eyes towards a new female housekeeper and the cycle of distrust between the Moran's started up all over again.

Lydia started to look elsewhere and commenced an affair with a much younger man who she had met during a charity event in Brighton. Sebastian found out and wanted to kill his wife. He'd resisted that extreme option, but he filed for divorce. He cited his wife's adultery.

However, once the dust had settled following the divorce, Sebastian realised that he'd been a fool and had really loved his wife. His continuous bad behaviour had driven Lydia into someone else's arms and he was to blame.

He'd been determined to turnover a new leaf and to make something of his life as a serious business person.

CHAPTER 15

London
1972

'Have you all set your goals for the week?'

Dominic Rivers, the branch manager of the East Oxford Street branch of Intermezzo Financial Services, was conducting the weekly Monday morning meeting, which was compulsory for all consultants to attend. Although the consultants weren't actually employed by the company, their status being self-employed commission only sales people. A number of the salespeople in attendance at the meeting, were managers as well, having recruited their own team, and earned override on the recruits sales – nevertheless, the company held all the ace cards and could instantly dismiss a consultant for any minor infringement of the rules that were devised by the company's founder, Sebastian Moran.

All hands firmly shot up to confirm Dominic's question about goals. Dominic, looking around the room, was drawn to a new recruit, Barry Jensen, whose arm seemed only reluctantly risen, and who was looking a bit down in the mouth.

'How many sales did you make last week, Barry?'

Barry, with all the consultants looking at him, his face deeply red, hesitantly responded, 'You know Dominic, that I didn't manage any sales last week'

'Look here, Barry, we're not a charity organisation, you've had the benefit of a desk in our offices, including heating, lighting, telephone and our new fax machine. If you're not producing sales for the company, we'll have to let you go.

'Ricky Wegner, our regional manager, will be visiting the office later this morning, and he'll want a serious word with you.'

'Andy Mankin, tell us about your sales last week.' Dominic wished to change the mood in the room, by picking on one of the stars of the current crop of consultant/ managers.

Andy, who was full of himself, stood up tall and gave chapter and verse about his weeks successful sales.

'Did you hear that, guys? That's who you strugglers should spend time with. Andy will show you how to make lots of money!'

Andy knew exactly how the system worked. He'd kept a close eye on new recruits and made sure that the ones that were failing moved over to his team. Andy was most persuasive with his sneaky plan; he'd invite the struggling recruits out to the pub and over a few pints, he'd convince the poor guy or girl that their difficulties with sales were due to their working for a weak, ineffective manager, and that they'd be better off joining his own successful team...

His arm around the recruit's shoulder as they'd be on to their third pint, Andy would look them in the eye, and say, 'Let's fix up an appointment with Dominic or Ricky, and together, we'd make the case for them to agree to the switch.'

That way, Andy built up his team and it was a win-win, for him. If the consultant's sales picked-up – he'd earn the override. But the biggest win would come from a consultant, like poor Barry Jensen, who'd be sacked. Even the most unsuccessful consultant would have made some initial sales, even if they'd been with the consultant's relatives and friends.

When a new consultant was taken on – they'd be encouraged to initially talk to their family and close friends about the company's financial products, before seeking clients from further afield. On leaving the company, the consultant would be obliged to leave their client files behind. The files would be classified as 'orphan' clients. The manager of the sacked consultant would have the ownership of the orphans and have first rights to add the clients to their own portfolio.

It wasn't too difficult to realise that contacting an existing, client who'd already invested funds into the company's products, and offering to review the client's portfolio, was so much easier that trying to convince a brand new client to come on-board.

Over time, Andy built up a substantial client base, mostly built-up from the orphan client file. Andy went on to become one of the most successful consultant/managers in the company, from branch to a prospective regional manager, as the company grew even bigger and more successful.

CHAPTER 16

Dominic was in a bind. He'd become a branch manager by chance. The evening he'd met Ricky and Sebastian at Shirreffs wine bar in 1970 had changed his life. The two of them had convinced him to join the burgeoning sales force of 'Intermezzo Financial Services', despite his lack of sales experience and for being too reserved a personality to ever succeed in that field. However, as he was in from almost the beginning of the venture, he'd been immediately promoted to branch manager, without actually having to prove any sales ability.

He'd hated himself as having to embarrass Barry Jensen in front of the whole branch, but that was his job. The whole enterprise based on pyramid selling was dog-eat-dog – the survival of the fittest. People such as the awful Andy Mankin thrived in such an environment, but decent, sincere guys like Barry Jensen, fell by the wayside.

As Dominic's earnings from override plus a generous branch manager's salary, grew exponentially, he'd moved from Kings Cross and bought, with a huge mortgage, a luxury flat in fashionable Hampstead Heath, North London, and a brand new Alfa Romeo sports car. The lavish spending commitments kept him in situ with Intermezzo, despite his conscience nagging at him that the business model, and the way it treated their consultants was morally dubious.

Sebastian Moran, as well as being the owner of the company, was at the very top of the sales pyramid, earning override from every bit of sales activity, from consultants, managers, branch managers and regional managers. He'd dictated all the rules of the organisation, from where the various branch offices would be located to promotions and dismissals of personnel. He even insisted on a specific dress code. From branch managers down, everyone had to wear a dark suit, white shirt, with double cuffs and tie – finished with a pocket silk handkerchief. Shoes had to black leather only and always to be highly polished. Regional managers and the boss himself were free to dress as they'd please.

As Sebastian had taken over an existing insurance company, he'd marketed the tried and tested number of Life products that had been devised by the various senior underwriters and actuaries of the original company, and had kept on all the insurance experts in their positions, but had got rid of the senior management who'd been on massive salaries. He'd appointed his own technical director, who reported directly to Sebastian, and he'd understood from the very start that the company had only one boss, and that boss was Sebastian Moran.

 At the first meeting between Sebastian and the technical director, it was made clear that although the sales force would market the traditional life insurance policies, he'd wanted more sexy financial products that would be money-spinners for the company. New type of saving plans directly linked to the stock market, via fund managers, had started to appear in the industry and Sebastian wanted a slice of that lucrative cake.

The saving plans that were devised very much favoured Intermezzo, but had harsh penalties built-in for the client, if a monthly payment had been missed. The plans were for a period of twenty-five years, and if a client's situation changed at anytime during the lifetime of the plan and they'd stop their contributions, all their money paid in would be forfeited.

Ricky Wenger stayed close to his boss, Sebastian Moran, and worked on changing his accent to 'received English' by copying the way Sebastian spoke, ridding himself of his light-cockney accent that he'd grown-up with. He'd even picked up on Sebastian's opera enthusiasm, not so much as appreciating the particular art form, but being able to join in a conversation with Sebastian's crowd, who'd be people from a class of society that he'd never believed would ever be in his social circle. Ricky, who'd always, had his hair cut in the short-back-and-sides working class tough-guy style, had grown his hair, and he'd started to wear it shoulder length. He adopted a striking pose with his long wavy dark hair and designer clothes. His outfits, tailored by stage costume designers, included bold prints for brightly coloured waistcoats, worn over an open neck silk shirt, finished with a high collared double-breasted coat/jacket that went down to beyond his knees. His trousers were velvet, and his accessories include top-pocket extravagantly patterned handkerchiefs and a long scarf, which he'd wrapped around his neck, both items being in pure silk. Expensive leather boots from Jermyn Street, Mayfair, were his shoe choice. He also wore a stylish wide brim soft fabric trilby hat, designed especially for him, by 'Locks' of St James's. He'd also grown a beard, which was taboo in the office for the others. His appearance was very different from the 'Savile Row' dark business suit that one would have expected, but he'd been determined to look more like a poet or a theatre director than a regional manager of a life assurance company!

Ricky's get-up appearance had the desired effect of impressing the consultants and managers of the company who'd had to present themselves in the office soberly dressed in their business uniform. It was just one of the reasons, besides the money, why the ambitious ones wanted to rise up the ladder to regional manager status, to have the freedom to swagger around the office in gear that would drive the women crazy for them!

Ricky, who had become highly experienced as a female seducer, started to attract women from the expensive locations of London, such as, Chelsea, South Kensington, Belgravia, Richmond and Hampstead. They'd be a mix of bored rich married women, looking for extra marital adventure or younger single girls coming from wealthy families. He'd even successfully seduced young women from aristocratic backgrounds who he'd met through his association with Sebastian.

The relationship between Ricky and Dominic had morphed from boyhood friends to aspects of a master/servant set-up. Ricky, being the senior of the two, had taken the younger boy under his wing, following the tragic death of Melvyn, Ricky's younger brother and Dominic's best friend. During their time together in Brighton in 1960, Ricky became even more aware of his young friends innocence and his inexperience with girls. The first night in Brighton, when Dom had met a girl in a local disco club, the poor boy had thought he'd met the love of his life! The hair-raising shenanigans at the Morans' estate, when Lydia Moran tried to seduce the boy, awakened Dom's sexuality, but then the silly idiot thought he had fallen in love with Susie's young cousin from Devon, Barbara Fenlon. He'd tried to warn the lad not to take it too seriously, but to no avail. When Dom described to Ricky the bedroom scene at Bristol University, when he'd caught Barbara in-flagrante-delicto, Ricky thought it had been hilarious and couldn't contain his laughter. Dom was disgusted with his so-called friend's reaction that he'd decided to cut all ties with Ricky. They'd not seen or been in touch with each other for several years, until Ricky had met up with Sebastian again and had been persuaded to join Moran in his new exciting insurance venture. When Ricky understood how important it would be for his advancement in the company to recruit as many people as he could, he thought of Dominic, who'd he'd heard was working for an insurance company in an administrative role. Ricky knew that Dom was still occasionally in touch with his parents, the Wengers, especially on or near the anniversary of Melvyn death, and they'd not hesitated to give him Dom's address and telephone number in Kings Cross, hoping that their older son and the friend of the their late younger son would settle their differences and be buddies once again.

Dominic's wasn't one to hold a grudge, but he hadn't considered that there'd been an ulterior motive to Ricky getting in touch just to make peace between the two old friends. Of course he should have realised that Ricky had always been a highly calculated individual. He had just chuckled to himself about his own naivety when it became clear that Ricky only re – contacted him with recruitment on his mind!

But Dominic was curious about the fabulous opportunity Ricky had gone on about, and he'd been even more curious to meet up with Sebastian again, the man who'd given him so many nightmares over the years, every time he'd thought about His Lordship.

So that's how Dominic came to be at the bar in Shirreffs on the night of the reunion of the Brighton trio.

CHAPTER 17

At the end of each quarter, the London offices of Intermezzo, comprising the four West End offices, plus the two city offices, held a regional meeting at one of London's plush hotels to hand out rewards to the top performing consultants and managers. Only consultants who'd reached a certain level of sales for the quarter were invited to the meeting, which would normally include a guest speaker, which might be a well-known sports celebrity, or one of the new fangled authors, who'd written bestselling books on 'how to be successful,' and styled themselves as a 'positive mental attitude coach.' The alternative to a guest speaker was the company's boss, Sebastian Moran, who'd attend the event and make the main speech. Ricky Wenger, the regional manager, and each of the six branch managers, would always be in attendance. Following the presentations and the speeches, a slap-up lunch was included.

At the 1972 spring quarter meeting, Sebastian Moran would be the main speaker and the venue was the famous Ritz hotel in London's Piccadilly, in one their function rooms.

Each branch manager highlighted their best-performing consultants for the quarter and handed out a cash bonus to each of the winners. Ricky made a speech praising each of his six branch managers and choosing the one consultant who'd be the performer of the quarter. The special prize was not necessarily for the consultant with the highest sales figures, but could be for their overall attitude to the company, or for general improvement in their sales performance, or for helping a struggling new consultant establish his or her selves in a hugely competitive environment. The prize was a weekend away for two in a European city of choice – all expenses paid and with them staying in the finest hotel of the chosen location.

Sebastian made a long rambling speech – a mixture of encouragement and threat.

He was determined to keep everyone on their toes, making sure no complacency crept into anyone's mind set. Consultants were frightened of the boss, as he could be ferociously tough on any miscreants, as well as being massively generous in praise of the striving consultant.

In his presentation he'd made some interesting observations about the industry.

'I know you all prefer to market the new fashionable savings plans to the traditional life insurance products. And I predict that in the years ahead we'll be selling personal pension schemes and sorting out clients mortgages, as well as estate planning and wealth creation. In other words, we'll become the complete financial adviser and competing with city traders in all sorts of financial products.

'That's great, my friends, and it's all our futures that we look forward to.

'However, today I want to make a plea for the massively important life assurance schemes – which is, and always will be, the bread and butter of the industry.

Unfortunately, selling life insurance policies in past decades were considered an almost desperate way to make a living and the butt of jokes with the chaps in the local pub, who propped up the bar in one's local pub.' (Stifled chuckles from the audience...) 'It was often sold by door to door salesmen. "Good morning madam, can I interest you in this new magic washing detergent that would get rid of the most persistent of stains on your white blouses and your husband's shirts." And as the housewife shakes her head and starts to close the front door, the salesman apologetically asks if her family had a life assurance policy – the mentioning of the dreaded life assurance would have got the door immediately slammed shut in their face.'(More chuckles... but this time it was been a bit more raucous)

'Hands up if anyone here had heard of the name, Charles Ives? Hmmm, I though not. You'd all be surprised to know, that Ives, born in 1874, was an American classical music composer. But Ives was no standard tunesmith musician – he'd written modernist music way ahead of his time, with unexpected dissonant passages in the most unlikely places in his scores. The audience at his concerts were shocked and his compositions were subsequently ignored. What did he do? He'd had a living to make and a family to support. He went to work in a life assurance company – eventually, forming his own insurance business. He'd become hugely successful in the budding industry, and despite being an intellectual of the highest order, he'd genuinely believed in the concept of life assurance and was proud of his success in persuading so many people to purchase his products which would have given then them peace of mind in family security. Ives, in our own time, is duly recognised as one the great modern composers of the early twentieth century – up there with the likes of Arnold Schoenberg et al.

'So, my friends, don't let anyone try to put you down, by being a life assurance salesman – be proud of your career and remember; if selling life assurance was good enough for the great Charles Ives, it's good enough for you.'

Following loud applause, Sebastian concluded: 'Now off you all go – enjoy a delicious lunch. You've certainly deserved it.'

CHAPTER 18

Ricky had kept a log of all the girls and women he'd seduced over the years, and the numbers had increased exponentially since his change of circumstances, from a basic sales person to a regional manager of a successful life assurance company. He'd never been short of confidence, but since the career elevation and the complete overhaul of his appearance, he'd never found it easier to get his way with whoever he'd fancied.

As he was Dominic's immediate boss, he'd use the younger man to keep score of his conquests. It was a way of showing off to Dom and to make him jealous, as the poor boy hadn't had a girlfriend since the disastrous episode with Barbara, which had happened years before, and had severely hurt his pride, denting his sexual confidence. Dom wasn't one for casual dating, being a romantic soul at heart – he'd always sought to meet someone who would lead to a full-on monogamous long-term relationship.

Sexually, he'd secretly fancied older women – his brief tryst with Lydia Moran in Brighton when he was only aged seventeen, had had a lasting effect on him, but he'd never had the opportunity to repeat the experience with anyone else.

The few women consultants in the office, plus the branch female secretary and its receptionist, were all lusting after Ricky, so he didn't stand a chance with any of them even if he'd been interested, which he hadn't been.

Ricky's main office was at the London, Haymarket branch, so when he visited the other offices in his region, he'd commandeered the branch manager's office, which was the only private room in the various office buildings. The consultants all worked in an open-plan environment, designed that way by Sebastian so that everyone saw and heard what everyone else was up to, leaving no room for shirkers and slackers.

The morning of the branch meeting when Dominic had chastised Barry Jensen, Ricky paid his weekly visit. Following a coffee and a business catch-up with Dom, he'd called Jensen into the office and laid down the law with a final warning. 'Pull your weight or you're out of the company – full stop!'

He'd then asked Lilly – the pretty young secretary – to see him in the office. 'Please lock the door, Lilly.' She entered with a knowing grin on her face. She'd understood exactly what Ricky was after, as she'd been there before, and she'd had no objection to enjoying a bout of sexual activity with his nibs.

What Ricky didn't know was that Dominic could watch the whole performance from a secret hole in the wall of the storeroom that was adjoining his office. He'd discovered it by accident when Ricky was entertaining one of the female consultants on a previous occasion.

Dominic got a thrill watching his old friend in action and was a bit ashamed to realise that he'd become a voyeur.

Through the peep-hole Dominic could see that they'd fully undressed and Lilly was vigorously giving Ricky oral sex. He'd then arrayed her over the desk and they'd copulated eagerly. He'd turned her over and entered her from behind. As they'd both reached a climax, Dominic, viewing all the action from the storeroom, masturbated.

Ricky, although being sexually obsessed, had been finding it all too easy to get his way with women of all descriptions. He had zero interest in adolescent girls – they had to be at least age eighteen – but preferred the early twenties age group. He'd amused himself by having given Dominic the role of logging all his conquests. The log was getting bigger and bigger and he'd seen himself as the twentieth-century Don Giovanni, the title character in Mozart's opera. He'd attended the opera at

Glyndehurst as a guest of Sebastian, and although knowing nothing about the opera, or about opera in general, he'd been absolutely fascinated by the operas inventor; the poet and writer, Lorenzo Da Ponte. Da Ponte had been a bit of a rogue and a serial womaniser; his friend had been Casanova – the most famous seducer in history!

Ricky had also got the idea of a conquest log from *Don Giovanni,* the opera. In the opera, the Don's manservant, Leoporello, had kept a log of the Don's conquests, and sang a hilarious aria to one of the Don's abandoned women, Donna Elvira, who'd been in love with the Don. The aria was trying to tell the Donna, 'don't bother with him, as you're just one of hundreds of women who's been seduced by the Don.' Leoporello then goes into detail about the Don's numerous conquests – how many he'd met in each different country that he'd visited, as well as their ages, their looks etc, etc.

With himself being the Don, Dominic had had to be the manservant, Leoporello; hence he'd be the one to keep the conquest log. Dominic had been reluctant to be the chronicler of Ricky's seductions, but the more Ricky tried to remember all of the females he'd seduced over the years, relating them to Dominic, who'd added each one to the list, the more his young friend, found that by osmosis, a lustful thrill occurred – he'd be imagining, in graphic detail, the unfolding of the sex act.

Ricky had been spending more and more of his leisure time with Sebastian and his wealthy crowd of friends in Belgravia, where Sebastian resided, in an historic townhouse of a considerable size. He'd become bored with women from his sort of lower- middle-class background, finding rich women far more alluring – especially women from an aristocratic background. They'd dressed and smelt better and possessed an air of confidence, and even a touch of arrogance, that turned Ricky on. He looked forward to seducing high-society women and had achieved many conquests. And the ones who he enjoyed the most were those who put up the most resistance initially. The women from Sebastian's circle that Ricky had sexually conquered would not for one minute consider Ricky as boyfriend material, or someone they'd consider marrying. Marriage would always be with someone from their own class that Daddy would approve of and provide the funds for a luxury lifestyle that they felt was their birthright. Despite Ricky's elocution improvements and his poetic style of dress, they considered him their bit of rough. Ricky didn't mind at all, as he wasn't seeking a girlfriend either and the idea of marriage was anathema for him.

Anna Kimber-Smythe was becoming a challenge for Ricky. Basically, she'd refused to play ball with him and turned-down any sort of sexual approach. She'd been amused by Ricky trying to edge himself into society by his garish clothes, long hair and beard. She'd considered him a bit of a fraud and basically, just an oik in fancy dress!

 Her friends, when they'd got together, had a good laugh at Ricky's expense.

So why did Anna lead Ricky on? It was for her, purely a bit of sport. Anna was the daughter of a hereditary lord, and, his family were long-time friends of the Morans. Sebastian had known Anna since childhood, and they'd be like brother and sister, so neither had any notion of getting together sexually or romantically. Country Sports were in Anna's blood, especially anything to do with horses. She'd adored going out with the hunt where the foxes were torn apart by the trained foxhounds. She'd found the whole experience sexually arousing, and would often go off with the 'master of foxhounds' for a sexual tryst following the hunt after a few drinks in one of country inns.

So Anna was certainly no innocent – why then had she led Ricky a merry dance? It was just another sport for her. Lead the fool on and watch his frustration. He'd been used to having his own way with many women, and even some of her aristocratic girl friends had succumbed. But Anna experienced the greatest pleasure by refusing his advances.

Ricky just couldn't abide that, so one night when she'd foolishly agreed to go back to his place following a night out, he forced himself on her. She ran out of his flat in a dishevelled state of undress, got herself to a phone box and got through to her Daddy, who'd sent the chauffer in the Rolls-Royce to pick her up.

Daddy sought revenge and let Sebastian know in no uncertain terms that if his so-called friend ever showed himself again at his residence, he would have him killed.

'I'm not sure you should log onto the catalogue my latest escapade Dom'

'Why's that?'

'Because for the very first time – in all the hundreds of escapades – I've had to force my way with her.'

'Who's her?'

'You wouldn't know her – the stuck-up bitch. Her name was Anna – the daughter of Lord Smythe – friends of Sebastian's family.'

'Whoops – that sounds dangerous, Ricky.'

'That's not half of it. Sebastian told me that Daddy Smythe had threatened to have me killed if I'd ever showed my face again at the Smyths' residence.'

'Oh my god – my advice would be to keep away from any of Seb's crowd, at least till this thing dies down.'

'Absolutely, Dom, and Seb's furious with me, as he'd known Anna since they were both kids. I just hope he doesn't sack me.'

'Well, that's rich coming from Moran, as we're both fully aware of his lecherous history. It's a laugh him being all high and mighty now that he's the successful business tycoon. That speech he gave at the regional meeting about a bloody classical composer – what was the git's name?'

'Ives'

'Yes, bloody Charlie Ives. You'd think that our Seb was some sort of classical music expert the way he'd carried-on. He's maybe a lord and a successful business owner, but as a human being, he's been a complete failure.'

'Wow, Dom, I didn't know you had it in you – you're not as meek and mild as your projected image!'

'I have my moments, *old fruit.*' Dominic responded with a cheeky smirk on his face.

'Listen, my friend. I really do appreciate your support. We've been through a lot together over the years and I know that I've taken you for granted at times and had not treated you well, but I love you like the brother I used to have.'

Dominic had to turn aside to control his emotions.

That night Dominic had a dream – or more like a nightmare. *Anna's father had sought Ricky out to give him a piece of his mind on how the swine had raped his daughter. Ricky attacked and killed Lord Smythe.*

The following morning Dominic telephoned Ricky. 'Are you alright Rick?'

'Yes mate, I'm fine, why do you ask?'

'I had an awful dream last night in which Lord Smythe confronted you about your seduction of his daughter and you killed him.'

There was a prolonged silence on the telephone line. 'Ricky...
Are you still there?'

Eventually, Ricky's voice came through, sounding a bit shell
shocked.

'Well, you got part of your dream right. I hadn't had a
confrontation with Smythe yesterday and I certainly didn't kill
him. But his Lordship did in fact die last night. He suffered a
fatal heart attack at his home.'

Dominic couldn't believe what he'd just heard. But before he
could respond, Ricky continued.

'Your dream was partly precognitive, my friend. It seemed you
possess psychic powers.

'I'll tell you one thing though; in future, all my seduction
techniques would be concentrated on girls and women from
more ordinary backgrounds and I'll keep well-away from the
posh crowd who tended to play games with potential lovers and
are totally up themselves.'

Chapter 19

One could not envisage a situation where Sebastian would sack Ricky, or Dom, for that matter. Despite Moran's arrogance, he possessed a sentimental side to his character. Sebastian's relationship with the pair dated back to their Brighton days, and the trio had been soulmates in the creation of their successful company, Intermezzo.

Propping up the bar at their favourite watering hole, Shirreffs, Seb advised Ricky that he should keep away from the posh girls of Belgravia. He'd added that Anna Kimber-Smythe blamed Ricky for her daddy's death and she'd been considering reporting Ricky's sexual behaviour to the authorities. The only thing that had held her back was that they'd ask questions about her past sexual history, which was far from innocent; she'd attended many sex parties and had never been shy in participating in orgies. Sebastian also warned Ricky about the man she'd recently become engaged to: Sir Archibald Horatio-Irvine. He'd been spouting on about protecting Anna's honour and would be seeking revenge. He was handy with a pistol and came from a military background.

'Listen, Ricky – I'll be holding my annual summer party at my place in a couple of weeks, but in the circumstances it would be prudent that you stay away.'

'Fair enough, Seb. I'll keep a low profile. What about Dom – will he be attending?'

'I see no reason why Dom shouldn't be there – he hasn't misbehaved with any woman.'

Ricky spent the rest of the evening thinking that he'd been made a fool of by Anna, who'd never had any intentions of letting him have his way with her.

The night of Sebastian's party, Ricky found himself at his local pub, The Coach & Horses, in Marylebone, having a quiet drink and feeling a bit cheesed-off at missing out on Seb's event, which always had great food and drink, plus lots of women to try his luck with.

Nursing a pint of beer, he noticed a young couple sitting at a nearby table. The girl was extremely pretty, with a pert little nose and deep blue eyes; she looked about aged nineteen or twenty. The boy with her seemed a bit, but not much, older; Ricky reckoned early twenties. They looked very much in love, holding hands and sharing the odd little kiss every so often.

Ricky being the mood for some mischief decided to go to their table and introduce himself. 'Excuse me – I had to come over to say hello as you looked such a handsome couple.' They reacted in a sense of utter bemusement, wondering what the stranger had wanted from them.

Ricky, sensing that they'd had been perfectly contented in their own company, knew he had to act quickly to avoid being dismissed. 'Please let me buy you both a drink.'

'We're fine, thanks,' both uttered in unison.

'This is my local pub. I don't think I've seen you here before. Are you new to the area?'

'No....' they both chuckled at the man's presumption. We couldn't afford to live in Marylebone, no way! We have a council flat in Kilburn. We just wanted to spend a day up west to see what the moneyed lot are doing. We were just window shopping in Marylebone High Street, when we saw the pub and thought it looked nice, so here we are.'

It was the girl who'd answered his question – Ricky had thought that she possessed a very sexy voice.

'Let me introduce myself. My name is Ricky Wenger.'

'Hello, Ricky, my name is Matt Foster and my girlfriend is Zoe Billing.'

'I'm just going to top up my beer – what's yours, Matt?'

Matt and Zoe looked at each other and hesitated for a moment. 'OK, thanks. Mine's a lager and Zoe's drinking white wine.'

'Great, guys, be back in a few minutes.'

Whilst Ricky went to order drinks, the pair conversed.

'I don't trust that guy,' whispered Matt.

'He seemed fine. I think he's just a bit lonely tonight and looking for some company.'

'Hmmm... You're just a bit naive, Zoe. What does a guy from around this wealthy area want with us? Also, his accent is weird; it's like he had a London accent like ours but has tried to go posh but it hasn't really worked. And his clothes – who does he think he is wearing such outrageous outfits in those awful bright colours? Is he a poet, or what?'

'Calm down, my love. We don't know who he is or what he does; maybe he is a poet?

'Na, Zoe. That man's a fake, mark my words.'

Ricky returned with the drinks and Zoe indicated for him to sit next to her.

Zoe addressed Ricky. 'Are you a poet or something?'

Ricky laughed and said, 'No, I'm not.'

'What do you do then?'

'I'm part of a very successful financial organisation.'

'So why do you wear your hair so long and dress like an artist?'

'Well, because I've a top position in the company. I don't need to dress in a traditional business suit, and chose an individual style that stood out from the crowd!' Ricky stood up and did a twirl, laughing his head off.

Following several more rounds of drink, the situation at the table begun to get rather cosy, with Ricky openly flirting with Zoe and not meeting any resistance from her. However, Matt had started to become increasingly unhappy.

'Hey, babe, I think we ought to be getting along.' Matt said, as he stood up, gesturing to Zoe.

'What's the rush? The nights still young.' Ricky had sensed that Zoe was game and he thought of an idea of how to keep her close,

'Listen folks, you said earlier that you've come up west to see how the other half lived – I'm off to a posh party in Belgravia; why don't you two join me as my guest?'

Matt immediately turned down the invitation, but Ricky noticed that Zoe was intrigued by the idea of going to a party – especially a posh one.

'C'mon love, what's the harm? You'd know how much I love parties.'

Matt shrugged – had wanted to please his girlfriend – so he'd reluctantly acquiesced for Ricky to take them to Belgravia.

The party had been in full swing by the time they arrived at Sebastian's home. In the taxi on the way there Ricky told the couple about the party's host, Sebastian Moran. The fact that he was titled, Lord, as well as Ricky's boss and friend, really excited Zoe, but Matt seemed disinterested in the whole thing.

What Ricky hadn't disclosed was that he'd not been invited –
with Seb specifically advising him to stay away from Belgravia
to avoid any trouble from Anna and her fiancé.

Zoe eyes nearly popped out of her head when she'd first saw
Sebastian's white stucco-fronted house, never having believed
that she'd be visiting such a stylish residence in one of the most
expensive areas of London. As they stepped out of the taxi
Ricky lightly touched Zoe's bum, having made sure that Matt
didn't see the incident.

Despite not being invited, Sebastian, well on at inebriation,
having started drinking at lunchtime, seemed to have forgotten
uninviting Ricky, and gave his colleague and friend a massive
tight hug, proclaiming, that the party wouldn't be same without
Ricky's attendance.

'Sebastian, I've brought some new friends along to the party. I
hope you're OK with that.'

'Any friend of yours, Ricky, is a friend of mine.'

Ricky made the introductions and hands were shaken, with
Sebastian offering the newcomers his most warm smile, adding.

'Everyone is out on the terrace enjoying the beautiful summer
evening and the champagne's flowing.'

Sebastian led them out onto the terrace where indeed the
vintage bubbly was being served by very smartly dressed male
staff. The hooray-Henry's, with loud upper-crust voices, were
holding court, whilst their elegant wives and girlfriends hung
onto their every word, even if they were talking garbage, which
they were, most of the time.

'Ricky had made sure that Matt and Zoe each had a glass of
champagne as he excused himself to say hello to Dominic,
who'd been standing in a corner, chatting to Finley and Susie.
He was surprised that they were at Sebastian's party.

'It's so good to see you both.' Ricky had given his friends, Finley and Susie, big hugs and kisses.

'Well, *my old fruit,* we were surprised to receive to an invitation from our old nemesis, Lord Sebastian Moran.'

'He's not so much his Lordship these days but the successful businessman.' Said Dominic, looking at Ricky with some concern, wondering why he was there at the party at all. Did Sebastian know that Ricky had gatecrashed the event?

'Don't worry, Dom, Seb knows I'm here. He welcomed me with open arms. He's obviously forgotten his earlier decision not to invite me.'

Finley and Susie listened to the exchange between Dom and Ricky with some bewilderment, knowing the recent closeness, as colleagues and friends, between Ricky and Sebastian.

Ricky, seeing Finley's furrowed brow, just said. 'It was about a bird, mate.'

Finley laughed knowing about Ricky's sexual obsession, and put his hands up in the air.

'You don't need to tell me anymore, Rick, I've always told you to be careful, that you'd get into trouble one day through your constant need for sex.'

 Susie wasn't always utterly comfortable around Ricky, even though she'd, deep down knew that he being such a close mate of Fin, would never dirty his copy book making a move on her. Remembering the awful problems she'd had with Sebastian during their time in Brighton, she was curious about how much Sebastian had changed his spots.

'Is Sebastian really a changed man?' Susie half whispered her question, not wanting other guests to overhear the conversation.

Dominic took on the question, also speaking in a quiet voice.

'Don't fall for all the whitewashing of Moran, even though his ex-wife, the lovely Lydia, is amongst the guests here at the party. He's just exchanged his aristocratic power and superiority to the business world. To be fair, he's now less of being a female seducer and understands that business success had to go hand in hand with a clean moral record, both in financial and sexual matters.'

Whispering in Susie's ear, he added.

'He's an absolute bastard to work for. Rick and I are fine, because we were there with him in the early days of the company, and, he considers us friends. But others, have been treated very badly, the arrogance and entitlement are still very much part of his persona.

Ricky interjected. 'Sorry to interrupt guys, but I've brought a couple of guests with me and I need to check that they're OK.'

'No problem, Rick — we know some of the people here who've been to our hairdressing salon and we should say hello.'

The guests at the party were a mixture of Sebastian's aristocratic friend, some who he'd known since childhood, with a good selection of more recent friends and contacts from the business world, including the well-known figure from the fashion industry, Raymond Hartman, who'd become Sebastian's regular drinking buddy at Shirreffs wine bar. Raymond, being very tall, was always the centre of attention, whether drinking with the business crowd at Shirreffs, meetings with his work colleagues or socialising with toffs at Sebastian's summer shebang.

Sebastian was rather envious of Raymond, whose Jewish parents had had to flee from Austria to London during the 1930s, leaving all their worldly goods behind. Raymond was therefore, a self-made man with a big personality, and, an even bigger ego and was lauded for his business success, whereas Sebastian, whatever business achievements he'd attained, was judged differently by his peers. Behind his back, people sneered with comments, such as, 'silver spoon,' 'trust fund heir' or weak-chinned toffee-nosed aristocratic Lord-of-the-Manor.

Finley and Susie moved through the crowd on the terrace to hello to Raymond Hartman. There he was, towering above the throng of people, who'd gathered around the popular fashion figure, busy holding court amongst his well-wishers. How did Finley know Raymond? The hairdressing talent of Finley was well known beyond Soho, where the salon was situated. The word had spread around the new fashionable media, sport and design operators, and men of London rejected the staid look of the traditional way of dressing and grooming. Out went the three piece dark suit and watch-chain, short back-and-sides hair and bowler hats. Granted, they'd not all dressed as extreme as Ricky, but 'in' came more stylish single breasted suits, with wide lapels and sailor-like wide trouser legs; the look was finished off with pointed leather shoes. The more adventurous wore the newly popular Kipper ties, designed in outlandish colours with pop-art patterns.

Until recent times gentlemen had always wore hats, but the new generation of young men rejected hats of any kind and grew their hair long. Consequently, the traditional barber shop had been transformed into gentlemen's hairdressing salons. Finley's salon had become an in-place to go for a stylish haircut. Raymond Hartman, and his executive colleagues, from the fashionable Pop Shop store in Oxford Street all had their hair cut, washed and blow-dried at Finley's in Soho, with Susie expertly doing the manicures.

Raymond, no snob, greeted Finley and Susie as old friends, introduction them to all who'd gathered around the popular businessman.

Meanwhile, Ricky had led Dominic away from the crowd to a quiet part of the terrace. He'd explained about his newly acquired friends and how he was lusting after the gorgeous Zoe.

'I want you to take care of Matt – distract and amuse him, whilst I look after Zoe. You know what I mean Dom.' Ricky gave Dom a nudge and a wink. Dom knew exactly what Ricky had in mind and wasn't happy about it.

'You can't do that here Rick, especially with her boyfriend around.'

'That's not you concern. I'll give you the details tomorrow and you'll be able to catalogue another of my conquests.'

They spotted Ricky's new friends sitting on a white wrought-iron latticework garden chair for two, sipping champagne just down a few steps from the terrace, into the garden, both looking bored and out of place at the posh people's event.

'Sorry, folks to have neglected you, but let me introduce you to my friend, Dominic. I'm sure, Matt... You'd like to meet some of the people here. You'll go along with Dom and I'll give Zoe a tour of the house – I know she'd love see the elegant rooms.'

Matt looked very unsure but as Zoe seemed so enthusiastic he reluctantly agreed to go off with Dominic.

'C'mon Zoe – let's go indoors.'

Zoe was flirtatious and found Matt, although loving him, a bit on the dull side. But in truth she was an innocent and inexperienced in sexual matters. She'd met Matt at school and they'd been boy and girlfriend ever since.

Ricky could be a brute with women, especially with the ones that he'd sensed had been around the block – so to speak. But when his instincts were that the woman he was trying to seduce, needed a softer approach, he'd learnt to turn on the charm.

Ricky had led Zoe around the garden to the kitchen entrance, where the chefs and the waiting staff were busy preparing the food to be served later in the evening. Passing through the kitchen without anyone taking much notice, he took Zoe's hand and headed to the drawing room, which Ricky had known from previous visits to the house. The room was decorated in an ostentatious style – the walls and the ceiling had been painted in bright yellow, with two magnificent chandeliers dominating the space. A Steinway grand piano was placed in one corner of the room and a Bang and Olufsen stereo system in the other corner. A Lucien Freud portrait of Sebastian was placed right in the centre of room, making sure that no one missed seeing it.

Zoe was overwhelmed with the surroundings, thinking what it would be like to live in such opulent luxury. Sitting down together on the black leather sofa, Ricky sensed the bird's unease.

'I think we'd better get back to the party... Matt will be wondering where we were. I thought you were giving me a tour of the whole house,'

'That was an excuse, my lovely. I wanted us to be alone together.' Ricky put his arm around Zoe and drew her close.

'I'm not sure about this, Ricky, please let's go back'

'What's the hurry, doll? Don't you fancy me?'

I think you're really nice looking; it was fun meeting you and coming to the party, but I don't want to do anything that would upset Matt.'

'Forget about Matt – let's have some fun together.'

'Don't you have a girlfriend, Ricky?'

Ricky lied. 'I was in love with this beautiful girl but she got very sick and then she died. After the tragedy, I couldn't ever think about making love to another girl ,but when I saw you, I was reminded of my beloved Donna, and felt an overwhelming passion for you.'

'I'm sorry about Donna, but I'm sure there is someone special for you out there.'

'You don't understand... it's you I want, my gorgeous sexy Zoe.'

Zoe, with very mixed and confused feelings, indicated that Ricky could kiss her, but then they'd have to get back to the party.

Ricky kissed Zoe, got up from the sofa and went to turn the lights off.

He returned to the sofa and jumped on top of her. He'd started to undo her blouse and the hook of her skirt.

'Zoe, alarmed, shouted, 'what are you doing, Ricky? Get off me!'

Putting his hand over her mouth, he whispered into her ear in his most seductive voice. 'You know you want this, don't you.'

Zoe jumped up and let out a huge scream.' Help me someone! I'm in the Drawing Room!

The cry was heard by Sebastian, Dominic and Matt as well as by Anna Kimber-Smythe and her fiancée... Archibald Horatio-Irvine. They all happened to be in the next-door room and came rushing in.

Anna immediately recognised Ricky before even someone turned the lights on.

'There he is, the man who raped me. Get him Archie, and teach him a lesson with a jolly-good thrashing.'

But Ricky was too quick for them and had easily managed to push past Horatio-Irvine, who'd been a bit unsteady on his feet having drunk too many glasses of champagne. He ran out of the door and made his way back to the garden, where he escaped via the back entrance to the house, jumping into a passing taxi.

Back at the house, Zoe was crying and Matt was trying to sooth her. Dominic, feeling a bit guilty himself for helping to facilitate the assignation, offered to drive the couple home to Kilburn. He didn't stop apologising for his friend's bad behaviour.

CHAPTER 20

Ricky and Sebastian were propping up the bar at their regular drinking-hole, Shirreffs. The usual Bonhomie between the two friend and colleagues was more subdued than usual. And even when Raymond Hartman joined them at the bar directly from a successful board meeting at his Pop Shop, they'd found it hard to match Raymond's humorous anecdotes in his larger-than-life attitude to all things, important or trivial.

Raymond moved off the bar stool to chat to some other people, who were situated at the other end of the bar, Sebastian put his arm around Ricky and said quietly...

'Ricky, I didn't want to do this to you and I definitely did not want it to have happened officially at the office, but you'll have to go from the company. Anna and that Archibald twerp have teamed up with Zoe and Matt; they've made a complaint to the police about your sexual behaviour. Even if nothing comes of it, you'd know as much as I that just a sniff of a scandal could ruin our business. Personally, I think you've been a fool, but I'm not judging you as I'd be the last person to point fingers, what with my past record in unacceptable sexual conduct.

'I understand, Seb. I'd do the same if the shoe was on the other foot.'

'I've arranged a decent financial package for you, but I want you to clear your desk tomorrow morning and quietly disappear from the business. My advice to you is to keep a low profile for a while.'

The following morning, Ricky arrived at the office at the crack of dawn before anyone else would have made an appearance, gathering all his things together, leaving the building for the very last time.

Sebastian appointed Dominic in Ricky's place, so he'd become the regional manager of all of the Central London branches of the company. Dominic moved his office from Oxford Street to Haymarket, where Ricky had been based. Andy Mankin was appointed manager of the Oxford Street branch, taking over the role from Dominic, following the latter's promotion.

Despite Ricky's sacking from Intermezzo, he'd be confident enough of finding another job in the industry, provided he'd be able to get over his current local difficulties with the police.

The advice from his solicitor was that the complaints would be very hard to prove taking into account Anna's past sexual history and Zoe's leading you on with the kiss.

Ricky decided to keep away from Shirreffs and had kept his drinking forays to his local pub in Marylebone, The Coach and Horses. Dominic had kept loyal to his friend and joined him for drinks there on a regular basis.

One evening, on Dominic entering the pub, Ricky noticed a worried look on his friends face.

'You ok Dom? Let me get you a pint.'

'Thanks Rick.'

Ricky came back with two pints of bitter asking Dominic what was bothering him.

'It's that dam dream again, and why, for God's sake, do I dream about you!

'The one I had last night was really weird. I saw an image of the late Lord Smythe speaking with you, Ricky. He'd accused you of killing him and he sought revenge. Your attitude towards Smythe was dismissive and cruel. You didn't believe he was dead and challenged him to a dual. Smythe agreed to a dual and requested a meeting between you. You then invited him to a party at your apartment building, where the two of you can have it out and let the best man win.'

'Ha ha ha... that's the most hilarious thing I've heard in ages, Dom. I'll tell you what – let's find out where his lordship is buried. We'll visit the gravestone and officially extend an invitation for him to attend my party.'

'I didn't know you're having a party, Rick.'

'Well, we are now, Ha ha ha.'

One evening in dark, dank, foggy November, the two friends took a trip up to Highgate.

They visited the cemetery where Lord Smythe was buried. The grave wasn't difficult to locate as it contained a huge tombstone that listed the Lord's many accomplishments, as well as the names of the family members who'd been the main mourners.

'Go on... Dom, you had the dream – invite the lord.'

'Ricky, this is all so weird, I can't believe I agreed to come here.'

'Listen Dom. You owe me big time – you're now a regional manager in the fastest growing life assurance sales force in the country. Who recruited you in the first place? Hey, without me you'd still be earning peanuts in that two-bit company, pushing around bits of paper. Besides, you'll always do what I ask. I've that power over you... Ha ha ha.'

In a nervous stutter Dominic spoke to the gravestone and invited Lord Smythe to Ricky's party.

Were their imaginations running riot in the gloomy darkness? Both men went white with absolute horror.

'Did you hear a voice...?'

'Yes, I heard a deep bass voice, very croakily, announce that he'd attend my party... spooky or what?'

Ricky, this place is haunted. Let's get out of here.

Ricky and Dominic made a hasty retreat from the cemetery, shaken to the core.

A few weeks had passed and the two friends looked back on their escapade to the Highgate Cemetery and laughed it off, realising that the unreal atmosphere by the graveside had got the better of their imaginations as Ricky pronounced, 'Dead men don't speak!'

Ricky's party was in full swing. He'd booked the party room, with a fully fitted kitchen, situated on the ground floor of his luxury apartment in Marylebone, which was only available to residents for their special events. He'd had the best caterers in town, specialising in the finest French cuisine, to organise the food and the drink. Champagne and canapés to start, then a sit down dinner with the best seafood dishes followed by roast pheasant in a creamy calvados sauce accompanied by *pommes frites, petit pois,* and a green salad, served with the best vintage wines. Peach soufflé was the dessert, followed by liquors and cigars. Ricky hired a string quartet to play during dinner and he'd specially requested an arrangement for string quartet of Mozart's three Da Ponte operas, *Le Nozze Di Figaro*, *Don Giovanni* and *Cosi fan tutte.* Dancing was to disco music after dinner for which Ricky hired a well-known disc jockey. No expense was spared as Ricky wanted to show that despite his current travails, he hadn't been hiding himself away. Nothing bothered him – he was completely shameless.

They were all there at the party – Dominic of course, Sebastian with his ex-wife, Lydia, and a smattering of his Belgravia crowd, excluding, of course, Anna and Archibald, and, anyone close to that couple. Finlay was there with his lovely wife, Susie. Raymond Hartman was in attendance, with all the Shirreff regulars, as well as many ex-colleagues from

Intermezzo. Also, many friends from Ricky's younger days, whom he hadn't seen for years and had managed to contact; they had been delighted to receive an invite.

Everyone at the party was having a great time. The champagne flowed and the dinner had been absolutely delicious – beautifully presented by the French chef and beautifully attired waiters. The string quartets arrangement of Mozart's famous operas, were hugely enjoyed, especially by Sebastian's Belgravia crowd, who were regulars at the Royal Opera House and Glyndehurst.

Raymond Hartman made a speech, thanking Ricky, and, telling the guests that it had been the very best party he'd ever attended. At the end of Raymond's speech, Ricky whispered to Dominic, who was seated next to him. 'Raymond had offered him an executive job at Pop Shop, and had added that he thought Sebastian was an idiot to have sacked him. He'd said that a successful businessman in the 1970s needed a big libido to succeed. He'd only take on executives that were sexually prolific and he, being the boss of Pop Shop, was the most sexually prolific of all!'

Dominic laughed his head off giving Ricky a firm pat on the back, congratulating him on being offered a job by the big shot himself, the one and only Raymond Hartman.

As the evening wore on, with the disco music being at full blast, the atmosphere had become electric, with guests singing along to the pop tunes of the day, that the disc jockey had cannily chosen to play. A lot of drink had been consumed and a few couples, not necessarily the partners they'd arrived with, had disappeared into side rooms for some sexual activities. Others, the more romantic ones, stayed on the dance floor, and, when the disc jockey played slow numbers, hands were everywhere, with much sexy kissing going on.

The night was coming to a close with the music slowing down, guests a bit unsteady on their feet and some looking a bit dishevelled, either from alcohol or from sexual activity. Some of the more senior guests, perhaps a bit worn out from too much dancing, were sitting down and smoking cigarettes.

Ricky and Dominic had their arms around each both feeling satisfied at the success of the evening and a bit smug too. After all, they'd outwitted Sebastian years before in Brighton, when the lordship had tried to seduce Finley's Susie, but was cleverly foiled, and now he'd been made to look a fool again for sacking Ricky. Here Ricky was the toast of the evening, and was about to join the most successful fashion store in the country as a senior executive. Life was good!

Just then, there was a loud knock on the door. Ricky and Dominic, both rather drunk, looked alarmingly at each other both with thought of that strange evening at the graveside of the late Lord Smythe, thinking they'd heard the dead man speaking, accepting an invitation to Ricky's party.

Both Dominic and Ricky uttered the same words.' It can't be ... can it?

The door opened and all the guests went deadly quiet. Two big burly men in shabby suits and crumpled trilby hats, entered the room and following behind them, were, Anna and Archibald, and behind them, Zoe and Matt.

Anna pointed to Ricky. 'That's the man – Ricky Wenger, the man that raped me.' She'd said her words in a very loud voice, so everyone in the room could hear. Zoe came forward and said in a quieter voice, that yes, the very same man sexually assaulted her at a party in Belgravia.

At the mention of Belgravia, everyone turned to Sebastian who turned crimson with embarrassment, although, nobody was accusing him of anything.

The two burly men stepped forward. 'I'm Chief Detective Simpson, and this is my colleagues, Detective

Sergeant Burrows. Turning to Ricky, he asked. 'Are you Ricky Wenger?' Ricky, with his head bowed, confirmed that yes, he was he.

'Mr Ricky Wenger, I am arresting you for rape and sexual assault. Anything you say could be taken down in evidence against you. Sergeant Burrows, please handcuff the suspect and take him away'

Ricky, without turning around, went, without protest, with the detectives out to their police car, which sped away to the police station.

Anna and the other accusers left the building together and drove off into Archibald's Jaguar.

The party broke up, with everyone in total shock, all leaving as quickly as possible.

The last two to leave the building were Dominic and Sebastian. Sebastian, turning to his younger colleague, remarked. 'The party that had started on such a high finished in the lowest possible way.'

All Dominic could do was nod in agreement with Sebastian, without adding a word.

Both left the building and went their separate ways home.

CHAPTER 21

Hertfordshire 1993
DON GIOVANNI

ACT 1

Don Giovanni, a Spanish nobleman, is renowned throughout Europe as a seducer of women. Leporello, his servant, reluctantly aids him by keeping watch. Giovanni attempts to leave the house of Donna Anna, his most recent conquest. He kills Anna's father, the Commendatore when the Commendatore tries to stop him. Anna tells her fiancé, Don Ottavio, that she was raped by an unknown man and they vow revenge on the murderer.

Leporello attempts to persuade his master to reform are interrupted by Donna Elvira, a former mistress of Giovanni's, who is travelling to look for him, Giovanni leaves it to Leporello to explain the extent of his master's womanising.

Masetto and his bride Zerlina are to be married at a peasant wedding, but Giovanni sets himself to seduce Zerlina. Elvira interrupts and foils Giovanni's attempt. Ottavio and Anna appeal to Giovanni for help in their pursuit of the murderer of Anna's father. Elvira again interrupts and warns Ottavio and Anna about Giovanni's true nature. Anna tells Ottavio that Giovanni is the man who murdered her father.

Leporello discusses with Giovanni the plans for the masque ball his master is hosting that evening. Zerlina assures Masetto that Giovanni had not touched her. Elvira joins forces with Ottavio and Anna; they are going to the ball and intend to exact vengeance on Giovanni. Whilst everyone is dancing at the ball Giovanni attempts to ensnare Zerlina, but she rallies all behind her to try to entrap Giovanni. All accuse him, but he and Leporello elude them once more.

Hoping for success with Elmira's maid, Giovanni exchanges clothes with Leporello, who is instructed to lure Elvira away. Giovanni is interrupted by Masetto, who is intent on killing him, but his disguise is successful and he beats Masetto up and escapes.

Returning with Elvira, Leporello is mistaken for Giovanni by Anna, Ottavio, Zerlina and Masetto. Removing his disguise, Leporello convinces them that he is not the guilty one. Ottavio swears vengeance on Giovanni, whom, in spite of everything, Elvira continues to love.

Giovanni hears the voice of the Commendatore, who he killed warning Giovanni of impending retribution. Giovanni orders Leporello to invite the ghost to supper. The ghost of the Commendatore accepts Don Giovanni's and arrives to send him to hell.

As it happened, I'd decided not to play the opera, *Don Giovanni*, at the remaining hosting evenings during 1992. I'd received some resistance from some of the members, as to the length of the evening, but there was more to it than that. Although the schedule of gramophone club events had remained as planned, relationships between two married couples, whom had formed the core membership of the club, had hit the buffers.

Tobias and Verity, Ronald and Dulcie, as well as Hannah, had stopped attending the gramophone club for the remainder of 1992, so, as well as losing five founder members of the club, the attendee numbers at events were decidedly low. It felt as if the heart of the club had been ripped apart. Although I was fairly new to the club, I felt a strong motivation to keep the group together, however small, and I'd hoped that the missing five would return when whatever had been bothering them, had settled down.

For my hosting evenings during that period I kept to core repertoire of well-known classics; nothing to challenging or controversial and I kept the programmes short.

Four of the missing members came back at the beginning of 1993 – the rest of us were delighted to see them back, although, for one reason or another, Hannah did not return. We'd all realised that there had been some serious upheaval and changes in the various relationships, but we'd all been sensitively discreet, and apart from giving them warm welcome hugs, no questions were asked and no exclamations were offered.

For me, it was time for *Don Giovanni*, and, interestingly enough, the previous murmurings of too long a programme disappeared.

We had a full house for *Don Giovanni* and the fact that we were doing a complete opera, meant we'd attracted a number of new people whom were opera enthusiasts, and they were particularly keen on *Don Giovanni*, the opera.

I was proud of my recording of the opera that I'd purchased about five years previously, the Georg Solti recording on the Decca label. The recording dated from 1979 with a wonderful cast. As well as being a Solti fan, I was attracted to the evocative illustration on the front cover of the box of the three LPs. It was by the British artist, Charles Ricketts and titled, *Don Juan*. The cast included a mouth watering array of operatic stars. They were: Bernd Weikl (Don Giovanni); Gabriel Bacquier (Leporello); Stuart Burrows (Don Ottavio); Margaret Price (Donna Anna); Sylvia Sass Donna Elvira); Lucia Popp (Zerlina).

I had printed copies of the libretto to distribute at the start of the evening, as well as copies of the plot.

I gave a short talk about the opera before playing the records, stressing the uniqueness of the Mozart masterpiece, and asking the question:

'Is the opera a comedy or a dramatic work?' The answer was it was neither one nor the other, but actually both. The genre in Italian was called *dramma giocoso,* which translated, 'humorous drama'. To sum up, *Don Giovanni* was by turns absolutely horrifying, but also comically hilarious. There lies its uniqueness.

The evening had been long and a few of the attendees were tired at the beginning of Act Two, which was perhaps the least inspired section, musically, of the score, but by the time we arrived at the scene of the statue arriving for supper, the audience was again wide awake, caught up in the sheer audacity of the creation. Solti had handpicked great singers and they'd sung their arias beautifully. And Solti himself brought energy and excitement to the wondrous score.

There was enthusiastic clapping at the conclusion, like we'd been at an actual live performance of the opera. Everyone went home exhausted, but on a cultural high.

I found it hard to sleep that night, with the music of *Don Giovanni* running through my head. Stuart Burrows' mellifluous tenor voice, in particular, kept teasing me as I was humming to myself his two arias, *Dalla sua pace* from Act One and *Il mio tesoro* from Act Two. Burrows character in the opera is Donna Anna's fiancé, Don Ottavio, a rather stiff figure, dramatically, that the librettist, Da Ponte, seemed to have little interest in developing, but I know people who'd only attend a performance of *Don Giovanni*, to hear a good tenor sing those two incredibly beautiful arias. In fact, there should only be one of those arias, because *Il mio tesoro* was so difficult to sing that Mozart substituted it at later performances. He'd composed instead, *Dalla sua pace,* which in itself was not an easy sing. Although the tradition over the years was to include both arias in performance, some recent productions, especially from directors from non-operatic backgrounds who never knew what to do with the wooden character of Don Ottavio. I know that I'd feel short-changed if one of the arias was dropped from a performance.

Sleep eventually arrived, with me dreaming about the beautiful aristocratic character of Donna Anna.

I had taken some overdue leave from work, so the next morning, I was free to spend the day at my leisure. The nagging thought was to use the spare time getting on with my novel, but I needed a break from writing, before commencing on part three of it.

It was a lovely sunny morning so I decided to go for a long solitary walk. I was living near the oldest agricultural experimental farm in the world, Rothhamsted. The farm was situated in Harpenden, Hertfordshire, and a long walk through their farmlands seemed a good plan for the day. Whilst walking through green fields, but feeling exhilarated taking in the fresh country air, my thoughts turned to my novel, especially the chapters I had recently completed. I'd intended to take aspects of the opera, *Don Giovanni,* and merge them into the story of twentieth-century characters behaving badly. I wondered how successful I had made the link. Of course, it would be for others to judge in due course, but I was hoping that the book would convert some readers to becoming opera lovers.

As I continued my walk, I reviewed, in my head, some of my novel's characters, and, which of *Don Giovanni's* cast I had left out of the plot. I had certainly left out Donna Elvira, an awkward character in the opera who veers between love and hate for Giovanni. My creation of the character, Sebastian Moran, who'd been my Count in the Figaro chapters, does not have a *Don Giovanni* match – nevertheless, he plays a major role in my story around the opera. Again Finlay and Susie, the Figaro and Susanna in the earlier chapters, only have walk-on parts in the *Don Giovanni* sections. The matching characters in the novel were, Ricky Wegner who was the Don Giovanni; Dominic River – Leporello; Anna Kimber-Smythe – Donna Anna; Archibald Horatio-Irvine – Don Ottavio: Zoe – Zerlina and Matt, Masetto: The Commendotore was Lord Smythe.

I had walked for several hours and arrived back at Harpenden's
West Common, just at the time that the Harpenden Arms pub
was opening, and I was thirsty for a pint of local beer.

CHAPTER 22

Hertfordshire

1992

Tobias Elden

Tobias was nervous about his appointment with Bettina Emberton, having reluctantly agreed to the consultation, purely out of curiosity. The two of them had accidently bumped into each other, twice, travelling from London home on the train home. He'd got the wrong end of the stick about what Bettina had suggested. Initially, he'd embarrassed himself by stupidly thinking that Bettina had made a pass at him. He'd quickly recovered from that faux pas and then he'd understood (wrongly, as it so happened) that the consultation suggestion was in the role of a marriage guidance counsellor. It was only when he'd telephoned to arrange the appointment that the penny dropped that Bettina was actually running a dating scheme for married men and women. Getting over his initial shock, he'd fixed up the appointment. Once he'd put the phone down, he thought. *What the hell am I doing, and, what sort of business is Bettina' involving herself with?*

Bettina preferred to hold the consultations in a five-star hotel drawing room than in her offices. The appointments would be in the daytime, as in the evenings, hotel drawing rooms took on a different vibe, with softer lighting and more alcohol consumption, which would increase the noise volume at other tables. Only if clients were unable to attend during the day, due to their own work commitments, would Bettina agree to arrange the consultation in her London offices, for an evening appointment.

Bettina named her matchmaking scheme Love Me Do, in homage to the Beatles debut single, issue in 1962, when Bettina, aged eighteen, moved with her family to London.

The hotel Bettina had chosen to meet her clients was the Ainsborough, situated in the upmarket area of Knightsbridge, close to the famous store Harrods. The ornate drawing room had two tables in each corner of the room; both tables had a screen around them for privacy purposes. Bettina had an arrangement with the management of the hotel, where she could reserve one or the other of the private tables for her consultation meetings.

Tobias, although he'd made a point of dressing in his smartest suit, still felt a tad uncomfortable arriving at the hotel's main entrance, with a Rolls Royce, a Bentley and a Jaguar parked ostentatiously outside the front. Tobias had travelled by train from Hertfordshire, and the underground from Kings Cross. A smartly dressed porter with a top hat had opened the entrance door, tipping his hat in greetings. 'Good morning sir.'

Tobias made his way to the drawing room. On entering, he'd immediately noticed the smiling, standing-up Bettina, gesturing him over to her corner of the room. As they shook hands, Toby kissed Bettina on each cheek and took a seat behind the screen. A waitress immediately appeared offering refreshments, and coffees were duly ordered.

Whilst waiting for coffees they chit-chatted about the gramophone club and other non-personal this-and-that. Once coffees had been brought and sipped, Toby having adopted a serious expression, he asked Bettina, 'please tell me what your matchmaking scheme is all about and how does it work?'

'Well, I started Love Me Do ten years ago, when my marriage broke up. I'd been a school teacher for many years, but I'd always had a knack of matching friends and colleagues together. Being divorced made me revaluate my life in every aspect, and I'd had the crazy idea for starting my own business as a matchmaker.

'Anyway, we're not here to talk about me; the meeting's about you.'

'OK, understood, but why matchmaking for married people'?

Bettina explained briefly to Toby the reason why she'd added the special scheme to her portfolio of Love Me Do, emphasising that it was very much a small side of the operation – dating for singles was still over 90 percent of her business. 'But I had so many inquiries from people stuck in relationships that weren't working, for all sorts of reasons, and they'd wanted a discreet outlet for their frustration. Divorce was off the table for some, as their religion forbade it. In other cases, it was for prosaic reasons – namely financial. So Toby, the scheme is in no way salacious. It's still about relationships, but of a niche type.'

They spent the next hour or so, completing the application form to be able to join the scheme, filling in details about Toby's physical appearance, his health, his family and educational background, his interests including cultural, sporting, food, drink and travel.

Moving on from general information, Bettina asked for a summary of Toby's career.

'Well, I spent my whole career in the media world, specifically the TNB. I'd started at the corporation straight from university, as a junior trainee, slowly rising through the ranks, ending up as editor of the leading nightly news magazine programme. I retired early for various reasons, and I now do some freelance work for different media companies.'

'Toby, not wishing to be intrusive but I'm curious to know why you retired at such a young age when you were at the top of the tree there.'

The atmosphere around the table had become a bit frosty. 'I don't see how my retirement from the TNB is relevant to your profile building. Besides, this whole exercise is making me feel uncomfortable. Why do you need all that information? I thought that you'd just introduce me to some suitable women, who'd be in a similar situation to me?

Bettina immediately closed the file and looked straight at Toby. 'I'm a professional and try to do a thorough job for all my clients. The only way I'd be able to do that, is by making dating introductions on the basis of full knowledge and understanding; the profile building is an essential first step towards that goal. If you'd rather end the consultation here and now, that would fine by me, and I'll destroy the incomplete profile form.'

'No. No, Bettina, I'm sorry I over-reacted. It's just I didn't expect such a formal-type interview – I'd thought we'd have a little chat, over a cup of coffee, and sort of take it from there. '

'Bettina smiled. We had the coffee, anyway!'

'Please continue, Bettina.' The waitress appeared with fresh coffees, knowing by a sort of osmosis that they'd be ready for more coffee.

Not opening the file, Bettina continued. 'What's the current state of your relationship with Verity?'

'Hmmm...To be honest, it could be better. She decided that her friend, Dulcie, you know, Roland's wife, is someone she'd rather spend time with, than her husband.'

Bettina furrowed her brow. 'Would there be same-sex interest between the two women?'

'Ha ha ha. That's the funniest thing I've heard in ages; my wife and Dulcie – lesbians? Don't be silly – no way!'

Bettina put her hands-up. 'OK, Toby, ignore that suggestion.' But Bettina had seen the two women close up at the gramophone events and had had her suspicions that something could be afoot there.

'Let's move on from your profile.'

'That's a relief.'

'I need to know the type of woman that you'd be attracted to.'

'OK... that sounds good; it takes the heat off me, ha ha ha

'Right... Do you have an age preference?'

'No... not really. Let's say about my age, or maybe, a few years younger, or even a few years older.'

'What about physical appearance?'

'Mmm, I've been thinking about that for a while, Bettina. You know Verity, she's very feminine looking, a pretty woman; would you agree?'

'Yes, Toby, Verity is an extremely pretty woman.'

'You should have seen her when we'd first met, she was gorgeous!'

A far-away look appeared in Toby's eyes as he had fleeting thoughts about regret for what had been, and what was now developing between them, following a long and mostly happy relationship.

As he shook himself out of his reverie, words came out of his mouth that surprised himself.

'In later life, I'd come to realise, that actually, I'm more attracted to women with a more masculine look, having always assumed that it be the feminine, aka Verity, that would float my boat.'

Bettina was equally surprised by Toby's admission.

Following some more general questions about the type of woman Toby would be interested in being introduced to, with the idea of pursuing a discreet love affair, Bettina wrapped up the meeting. She'd felt that she'd put Toby through-the-ringer and that he'd attended the consultation purely out of curiosity, and, politeness to a music-loving acquaintance.

'Thanks for coming, Toby, it was very much appreciated.' They both stood up and shook hands.

'I need to peruse your profile and give some thought to your comments. I'll then be in touch with some suggestions.' Handing Toby a tariff card with the Love Me Do's terms and conditions, Bettina concluded, 'There's no sales pressure here, Toby. You need to be absolutely sure that it's what you want to do, before we go ahead.

'Thanks, Bettina, I'll wait to hear from you. And, by the way, I hope to see you at Roland and Dulcie's gramophone evening later in the week. '

Bettina, a big smile, said, 'Yes, Toby, I'll be there.'

Once Toby had left the drawing room of the Ainsborough, Bettina sat down, ordered another coffee, and thought about Toby. Her initial instincts were that he'd be unsuitable for her dating scheme, too sensitive, and unlike her typical male clients. The male clients that had had the confidence to attend the consultation, both the singles and the married, were generally full of themselves, believing they'd be God's gift to the female race. Also, the men had always requested that they'd be introduced to women much younger than them. Toby, said his interests would be of women either his own age, just a little bit younger, or even a bit older than him. As well as, his professed desire for a masculine-looking woman was unusual. Yes, Toby was a bit odd. Certainly it gave Bettina plenty food for thought.

Toby was also wrapped up in his own thoughts on the underground and train journey, travelling back to Hertfordshire. Where his thoughts took him was to sex. How ironic was it that a man was most the potent being full of testosterone when he was in late adolescence and early twenties; but at that age, he'd be sexually inexperienced. He'd be ignorant of the potential multiplicity and variety of the sex act. In one's forties and fifties, just at the time when men became more sexually knowledgeable and confident, potency and testosterone tended to drop, and would kept dropping, as one became older still. It was one of life's cruel curve-balls. When he'd met Verity, they were both young and sexually naive. They'd started to have sex together a couple of years after they'd started going out, and they'd settled into routine sexual practices that had sustained them throughout their long married life. The relationship hadn't been about lust, or sex, for that matter, but about love and friendship. They'd loved each other and had considered themselves lucky and even a little smug. But time and ageing had bred a certain questioning. When they were young and romantic, sex was just a routine part of the overall package of their successful relationship. Later on in life, when he'd begun to think about mortality and had started to examine the really important things in life, sex reared its head in different ways to how it did when young and fresh, believing then that he'd owned the world.

He'd not regretted attending the consultation with Bettina, because it had opened up his revaluation of what he sought in sexual matters. He'd realised that both he and Verity had become stale together, and he, anyway, wanted to grab life by the throat and move on from the cosy life that had sustained them for many years.

One thing, though, that was absolutely sure about, that the answer for him wasn't signing up with Bettina. She'd been totally professional in the way she'd conducted the meeting and he'd thought her a delightful person. But the scheme wasn't for him; it was too business like and rather cold-blooded. He'd also come to the conclusion that Bettina hadn't been convinced that he'd be a suitable client for her scheme. He'd have a quiet word with her at the upcoming gramophone event.

It was then that Toby began to think about Hannah. Next to Verity, she'd be considered less attractive with a slight masculine look – with her short cropped hair and dressing in formal structured suits. Yet, as he'd indicated to Bettina about being attracted to a masculine look in a woman, and despite dismissing the idea in his head for various reasons, he'd become sexually drawn to her. It was her no-nonsense manner and intelligence that when he'd thought about sex with someone other than Verity, Hannah kept cropping up in his head,

There would complications a plenty. Although Hannah's love life was an unknown quantity, it was common knowledge that she was in a relationship, despite the fact that none of the gramophone set had ever seen this mysterious gentleman, and knew nothing about him.

But, the main stumbling block was that there had been history between Toby and Hannah. One of the reasons that Toby had told Bettina, during the consultation that he hadn't been interested in being introduced to a much younger woman, was that during his career at the TNB, he'd had his feet burnt due to an involvement with a young female colleague that almost cost him his job.

When Toby introduced Hannah to the gramophone members, it was just assumed that they were local Hertfordshire acquaintances, but the facts were that they'd known each other through the TNB. Some years earlier, when Toby had got himself into a bit of bother over a young woman, Hannah Longsmith had been part of the TNB's independent panel that had sat in judgement as to whether he'd been guilty of sexual misconduct. The complaint was not upheld and Toby had been forever grateful to the panel, and to Hannah, in particular. She'd read the trajectory of events correctly between Toby and the young woman in question, arriving to the conclusion that no sexual impropriety had taken place.

Lucille Bennett had been Toby's editorial assistant at TNB, and had worked very closely with her boss. Toby had always been faithful to Verity, and had no designs on Lucille, who was twenty years younger than Toby. Lucille had a crush on him and would occasionally join the team for a late night drink following the evening TV news programme.

'Haven't you got a home to go to, Lucille?

Toby and Lucille were the only two of their team still in the pub; the other had left for home.

'I could ask you the same question, Toby, Ha ha ha.'

'Well, I'm lucky, my train to Hertfordshire runs all night; I just have to grab a cab to Kings Cross.'

'Snap, boss, my bus to Crystal Palace, South London, also runs all night!'

'Fair enough Lucille. but that's no excuse to be drinking all night.'

'OK '–Toby, but let me buy you one more drink for the road. What will it be?'

'I'll have one more pint and then we'd both better head home – tomorrow's another day.'

The pub had emptied out whilst Lucille was at the bar getting the drinks, a pint of beer for Toby and a vodka and coke for Lucille, probably one too many for her, as she'd drunk more than her usual ration of alcohol consumption, which tended to stop following the second round of drinks.

'Let's sit on the banquette in the corner, Toby.' Lucille, with the drinks in her hand, swerved away from where their news team colleagues had congregated earlier on. 'It's cosier over there, Ha ha ha.'

It was also much darker in the corner, and the bar staff were unable to see them. Why don't you move a little closer?' Lucille whispered in Toby's ear whilst she looked straight into Toby's eyes. Toby shuffled up to her, being conscious, through the glassy haze of alcohol that his editorial assistant was flirting with him. He'd not been looking for an affair, especially with a woman so much younger. And the fact that he was Lucille's boss, ruled out even the very thought of it. Although Lucille had been his assistant for a couple of years, he'd known very little about her. She'd been excellent at her job, especially her research on the news items chosen for the nightly programme. She'd occasionally mention a boyfriend, but the boyfriend had not been spoken about for a while; maybe they'd broken-up? In any case, he'd never considered her in a sexual way. She was a typical young woman of her age. Stylishly cut blonde hair but with rather bland facial features. She'd had a trim figure, perhaps a bit skinny for Toby's idea of an attractive female, but the twenty-something age group were obsessed with not putting on weight and skipping meals in pursuit of the perfect slim figure. It seemed to Toby that all her clothes had been bought at Pop Shop in London's Oxford Street, where most of London's young women shopped. Her skirts were very short, which showed off her well-shaped legs. From Toby's point of view, Lucille could have been interchangeable with hundreds of young women in London, of a similar age group. There was no individuality anymore; they all wanted to look alike.

'How's your boyfriend, Lucille? You've not spoken about him for a while.'

'Oh, I broke-up with Adam. He was far too young for me. I'm looking for a real man, like you, Toby. 'Lucille put a hand on Toby's thigh.

'I'm far too old for you, Lucille. Besides, I'm married and I'm also your boss.'

'So what, all the married people I know are having affairs. And you being my boss would make it extra exciting. Risk is sexy, Toby, ha ha ha.' She'd been rubbing her hand up and down Toby's thigh whilst she made the bold statement.

Lucille put face up to Toby's and gently brushed her lips with his and then putting her arms around his neck manoeuvring their heads together – kissed him passionately in the sexiest way, her tongue making its way around his mouth. Despite his misgivings, Toby couldn't resist that all-consuming kiss and responded enthusiastically. He'd never experienced in all his adult life a kiss quite like what Lucille had initiated, her tongue extending right down his throat.

They'd continued for a while, neither of them wanting to stop. Then they'd noticed that the barman had spotted them and to lower their ardour, he'd turned the lights up and a few other stray drinkers could also see them.

They'd looked at each other partly in embarrassment that they'd been seen and partly with the acknowledgement that a massive sexual arousal had lit a fire in them both.

'We'd better head for home, it's very late,' whispered Toby, holding Lucille's hand.

'Lucille whispered back. Come home with me.'

For a moment Toby was tempted, but common sense prevailed. 'I can't do that as much as I'd love to. My wife is waiting for me at home.'

'Phone her on your new mobile phone and make some excuse that you've had to stay over in London.'

There was some more hesitation from Toby. His mind was on that amazing kiss and he wanted that kiss to continue all night long.

'No, No, I can't do that, I must get home, and I'll walk you to your bus stop.'

Toby waited at the bus stop with Lucille until her night bus arrived. He wanted to be sure that she'd be OK with all the alcohol consumed. Goodnights were uttered, with Toby giving Lucille a sanitised soft kiss on the lips as she alighted onto the bus taking her home to Crystal Palace.

Toby sobered up both from drink and lust on his journey back to Hertfordshire. As much as he'd been overwhelmed with the type of kissing they'd engaged in, he was well aware that it was stupid of him to have succumbed to Lucille's come-on flirtatiousness, and he should have refused that final drink before things kicked-off, getting out of hand.

At least he hadn't been crazy enough to spend the night at her place, however alluring the thought had been when she'd suggested it. He'd remained faithful to Verity over the years, and was not going to change that with someone who really wasn't his type at all. But the kissing, *oh-my-God,* was so memorable. That in itself was being unfaithful.

Verity was none too pleased that Toby had been out so late into the night drinking with colleagues, but if she'd known about the kissing, well, that was not worth thinking about.

Once Toby had pacified Verity, he started to think about seeing and working with Lucille the next day and didn't feel good about the prospect.

At work the next day they'd both carried on as normal, as if nothing had happened between them the previous night. But in the break before the live show went out, Toby took Lucille aside into a quiet area of the studio, explaining to her that although he'd really enjoyed what had occurred between them in the pub, it was, and could only be, a one off. It would not happen again; it would definitely not go any further. An affair between them was totally out of the question.

Lucille said nothing and went back to the main studio, seemingly showing no reaction to Toby's rejection. But inside she was seething; her crush on Toby had turned to bitterness. She thought... *How dare he treat me like that, to engage in passionate kissing on the night and reject me the following day.* She'd have her revenge and the next day, she made a complaint to the human resource official, reporting that Tobias Elden had been pestering her for ages, leading to forcibly kissing her at the pub, then begging her to invite him to her home stay the night.

Toby was put on gardening leave with full pay whilst the complaint was investigated; Lucille, not only carried on working at the corporation, but was promoted to temporary editor in place of Toby.

It was the first chink in Toby and Verity's marriage. Being forced to stay at home, Toby had no option but to fess up to his wife. He'd explained, with embarrassment, exactly what had occurred between him and Lucille in the pub, not going into too much detail about how much he'd enjoyed the kiss, secretly wishing that Verity would kiss him like the way Lucille had.

Verity had taken a dislike to her husband's assistant at the odd times she'd met Lucille, when visiting Toby at the studio, noticing how Lucille would look at Toby with a certain longing. That was an instinct pertaining specifically to women, who were able to notice little details about human behaviour and body language that men seemed to be blind to.

At least the corporation's inquiry into the complaint would be strictly in-house. Legal authorities had not been notified, and would not be; nor had the press or the media. So other than Verity, no one else within Toby's circle of friends had any idea about Toby's work difficulties; the assumption had been that he'd taken extended holiday leave.

Verity, knew her husband after so many years. She always knew when he was be lying or telling the truth. His body language gave him away. In the case of his explanation of what actually happened with Lucille – she'd totally believed him. That's not to say that she hadn't been devastated that Toby had misbehaved, but she was no prude. She understood anyone could veer into flirtatiousness, with the right encouragement and being full of alcohol.

The panel that would judge Toby was made up of three women and three men; plus a chairperson – who'd have the casting vote, in case of a tie, was a woman. None of the panel had any association with TNB or from the media, but were individuals representing various industries, including finance, fashion, insurance, manufacturing, trade unions and the medical profession. The chairperson was Hannah Longsmith, who was a most respected director of a leading fund management organisation.

The panel interviewed both Lucille and Toby separately, and when the panel reconvened to discuss the interviews, the consensus was that Lucille was believed more than Toby.

They'd both had permission to invite one witness to the proceedings. Lucille turned down the invite, but Toby asked the barman, who'd witnessed some of the shenanigans between the man and the woman. The barman, Mr. Joe Sawbridge, told the panel, that although he'd not seen everything that occurred between the pair, what he'd observed confirmed Mr Elden's version of events. The woman, Ms Bennett, seemed to be the one leading Mr Elden on, not the other way around.

When the panel reconvened to decide the outcome, Mr Sawbridge's evidence was met with a certain amount of scepticism. The research the panel had carried out before the interviews, established that the pub, the George and Dragon, located in Portland Place, close to TNB's headquarters, was a pub that Mr Elden and his colleagues, used frequently. The management of the George and Dragon knew that Mr Elden was the boss of his team, and he bought a lot of business to the establishment. They wouldn't want to lose that business, so they might have taken that into account when prepping the barman, Mr Sawbridge, on the tack he should adopt with the panel.

When a vote was taken, the three female panellists came down against Mr Elden, and the three male panellists voted the other way, believing that both Elden and Sawbridge had told the truth, dismissing the notion of the barman being economical with the truth. They also took the view that Ms Bennett wasn't being totally truthful with her account of the facts.

The women unanimously rejected the men's suggestion regarding Ms Bennett's truthfulness, doubling down on their previous position that fault lay with Mr Elden.

Ms Longsmith summed up by admitting that the case couldn't be proved one way or another, but she was concerned about the female panellists' assertion that the barman, Mr Sawbridge, would have been coerced in speaking in favour of Mr Elden for purely commercial reasons. She'd thought that had been an unfair slur.

'Who has more to lose here?' She put to her colleagues that Mr Elden would lose his job that he'd been in for many years, jeopardising his pension and his reputation. Ms Bennett, meanwhile, even if we came down in favour of Mr Elden, would not suffer anything like the same consequences. There would be embarrassment for her in the organisation and perhaps some colleagues gossiping behind her back. But that's miniscule, next to what Mr Elden would have to endure. So perhaps, lady colleagues, you'd like to reconsider your verdict.'

The three men stayed with their initial verdict in favour of Mr Elden. The three women had a longer conversation, taking into account Ms Longsmith's comments, but in the end they'd decided not to change their minds.

So it was a dead heat.

Hannah Longsmith had the casting vote and requested an overnight pause, staying awake all night with all the pros and cons running through her head. Maybe the whole thing was a storm in a teacup. After all, what one was talking about was a kiss, that was either consensual or not. But of course Ms Bennett's complaint was about more than a kiss. It was about being consistently pestered for sex by ones immediate boss and that, unfortunately, goes on too much in the media and business world, and that needed to be stamped upon. On the other hand, she'd not accused him of rape, or, for that matter, anything of a sexual nature or unwanted touching. Hannah, a plain-speaking person, not attracted to frippery in language or in anything else, nevertheless, had a lighter side to her persona, which few people saw. As she awoke in the morning, she was unable to stop humming a famous musical earworm, a song from the film, Casablanca... *'As time went by... a kiss is just a kiss...*

Her mind had been made up. She'd use her casting vote in favour of Tobias Elden.

Toby had kept his job and his pension. Lucille carried on as his editorial assistant for a few months before handing in her notice to leave TNB.

CHAPTER 23

Hertfordshire

1992

It was typical middle-class English behaviour. Five of our leading members had stopped attending gramophone evenings for the best part of six months, but the missing members were barely mentioned at the events, which continued as best as they could without them. Other members, including me, stepped up and hosted extra events, over and above our previous scheduled ones.

As I had established a personal friendship with Toby, we'd met a few times in London during the period of the missing five. Toby was reluctant to open up to me about what was going on with the absentees. I assumed the problem was connected, not only with Verity, but with their close friends, Ronald and Dulcie. But why had Hannah been missing from the gramophone events?

To save having to spend the evening chatting, Toby was always suggesting attending a concert instead of drinking in one of our favourite pubs or wine bars around the West End of London. Toby, as well as loving Bruckner, was also a great enthusiast for the music of Brahms, in particular the composers four symphonies. His favourite of the four was Brahms first symphony, which he loved to distraction.

'The first concert I ever attended at the Festival Hall in the early 1960s had the Brahms No. 1 on the programme.' Toby was holding forth about his love for Brahms, having a drink with me at the bar, before the concert. 'I had attended a few Sunday night concerts at the Royal Albert Hall before then, but they'd always consist of popular classical music favourites, finishing off with Tchaikovsky's 1812 overture, complete with bells and cannons. Later in the 1960s I'd started to attend the Proms at the Albert Hall, but that's a whole other story.'

Toby was in a reminiscing mood, which took him away from his current personal travails.

My friend, continued. 'I remember that Brahms 1 concert as if was yesterday, not thirty years ago. The orchestra was the London Symphony and the conductor was a young Lorin Maazel. The concert began with a short symphony by an eighteenth century German composer, which was instantly forgettable. The composer was Karl Stamitz. Unusually, they'd played the Brahms in the first half of the concert and the concerto, which was also by Brahms, his second piano concerto. The soloist was Vladimir Ashkenazy, who'd recently moved to the West from the Soviet Union. But for me, it was the symphony that was life-changing, and I realised for the first time that I couldn't live without music.'

I loved it when Toby was in full flow. He was so expressive with his lilting Welsh accent. I just enjoyed listening to him, whatever he said.

'The symphony goes from a massive serious opening in C minor to a blazing finish in C major, and in between, we get a most beautiful slow movement with a wonderful violin solo. The third moment is a gentle intermezzo incorporating a hint of the great tune to come in the finale. The finale... Wow, what can I say? How could I describe it without sounding trite? But, Alex, once heard, never forgotten. The great tune stays with one forever. The stately horns introduce the tune in ceremonial fashion and then the tune slowly creeps in, to expand into the most glorious sound that makes the world stand still... one is totally spellbound, feeling a sense of pure happiness and contentment.'

'Sorry to interrupt, Toby, but the bell has gone for the concert to begin. We'd better take our seats.'

'OK, Alex, let's go and hear how the Philharmonia, with their chief conductor, Giuseppe Sinopoli, play and interpret the symphony that I love above all others.'

The two friends were travelling home from the concert to Hertfordshire, and both had been quiet and subdued since they'd left the Festival Hall, taking the underground from Waterloo to Kings Cross, to pick up the mainline train.

Once sitting comfortably on the train, I asked Toby what he'd thought of Sinopoli's performance of the Brahms symphony.

'Well, it certainly was a good performance, but for my taste, some of his tempi were a bit slow. And he didn't take the repeat in the first movement. Mind you, very few conductors take that particular repeat these days, especially in a live performance. But, as far as I'm concerned, if a composer puts a repeat mark in his score, performers should respect that instruction. And let's face it one can't have too much Brahms, can one?'

'No, Toby, I couldn't argue with that. Anyway, I loved the performance and when that glorious tune arrived in the finale. I got Goosebumps, and as the symphony reached its final peroration I wanted to shout out, "Yes... yes and yes!"'

'Good for you, Alex, you're a man after my own heart. But I'd add one thing. When one discovers a great piece of music, it's that very first hearing of it that stays in one's musical mind. And every performance of the Brahms I've heard, both in live performances or on disc, since that memorable night, when Maazel's reading of the score changed my life, has never really lived up to how he'd shaped the symphony, and I've always been hoping that the next performance would equal the feelings I'd experienced on that occasion. Maybe, it had nothing to do with performances; perhaps I'm just yearning for my youth back.'

I had been listening to Toby's comments intently, realising that his stream of consciousness had a wider context than just reviewing the concert; he'd actually been reviewing his life. I thought to bring the conversation back to the concert.

'I also enjoyed the first half of the programme, the performance of Schoenberg's "Verklarte nacht."

'Toby lightened up on the word Schoenberg. You mean music's bogeyman, ha, ha, ha. As a matter of fact, Alex, "Verklarte nacht" is an early Romantic piece of his, lyrical and rather beautiful. It was written before Schoenberg tried to change music forever by adopting his twelve-tone system. And I appreciated Sinopoli's cool approach to a piece that could become overheated in the wrong hands.'

'I must add, Toby, that the Philharmonia played their hearts out for Sinopoli, their chief conductor, in both works.'

'Yes, I agree with you on that.'

The conversation petered out for the rest of the journey, both men feeling tired and looking forward to getting home.

I met up with Toby again in London a couple of weeks later. He wanted us to go to the Barbican in the city of London, for a recital by the great Austrian pianist, Alfred Brendel. He explained to me on the telephone, whilst suggesting attending the Brendel recital, that he hadn't been a fan of piano recitals as such, especially one's with a mixed programme of short pieces, mainly designed to show off the virtuoso of the pianist. But Brendel was different; he wasn't a pianist, but a musician of the very highest calibre. The programme consisted of the three last piano sonatas by Schubert. As far as Toby was concerned, Brendel playing Schubert, especially the final sonatas in one lengthy programme, was a concert not to be missed. In his opinion Brendel was the finest Schubert keyboard interpreter of the current generation.

As it turned out the concert was cancelled due to Brendel being unwell. Toby was hugely disappointed and said that we should meet in London anyway and have a consolation dinner together. A popular Italian restaurant which attracted many people from the arts world was Orso's in Covent Garden, and as both Toby and Alex enjoyed Italian cuisine, they booked a table there.

The restaurant was in a basement down spiral stairs in Wellington Street, close to the Royal Opera House. The atmosphere was buzzing and having been warmly greeted, we were shown to a table in the centre of the restaurant, giving us a great view of other tables, and we noticed well known celebrities, including the Hollywood actor, Richard Gere, seated at a nearby table.

'This is nice, Toby, a good choice of restaurant.' The waitress brought the menus and wine list to our table.

All the classic Italian dishes were listed on a longish menu.

'What would you like to drink, gentlemen?' The waitress offered us her warmest smile.

Toby, without hesitation shot back. 'Two Bellinis please.'

'Yes sir, I'll get those ordered straight away.'

Alex looking suitably impressed, said, 'You seem to know the ropes here, Toby,'

'Well, you know that Verity and I attend the opera at the Royal Opera House fairly frequently, and, as it's just up the road from here, we find that this place is ideal for dinner, either before the show, or after.

'Great then, so what do you recommend to eat?'

'I normally go for vitello tonnato for starters, which is, cold sliced veal, with a tuna flavoured mayonnaise sauce, and, then I would go for the osso buco to follow. Verity would generally start with a tomato and mozzarella salad and then go on with some sort of pasta dish as a main course.'

'I'm sure I've had osso buco somewhere in the past, but please remind me what the dish consists of?'

'It's a braised veal shank risotto. Osso buco means "hole of bone" because it has a marrow bone, which is delicious to suck. The dish is finished off with a *gremolate,* which consists of lemon zest, parsley and garlic. They do it brilliantly here, but it's a rich dish.'

You've sold me, Toby, I'll go with your recommendations for both starters and main, I'm starving.'

Having ordered the food, they settled on a bottle of Valpolicella to drink.

The food was delicious and much enjoyed, with both men too replete to even look at the dessert menu. When they'd finished the meal and were nursing coffees accompanied by small glasses of grappa, Toby was feeling expansive and got onto the subject of music once again.

'Hopefully, Brendel recovers soon and the cancelled concert rescheduled. I've heard him tackle those wonderful late Schubert sonatas twice before in London. Well, actually, it was one and a half times.'

'What do you mean, Toby?'

'Hmmm, it was the first time Verity and I had had serious fallout. It was about twenty years ago, at the time that Brendel was just morphing from a good to a great pianist, As far as I could tell, it was the first time he'd programmed the three late Schubert sonatas in one programme. Well, in London anyway. The concert was at the Queen Elizabeth Hall, the smaller hall next door to the Festival Hall. Brendel wasn't yet a big enough name to command the much larger venue for a solo piano recital. Anyway, I was really excited in anticipation of the concert, and as you know, I'm never late for anything, especially a concert or an opera.'

I nodded vigorously, knowing how punctual Toby was.

' It so happened, Verity and I were off on holiday to Greece a few days later and we needed to buy a new suitcase, as the one we'd been using was worn and rather battered. We'd got waylaid in the store choosing the suitcase. Consequently, for the first and only time in my life, I missed the first half of a concert. We'd arrived just a few minutes after the start of the C minor piece. And what made it so heart-retching was that we missed two out of the three sonatas, as Brendel decided to play the C minor and the A major pieces consecutively without a break, not giving us an opportunity to slip into the hall for the second piece. We had to wait for over an hour before we were allowed entry to the auditorium, and then another twenty minutes of the interval, before we finally saw Brendel striding toward the piano to play, what was perhaps, the most beautiful piano sonata in the entire repertoire, Schubert's last composed sonata, a glorious outpouring of lyricism, in the key of B flat major. Alex, I remember my reaction so well when Brendel started to play the opening theme with such beauty of tone, with such utter poise, tears just kept pouring down my face. Verity nudged me to control myself as other patrons were staring at me, but I couldn't stop the tears, a mixture of frustration of missing two of the sonatas, and ecstatic joy at hearing Schubert's heavenly melody.'

'Oh my God, Toby, I feel tears forming in my eyes just listening to your rendition of the incident.'

'Later, I heard other distinguished pianist programme Schubert's last three sonatas – great artists such as Maurizo Pollini and Richard Goode, but for my money, nobody ever came close to Alfred Brendel in Schubert. Ten years after that first part-disastrous part-glorious evening, Brendel repeated the Schubert programme, but this time at the much larger Festival

Hall, and it was, of course, magnificent. But the emotion of that first time at the Queen Elizabeth Hall is something I'll never forget.'

'Did you forgive Verity for making you late for the concert?'

'Of course I did. Ha ha ha.'

'Let's get some more coffee and a couple of more Grappas.'

'Good idea, Toby.'

The restaurant was starting to empty out, including the table where Richard Gere had been sitting, but some late diners, who'd come straight from the opera, were still tucking into their main course.

'Tell me, Alex, can you read music?'

'Unfortunately, I can't. I never learnt an instrument as a youngster, or had never joined a choir.'

'Same with me Alex, but I do read scores'

'How did that come about?'

'I enrolled for music evening classes at Morley College, when I was in my twenties. Not to play an instrument but to study theory and musical history. I didn't realise at the time, how much pleasure, the ability to read a score, would give me in later life. When listening to music with a score, the music comes alive. You see and hear the notes simultaneously. With a big orchestral piece – for instance, a Mahler symphony, to follow the huge panoply of its instrumentation literally blows the mind!'

'Phew, that's amazing, Toby. I could perhaps understand you reading a score of, say, a Mozart or a Haydn symphony, which are scored for a compact orchestra of strings, a few woodwinds, the odd brass instrument and the occasional timpani. But a huge Mahler score, oh boy, that must be so difficult for a layman to read; I imagine even hot-shot conductors would have their work cut out absorbing Mahler's scores.'

Toby, laughed his head off. He moved closer to Alex, and whispered in his ear. 'I'll let you into a secret. It's easier to follow a Mahler score than a Mozart one.'

'How come, Toby'?

'Well, a typical Mozart or Haydn movement of a symphony, is linear in layout, following more or less, a straight line, with one or two harmonic surprises on the way, so, on the one hand, easy to follow. On the other hand, one could be lulled into complacency and lose concentration. Complacency would not be an option with Mahler. With so much going on, if one drops concentration for a moment, all could be lost, so one is glued to the score from the very first note to the very last one. But, oh god, what joy and satisfaction I feel at the conclusion of the symphony.'

'I've never seen you with a score in hand, either at a gramophone event or when we've been to a concert.'

'No, that's true. To be honest, I've always been self-conscious of having a score with me at concerts specifically, not wanting to disturb the person sitting next to me by turning the scores pages. However, when I've been to a concert with Verity, I always book a gangway seat, with me sitting on the end of a row and Verity sitting next to me on the inside. So, in that situation, the only person I'd disturb would be my wife. But listening to music privately at home gives me an opportunity to follow the score. I'm just surprised that more, non-musician music lovers don't follow scores whilst listening. They're missing, in my opinion, one of the greatest pleasures life could offer!

'There ends the lecture, Alex, let's get the bill and get out of here.'

On the train home, Toby had been conscious of having dominated the conversation during the evening, so he turned to Alex with the question, 'You're a bit of a dark horse, Alex. You don't talk much about yourself and I know very little about you.'

Toby caught me unawares with his turning the spotlight on me. 'There's not much to tell, as I've lived a very unassuming life.'

'Hmmm, I think you protest too much. After all, you're writing a book, and a lot of fiction these days is autobiographical, or at least semi-autobiographical.'

'Well, my book isn't about me, and if it was, it would be the most boring book ever.'

'Hmmm, I sometimes think that there's a whole history of Alex that we don't know about. Anyway, I'm curious to know what made you work for the Labour Party.'

'My parents were typically middle-class conservatives, always, without really thinking about it too much, voting for the Tories at election times. During the early 1960s the Toffs were still running Britain, and, parliament was rife with scandals, specifically, the Profumo affair, which made the Tories a laughing stock all around the country. I'd started to question my parents support for the Tories when I was at university, as I was mixing with left-leaning students, but I wasn't personally, during my university days, fully engaged in politics, or political thinking. In fact, I was ineligible to vote until I was aged twenty-one, which was in 1964. Everything changed in 1964, when the disastrous Tory prime minister, the aristocratic, Alec Douglas Hume, who'd used matchsticks to work out simple arithmetic, lost the general election, with Labour taking office again following thirteen years of opposition. The new prime minister was Harold Wilson, *a man of the people*, and that's when the swinging sixties officially began.'

Toby was in listening mode, having dominated the chat for most of the evening. 'So, what did you do after university?'

'I had a boring job in an administrative role, and then later, my life took an unwelcome turn, which I'd prefer not to go into.'

'Fair enough, Alex, I respect your desire for not wanting to share your personal history, but you still haven't told me about your career with the Labour Party.'

'During the late 1970s I'd become more politically aware and became a supporter of the Labour Party, helping out during elections with delivering leaflets, and other dogsbody tasks. Following Margaret Thatcher's election win in 1979, and consequently becoming the first female prime minister my left-wing views became more trenchant. I hated everything that she stood for, and began to think about getting into politics as a potential Labour Member of Parliament, but for different reasons, that was never going to happen. But the Labour Party was advertising for someone with administrative experience. I fitted the bill and I've been working at their central office ever since, but, as you know, I'm going for early retirement next year.'

The train had just departed from St Albans station and their own station was the next stop on the line, so there was no opportunity for Toby to ask Alex anything else, but his feeling was that he got less than a full trajectory of Alex's adult life's journey.

CHAPTER 24

Hertfordshire 1993

Feedback regarding my extended gramophone event, when I played a complete performance of Mozart's opera, *Don Giovanni,* was very positive, so for my next scheduled hosting event, I decided to take the plunge again, and play the final opera, complete in one evening, of the Mozart/Da Ponte trio of operas, *Cosi Fan Tutte (ossia La scuola degli amanti).* The opera is a tricky one to translate into English, and one has a choice of: 'They all do it' or 'Women are like that' or 'The School for Lovers.'

As I'd done for the previous Mozart operas, I printed copies of the libretto to hand around to the members and to other attendees who'd heard about the complete operas being played and inquired about attending the event. We welcomed everyone and were delighted that we obtained and absolute full house, as many people as my living room could accommodate. The popularity of playing complete operas gave me a lot of kudos with the founding members, especially with the unofficial leader of the club, Greg Witton. Greg, being a pessimist, had been indicating for a while, especially, when we missed the five stay-a-ways that the club suffered during part of 1992, that the future of the club was looking bleak. But here we were, a packed house for a long evening of a complete opera.

I also printed out a short synopsis of the plot to distribute to everybody with a copy of the libretto. I kept the synopsis short, as the plot of *Cosi Fan Tutte* was rather vacuous and one didn't need to know all the details of the various comings and goings, but just to have an overview of the story, which was about human behaviour when lovers are tricked and tested.

The opera is set Naples during the eighteenth century.

Don Alfonso is determined to prove to Guglielmo and Ferrando that all women are alike, and wagers them that in their absence even their fiancées, Fiordiligi and Dorabella, would be unfaithful.

Don Alfonso enlists the help of Despina, Fiordiligi's and Dorabella's maid, and announces to them that Ferrando and Guglielmo are being called away on active service. He then introduces them to two Albanians who are none other than Guglielmo and Ferrando in disguise. After unsuccessfully trying to make advances to each other's fiancées they pretend to take poison. Despina, disguised as a doctor, magnetises them back to life.

Gradually Fiordiligi and Dorabella succumb to the two Albanians and Ferrando and Guglielmo concede defeat to Don Alfonso

News that their former loves are returning bring Fiordiligi and Dorabella to despair. Ferrando and Guglielmo change from their Albanian disguise and confront Fiordiligi and Dorabella with the marriage contract that Despina had prepared for their marriage to the Albanians. Don Alfonso reveals his plot. Ferrando and Guglielmo are reunited with their original lovers or maybe they switch to the Albanian counterparts?

I gave a short talk before starting the opera. I explained that, unlike the other two Da Ponte/Mozart operas, *Cosi Fan Tutte*, was not based on any existing dramatic work or, in fact, any literary source whatsoever. The idea seemed to have originated with the emperor himself, Leopold 11, who'd commissioned Da Ponte to write the libretto.

'Not to beat about the bush, the plot of *Cosi Fan Tutte* is about the silliest plot imaginable for any opera, and no wonder did not only Beethoven disapprove of the opera, but also the whole of the nineteenth-century practically ignored the work. The opera began its comeback in the second half of the twentieth-century, when Mozart's music, generally, had become much more part of the standard concert and operatic repertoire than it had previously.

'But, and this is a big but, Mozart's music for *Cosi Fan Tutte* is absolutely sublime. Not only is it the equal of *Figaro* and *Don Giovanni*, but arguably even finer. The opera contains a host of wonderful ensemble numbers as well as stunning solo arias. And if one looked beyond the surface of the plot, one could even make a case for it. It asks us questions about love and fidelity, which was as relevant in the eighteenth-century as it is for us today.

'One other drawback to the plot, which can't be ignored, is its misogynistic message, that women can't be trusted to be faithful to their partners and they'd be easily led astray by any man persistent enough with his wooing. Hmmm, I can already see some disapproving looks from some of the ladies here, but there are ways around the dilemma. A clever director could switch the genders around, so it would be that men that had been hoodwinked. Another way to deal with the issue is for the women at the finale, instead of choosing either to revert to their original lovers or the newer ones, decide on neither, storming out of the theatre in absolute disgust.

'Actually, I have in my mind a third way, but I'm not sure that I'm courageous enough to share it with you right now, as I'm still totally sober!'

The members and guests looked at each other, wondering about what salacious idea I'd concocted for the plot of *Cosi Fan Tutte*...

Before anyone had a chance to speak, I put the first side of the LP on the turntable. The first bars of the opera wafted through the room and everyone started to relax.

CHAPTER 25

ALEX'S NOVEL

OPERA (3)

Dalkey Village
County Dublin,
Ireland.

1978

'How many covers do we have booked in for tonight, Dom?'

Sixty, we're absolutely chock a block. We can't accept any more bookings, unless we received some cancellations, and I can't see any in the book.

'Is Ricky up to speed in the kitchen with supplies?'

Ricky popped his head out of the kitchen with his thumbs up.

'There's no need to fret, boss, everything's under control in all areas of the restaurant.'

The brief exchange between Sebastian Moran, Dominic Rivers and Ricky Wenger took place on a beautifully sunny Friday afternoon in early autumn, in the Crab restaurant, which was situated in the attractive village of Dalkey. Dalkey, was fourteen kilometres from the centre of the city of Dublin, by the coast between Dun Laoghaire, Glenageary and Killiney. Along the coast was the natural harbour at Bullock, with a couple of small inlets. Sorrento Point was just east of the town proper, and the northern part of Killiney Bay. Dalkey Island, an uninhabited Island, near to the village of Dalkey, was famous for its wild goat population. Dalkey was also home to Dalkey

Castle, a fortified, medieval, townhouse castle, dating from the fourteenth century.

Dalkey had had a rich literary heritage, being home to many writers and artists, past and present, including George Bernard Shaw, the nineteenth-century Irish poet, Jane Emily Herbert, the British artist, Julius Olsson, who'd moved to Dalkey, when his house in England, was bombed during World War Two. He died at his home in the village during 1942. The writer, Maeve Binchy, was born in Dalkey, and the playwright, Hugh Leonard, was born and had lived most of his life in Dalkey.

Following the debacle at Ricky's London party in 1972, which ended with Ricky's arrest, Sebastian reassessed, yet once again, both his business and his private life. In a few short years, he'd built a small insurance company from a door-to-door, traditional, almost apologetic way of convincing householders the need for life assurance into a sophisticated, financial advice, countrywide operation, with a sales force exceeding two thousand advisers. But when he'd lost his two close lieutenants who'd become dear friends, since they'd got to know each another years earlier in Brighton, his heart went out of the business, and, he put the company up for sale. He received many attractive offers for the business, but a major international French life assurance company, owned by the French government, made Sebastian a spectacularly massive offer; it being an offer he just couldn't refuse, the deal was done. Sebastian walked away from the financial industry with more money in the bank than he knew what to spend it on. For the second time, he decided to take his life in a new direction.

One thing Sebastian did with his money was to pay for Ricky's and Dominic's defence by engaging the best and the most expensive barrister in the business, a colleague from the House of Lords, to defend his two friends of serious criminal charges.

Dominic? Well, yes, subsequent to Ricky's arrest, Matt Foster and Zoe Billing, made an official complaint about Dominic that he aided and abetted Ricky, in his friend's pursuit and sexual assault of Zoe, whilst he kept Matt amused in the grounds of the Belgravia house, where the crime took place, knowing full-well, what Ricky's intentions were with Zoe.

The hot-shot barrister managed to persuade the judge to change, and, water-down the charge of rape of Anna Kimber-Smythe, to 'serious sexual assault' and to water-down the 'sexual assault' of Zoe to 'sexual misconduct'. Unfortunately, the barrister's attempt to completely throw out the charge against Dominic failed, and the 'aiding and abetting' charge stayed.

Despite the lesser charge, both men were found guilty. Ricky was given a ten-year jail sentence, and Dominic was sentenced to one year imprisonment.

Sebastian stayed loyal to his two friends and visited them in jail frequently. Dominic was released after serving six months, but Ricky served a full five years of the sentence. Whilst in prison, Ricky took up cooking as a prison occupation, and by the time of his release he'd become a seriously good chef. On his release, he'd managed to secure employment in a top London restaurant, as a commis chef. The restaurant made a point of employing released prisoners, as long as they'd be satisfied that the miscreant had turned over a new leaf. Not that he needed the money, as he'd accumulated substantial sums from his time with *Intermezzo,* which had been earning interest in the bank during his prison years. But he'd taken to cooking like a duck to water, and he didn't want to spend his days, following his release, dwelling on his past misdemeanours. He wanted make something of himself in his new chosen career.

Dominic hadn't been so lucky. Like Ricky, he still had his money and his flat in Hampstead, but was bored and wanted to get back to work. But because of his criminal record, anything to do with finance or insurance had been completely closed to him, even for a lowly administrative job. Sebastian came to the rescue by recruiting Dominic to look after his vast personal financial interest. Despite Dominic's unfortunate criminal record, he still trusted his friend implicitly.

Sebastian and Lydia remarried. They'd remained close once the dust had settled on their divorce ten years earlier, realising that despite all that had occurred, the love between them had been genuine, and there was much that they actually liked about each other. Of course, on a purely practical matter, attending aristocratic and royal functions as a married couple, being announced as The Lord and The Lady Moran did not raise any eyebrows, as perhaps, attending functions together, as a divorced couple, might have done.

Sebastian stayed living at his Belgravia residence, whilst Lydia remained at her Chelsea townhouse, which were close each other. Their lifestyle was more like a courting couple than a married one, spending the night at each other's homes, either when they felt like sleeping together, or when the occasion demanded, for instance, at one of Sebastian's regular home dinner parties, catered by professional staff, in which they'd always present a united front.

In one respect though, their relationship was quite unlike a courting couple. They'd both given each other license to enjoy relationship with other people, as long those relationships remained on a casual basis. Lydia had recently celebrated her fiftieth birthday and she enjoyed the company of younger men. Sebastian, being the same age, had begun to be attracted to men, and attended gay parties, often given by gay members of the House of Lords. The parties were very discreet; they made sure that journalists had not infiltrated an event, as none of the Lordships had come out as being of a homosexual disposition. The majority of them had wives and children, tucked away somewhere in the Home Counties. The men all had weekday flats in Central London, returning to their families at weekends. It was an ideal arrangement for a closet homosexual. The situation for Sebastian was different. He shared his peccadillo with Lydia which she quite enjoyed hearing about. She was sworn to secrecy, to protect his fellow gay friends. He also liked to hear about her sexual adventures with whatever young man she be currently seeing. Sebastian and Lydia unconventional relationship suited them extremely well. In a funny sort of way, they were happier together in their odd arrangement, than they'd been in the early days of their first marriage twenty years before, when their love was all consuming. But being young and naive in matters of love and sexual mores, they'd automatically followed the cultured norms of their peers and their class.

Sebastian, coming from a long line of aristocratic ancestors, had followed the usual custom that his father and grandfather had done in their time. Marry a girl with the right class pedigree; procreate as quickly as possible, making sure that at least one of the offspring is male. Once duty was done in producing a son – ideally two sons, an heir and a spare – one was free to roam in any sexual way one wanted; take a mistress, insist on conjugal rights with female members of staff, or even indulge in homosexuality. However, if the lady of the house ever dared to look at another man, one would have grounds for divorce, the wife losing her children and financial security. Worst of all, she'd be shamed and ostracised by society.

The difference with Sebastian and Lydia was, at the start, anyway, they'd genuinely loved each other. Nevertheless, especially when Lydia was unable to conceive, because of a fault with Sebastian's sperm count, he reverted to a gentleman of his class and background. That was when the marriage went wrong. The rot had set in during their Brighton years.

Sebastian and Lydia had decided to spend a long weekend in Dublin, to coincide with Saint Patricks Day in March 1978. They booked a suite at the Shelborne Hotel, located opposite St. Stephen's Green and close to Grafton Street, Dublin's famous shopping spot. They watched the St. Patrick's Day parade, frequented some of the city's famous pubs, drank pints of Guinness, ate at great restaurants, visited a few art galleries and booked tickets for a Sean O'Casey play at the Abbey theatre. The weekend was thoroughly enjoyed and they rounded off their stay with a visit to an old girlfriend of Lydia, who lived in the village of Dalkey.

Lydia's friend, Mandy Wilton, had explained to Lydia, that Dalkey had become a restaurant destination, with a great variety of top-class establishments, all in close proximity around the village. So the invite included lunch at one of her favourite Dalkey restaurants and afternoon tea at her home. Mandy lived in an apartment block called Pilot View, situated by Bullock Harbour, off Dublin Bay and close to Dalkey village. Mandy, being spoilt for choice, decided on The Crab restaurant, just off Castle Street. Spanking fresh seafood was The Crab's speciality and the restaurant was spaciously airy, designed in a rustic style, ideal for a lunch in a coastal location.

Sebastian and Lydia had fallen in love with Dalkey at first sight. It was a very small coastal town, although generally considered more of a village, not pretty or cute, but a compact centre with elegant brightly coloured buildings, a good variety of shops, great restaurants and superb pubs. Above all, it was a space that was full of people. They greeted and laughed with others, whilst making their way through Castle Street, Dalkey's main thoroughfare.

The lunch at The Crab was every bit as good as Mandy had said. We were greeted by the owner, Sean Dilly. He welcomed Mandy as an old friend, with kisses on both cheeks and warmly shaking Sebastian and Lydia's hands. Following the introductions, Sean, despite being host to a busy restaurant, spent a few minutes chatting to the Morans, being especially keen to know how they'd been enjoying their long weekend in the Emerald Isle. They were led to a good table in the centre of the restaurant. They ate a delicious lunch, which had included lobster salad, crab claws with garlic butter and a lovely sherry trifle, all washed down with a cold dry Muscadet white wine.

Pilot View, where Mandy lived, was an amazing building, facing out to the sea. Her flat, on the third floor, consisted of an amazing living room, with a balcony overlooking the ocean. Sitting in the room and looking out, one had the feeling that they'd been on a cruise ship!

Lydia said, 'What an incredible view you have here.'

'Yes, well, thank you. I'm very lucky to reside here, thanks to my ex-husband's generous divorce settlement. It's a much sought-after place to live. Several government ministers have apartments here and my neighbour along the corridor is the well-known popular Irish playwright, Hugh Leonard.'

They struggled to eat Mandy's delicious homemade fruit cake, which she'd served with afternoon tea.

'Thanks so much for a delicious lunch, Mandy. It was so kind of you to invite us.'

'You're very welcome and it gave me a chance to reciprocate, having been entertained so many times by you two in London.'

'It sounded like you've enjoyed your trip.'

Lydia replied that they'd had a great time in Dublin, and, that today was the icing on the cake.

'I'm so pleased. Maybe next time you'd spend longer over here. It's a shame though that Sean Dilly had put The Crab up for sale.'

Sebastian, put his bone-china tea cup down on the saucer and looked up with interest.

'Why would he want to sell such a thriving business'?

'Well, his elderly mother, who lived on her own in England, was very poorly, and needed to go into a care home, and Sean needed to fund it. He lived in a rented house here in Dalkey, having put all his money into the restaurant. The building of The Crab was originally a deep-sea diving equipment warehouse. He sold his house to fund buying the restaurant, which he then converted into a restaurant. You must surely agree he made a grand job of it'!

Sebastian's mind was working overtime.

What if...?

He'd been looking for a new business venture since selling his insurance company and he so enjoyed their few days in Dublin. Dalkey, it seemed to him, was a real gem of a place. Perhaps he could buy The Crab?

'Sebastian, you've gone very quiet.'

'Lydia, I was just thinking about buying The Crab.

Both Lydia and Mandy stared at Sebastian in amazement.

'You're joking, of course, ha, ha, ha. What do you know about restaurants except regularly eating at London's finest?'

'You're right, darling, but Ricky Wenger does, and I'll bring him over with me as the chef, as well as his buddy, Dominic Rivers, currently my financial secretary.'

'Hmmm, Seb, with those two in tow, maybe it could just work for you.'

Chapter 26

Dalkey, Ireland
1978

The purchase of The Crab restaurant from Sean Dilly was achieved remarkably quickly and stress free. Sebastian agreed the substantial sum that Sean was asking, without even trying to negotiate a price reduction. Sebastian really wanted to own the restaurant, having been conscious of the reason that Sean was selling. Although, Sebastian had been a tough deal-maker in previous enterprises, he hadn't decided to buy the restaurant with a pure profit motive as the main driving force. He fancied the idea of spending considerable time in Ireland, especially in Dalkey, which was a place he found most convivial, a real contrast from Belgravia, London. He'd buy an apartment where Mandy was living, in Pilot View, if one would become available. Most importantly of all, what he'd been keen to achieve with the purchase was to give career opportunities to both, Ricky Wenger and Dominic Rivers. Ricky had become a reformed character since leaving jail. He'd thrown himself into the task of becoming a top chef and taking over the kitchen at The Crab would be a great step forward for him on his journey towards his goal. However, poor Dominic, who'd taken part of the rap for Ricky's bad behaviour with women – being loyal to his older friend had cost him his freedom, landing him with a criminal record. A new start for him, away from London, as manager of The Crab would do him a world of good.

The Crab had had a formula for success under Sean Dilly's ownership. Following the sale of the restaurant to Sebastian Moran, the new proprietor decided to keep things very much as it had been – namely, a fish and seafood specialist establishment, offering the freshest fish available from the local fishermen in the first instance, topping up with the variety of species on offer from the fish market. Sean had never made any pretence that his restaurant had been haute cuisine in its aspirations, but he was on a mission to encourage more Irish people to enjoy eating fish, which in Ireland, hadn't been a given. However, Sean had done some research and more Dublin people were taking their holidays abroad and they were getting a taste for fish at the beach tavernas in Spain, Italy and Greece. The Crab originally opened at the end of an August that was unusually warm for Ireland, with holidaymakers recently back from those sunny climes, Sean caught the zeitgeist of the day and his early customers were reliving their holiday experiences by eating fresh fish at The Crab.

Sean had made friends with the local fisherman who'd provide a sack-full of crab claws that he otherwise would have discarded, as he'd only been able to sell dressed crab, neatly packaged in a crab shell, containing a mixture of white and brown crab meat, but usually more brown than white. The redundant crab claw was full of the more highly prized white meat, but was too fiddly for the fisherman to deal with, so he offered them to The Crab free of charge. The restaurant chef had become highly skilled, with the right kitchen utensils .to work around the claw to make it presentable to the customer. White crab meat served with piping hot garlic butter, put back in the shell, was the most popular dish on the menu, and it had been 100 per cent profit. Besides crab, lobsters, prawns, mussels and a varying selection of white fish were the menu's constants, with traditional deep-fried fish and chips always available. For the die-hard non-fish eaters, the restaurant offered a variety of cuts for steak and chips, served with a béarnaise, red wine or black-pepper sauce.

Sean couldn't have been more helpful to Sebastian once the sale had gone through. He explained about the alcohol licence situation in Ireland which was different to England. As pubs were a protected sector in the country, restaurants were forbidden to encroach on the pubs by selling beer or sprits. The restaurant alcohol licence was specifically a wine one. Various aperitifs and liqueurs were also allowed. Sebastian was surprised about the licence arrangements but as there was a police station next door to the restaurant, he decided not to dirty his copy-book; he'd strictly abide by the rules.

Sean had mentioned that other restaurants in the village turned a blind eye to the rules, and certain customers would be able to order a whisky, or a gin and tonic. Sean mentioned a well-known Irish playwright, Harvey Lampard, who'd regularly frequented the Dalkey restaurants and with a nod and a wink, he'd get his preferred tipple, which was in fact a whisky and water, which he'd drink throughput the meal. When The Crab first opened, Mr Lampard booked a solitary table for the Saturday night. On being warmly greeted and shown to a table for one, he'd immediately ordered a large whisky. Sean politely explained to the gentleman about the licensing laws, and refused the request. He nodded without comment and ordered his meal with just a glass of water to drink. Paying his bill, not adding anything for service, he exited the restaurant without further comment, never ever returning to The Crab. The playwright wrote a regular column in a Dublin social magazine, and some months later, in a food section of the magazine, Lampard wrote a scathing review of The Crab, having a sly dig at the proprietor, accusing him of being dressed in a slovenly manner, with his shirt tail hanging out of his trousers.

That was a cautionary tale for Sebastian; to be aware of a certain playwright, if he ever thought of testing out the new English owner. Moran, an English lord, operating in Ireland, was certainly not going to hold hostage to fortune by upsetting the local Gardai, whatever his competitor's attitudes were to the licensing laws.

The chef, who had been with Sean from the beginning, was head-hunted by a top Dublin restaurant at the time of the sale to Moran, opening the door for Ricky Wenger to take up the position. The two assistant chefs stayed-on, to work under Ricky, as did the young waitress, Roisin Walsh, a delightful local girl from Dalkey.

On the recommendation of Lydia's friend, Mandy Wilton, Sebastian offered part-time employment to Connor Clarkson. Mandy had been friends with the Clarkson family for many years. The family lived in the neighbouring village of Killiney. Connor was the Clarkson's eldest son, aged twenty-five, and was a struggling classical musician, a violinist. Connor wouldn't take on any endeavour without his boyhood friend, and musical partner, Sandor Kovacs, a pianist aged twenty-six, who lived in the same street as the Clarkson's. The Kovacs were originally from Hungary; they'd settled in Ireland during the 1940s. Sandor was known in Ireland as Sandy. The two boys became inseparable; consequently, Connor refused to accept the offer of work from The Crab, without a similar offer to Sandy. So Sebastian, who'd bought a grand piano for the restaurant, offered the two guys an arrangement that they both share the task of waiting on tables on busy nights, and on quieter nights, they'd musically perform as a violin and piano duo, or Sandy on the piano, and Connor, who possessed a reasonable baritone voice, would entertain the guests with some Irish songs.

Connor and Sandy had attended the same local school, with Sandy, being two years older, in a class above his friend. They'd both won scholarships to the Royal Irish Academy of Music in Dublin, respectively in their keyboard and string departments. They'd both graduated with honours, but opportunities for classical musicians were limited in Ireland, with both lads settling for the odd engagement, either as a violin and piano duo, the occasional solo piano recital for Sandy, or for Connor, occasionally, an extra violin was needed for an RTE Symphony Orchestra concert, if they were programming a big piece, such as a Mahler symphony. To supplement their income, they both took on private pupils amongst the moneyed classes of the affluent suburbs of South County Dublin. They both had done the odd waiting stint in various restaurants around Dublin, but for them both having a regular job five nights a week (the restaurant being closed on Sunday and Monday) gave them a bit more financial security. They weren't needed for the lunch service (Wednesday, Thursday and Friday only), which suited the lads, as they taught their private pupils during daytime. A couple of local girls, friends of Roisin, were able to do a lunchtime shift, if required. Sebastian terms had been most generous in wages he offered his waiting staff, and all tips were shared between the staff at the end of each week. Sebastian had also agreed to give the boys a night off, without pay, if they were booked for a musical engagement. The lunchtime girls could always be called in as the situation required.

Music students, Niamh and Bridget Kennedy, who were sisters, met and had become friends with Connor and Sandy at the Royal Academy, the foursome becoming inseparable during the college years morphing into double dating. Niamh and Sandy became an item and so had Bridget and Connor.

The Kennedys lived in Monkstown, another affluent Dublin suburb, not far from Killiney and Dalkey. Both girls studied singing at the Academy, Niamh, aged twenty-eight, was a mezzo-soprano, whilst Bridget, a couple of years younger, was a soprano. They'd excelled at college with operatic agents from England, already sniffing around the girls with a view to auditioning them with leading opera companies for roles in the Mozart opera repertoire which they'd be ideally suited.

The sisters turned heads whenever they were out together. Niamh was dark haired, worn short, with beautiful brown eyes, medium height, with a pleasing curvy, voluptuous figure. She possessed the warmest smile when her whole face lit up and a soft but deep speaking voice. Bridget was the opposite. A tall blonde with blue eyes, she was statuesque in figure, with high cheek-bones, but with a more amused smile than her sister, whilst her speaking voice was soft and feminine. The agent had managed to get both sisters auditions at the prestigious summer opera festival, Glyndehurst, by the South Downs in Sussex, England. Glyndehurst Festival had been putting on opera since 1934 and Mozart operas, in particular, had always been a speciality. They were more interested in ensemble singing that blended into a believable whole, than engaging a star diva, who'd be showing off her vocal skills than being part of a team that presented credible music-drama. The company had always been keen to engage up-and-coming singers before they'd become famous and too expensive to hire, and they took the agent's recommendation, arranging for the sisters to travel to Glyndehurst for an audition to perform in the 1979 new production of Mozart's opera, *Cosi Fan Tutte*.

The leading female leads in *Cosi Fan Tutte* are two sisters, Fiordiligi, a soprano role, and Dorabella, a mezzo-soprano role. So when the agent presented, Niamh, and Bridget Kennedy, to the director and the conductor of the opera, they uncannily just fitted the two operatic sisters. Niamh, in the director's eyes, was physically an ideal Dorabella, with her open sunny personality and her, seemingly. flirtatious nature, with a twinkle in her eyes. Whilst Bridget looked like a Fiordiligi of one's dreams; she was imposingly tall with elegant features, a facial expression that was harder to read. In the opera, Fiordiligi's resolve not to cheat on her lover is much harder to break down than her sister, Dorabella, who tried to convince Fiordiligi that a little flirtatious fun wouldn't do them any harm.

Looking like the opera characters was one thing, but the conductor turned to the director, out of earshot of the girls.

'They may look the perfect pair, but can they sing their parts?'

The conductor went over to the piano to accompany, firstly, Bridget, who would sing the aria *Per piata, ben mio*, from Act Two of *Cosi fan tutte*, and followed by Niamh, whose aria would also be from Act Two of the opera, *E amore un ladroncello*.

Both sisters were extremely nervous but felt that they'd give it their best shot. What concerned them more than anything else, was that only one of them would be engaged, leaving the other one totally crestfallen.

Having sang their arias, they were asked to wait in another room, whilst the director and the conductor discussed their various options. They could engage them both, engage just one of the girls, or, offer them a place in the chorus as a consolation prize, and, try to find two more experienced artists.

The Director said, 'We could do a double "Kiri" here'

The conductor, looking rather puzzled, asked what he had meant by 'Kiri'

'Well, remember I directed the new production of *Le Nozze di Figaro* at Covent Garden in 1971, and we took a punt on the then unknown soprano, Kiri te Kanawa. During the interval, I'd heard various comments in the Crush Bar from people who were wondering why we'd chosen an unknown young soprano for the role of the Countess. But now, Kiri is a famous operatic diva!'

'If the girls have a success we'd get the credit of launching their careers.'

'Yes, of course, I heard you, and Glyndehurst is well known for launching young artists, but these two have done nothing, no performance history of any kind, or winning any vocal competitions. They just studied at the Irish Academy.'

'But Ireland had a track record of producing successful opera singers.'

'Hmmm.' The conductor was deep in thought.

'OK,' he suddenly said. 'It's a big gamble, but we're not throwing them on the stage right now; after all, Glyndehurst has a long rehearsal period, so let's go for it.'

The Director smiled and gave the conductor a reassuring pat on the back.

'Our task now is to find two handsome lovers to match with our lovely opera newbies!'

CHAPTER 27

Dalkey – Ireland

1979

It was 14 February, known universally as Valentine's Day, six months on from Sebastian Moran's buying and running The Crab restaurant in Dalkey. It had been a busy, but happy six months, in the lives of all those associated with the restaurant.

Sebastian and Lydia's relationship was as good as it had ever been. When two flats became available in the sought-after Pilot View apartment block, he snapped up both flats by cash payment. One flat was for him and Lydia, whilst the other was a gift for Ricky Wenger and Dominic Rivers, for them to share. He felt responsible for what had happened to his friends in London, in some ways encouraging Ricky in his behaviour with women. And, Dominic was like a loyal puppy dog to Ricky and that loyalty had cost him six months in prison.

Sebastian, an aristocratic English gentleman and a hereditary lord, was part of the popular restaurant scene in Dalkey, which amazingly, managed to host four other restaurants. Besides The Crab, they were all a few doors away from each other in Castle Street, or just off the main thoroughfare. As well as the restaurants, the two excellent pubs, both in Castle Street, also served food that was more than decent. At first, Sebastian was a bit reticent to mingle with the other restaurateurs in the pub; he kept to himself or with his colleagues and staff from The Crab. This was the pub directly opposite his restaurant, and the Crab crew were regulars in there between shifts.

Sebastian and his English colleagues had been fully aware of the 'troubles' taking place north of the border, in Northern Ireland, and some of the terrorist attacks did in fact spill over to the Republic, and that included Dublin itself. Strangely, it was rarely mentioned around Dalkey, or even in Dublin, when he and Lydia spent time in the fair city for a theatre performance or for an art exhibition. Nevertheless, considering his background, he worried about the perception locals had of him and his English pals.

On Lydia's birthday, Sebastian booked a table at one of Dublin's finest and oldest fish restaurants, The Lord Edward, situated in the city centre. They were seated at their table and perusing the menu when a vintage bottle of champagne was brought to the table. When Sebastian said to the waiter that he'd not ordered the bottle, the waiter just pointed to gentleman sitting at a nearby table who'd stood-up, smiled and waved, mutely uttering, 'Happy birthday Lady Moran.'

He recognised the gentleman as Liam Kelly, the owner of The Crab's nearest competitor, Chez Liam, Dalkey's restaurant specialising in French cuisine. As the two men had never been more than nodding acquaintances, Sebastian was more than surprised to have received the bottle of champagne. Sebastian went over to Liam's table where he was dining with his wife, Orla.

'Well, you certainly picked the restaurant with the right name, The Lord Edward, for the lord and lady to be having a celebratory dinner.'

Sebastian was momentarily thrown off-balance, by the sarcastic tone of the remark. He'd noticed with certain introverted Irish people that they use sarcasm to overcome their natural reticence to commencing a conversation. Without reference to Liam's remark, Sebastian responded, 'Liam, it was so kind and generous of you to send over the champagne. But, how did you know it was my wife's birthday?'

'Sit down and join us.'

'No thanks, I wouldn't want to intrude on your evening'

'Oh, the birthday girl is sitting on her own, so I'll be quick with what I wish to say. You're very welcome to the champagne, and I knew about your wife's birthday because your chef and mine are buddies and go drinking together.

'Anyway, what I want to say to you is that the Irish crowd in Dalkey have no objections to you or your English colleagues living and working here. None of us here support Irish terrorism, and although we'd like to see a united Ireland one day, but only by peaceful democratic means. English people are welcomed here as much as, we'd like to think, that Irish people would be welcomed in Britain. You're contributing to Ireland's economy and that's appreciated. I've not heard one word said against you or about your team. So relax, and enjoy the Craic with the other restaurateurs. We all specialise in different cuisines, making Dalkey a massive draw for diners from all over the county.

'Please give my apology to your wife for keeping you here, and enjoy your evening.'

'Thank you, Liam, you too enjoy your meal – your comments meant a lot to me.'

Shaking hands again with them both, Sebastian returned to his table apologising profusely to Lydia for leaving her on her own.

'It was nice of him to send over the champagne, but what was he going on about for so long?'

'I'll tell you later, let's just open the champagne and toast your birthday!'

Back at The Crab, Sebastian and the restaurant team were amazed how popular Valentine's night dining had become in Ireland. Even with so many eating-out options in Dalkey, The Crab, was booked out with a waiting list for cancellations a mile long. All hands were to the pump on the night, with the lunch waiting staff added to the normal evening roster. In the kitchen, as well as Ricky's two assistant chefs, Dominic exchanged his front-of-house role, with helping his friend to get the food orders out in a timely fashion.

Sebastian on most nights took his place at his permanently reserved table, a table placed at an angle that gave him a perfect view of all the other diners, so he could keep an eye on the efficiency of the service. Generally Lydia was at his side, and they'd be served dinner just like treasured regular customers, but on Valentine's night, he took over the welcome and greet role from Dominic, and he even helped the waiters by taking food orders from customers, who he felt had waited too long to be served.

There were many customers on the night that were unknown to the owner and the staff, but there was one couple, although having booked a table late in the day, were given a five-star treatment and the best table in the house. They were Ricky's great friend from the old days, Finley Reason, and, his lovely wife Susie. Having been married in a farcical manner, during the final days of his and Susie's time working for the Moran's in Brighton, nineteen years previously, they were still deliriously happy together, and very much in love. Finley, a successful hairdresser in London's Soho district, had the romantic notion to take Susie to Dublin for Valentine's Day, and whilst there to look up Ricky and his mate, Dominic, as well as his old philandering and ferocious boss, Sebastian Moran, who'd he'd long forgiven, noticing over the years, since the Brighton days, that not only had Moran mellowed, but had segued into a decent human being; well, semi-decent, anyway!

On many nights at The Crab, especially on busy one's when the service was over and the last few customers were paying their bill and getting ready to leave the restaurant, Sebastian, with any of the crew who'd wished to stay on for a late night drink, would pull a few tables together and open a bottle of green Chartreuse, the restaurant customer's favourite liqueur, the colour green being very much associated with Ireland.

Following a high-pressure shift, it was a great way to unwind, sharing a convivial drink with colleagues and friends. The two musician waiters, Connor and Sandy, who'd become very much part of the team, often stayed on and joined in with the craic.

When it was announced that Niamh and Bridget had been engaged for the two leading female roles in *Cosi fan Tutte* at Glyndehurst Opera, Sebastian had generously invited them to a complimentary dinner at The Crab together with their respective boyfriends, giving the lads a night off as waiters, and the foursome were treated to a sumptuous dinner – champagne to start, followed by a superb burgundy white wine to accompany the lobster main course. It was one of those special evenings at the restaurant with everyone going over to their table to congratulate the girls on their amazing achievement. News travelled fast around the Killiney and Dalkey areas, and the locals took pride that two of their own had been picked for such a prestigious English opera festival.

The four stayed on until the early hours drinking Chartreuse with Sebastian, Lydia, Ricky and Dominic. The Morans had been more than curious about Connor and Sandy's girlfriends; the boys constantly talked about them, and both seemed to be besotted with their respective partner. The others studied the interactions and body language of the foursome and arrived at certain conclusions about the couples' relationships, with thoughts on the differences between Niamh and Bridget.

Sebastian continued discussing the topic with Lydia late into the night, when they finally walked back to Pilot View; too tired to go to bed, they opened a bottle of wine and talked.

What did you make of the girlfriend's, my love?'

'Hmmm, I think the lads will struggle with those two beauties; you saw the way they hung onto their every word tonight looking into their eyes with such admiration. It's sort of romantic from the boys, but I'm unsure how much it's reciprocated. And once they've made their operatic debut, the press would be after them for interviews and features. How will the boys keep up with that? It's a shame they'd not got a similar break in their musical careers – that would make it more even between the couples.'

'I'm not sure you're reading the situation correctly.'

What do you mean, Seb?'

'Well, I think the young women are genuine enough and in love with their respective man, but I did notice a flirtatious nature to Niamh, who was eyeing up all the various men in the restaurant earlier. Bridget, seemed more self-contained and secretive, but I wouldn't put it past either of them to play around when they're away in England. I also don't think the boys are as innocent as they appear to be.

'One evening when you weren't at the restaurant Ricky and Dom had headed off home at closing time and it was just three of us sharing the bottle of Chartreuse. We were all a little worse-for-wear and Sandy admitted that although he loved Niamh, and looked forward to, hopefully, eventually, marrying her, he sometimes fantasised about having a sexual tryst with a man.

'By the-way, the comment was made when Connor had gone to the loo.'

'That's weird darling, because out of the two lads, I guessed it would be the effeminate Connor that would have gay tendencies. There's nothing camp about Sandy.'

'You're making the same mistake that many people do. Being camp does not necessarily equate with being gay; it could be just an introverted personality pretending to be an extrovert, by adopting a theatrical camp-type mask.'

'Hmmm... Seb. Lydia said, I'm not sure about your theory.'

'Anyway, what would interest you more, my dear Lydia, is that pretty boy Connor admitted that his secret fantasy was going to bed with a much older woman; maybe you, my darling?

With that thought in her head, Lydia went off to bed, and Sebastian soon followed her into the bedroom.

At closing time at The Crab on Valentine's night the busiest night in the restaurant since Sebastian bought it, the Chartreuse drink session had more participants than usual. The usual suspects, Ricky and Dominic, joined Sebastian and Lydia, together with Connor and Sandy. The two assistant chefs had also needed to wind down, after churning out so many meals under tremendous pressure, and joined the group. Sebastian persuaded Finley and Susie to join them, the first and only time restaurant customers had been invited to join the 'Chartreuse' set after closing the restaurant doors. The reason for keeping the group to staff only was because the usual first part of the chat would be a post-mortem of the evening's successes and failures, with a chance for the staff to get any frustrations off their chests, which could include being rude about any impolite customers. But, Finley and Susie were like family, and it was great for the original Brighton mob to be reunited once again.

Once everyone had had a chance to talk through their experiences of the evening, with a second bottle of Chartreuse magically appearing at the large table, the minutiae of the ins and outs of discussing the food, the service and opinions about various dining lovers, who were celebrating Valentine's night, started to fade from the conversation, with a more general chat about love emerging.

'So tell me, Susie, what's the secret about your long relationship with Finley?'

She was the only other female present, Lydia, who'd asked the question, and it shook up Susie who'd nodded off whilst listening to all the in-house chitchat.

Susie, feeling embarrassed and not knowing how to respond, just looked at Fin for support.

'Let me answer the question, Lydia. I believe in the saying; "Variation's on Love."'

'Whose saying was that quote?' piped up, Ricky.

'Original, mate, didn't you know that I was a philosopher as well as being the best hairdresser in London? Ha ha ha'

Everyone joined in the laughter, with Connor and Sandy being curious about the old friend of their restaurant colleagues.

'Anyway, to answer your question, Lydia, we all seek love in different ways. Although, in my young day, I was a lad about town with my friend, Ricky, and we'd get into all sorts of scrapes together, especially with the girls. I moved to Brighton and opened my first barbershop there. At about the same time, I met the love of my life, my beautiful wife, Susie'

Finley made a hand gesture towards Susie – she went beetroot red in the face.

'We had a madcap time, working for His Lordship.' He pointed a finger at Sebastian with a mock stern look on his face.

'He was determined to seduce my Susie, but with the help of my wonderful friends, Ricky and Dominic, and of course, her Ladyship, we tricked Moran into making himself into an utter fool.' Then it had been Ricky and Dominic who looked sheepish. Connor and Sandy had information about their boss which was contrary to everything they thought they knew about him.

'But let me add,' Continued Finley, 'there's redemption for everyone in our world, and Sebastian's development since that time, has been nothing short of transformative. I'd now describe my old nemesis as a proper *mensch*.' A look of puzzlement appeared on Connor and Sandy's faces.

'It means Moran has become a man of integrity and honour.' Finley uttered with a smile. You see, friends, for a gentile chap like me with so many Jewish customers, I've even picked up some Yiddish lingo. Yiddish could express something in one word that would be three or four words in English.

'We've strayed somewhat from the path of discussing "love." So let me expand my thoughts on the subject. I lived and worked in London and Brighton. I encountered many different people with varying lifestyles, and none of the lifestyles are right or wrong. Not everyone is lucky enough to find the love of their life with their first proper girlfriend. I bless my lucky stars every day. But, as a hairdresser, I'm like a priest taking confession, hearing, almost on a daily basis, some hair-raising stories about relationships and non-relationships.

'Last week I had one of my regular gentlemen clients in the salon. The gentleman was a lovely man, kind and generous with his tips. He was a record producer, at the top of his game, with not a whiff of scandal about him. The gentleman was married with two children and he spoke about his family, saying he was in love with his wife and adored his kids. But in confidence, he admitted to me, whilst I'd be styling his hair, that not only had he had a long-term mistress, but that recently, he'd fallen in love with another woman, but he still kept loving his wife and his mistress. Now, one could be critical of the gentleman on so many levels; for instance, what his feeling would be if any of the women involved took up with another lover themselves? I didn't ask, so I don't know. But who am I to judge? Is it possible to love more than one person at the same time?' A definite "no" from my point of view, but we're all different, and I'd come back to my opening remark, "Variations on Love."'

The others, especially Connor and Sandy, were looking at Finley with interest and admiration thinking him to be a most fascinating individual.

Finley, having taken a good swig of Chartreuse, continued, 'Soho, where my salon is based, is known for people out of the mainstream of society, and the area inhabits a fair smattering of gay and lesbians. Yes, I know I'm a gentleman's hairdresser, but I get a certain type of female client who wanted a male haircut. They are very open with me describing their respective partner – explaining the allure of the more feminine of the pair; whilst the client, entering my salon, had been dressed as a man, sporting a tailored suit, shirt with cufflinks and a tie.

'Gay men come in a variety of guises. There are gay couples that are no different from straight ones. They'd be in a committed relationship, living together with all the ups and downs of everyday life. Sometimes they stray into casual sex, just like straight couples. The idea that gay men are more promiscuous than heterosexual males is a myth, in my opinion. The only difference was that, although gay adult sex is now legal, gay marriage isn't. But that will come, although it may take another thirty years.'

Sandy... who'd been listening very carefully to Finley's stream of consciousness verbal thoughts, piped-up. 'Gay adult sex is still illegal in Ireland.'

Finley had a look of surprise on his face. 'I didn't know that, Sandy, but I'm sure that will change over time, and even gay marriage in Ireland will happen, eventually.'

'Sorry for hogging the limelight, friends, but both Susie and I, loved being amongst you tonight.'

'We've loved having you and Susie here on Valentine's night,' said Sebastian, as you're the most romantic couple known to us, so please carry on with your thoughts.'

'Hear, hear,' the others added.

'Thanks, Seb, for your kind words. We're not the perfect couple, and we've had our moments, but our love has always overcome any minor differences we've had.' Finley had winked at his wife with a kissing motion, following his comments.

'But it's the bisexual men and women who'd be the most verbally abused by, both gays and lesbians. Some gay men believe that bisexuals are really gays in disguise, but too cowardly to admit the fact. On the other hand, straight people often believe that bisexuals are just sexually greedy, or even worse, sexual opportunists.'

Sebastian was looking a tad uncomfortable, having not shared his bisexual tendencies with anyone other than Lydia.

'Of course, "Variation on love" comprises many other categories, including swinging, open relationships, polyamory, private parties and sex clubs.'

Connor, who'd lived a fairly sheltered life, was fascinated with the way Finley, a monogamous happily married man, was able, in the company of his wife, to speak so openly about things that in Ireland would be hush-hush. Looking at Finley, Connor asked, 'Why did you call it "love" when what you really meant was "sex?"'

'Hmmm, I call everything "love," Connor, because the word "love" is very broad. All sexual activity, as long as it's between adults and consensual, will contain an element of "love." I believe in the slogan, "Make love, not war."'

Susie was well aware of how much her husband enjoyed holding court with friends, as in his hairdresser salon; he was more of listener to his clients than a speaker. Besides, she'd heard it all before and was feeling very tired. 'I think it's time to get a taxi back to our hotel in Dublin, darling.'

Goodnights were said – hugs and kisses with everyone, as Finley and Susie alighted their taxi.

The late-late night reverie was down to six people – Sebastian, Lydia, Ricky, Dominic, Connor and Sandy. They had all drunk too much of the green-stuff. So Seb cracked open a bottle of champagne. Addressing the Irish lads, Seb asked them how familiar they were with the opera their girlfriends were starting rehearsals for in England.

Sandy responded…'well, we've never seen *Cosi Fan Tutte,* but of course, Connor and I will be attending the opening night in May.'

Connor added, 'We know and perform a lot of Mozart's music, but the only opera of his we've seen, at the Dublin Grand Opera Society, was *The Magic Flute*, which we both loved to bits.'

Sandy nodded in agreement.

Sebastian outlined the plot of *Cosi Fan Tutte* to the two lads, adding, 'Niamh and Bridget would be acting out love scenes with two, probably handsome men. Are you sure that they'll remain faithful to you two, and not get carried away with the theatrical glamour of it all, morphing from stage lovers into actual ones?'

 Both Connor, and Sandy, jumped up and protested, annoyed that Sebastian would even think of such an outcome.

Sandy, the most vocal of the pair, was quite adamant that their girlfriends would never cheat on them. 'We, in Ireland, don't have the loose morals as some in England, as your friend Finley described.'

The atmosphere became a touch frosty around the table, and Seb decided it was time to call it a night.

The following night, the after-closing drinks session was a smaller affair, just Sebastian, Lydia, Ricky and Dominic. 'The original Brighton four,' had been mulling-over the shenanigans of the previous night. Connor and Sandy had been quiet during the evening service, undertaking their chores without taking part in the usual banter. Had they been upset about the suggestion that their girlfriends might flirt, or even worse, cheat on them, with their operatic lovers? But on a previous night, Sandy had confided in Sebastian that he had gay fantasies, and Connor had admitted fancying much older women. Maybe their male-centric influences had given them an old-school notion, that moral standards were different for females.

Realising how non-communicative they'd become with no-one topping-up their glass of Chartreuse, Sebastian remarked, 'Our mutual friends, Finley, and Susie, were on great form last night. Finley, in particular, had developed some extraordinarily thought-through notions about love and sex.'

Ricky, who'd known Finley for a lot longer than the others, spoke-up. 'Finley had always been an extraordinary human being. Even as kids, he never said, or did, anything to impress other kids, or to show off to adults. He was a deep thinker from the time we met at school. Last night, he described himself, in a self-mocking way, as a philosopher hairdresser, but that's exactly who Finley is. I've been blessed with two of the most wonderful friends, in Finley, and Dominic.'

Suddenly realising that he'd left out Sebastian and Lydia, he quickly added, 'and the two of you, pointing a finger at the Moran's, in recent years, have joined this exclusive club.

Sebastian, not one for sentimentality, changed tack; 'Do you guys think that Niamh and Bridget will stay completely faithful to their boyfriends, when in England, performing in the opera?

The two friends looked at each other, both knowing that they felt the same way about the issue, having discussed it together earlier in the day.

Ricky, speaking for them both, responded, 'Absolutely yes, we believe that they will remain completely faithful to Connor and Sandy.'

'Hmmm, Lydia and I take a different view. They'll be so caught up with their opera characters and with the men they're tangled up with operatically, they'll succumb to any moves the men might make, putting Connor and Sandy temporarily to the back of their minds.'

'Hey, guys,' continued Sebastian. 'Let's have a little flutter. The Royal Opera, in London's Covent Garden, has announced a Mozart Festival in the autumn. The three Mozart/Da Ponte operas, *Le Nozze di Figaro*, *Don Giovanni* and *Cosi Fan Tutte* will be programmed on three consecutive nights. I'll buy four best stalls tickets for all three operas when the booking opens, and if you're right about the girlfriends, it will be my treat. On the other hand, if we're proven correct, the two of you will reimburse me for all the tickets.'

'That sounds like a good flutter,' said Dominic. 'But the obvious question is, how will we know if the girls are being unfaithful?'

'Ha, yes, that is the question. A good friend of mine is the production director at Glyndehurst. I'll have a word with him, and he'll promise to keep a discreet eye on the two women throughout the rehearsal period and for the run of performances. I believe that my friend would be totally honest with me. But, "hush" would be the word around Connor and Sandy, as the flutter was strictly a game between us four.'

The three men shook hands in agreement. Lydia walked away from the men, thinking, 'boys toys,' it all being a game for the men. Although, instinctively, she believed that the two sisters would indulge, at the least, in flirtations at the opera house, but she also thought that to place a bet on the matter was somewhat distasteful.

CHAPTER 28

East Sussex, England

1979

'I prefer yours, Niamh.'

'Mmm, Well, yours is also quite tasty, Bridget.'

The sisters had arrived in Glyndehurst, for the beginning of the long rehearsal period, and had just been introduced to the rest of the cast.

Cosi Fan Tutte's cast was a compact one of six singers. Don Alfonso, a bass/baritone, who was the cynical older friend, who was the master of ceremonies of the plot, manipulating everything and everyone. Despina, a soprano *soubrette,* Alfonso's maid, and co-conspirator, who also doubled up in disguises as the doctor and the notary; Fiordiligi (Bridget), and Dorabella (Niamh) were betrothed, respectively, to Guglielmo, baritone, and Ferrando, tenor, but as the plot progressed, with the males returning in disguise, the couples exchanged partners.

'Well, during the opera, we've a choice of lovers, so let's decide later which ones we want off-stage, ha ha ha.'

The tenor and baritone were both Italian, handsome, married (though they'd left their wives in Italy) and touchy-feely, with the girls, in particular.

Over the weeks, as rehearsals became more intense, off-stage relationships began to develop. Niamh, the more lively personality of the two, was attracted to the tenor, a good natured man and extremely romantic in his wooing of her. Bridget had become enamoured with the baritone, who was full of quick witted repartee (both the Italians had excellent English), as well as being charismatic and persuasive.

 The production director, Stuart Montgomery, had been keeping an eye on the sisters, as he'd promised his old friend, Sebastian Moran. They'd known each other from the Morans' time in Brighton. Moran had helped him out of a financial hole, due to his, then, gambling habit. Although he had not been keen to spy on the girls, he felt obliged to cede to the request.

The opening night of the opera in May was a sensation. The critics, there in droves, were full of praise for the whole show, but especially for the two Irish sisters, making their debut at a major opera festival. 'Born to play and sing their parts,' was just one of the comments in one of the nationals. Connor and Sandy travelled to England for the first night, and were extremely proud of their respective girlfriends. Any flirtation they'd seen on the stage was completely within the context of the plot. The Italians stayed at arm's length from the girls at the first night party and they all drank too much champagne. The boys flew back to Dublin to next day. Both Niamh's and Bridget's parents were due to attend a performance later in the run.

During the Glyndehurst opera season, *Cosi Fan Tutte* was performed every three or four days, During the non-performing days, one day was for resting, one day was to spend time with the Glyndehurst vocal coach and the theatre director, to iron out any stage or vocal issues that had arisen in a previous performance, that usually left one day completely free to have fun.

Off stage, Bridget and her initial stage lover, the baritone-singing Guglielmo, whose real-life name was Luigi Conti, became a regular pair during downtime. Niamh and her tenor stage love, Ferrando (Roberto De Luca, in life) were slower in adopting their stage coupling than her more impulsive sister. But as the weeks went by, an off-stage foursome seemed to be acknowledged around Glyndehurst, both with the other artists and the production team.

On week four, during the run of *Cosi Fan Tutte*, the schedule allowed an extra day of leisure for the cast, so there were two days in succession when the cast had no artistic commitments. Luigi, who'd always be full of ideas for playtime, suggested an overnight trip to Brighton, which was just over an hour's drive away from Glyndehurst, and booked a night at the famous Grand Hotel.

The foursome had booked two large double rooms at The Grand Hotel. Although, at that stage, sexual relations had not occurred between either couple, but they all knew that it would happen before the end of the opera run. They'd been quite public about indulging in kisses, and cuddles in the Glyndehurst bars and restaurants. As the winter months turned to spring, the two couples were seen swanning around the beautiful opera house gardens, holding hands, amongst the array of gorgeous roses, geraniums and lilies, surrounded by tall yew hedges.

Was there gossip amongst the artists, and others who were engaged in all sorts of employment activity, around the opera house complex? Far from it, as over many summer seasons they'd seen it all. Many romances blossomed in the exquisitely scented atmosphere of Glyndehurst, some segued into relationships that survived, once away from the heady perfume of the country house, whilst others were just ships passing in the night, but beautiful, during the period they lasted.

Stuart Montgomery overheard Luigi in his loud, Italian accented English, talk about the trip to Brighton with his friend Roberto, and their Irish girlfriends. Montgomery made a call to Sebastian Moran, updating him on his spying mission, specifically, the foursome's plans for a night at Grand Hotel in Brighton. Moran reckoned on the basis of Montgomery's previous reports, he was about to win his bet, but just to be certain, he told Stuart to book a room at the hotel on the same night, and, to check the bedroom situation – who was sharing

with whom? Moran concluded by telling Montgomery to send
him the bill for dinner, bed and breakfast at the Grand and that
he'd reimburse him with a cheque in the post.

The weather in Brighton was glorious, a perfect early June day,
when spring began to turn to summer, the temperatures
rising, but still retaining the freshness of late spring. To
maintain a sense of propriety, one double room at The Grand
hotel was booked in the name of the sisters, and the other room
was for Luigi and Roberto to share. Both rooms were on the
same floor. A nod and a wink, though, was that Luigi would
slip into the girl's room and that Niamh would move in with
Roberto.

Stuart Montgomery, having checked into The Grand, managed
to have a quiet word with the hotel's chief receptionist,
explaining that he was an agent for a lawyer in Italy, who was
representing the wife of Luigi Conti, the gentleman who'd
checked into the hotel earlier, booking a double room with his
friend, Roberto De Luca. Mrs Conti was seeking proof of her
husband's infidelity, to be able to have grounds for divorce.

'How can I help you, Mr. Montgomery?' The receptionist's was
looking at Montgomery with a cynical half smile.

'I'm not looking to cause any trouble here; complete discretion
is my number one rule in my job. I would just like to know the
room number of Mr Conti and Mr De Luca, so I can secretly
keep an eye on Mr Conti, as far as his inviting a female into the
room.'

The receptionist knew that the two men had arrived at the hotel
with two females. He'd known at the time of them checking in
to the hotel exactly what they had in mind; he'd been at the
Grand long enough to know the drill. Either the men or the
women would switch rooms to sleep with their respective lover.

With an inscrutable expression, he addressed Montgomery.

'That's impossible sir, more than my job is worth.'

Montgomery discreetly put fifty pounds into the receptionist's hand. (He'd charge the fifty pounds to Moran)'

'Just wait here, sir. The receptionist, still looking totally inscrutable, asked Montgomery to wait where he was. Returning a few minutes later, he handed a note to Montgomery, which had the gentlemen's room number written down. The note also confirmed that their female companion's room was on the same floor, along the corridor. Adding a further twenty pounds to the receptionist tip, he requested a change of room that was located on the same floor as the foursome. Following the negotiations with the receptionist, Montgomery went directly to his revised room number, having decided to stay out of the public areas of the hotel, so that the Glyndehurst foursome wouldn't spot him. Dinner would be by room service. He just needed to keep an eye on the comings and goings along the corridor.

The young couples had gone for a long walk on the Brighton sea front, stopping off at one of the beach bars for beers, burgers and ice creams. Back at the Grand, afternoon tea beckoned on the terrace. They tucked into smoked salmon and cucumber sandwiches, delicious selection of cakes with large pots of English breakfast tea.

The pairs split up, each going to their respective rooms, the girls to rest, to enjoy a long bath and to dress, both choosing elegant outfits that enhanced their perfect figures, wanting a different look to their stage presence, where they'd been made to look younger than they were, dressed in loose casual shift dresses.

The two men, who needed less time to shower and dress for dinner, went off to the hotel's bar and ordered a couple of beers. Nursing his beer, Luigi thought about lighting up a cigarette, but decided against it. Smoking was deadly for singers, and he only smoked when he was opera-engagement free.

'Roberto, my friend, I was just thinking. We both chose our particular girl to love, whilst in England. Bridget and I, are a great couple; she's quieter than me but loves my jokes, always telling me how much I make her laugh. Hopefully, we'll make love tonight for the first time and I know that it will be great. But I was just thinking that in the opera, Niamh becomes my lover in the second act, although we'd return to our original loves at the end of the opera. But that's our director's choice. In other productions I've sung in, we remained with the others lover. To be honest, during the performance I'm always aware of Niamh hugging me tighter than she's been coached by the director, which is a big turn on for me. In contemporary language, *Cosi Fan Tutte* is a swinger's opera!'

Roberto was taking-in everything that Luigi was saying, and instead of the expected Italian *geloso*, he often thought during a performance that he fancied Bridget physically. However, he realised that as a personality, Niamh was a better fit for him.

As Luigi wasn't getting any reaction from Roberto, he'd boldly stated, 'Let's swing tonight; we'd both make love to both girls.'

'Mmm, Luigi, you're getting carried away. As much as I feel the same as you, to be able to replicate the operas scenario in real life, but if we're not mindful, we won't be making love to either girl.

Roberto looked at Luigi, wondering what mad-cap notion he'd come-up with.

'You're right, Roberto, we must tread carefully or we'll freak-out our *belle ragazze*, so let's change our plans for tonight'

'What did you have in mind?'

'*amico mio*, we must not to spend the whole evening drinking, stuffing our faces and then retiring to our rooms. We'll have a few drinks here, to kick things off; we'll then go out to eat.

We'll need to build up to the right emotional atmosphere before we even suggest a partner swap.'

'How would not eating in the hotel and going to a restaurant instead, create the right emotional atmosphere?'

'Think about it, Roberto, A big meal here would make us all tired, and we'll all be sleepy, and we'll want to go to bed. What we need is to keep the energy levels up and to make a night of it out in Brighton.'

Roberto was looking puzzled.

'I'd been told from another singer at Glyndehurst, that there's a very sexy exclusive night club in town. Yes, not only do I have the details, the singer has also given me his membership pass.'

'You're a sly fox, *amico mio.*'

'It's always good to plan, my friend!' OK, we go to the club. From what I'd been told, the vibe there is very lustful; swapping couples occurs regularly with the members of the club. We'll get hot, with both our own and each other's *amante.* We'll go back to the hotel with lust in our thoughts and in all our minds, but it will be late into the night, and we'll go back to our own rooms...to sleep. We'll have to book a second night at the hotel, which will be fine, as we're not due back to Glyndehurst to the following day. We'll spend the whole day and night tomorrow, making love with Bridget and Niamh!'

'You're wasting your time as an opera singer, Luigi, You'd make a great novelist.'

'Ha ha ha, I'd hate to go back to Italy and regret that we'd messed-up with our Irish sweethearts. I think the plan is good, no?'

'You're such a clever rascal, Luigi. I'll nip down to the reception and explain that we and our friends would like to extend our stay for one more night.'

'Yes do that, and let's hope the girls will be OK with staying on.

The men, having showered and changed were back at the hotel's bar awaiting their women. They arrived at the bar looking spectacularly glamorous. The men had never seen them, up until that moment, looking so like Hollywood film stars. On stage, the director's concept was that they be pretty, with a young girlish appearance. And, off-stage, around the operas campus, they were dressed in T-shirts and jeans with no make-up. The men stared at Niamh and Bridget with longing in their eyes.

Sitting down, having ordered gin-martini cocktails for the four of them, the men explained about the change of plan for the evening. The women had been looking forward to dinner at the Grand, nevertheless, loved the sound of the exclusive *louché* nightclub. However, they were somewhat nonplussed that the men had arranged to stay over at the hotel for a further night, without them being consulted. But after a second martini, they began to see the logic of not rushing back to Glyndhurst the next morning, and after all, the whole escapade in Brighton was the men's financial treat.

A nice and friendly young woman, working on the hotel's reception desk, recommended a cosy French bistro situated in The Lanes, which was a famous shopping area of Brighton. The Lanes were within walking distance from the Grand, and off the four went, in high spirits, linking arms towards the restaurant.

The restaurant was ideal for them. It served rustic traditional French food. The women shared a coq au vin, whilst the men tucked into a *pot au feu*. Both dishes were meant for two persons. All four shared a big bowl of salade nicoise for starters. A full bodied Bordeaux wine was the perfect accompaniment to the meal. They decided against dessert, finishing off with strong coffees and cognac for the men, with the women going for a Pernod liquor.

The restaurant had a romantic vibe – red banquettes, soft lighting with candles on the tables and wine bottles lined up on the mantelpiece, below a large mirror. The clientele were mostly attractive young couples out on a date, anticipating a night of love.

Leaving the restaurant, they decided, as it was a lovely warm night, on a walk along the sea front to digest their meal. Being a bit early for the night club, they found an attractive looking wine bar, just off the sea front, ordering a bottle of the floral scented *Gewurtztraminer* wine from Alsace. The young man who took the order said to take a seat and that he'd bring the wine over. But when the wine came, an older smartly dressed man came over to the table carrying the tray of wine.

'Good evening ladies and gentlemen, I'm Harvey Monaghan, the owner of the bar. I just had to come over to say hello, because I recognise you all from the Glyndehurst production of *Cosi Fan Tutte*. I was at a performance the other night, and I thought that the four of you were absolutely sensational, so the wine is on the house.'

'Oh, that's very kind of you.' Luigi stood-up to shake the man's hand and made introductions all-round. 'Please join us Mr Monaghan.'

'Thank you, but please call me Harvey.'

Monaghan poured the wine, refusing a glass for himself.

The chat around the table centred on the opera, which Monaghan seemed not only to be an enthusiast but an expert, especially about the three Mozart/Da/Ponte works. The four opera singers were being polite to Monaghan, but it was their downtime; the last thing they wanted was to spend the night talking about work.

Roberto looked at his watch and indicated to the others that is was time to go. Harvey asked them where they were off to. Luigi mentioned the particular night club they planned to attend, so they'd be able to round off their night enjoying a fun time.

'Oh,' piped up Harvey,' I know the club well and the owner, Marc Littleton, is a good friend of mine. I'll telephone Marc to let him know that you're on your way there, and he'll make sure that you'll have a great night.'

Handing his card to Luigi, Harvey said that he'd order a taxi for them unless they had a car with them.

'No, Harvey, said Luigi, 'we left the car at the hotel, so yes, please order a taxi for us.'

Thanking Monaghan profusely for his hospitality, the four left the wine bar and headed for the club.

Marc Littleton greeted them warmly at the reception of the Temptation Club. He refused to accept the entrance fee, as not only were they friends of Harvey Monaghan, but he'd also been told that they were the current stars at the opera at Glyndehurst.

'But please, there's no reason to worry,' added Littleton. 'we're all 100 per cent discreet here – no-one would ever know that you'd been at Temptation, and, whatever you'd get up to at the club would stay within our four walls. Now, get in there and enjoy a night to remember.' Marc gave them a saucy wink as they entered the main area of the club.

A gorgeous-looking young woman, scantily dressed, showed them to a table in a quiet corner, but with a good view, despite the low soft lighting, of the dance floor and other tables.

Off the main floor there were several narrow corridors, leading, they suspected, to smaller public areas where lovers could indulge in whatever activity they wished to indulge in.

The young woman returned to the table with a bottle of champagne – compliments of the proprietor. Roberto commented with a little laugh, that no one wanted to take money off them that night.

The music was mainly the pop tunes of the day; predominately the slow romantic numbers, that encouraged close up dancing. The club was full, with every table taken, as well as some single men and women standing around the circular bar, eyeing up the talent.

Sipping their champagne, the two opera couples were looking around the other tables. The clientele were generally a glamorous one, both the men and the women. Ironically, they were escaping the opera house for a break, but the attendees at the club, especially with the way they were dressed, could have been at Glyndehurst. The big difference being that instead of dressing up for a dose of high culture, here, the glamorous men and women had debauchery in mind.

They were watching the couples on the dance floor – bodies squashed up together, the men's hand on their partners bum and one couple vigorously kissing. Bridget and Niamh noticed two men dancing together in a clinch, that shocked and fascinated them at be same time. They would never have seen that in Ireland, where homosexuality between consenting adults, was still illegal. Luigi and Roberto were watching a couple at a nearby table. The couple were passionately kissing, as another man, presumably a stranger to the couple, sat down at their table. He didn't say a word to them, just watching, as the man whispered something into his partner's ear. The woman looked at the strange man with a half smile on her face. The stranger moved closer to the woman, nonchalantly putting his hand on her knee whilst looking at the man, seeking tacit permission to touch his woman. He received a nod which gave the stranger confidence to continue. He moved his hand up and down the woman's leg taking his further up towards her wet vagina. He took her hand and led her towards one of the corridors, out of sight. The woman's partner kept to his seat looking not at all bothered. The two opera men became mesmerised with the goings on at the nearby table, giving them a sexual frisson watching their debauched antics.

Luigi related to Bridget and Niamh what they had witnessed. At the same time Luigi started kissing his opera girlfriend, Bridget, whilst Niamh and Roberto, holding hands, watched on.

'Let's have a look in the corridor to see what's going on there,' Roberto said interrupting his friends kissing. The two couples walked through the corridor, entering a dark room where they noticed the woman from the next table, in a state of undress, giving fellatio to the stranger who'd invited himself to sit at her, and her partners table. Standing behind Roberto, was the woman's partner who'd come through the corridor to watch his woman in flagrante. The man, looked around the room, saw a tall, dark-haired woman standing on her own watching the sexual activity around the room with lust in her eyes. He made a move towards the unknown woman, holding out his hand, which she grabbed whilst sinking into the man's arms, where they found each other mouths.

Roberto, Bridget, Luigi and Niamh watched the scene in astonishment wondering what sort of Sodom and Gomorrah club were they at. But, at the same time, the four felt sexually aroused. Niamh put her arm around her boyfriend Roberto, whilst Bridget and Luigi were kissing. Without either couple, becoming fully aware of what was happening, the couples switched. They began to passionately kiss each other's love. Niamh and Luigi were kissing with all the intensity of long built-up desire. Cool Bridget became hot for her sisters love, Roberto, something she'd wanted to do during their love scenes in the opera.

They stayed at the club until the early hours, arriving back at the Grand hotel all full of sexual desire, but also very tired. They headed to their separate rooms the men whispered to the women that they'd join them for love-making in the morning. Kissing their goodnights, they parted company.

'I can't believe what's happening,' Niamh remarked to her sister whilst they were lying in their separate small double beds, not being able to sleep despite both being exhausted.

 Bridget added, 'I was anticipating, with pleasure, making love with Luigi here in Brighton, but now I have an overwhelming desire for Roberto, as well as for my Luigi.'

'I feel the same' said Niamh. 'I want them both and wish they'd come with us into our bedroom tonight. Watching the sexy shenanigans at Temptations has made me feel extremely randy.'

'It's the same with me, sis.' The two of them drifted off to sleep.

Stuart Montgomery had stayed in his room all day and evening, ordering room service for supper. He constantly kept his ears and eyes to the corridor, watching the comings and goings in the bedrooms, so that he could confirm to Sebastian Moran that the two Italian men were sharing a bedroom with the Irish girls. As evening turned into night and he hadn't spotted or heard anything, he kept drinking coffee to stay awake. Finally, at 3 a.m., he heard voices outside his room. He opened his bedroom door slightly, seeing the foursome saying their goodnights and most importantly, going off to their separate rooms. Montgomery was surprised, to say the least, as he was sure that sexual activity had been going on or was planned during their Brighton stay. But he was unable to report to Moran that he had any proof of infidelities.

Due to a production meeting at the opera house at 10 a.m., Montgomery had gone down for breakfast at 8 a.m., checking out of the hotel, a disappointed man, at 9 a.m.

At 9.30 a.m., Roberto and Luigi knocked on the bedroom door of Bridget and Niamh, who were waiting for both men with overwhelming sexual desire. They made love all day, Roberto with Niamh, and Luigi with Bridget, then, they changed lovers, Roberto with Bridget, and Luigi with Niamh. They ordered room service for coffees and snacks, the men hiding in the bathroom when the waiter arrived. It had been a wet day in Brighton so they weren't missing any seaside sunshine. In the evening, they ordered steaks and red wine, again via room service. The men had stayed with their dual lovers the whole of the second night.

It had been their private performance, in real time, of *Cosi Fan Tutte,* where the men in disguise, made love with each other's lovers. But, the sisters must have seen through the disguises, so the opera was actually an eighteenth-century prototype of twentieth-century 'swinging!'

Stuart Montgomery telephoned Sebastian, explaining that although he could confirm that flirtations had taken place, he had no proof that either couple had actually slept together, although he suspected that they had. Moran was none too pleased, and some of his old arrogance was exposed, especially when Montgomery mentioned the extra seventy pounds he spent on tipping a manager at the Grand hotel.

'You can whistle for that, Stuart. I'll only reimburse you for what we'd agreed – bed, breakfast and a dinner.

CHAPTER 29

Dalkey – Ireland

1979

'I think we'll call it a draw.'

Sebastian was having the usual after-closing drink at The Crab with Ricky and Dominic.

'What are you talking about, Seb?' Ricky looked-up from the recipe book that he'd recently acquired.

The bet, Ricky, have you forgotten about it?

'Oh yes,' Ricky said, 'the bet. To be honest, Seb, I didn't take it seriously.' Dominic nodded from across the table.

'Well, guys, you should have, because if you've lost, I'll be looking for you two to reimburse me for the Mozart Festival tickets at Covent Garden; three operas for four people in the best stalls cost a pretty penny!'

At last, Sebastian was getting his friend's attention.

'So, what happened then,' Dominic asked?

'Well, we've received sufficient proof that the sisters had been flirting with their leading men, but as far as being unfaithful with them, it's inconclusive.'

Ricky asked Seb about his contact there who was supposed to spy on them.

'Yes... that idiot, Montgomery. He'd be useless working for MI6.'

Sebastian explained the saga of the Grand Hotel stay.

'They obviously spent the night with the Italian lads, but Montgomery screwed up and he never saw either of the men enter the women's bedroom. And to think that he bribed one of the managers to give him the guys' room number, then further bribed him to change his room to one on their corridor. He stayed in his room all day and evening and noticed nothing, except the four of them saying their goodnights to each other in the corridor at 3 a.m., with the men going off to their room and the women entering theirs and locking the door.'

'Ha ha ha, 'laughed Ricky. 'It sounds like a proper bedroom farce.'

Dominic guffawed. 'And did you reimburse him for his trouble?'

'I agreed to pay for his overnight stay, meals included, at the Grand Hotel, but he had the audacity to ask me to repay him the seventy pounds bribe, but I told him to take a run and jump. '

'Hmmm,' smirked. Dominic 'You sound like the Sebastian of old, lean and mean.'

Ricky and Dominic burst out laughing, and Sebastian, seeing the funny side of the whole escapade, joined in the laughter.

'But' – added Sebastian with a more serious look on his face, putting a finger to his mouth. 'Please guys, not a word to Connor or Sandy. They'd be absolutely devastated to know that their darling girlfriends were flirting with other guys, let alone being sexually unfaithful, if that indeed was the case.'

As it turned out, Bridget and Niamh, when back in Ireland, following the end of the opera run at Glyndehurst, had made limited confessions to their boyfriends. They tried to explain that working so closely with the two Italian men, as lovers in the opera plot, they'd indulged in a little flirtation with them, knowing they both had wives back in Italy, so it would be nothing more than just ships in the night. Between them the sisters swore secrecy with one another, as to never ever confess to having had full sexual relations with the men. They'd shuddered to even think about the consequences of Connor and Sandy ever finding out that the two couples swapped partners, enjoying sex with each man whilst the other couple looked on.

They'd actually been foolish to even confess a mild flirtation, as the lads took it badly. As far as they were concerned, trust had been broken, and each man would be reconsidering the future of their relationship.

When Sebastian and Lydia became aware of the girls' mini confession and the boys reaction, Sebastian remarked. 'The boys need to learn about real life; what the hell. A little flirtation in the hot house of an opera house should have been no great deal.'

'Mind you, I doubt that it was only flirtations. I suspect that it went further, possibly much further than that. But, whatever they did or didn't do, flirtation is what they owned up to'

Lydia, listening carefully, added, 'The lads have lived sheltered lives and have some very fixed ideas about the roles of men and women in relationships. It could be through various influences, partly family, maybe church doctrine – that's very strong here in Ireland, or just the conservative society they've been surrounded by all their lives.'

'Are you suggesting that for men, as would be the case with traditional cultures, have license to stray, sexually, but women, will be treated harshly if they did the same thing?'

'Well, yes, that would explain the lads confessing to you, after a few drinks, their respective fantasies of gay sex and sex with older women.'

'Hmmm, Lydia, I almost forgot about that chat with the lads.

'I must admit that I feel sorry for Bridget and Niamh. Unlike the lads, whose careers so far had been solely around their own Irish environment, the girls have been thrust into the limelight, in a theatrical milieu within a different country that was strange and startling to them. No wonder they were tempted to stray from their known norms of behaviour.

'Perhaps if we encouraged Connor and Sandy to live out their sexual fantasies, they'd have more understanding about their girlfriends having succumbed to temptation.'

Lydia, with a far-away look on her face, thought about the fresh-faced Connor and how she'd like to spend time with him.

Sebastian, reading his wife's thoughts, knew instinctively that they couldn't allow either of them to become involved, sexually, with the lads.

'We can't personally be the ones that lead them astray; they're employees of ours.'

'Of course, you're right, Seb.'

'But we could steer them in the right direction, my love.'

'What are you suggesting?'

'Your friend, right here in Dalkey – Mandy Wilton. She's an attractive woman, late forties-early fifties?'

'Mandy is the same age as me.'

'And you've confided in me that she had a thing for younger men.'

'Yes, that's true but she is a friend of Connor's family'

'That would make an introduction easier.'

'What about Sandy? A gay affair would be a bit tricky in Ireland.'

'No, not in Ireland, I'll take him to my private gay club in London, but I promise you that I'll be a mentor to him only, show him the ropes, but not become involved with him in any way.'

CHAPTER 30

London

1979

It was a lovely early October day in London, the city at its best – blue skies, warm, but mellow sunshine, and the trees in London's great parks beginning to show their autumn leaves. Sebastian had invited Connor and Sandy to stay with him for a week at his Belgravia home. Lydia alternated between living in her Chelsea town house and spending the odd night in Belgravia with Sebastian. The restaurant in Dalkey had been left in the capable hands of Ricky and Dominic who'd taken on some temporary staff to fill in whilst Connor and Sandy were in London. In any case, it was a quiet time in the restaurant, being between the busy summer season and the festive period leading up to Christmas. They would close altogether for a week at the end of the month, when Ricky and Dominic went to London to join Sebastian and Lydia, for the Mozart Festival at Covent Garden.

Lydia had invited her friend from Dalkey, Mandy Wilton, to stay with her for a few days in Chelsea. Mandy wanted to catch the Vincent Van Gogh exhibition at the National Gallery, as well as catching up with some other old London friends.

Lydia made a point of inviting Connor to dinner whilst Mandy was her house guest, and at the same time informed the pair, that she'd actually be staying overnight with Sebastian in Belgravia on that particular night, leaving the two of them together. She made some feeble excuse, concerning a new medication that Sebastian had been prescribed, by his doctor for high blood pressure, and she wanted to make sure that he was OK with it.

However, she cooked an Italian meal for the three of them. Prawn cocktail, a fabulous home-made lasagne, accompanied with a green salad. She baked an apple tart for dessert, served with her own ice cream. Several bottles of good-quality red and white Italian wine were opened, left on the table to help oneself without an undue pouring ceremony. They began the evening with generous measures of several rounds of gin and tonics. The lights were low and she'd put Chopin nocturnes on her turntable.

When Connor and Sandy had let their respective girlfriends know, once they'd confessed about flirting at the opera, that any thoughts of imminent engagements and subsequent double weddings, that had been talked about previously between the four, had become out of the question for the time being, or maybe forever, the lads had become very moody around the restaurant, not being their usual charming selves with the customers.

Sebastian took the lads aside, individually, and let them know that they needed to buck up their ideas, or he'd have to dispense with their services; but he'd also offered them an olive-branch, which was also a piece of personal advice.

He reminded Connor that he'd confessed to fancying older women; Sebastian could help him out in that regard. That would be sweet revenge on Bridget. Sebastian mentioned Mandy Wilton, who Connor always had a secret crush on since boyhood, so he was happy to go along with Sebastian's plan. Mandy was not what one would call beautiful, being tallish, with a voluptuous figure, medium brown hair worn in a ponytail. But her brown refulgent eyes and sensuous full lips suggested a woman full of sexual possibilities.

Mandy, an art lover arranged, through Lydia, to take Connor to an art show opening in Dublin, of the Irish painter and dealer Paul Dellans, whose gallery was upstairs the famous Irish pub, Fogans, on South William Street. Dellans was not only an original contemporary artist, but he was also a canny dealer, specialising in Irish artists, such as, Jack B Yeats and Percy French. In fact, Mandy was a friend of Paul Dellans', having purchased a beautiful Percy French watercolour from him that was proudly hanging in Mandy's Pilot View living room.

With a few pints of Guinness consumed in Fogans, after spending time at the exhibition and chatting with Paul Dellons, who had many contacts in Dublin' s musical world, promising to spread the name of Connor Clarkson to the city's concert promoters, Connor left the building feeling pretty chuffed.

Mandy invited Sandy back to Pilot View, where following a few gin and tonics, she made a pass at her young friend. Connor responded as they kissed.

 Connor left Mandy's flat with thoughts of *Phew, that was some sexy kiss*, Thoughts of taking things further with Mandy and having full blown sex with her, excited him hugely and he couldn't wait for a suitable opportunity. So when Sebastian invited him to London and then engineered the date with Mandy, he was unable to control himself with lust and longing for the sexy sophisticated woman who was almost double his age, and a family friend.

In London, at Lydia's Chelsea town house, her guests, Mandy and Connor had enjoyed the dinner and were full of compliments about Lydia's cooking. Leaving the pair together on the settee, Lydia made her excuses and headed off to the kitchen to see how her young helper was coping with the new dishwasher.

Alone, Mandy whispered in Connor's ear, 'When Lydia leaves, I'll invite you up to my bedroom.'

'Oh my god, Mandy, the thought of it makes me so excited, I can hardly control myself!'

'No so fast, young man, we'll have all night to make love.'

Connor put his arm around Mandy and laid his head on her shoulder.

Lydia came in and said that she was off to Belgravia.

Thanking Lydia profusely for her hospitality, she retorted with a wink of the eye. 'Have fun you two!'

The couple slowly headed upstairs, holding hands, and went into the guest bedroom where Mandy was staying.

Meanwhile, Sebastian took Sandy to his private gay club. The club was situated in Percy Lane, a small nondescript street, off busy Goodge Street, the area of London, known as Fitzrovia. The club, which attracted many members from the political world, was deliberately located out of the Westminster area, away from a journalist's prying eye. The membership scrutiny committee were extremely diligent about who received their nod of approval. It wasn't necessarily a snobbish thing, although there was an element of that, but the threat of blackmail of well-known political figures, had been a constant concern, especially those who were married with families, who'd be resident somewhere in the leafy Home Counties. The fact that Sebastian Moran had confided to the committee that he, and his wife, had an open marriage, and that Lady Moran, had given her husband tacit permission to discreetly indulge his sexual fantasies, had helped his membership application. One guest per member was allowed, but the member had to vouch for the guest. If the guest misbehaved in any way at the club, had become indiscreet about the club, or about anyone whom he met there, following a visit, the club would terminate the host's membership.

Sebastian took Sandy to lunch at the Pizza House, located in Goodge Street, the cosy friendly restaurant, with a short, rotund, bald-headed manager, whose jolly demeanour was a permanent fixture of the place that had pioneered pizza in London during the 1960s. Taking a seat at a table in the quietest corner of the restaurant, Sebastian ordered a mozzarella cheese, ham and anchovy pizza, whilst Sandy, not being familiar with pizza, ordered a pasta carbonara. They drank a fairly basic earthy carafe of red wine. Warm apple pies with Italian ice-cream had been the dessert finished off with espresso coffees. Over lunch, Sandy was given a run down by Sebastian of the club and its rules, stressing how important it was for Sandy not to ever share, whatever experiences he might, or might not have at the club with anyone, not even with his best friend, Connor.

Considering the type of up-market men the club membership consisted of, Sandy was surprised not to see expensive looking cars parked in Percy Lane, but Sebastian explained that members had been instructed to park their vehicles as far away as possible from the club, and to walk to Percy Lane. In no way, should members ever consider arriving or departing by taxi.

From the shabby outside, with no name sign on the door, to the inside of the club, there was a complete transformation, as the decor was of the luxurious kind. Named The Withdrawing Room, the area had been laid out as if one had entered a Turkish gay harem, with beautiful thick pile carpets, wall tapestries, painted with images of handsome naked men. A long L-shaped banquette was set against the wall with dozens of printed silk cushions that were scattered all along the fixed seating. Rich velvet purple drapes hung over different sections of the banquette. The central area was dominated by a large circular bar, and the bar staff were good-looking young men, all wearing white silk shirts, and purple waistcoats, to match the purple drapes.

There was no flashy multi-coloured disco type lighting, but just small lamps dotted around the space, the wall tapestries having overhead lighting. The men, mostly middle aged and above, were well dressed and groomed with an air of confidence, with not a hint of any 'camp' tendencies. Some of the men wore masks, probably being well-known politicians not wishing to disclose their identity. Smoking and all drug taking were outlawed in the club, but every type of alcohol drink was available at the bar, as well as good coffee and a selection of non-alcohol drinks and bottled water. No food, of any description, was served in the club.

Most of the social interaction took place around the bar where couples would pair off, transferring to the banquette. No sexual activity was permitted in the main area of the club other than kissing and holding hands. Men had to remain fully clothed at all times. Beyond the Withdrawing Room there was another open space, a dark and empty room leading to a series of small private rooms. The open area was for men, clothing optional, to consort with other men in a public space, and the private rooms were for those who preferred to do the same, without the prying eyes of the voyeurs.

Sebastian and Sandy found a spot around the bar and ordered a couple gin and tonics; Sebastian had nodded to several familiar faces with a silent 'hi.' Sandy was fascinated with the environment he found himself part of. He looked around the room and thought that, except for the men in masks, the other's generally looked as if they were attending a corporate board meeting not a gay club, but the decor around him spoke of decadence, not commerce.

Sebastian whispered in Sandy's ear that he'd leave him to his own devices, as he'd spotted someone that wanted to say hello to him. That was shorthand for Sebastian to respond to a man around a similar age to Seb, who'd given him a signal that he would like to spend time with him. Sandy watched the two of them disappear into the dark room together.

Sandy was watching two men kissing each other on the banquettes, and found it very weird to see such a thing, that he'd never seen in Ireland, despite being in the music business, where homosexuality was supposedly rife. He was pleased that he'd come to the club, but realised that the type of men there were not for him. What attracted him were younger men, somebody like his best friend, Connor. Knowing that Connor was totally straight he'd never risk their friendship by event admitting to him that he had gay tendencies. But coming to terms with that side of his sexuality, he understood that over time he'd secretly pursue young men, especially if in the future, Ireland would legalise homosexuality.

Sandy wrote a short note and gave it to one of the bar staff, to give the note to Sebastian. The note said that he was leaving the club and that he'd see him back at the house thanking him for the invite.

CHAPTER 31

Sandy arrived back at Sebastian's Belgravia house, his head full of what he'd experienced at the gay club. Although he hadn't stayed there long enough to participate in any physical involvement with another man, he'd confirmed to his inner being that, if there'd been a younger man that had appealed to him at the club, he'd have consorted with him happily and would had even been prepared to venture into the dark room with the young man. One or two of the bar staff had appealed to Sandy, but the rules of the club forbade staff to fraternise with members or guests, and if they did, they'd be instantly dismissed.

Connor was out and Sebastian hadn't yet returned from the club, but Lydia was at the house and staying the night there. When they came across each other, Lydia said that she'd had some important news from Dublin. Bridget and Niamh were unexpectedly travelling to London the following day for an audition. The great Austrian conductor, Otto von Hermann, had heard through his English agent, that the two sisters had been sensational at Glyndehurst, singing the two sisters in the opera, *Cosi Fan tutte*. Hermann, who ran the famous summer opera festival in Salzburg, Austria, was seeking replacements for his original choice for the sisters, who'd both had a major falling out with the autocratic conductor, during rehearsals for a recent production of the opera in Vienna. Hermann was flying to London for a fleeting overnight visit only, and as befitting his dictatorial reputation, he summoned the women to his suite at the Savoy hotel, to hear for himself – if they were the artists he wanted for his beloved Salzburg 1980 festival.

Connor only heard the news the following morning as he'd been at Lydia's house all night with Mandy. The lads had been scheduled to fly back to Dublin that day, but Sebastian and Lydia persuaded them to stay on and to meet their respective estranged girlfriends after their audition, to celebrate their success or console them if the result of the audition was negative.

The timing was unfortunate, coming the day after Connor had spent the night with Mandy, and Sandy had spent the afternoon at a gay club. But Sebastian realised that it could be an opportunity for reconciliation between the four.

Finley and Susie had heard through Sebastian and Lydia, that all had not been well, between Connor, Sandy and their respective girlfriends, who'd they'd never met, but were aware of the sisters' sudden operatic stardom. Finley had been meaning to reciprocate the Morans' hospitality in Dublin and had invited them for dinner at his favourite Soho restaurant,

The Gay Hussar, a famous Hungarian establishment that was popular with many left-wing politicians and journalist, that very night. Sebastian had rung Finley, to postpone the dinner, due to the new situation with the lads and the sisters. Finley wouldn't have it and had insisted that he host the six of them at the Gay Hussar, whether the women were successful, or not, with their audition with the great maestro.

Niamh and Bridget were scared stiff of the maestro, Hermann, as he lacked the warmth and friendliness they'd experienced when auditioning at Glyndehurst. Besides Hermann, his agent and a young male pianist were in the maestro's plush suite at the Savoy.

Having heard both women sing an aria each from *Cosi Fan Tutte*, he had a quiet word with his agent, Herr Schneider, and pronounced himself satisfied, but added that he'd personally give them some extra coaching when they arrive for rehearsals in Salzburg. 'Herr Schneider will arrange all the practical details and set up the contracts. I will see you two in Salzburg next summer,' said Hermann, in a gruff, heavily accented English, and then sort of ushered them out with a wave of dismissal.

'Phew,' exclaimed Bridget 'We've definitely put ourselves in the lion's den with that man.'

'Yes' said Bridget, but hey, he may be a bastard, but he approved of our singing and that's the main thing, and getting a gig at Salzburg is the equivalent of an actress landing a major role in a Hollywood movie!'

'I'll tell you one thing, though. We were so much better than at the Glyndehurst auditions, having sung the roles numerous times during their festival.'

The sisters hugged each other. Suddenly, the enormity of their achievement had hit home, realising that Glyndehurst wasn't a one-off fluke; they were on their way to international operatic stardom.

Once they arrived at the Gay Hussar for a celebratory dinner, hosted by Finley and Susie Reason, old friends of the Morans, the success of the auditions had finally sunk in and they stopped worrying about Hermann's authoritative manner; he's going to need them as much as they needed him.

The women, arriving in Greek Street, couldn't miss the bright red doors with a tan-coloured, bright, shiny fascia, boldly announcing: **GAY HUSSAR**. Above, and underneath the restaurant name, on the red paint were the words: **HUNGARIAN RESTAURANT**, just in case anyone was in doubt about what cuisine the restaurant served!

Although Finley and Susie had never met Niamh and Bridget, they recognised them immediately when they walked through the restaurant's door, and rushed to the entrance to introduce themselves, welcoming them to one of their favourite local eateries. The women thought they were in Budapest not London; the colourful interior had the look of a Hungarian folk operetta. The political left-wing element was represented by a series of cartoon caricatures of well-known British politicians spread around the walls. The seating was long benches on either side of main floor. There was an upstairs section as well, but Finley's party never got to see that part of the restaurant. Waiting staff were mainly middle-aged foreign men, with thick accents, but friendly and helpful to all the guests.

Sebastian, Lydia, Connor and Sandy arrived at the Gay Hussar. Greetings were exchanged and when the women explained that their audition had been successful and that they were off to Salzburg next summer, a huge cheer went up, with other customers around the restaurants looking up, smiling, and one or two even seemed to want to join in the congratulations. Finley immediately ordered a couple of bottles of their best champagne.

Connor and Sandy had felt a little awkward when they'd first entered the restaurant. The two couples had been estranged since the women had admitted the flirtations at Glyndehurst, but now the shoe was firmly on the other foot. Connor, in particular, had been reliving in his head the previous night that he'd spent with Mandy, having found it strange to be with another woman other than Bridget, but also tremendously exciting, that the older experienced Mandy, had chosen him as a lover. Less than twenty-four hours later, here he was, sitting opposite his girlfriend, as if the whole Mandy escapade had been a dream.

Sandy feelings were somewhat different. He sensed the irony of the choice of restaurant, with the word 'gay' in its title He had a sense of regret that he hadn't indulged in at least a flirtation at Sebastian's club yesterday, and looking over at his older boss, and friend, a feeling of envy came over him. There his was, sitting with his lovely wife, Lydia, grinning, as if the cat had got the cream. The envious feeling was not necessarily about whatever Seb had got up to in the dark room at the club, but the fact that Lydia knew about her husband's peccadilloes, and had given him tacit permission to indulge. Maybe that was the secret to a happy marriage? But when Sandy looked at Niamh, he knew that despite his unfaithfulness, he didn't want to lose her, and he realised that it had been his immaturity that had made him react so badly to Niamh confession of flirting with her stage lover.

For starters, they all shared a selection of dishes, *Liba-Sertes Pasteton* (goose and pork pate), *Debreceni Kolbasz* (smoked Hungarian sausage) Halpastetom, (fish terrine with beetroot sauce and cucumber salad), *Pacolt Hering* (marinated fillet of herring with soured cream) and *Szalami Tai* (mixed Hungarian salami). They all ordered *Marhaporkolt galiskaval* (beef goulash with galuska/dumplings).A large bowl of mixed salad was added to the order. Ice creams all round for dessert and lashings of Hungarian red wine was consumed throughout the meal.

Being a narrow room, conversations on the other long bench, could be heard, which, on the one hand, created a real buzz around the restaurant, but more intimate conversations would have been unwise in the environment. It was a restaurant for fun and enjoyment, especially in the evening, as all the politicos were on parade at lunchtime only. The focus around the table was on Bridget and Niamh, and their success with Herr Hermann, with Finley acting as master of ceremonies, keeping the celebratory mood on a high throughout, and as more and more wine was consumed by all, his task became easier.

Once coffee had been served, Finley suggested that they all come back to their place for a nightcap and once he settled the bill, they all trotted off, just down the road, to the Reasons' warm and welcoming flat.

Finley mixed cognac with port. He reckoned that the mix was an excellent digestive, and offered the drink to all his guests. The mood, that had been hyper jolly at the Gay Hussar, had become more reflective, mixed with tiredness, as they sat around the comfortable sofas at the Reasons' residence.

The liquors seemed to have done their trick, as the guests were beginning to become more alert, getting a second wind and recovering from tiredness.

Finley was holding fort and talking about all sorts of things, jumping from one subject to another. But, uncannily, without the guests being fully aware of where he was going, the subject morphed into personal relationships. As he'd spouted his philosophy on love and sex when they'd been Sebastian's guests in Dalkey, at The Crab, the subject was again on his mind, but here, on his home territory, he'd tackled it head-on.

'Look, folks,' he said, particularly gazing directly at Connor and Sandy. 'Firstly, let me assure you that nobody has been gossiping behinds anyone's back, but, instinctively, I know, since Niamh and Bridget had become overnight operatic stars, the relationships between the two couples, had become strained, which was such a pity, because each couple was a perfect pairing, in my humble opinion. But jealousy is a poison, just think of Shakespeare and his character of Othello. A love match with Desdemona was ruined by the poison Iago slyly whispered into Othello's ear. Yes, even a gentlemen's hairdresser had studied the great bard.'

The foursome, not looking at one another, but nervously laughing at Finley's Shakespeare comparison, were wondering what else Finley would say.

'Forgiveness is everything, my dear friends, either for real or for imagined slights, and was the basis of a happy love relationship. Niamh and Sandy, Bridget and Connor, please look at your lover in the eyes and hold their hand.'

A stunning awkwardness held the room, with nobody moving or speaking. Then, Sebastian got up from his seat, went over to Niamh and put out his hand to hers, entwining the hand with Sandy's, who'd changed seats to be next to his girlfriend. Sebastian didn't need to repeat the exercise with Bridget, as Connor had moved next her to her and grabbed her hand.

Both couples kissed their lover; the others broke out in spontaneous applause. At that moment, the slate was wiped clean, with any thought of cheating by either couple was completely expunged from their minds.

Finley's job, successfully completed, led to the breakup of the party. Hugs, kisses and hearty thanks were exchanged; the women hailed a taxi, to take them back to their hotel in Russell Square, whilst the remaining four grabbed another taxi to Belgravia.

POSTSCRIPT

Finley's magic had worked, as the two couples were engaged and married within the year, a double wedding in Dublin, with a fabulous reception at the famous Shelbourne hotel, located opposite St Stephens Green. Sebastian and Lydia were present at the wedding and so were Finley and Susie. The four were treated as guests of honour at the reception.

Niamh and Bridget went from strength to strength with their operatic careers and only slowed down when both sisters became pregnant at almost the same time. Meanwhile, as the women's careers took a break, Connor's and Sandy's careers took an upturn when they taken on by a hotshot London agent, whose name was Keith Floes.

Finley and Susie stayed happily married for the rest of their lives and the successful hairdressing salon in London's Soho, continued on for many years, until he eventually retired, selling the business and moving back to Brighton.

Sebastian and Lydia continued with their idiosyncratic lifestyle, to the satisfaction of them both. Sebastian eventually sold The Crab at a knockdown price to Ricky, but kept their residence at Pilot View in Dalkey, Ireland, with the couple flying over from London at every opportunity.

Dominic had decided to move back to London, and through Finley's many labour party contacts at the Gay Hussar

restaurant, looked towards left-wing politics going forward into
his future life and career.

217

PART TWO.

ART MEETS LIFE...!

CHAPTER 32

Hertfordshire, England 1993

'So, Alex, what's the title of the book you've recently finished?'

Toby Elden and I, were enjoying a drink at the bar of the newly opened Sopwell House Hotel, in the small historical city of St Albans, which was situated within a short drive from both Toby's and my own residence. The hotel complex included a state-of-the-art leisure centre, which contained a gym, swimming pool, sauna, steam room and Jacuzzi. The leisure centre operated a membership facility, which was specifically for non-residents of the hotel, and both Toby and I joined, being founder members of the fledgling health club.

'I'd titled the book, *The Variations on Love.*'

'Hmmm, that's an interesting title, Alex. What was the rational?'

'Well, it was in the third part of the book, when I was trying to mirror, as best as I could, the opera, *Cosi Fan Tutte*. One of my characters, named Finley Reason, who was a bit of a philosopher, sounded off, in a stream of consciousness, his attitude to sexual tastes.

His thesis was that there was no right or wrong with individual inclination in areas. just as, monogamy, infidelity, gay, lesbian, bisexuality and so on, and he described his overall thinking on peoples sexual peccadilloes in the soundbite, *The Variations on Love.*'

'Wow, Alex, you'll be treading on some sensitive souls with that kind of explicit narrative. In any event, what do you know about detailed sexual practices? As you've constantly made clear that you've lived an exemplary quiet life, but sometimes I do wonder about you. Have you created a personal bland facade about your past life trajectory, but maybe, the reality might be quite different?'

Toby had touched a raw nerve with Alex, who'd bristled at his friend's remarks.

'You obviously know nothing about novel writing. A novel isn't an autobiography – it's about using one's imagination. I'm a dedicated opera lover after all, so I've absorbed the kaleidoscopic variety of life's dramas through art, and I didn't need to experience unorthodox behaviour personally.'

Toby felt thoroughly chastised, and apologised profusely to me. Changing tack – Toby said, 'But tell me, how did you transpose the rather unbelievable plot of *Cosi Fan Tutte* into a viable contemporary story?'

I picked up on Toby's embarrassment, and his keenness to move away from his inquisitiveness about looking for skeletons in my personal cupboard.

'Good question, Toby,' I said. 'Actually, *Cosi* was, by far, the most difficult of the three operas to put a twentieth-century gloss on. I'd previously explained to you what I did with *Figaro,* concentrating on only two central scenes of the opera; the bedroom scene in Act Two and the garden scene of Act Four. With *Don Giovanni*, it was reasonably straightforward, as the opera was all about one deplorable debauched aristocrat character, but he was also a man full of charm and swagger. Ricky Wenger was the Don and Dominic Rivers was his servant, Leporello. I carried forward other characters from *Figaro,* such as, Sebastian and Lydia Moran, and also Finley Reason, with his wife Susie. The setting for the updating was a life assurance company, based in Central London.

Toby's eyebrows were raised when I mentioned insurance. I could read his mind. He'd be thinking, why life assurance?

What had that to do with *Don Giovanni*? Well, he'd have to wait until the book is published to see how it all fitted together.

I continued, 'the same main characters that I'd introduced in part one of the novel I've reintroduced, both in part two and three. I gave *Cosi Fan Tutte* a restaurant setting, based in an Irish village, in south county Dublin; Sebastian Moran was cast as the opera's Don Alfonso, the cynical seen and done it all mature gentleman, who'd set up the wager with the two young men, as to whether their girlfriends would remain faithful, if temptation reared its head. Ricky Wegner, Dominic Rivers, Finley and Susie Reason, all make an appearance in part three, but they are on the periphery of the *Cosi Fan Tutte*. My problem with *Cosi* had been that I believed, Da Ponte, the librettist of the opera, had not been serious about the disguise element of the plot. How would've the sisters failed to recognise their lovers when the men returned, soon after leaving them? But the clue to what Da Ponte had in mind was that when in the opera, the lovers returned from the Italian Mediterranean disguised as Albanians, they appeared to seduce the other man's lover, not their own. Why? My own interpretation was that Da Ponte, who was, after all, a friend of the notorious libertine Casanova, only gave a nod and a wink, paying lip service to the "disguise" element, which was for the benefit of the censors that enabled the opera to be approved for staging in Vienna in January 1790. No, What Da Ponte had been trying to convey was that the two sisters, Fiordiligi and Dorabella, fancied both men, and the men came back in "mock" disguise, so that the sisters fantasies could actually be realised. Anyway, Toby, that's how I interpreted the opera, incorporating a "swinging scene" into the opera's dramaturgy.

'Wow' responded Toby, 'that's a brave thing to do. I hope the moral police don't read the book, or come to that, some of our esteemed gramophone members might call for the smelling salts when reaching the chapter on "swinging", ha ha ha.'

Driving home from Sopwell House, Toby thought about the way Alex had critiqued his own book; how he'd explained his thought processes on the novel's mapping of the three Mozart/ Da Ponte operas in twentieth-century garb, which, after all, was something that opera directors were experimenting with, in current productions, at leading opera houses. Alex's take on *Cosi Fan Tutte,* in particular, was certainly bold, and, could cause quite a stir in some quarters. Toby reckoned that Alex's interpretation on Da Ponte's libretto, using 'disguise' as a cover for the couples desire to swap partners, was, as being a lover of the opera himself, perhaps, a rather dubious proposition. He personally had always taken the opera at face value, suspending his disbelief, and whilst watching the opera in the theatre, taking the men's return disguised as Albanians, literally. However, Toby could see the difficulties Alex would have had making the 'disguise' element credible, transforming an eighteenth-century opera plot into a contemporary novel. But Toby approved of Alex's decision to segue the same main characters through the three operas, even if the individuals that Alex invented for his novel mixed and matched in mirroring Mozart's and Da Ponte's invented characters.

Toby wondered, once again, about Alex's personal life, not really accepting his previous assurances that the novel was, in no way, autobiographical. He felt that he hadn't heard the full story about Alex's backstory. But, in any event, he couldn't wait to read the book, once it had been published.

CHAPTER 33

Kintbury Village
Berkshire, England.

1992

'What time is your massage, Verity?'

'I'm booked with Trevor at 11.15.'

Dulcie, checked her watch, the time being 10.55 a.m. 'You've got twenty minutes. Come and join me for a quick swim in the pool.'

The two friends dived into the swimming pool to enjoy a few vigorous lengths, before Verity emerged from the pool to dry down, getting herself ready for the massage.

Verity Elden and Dulcie Henrow had booked into Inglewood Health Hydro for a week of diet, weight loss and multi-spa treatments, set in a beautiful country house environment, which exuded total peace and tranquillity.

Inglewood was based in the picturesque village of Kintbury, with the Kennet and Avon Canal running through the village. Nearby was the historic market town of Hungerford.

Verity and Dulcie had booked a large twin-bedded en-suite room, with neither woman with any thought, other than the room was all about two lady friends sharing a bedroom, which was quite common in health farms, which attracted far more female guests than men.

The programme for the week was as follows: arrive on a Sunday to acclimatise to the hydro's facilities, and to attend a welcoming talk from the director, who'd set out the health and fitness goals one should aim to achieve by the end of the week. A fruit only diet was recommended for the first five days, which the ladies agreed to stick to, three meals a day, each consisting of a big bowl of a colourful selection of a wide variety of fruits. Fruit juices were banned; so was tea with milk and any type of coffee. A selection of herbal teas was the hot drink on offer. The dieters ate in the casual cafe area of the hydro, in their white Inglewood robes distributed to guests on arrival. The main dining room, a spacious wood-panelled area, serving a buffet selection of fish, meat and salads, was attended by the guests who'd decided not to take the diet option, and for the dieters from the Friday evening until, and including, Sunday lunch.

Verity and Dulcie had arranged that all their spa treatments would be in the morning, leaving the afternoons for outdoor activities, which included tennis, walking and cycling; bikes were available for guests to use during their stay. Being early October, the weather was autumnally mellow, ideal for fitness pursuits in the open air. They both enjoyed playing tennis together and going on bicycle rides around the village, but most of all, they enjoyed the walks around the canal towpath and exploring the beautiful surrounding countryside. Walking side by side, away from the other guests, although extremely friendly, were also curious about the relationship between Verity and Dulcie. Being in a hydro all week, away from the stresses and strains of everyday life, guests hadn't had much to occupy their minds, so groups of guests formed various cliques and gossiped amongst themselves about fellow guests.

'What's Ronald doing this week? Is he happy to do the household chores?'

Dulcie responded, 'No, Verity, Ronald's gone to Aldeburgh, in Suffolk, to attend the annual Britten weekend.'

'Oh, I see. Has he gone on his own, or with a friend?'

'He's gone on his own, as far as I know. Ronald is happy in his own company; that's been part of the problem between us. He always prefers to be on his own, rather than for me to be at his side.'

'Of course, Dulcie, Ronald is an enthusiast for the music of Benjamin Britten, but perhaps he felt that you don't share that enthusiasm, at least to the same decree.'

'No, No, Verity, that's not at all the case. I'll admit that I don't like everything that Britten wrote, and he did write a huge amount of music, in so many different genres. But I love Britten's operas, whilst Ronald is, at best, a lukewarm opera lover, even Britten's. Ronald, being a choir singer, prefers the composer's choral works to the operas, and is a bit sniffy about the popular orchestral pieces, such as. "Young Persons Guide to the Orchestra" and "Four Sea Interludes" from his most famous opera, *Peter Grimes.* To be honest, Verity, one of the things I'd always found irritating about Ronald, is that he is a musical snob. Even great musical masterpieces, if they become popular with the general musical public, and not just with the critics and experts, he turns his nose up at the piece.'

'Ha ha ha, that's typical Ronald,' Verity said with a chuckle. 'He can't help himself, the poor man has always felt that he is superior to everyone else, even when he knows, deep down, that his musical knowledge is limited to the specific areas he studied.'

The women were chatting whilst walking along the canal towpath, just wide enough for the two of them to walk side by side. Verity had felt guilty, not asking Dulcie about Ronald's plans for the week, until now, having been so caught up with explaining her feelings about the relationship with Toby, with Dulcie patiently listening. But that was what she loved so much about her dear friend – she was such a good listener.

The idea for the two women to go away together had come from the matchmaker, Bettina Emberton. Funnily enough, Verity had thought that Bettina was having an affair with her husband, Toby. The two of them had been huddled together during the interval of one of the gramophone club events. But no, she'd been advising him in a professional capacity only.

Toby had told Verity all about his chance meetings with Bettina on the train home from London, and subsequently, his consultation with her in a five-star London hotel. Bettina had been operating a matchmaking scheme for married men and women, and had suggested to Toby that she'd be able match him with a married woman who'd also be seeking a discreet affair, but, at the same time, not wanting to end their marriage.

Toby, although he found Bettina's approach totally professional, felt that the scheme wasn't right for him, it being too contrived and somewhat cold blooded. But it led him to reassess the type of woman he was looking for, someone as different from Verity as one could imagine. The woman was a member of the Gramophone Club, and someone who'd been a judge of him, during his ordeal at work, when he'd been accused of sexual misconduct – Hannah Longsmith.

Bettina had invited the foursome – Verity, Toby, Dulcie and Ronald – around to her house one evening, to try to help them in their relationship dilemmas, with the goal to stop their marriages completely unravelling. Her advice had been to test their current obsessions and not to run away from them. Toby thought that he'd fallen in love with Hannah, although the pair had only been out together a couple of times. Besides, Hannah had a long-term boyfriend, although they only saw each other occasionally. Verity and Dulcie, by contrast, had been close friends for many years. Dulcie, who had been very frustrated with her relationship with Ronald, looked upon Verity in terms of a potential physical affair or even as a long-term living together relationship by divorcing Ronald. Verity, although very fond of Dulcie, did not have lesbian tendencies, or didn't think she had. Ronald looked upon the whole shenanigans with wry amusement, thinking that the three of them were carrying on like adolescences and they should just grow up. He had not an ounce of jealousy in him, and would have been quite content to revert to a bachelor existence.

Bettina said very little, just listened and sympathetically nodded her head whilst each one opened up about their desires and frustrations. Her assessment, which she kept to herself, was that Verity and Toby were still very much in love but having known each other for ever, Toby, in particular, was seeking a different type of sexual stimulus from what he had with Verity. Verity really didn't want any of this and was just indulging Toby and instinctively knew that he'd come back to her. Dulcie was the most problematical one, as she thought that Verity and she were in love, whilst Verity thought of Dulcie in terms of friendship not of love. Ronald was a selfish cold fish as far she was concerned, and should never have got married, especially to such a warm-hearted woman such as Dulcie.

Once everyone had had their say, they moved from the dining room table to the more comfortable settees in the next door living room Bettina opened and shared around a good bottle of white wine, with nibbles of crisps and nuts, summing up everything she'd heard during the evening.

'Being a matchmaker, I've heard more about relationships going bad, than clients having well thought through aspirations for finding love again. The main problem with difficult relationships is that the couples don't talk about their frustrations with each other. So the fact that the four of you agreed to sit down together to express your feelings with me as some sort of arbiter, is hugely admirable, and I wish that in my business, I had dealt with clients as enlightened as my dear friends, sitting here with me. I think that Toby should explore his fascination with Hannah and see where it goes. Likewise, Verity and Dulcie need to spend time together to explore the potential, if any, of developing the idea of the two of you as a couple. Ronald,' Bettina, looking straight at him, said, 'It would be a good idea if you spent some time thinking about what you really want, relationship wise. Would you be happier on your own, or are you prepared to make certain compromises to woo Dulcie back?'

The four individuals listened carefully to Bettina, respecting her professional expertise in matters of 'love,' but not adding anything to her summary.

Bettina's house was an attractive, bricked, detached cottage-style building, looking more like a dwelling one would see in the countryside than in small commuter town. The interior was cosy, with two medium-sized bedrooms and one tiny one, which Bettina used as an office. Downstairs contained a standalone dining room, with a separate living room area; a medium- sized kitchen leading to a mature grass-free garden, with a pair of Italian cypress trees, shrubs and a herb bed. The house was perfect for a couple, but Bettina lived on her own. Toby was admiring the contemporary art displayed on Bettina's walls, but amongst the art works was a portrait of a strange Victorian-looking gentleman, with a round face and wide nostrils, wearing thin wire spectacles. His hair was a comb-over and he sported an under the chin off the face beard, popular in the nineteenth century. A large dark cravat under a stand-up-collar white shirt covered his neck.

'Bettina,' asked Toby, who is the gentleman in the portrait?

'Oh, that's an ancestor of mine, Fromental Halevy.'

Toby creased his forehead in thought. 'That's such an unusual first name. There was a French nineteenth-century grand opera composer called "Halevy," but I can't remember his first name.'

Bettina, said, 'It is the very same one, Toby. The name "Fromental" was indeed unusual. The name means "oat grass." The day of Fromental's birth in 1799 coincided with the day the oat grass plant was celebrated, known as *Prairial,* the third month of the spring quarter, in the French Republican calendar, which was then still in use.'

'Didn't Halevy write a famous opera on a Jewish subject?'

'*La Juive* was indeed a famous work, hugely popular in its time and for many years later. Gustav Mahler adored the piece and the role of Eleazar was a favourite role of the tenor, Enrico Caruso. Halevy's son-in-law was Georges Bizet, the composer of the opera, *Carmen.*

Toby, looked at Bettina with renewed interest, and asked, hesitantly, 'Are you Jewish then?

'Yes, Toby, I'm a proud Jew, coming from a long line of French Jewry, and Halevy's opera, *La Juive,* was one of the most famous operas, and certainly, in its day, the most popular of all operas that had been based on a Jewish story. '

Toby, asked, 'Have you ever seen the opera, Bettina?

'No, unfortunately, I haven't. It's rarely ever produced these days, but I have a recording of the complete work, and I have a feeling that it will come back into the operatic repertory again one of these days as it's such a great piece, although of course, being an ancestor of the composer, I am just a little bit biased, ha ha ha.'

'You should play the recording of the opera, when you next host a gramophone evening.'

'OK, Toby, it's a deal, but ideally, I would love to catch a live performance of the opera, and I always kept a look out for opera scheduling, in the UK and Europe.'

Ronald, listening to the exchange between Toby and Bettina, winced at the thought of sitting through a French nineteenth-century grand opera at a gramophone event. The thought of it almost made him want to throw up!

Bettina, offered to open another bottle of wine, but the mood of the room had changed. The focus of attention had moved from the foursome and their relationship issues to Bettina's fascinating heritage. The four nodded to each other to make a move.

Thanking Bettina for her time, hospitality and above all, personal advice, the two couples drove back to their respective homes; nothing had yet changed with their domestic arrangements.

The week at Inglewood Health Hydro had flown by. On the Friday, Verity and Dulcie were more relaxed and tension free than they'd ever been. The only thing they'd missed was a hearty meal, although the fruit diet had done its job. The women had lost weight and were both in great shape. Friday, of course, was the big transition day for the week's dieters. Breakfast and lunch were the last of the fruit meals, whilst for the evening it was a grownup dinner in the restaurant. But it wasn't just the food, it was changing out of the white robe one had been wearing all week, dressing up in one's best finery, and putting on makeup for the first time in the week. Arriving at the dining room felt like one had been transported from a rather dull cafe to an opulent five-star hotel restaurant. The menu was buffet style, beautifully presented on a long table, consisted of fish, meat, all kinds of salads and vegetables. If one had been on the fruit-only diet during the week – to be presented with such a mouth-watering choice of dishes was overwhelmingly enticing. Verity and Dulcie ordered a bottle of dry white wine to accompany their food. Having got through the bottle in double-quick time, they ordered a second bottle, one with a less-dry grape, to go with their dessert, a choice of trifle or rum baba. The second bottle went down a lot slower, with the women looking around the room at other guests. Some tables were occupied with people, like them, who'd been on the fruit diet and they were fascinated how different they looked, dressed and perfumed, and that was just the men. The women had the appearance of attending a society ball, in gorgeous attire. Other tables were of a mix of guests who'd been restaurant dining all week, and couples, mainly young, who'd arrived for a weekend stay and not bothering, or not needing, to diet. Dulcie was studying the women, with a sort of longing in her eyes, whereas Verity concentrated her gaze on the men, especially the younger ones.

Friday night was disco night at the hydro. The basement was transformed into a night club with live music on offer. The diners, including Verity and Dulcie, on leaving the restaurant, made their way to where the action was. Having abstained all week from alcohol, some of the guests were rather squiffy. Dulcie ordered two gin and tonics from the basement bar, bringing them to the table where Verity was sitting, and the women felt they were back to their younger selves, when they'd not had a care in the world other than who'd they'd end up pulling for the night.

Verity and Dulcie danced together but they also swapped partners with other guests, as much flirtation was taking place, mostly with people who weren't dancing with their own partner. Dulcie was slow dancing with another woman, whilst Verity was accompanied by a young man. As the lights went down, Verity saw Dulcie in a clinch with the woman she was dancing with. That galvanised Verity to grab the young man, leading him into an even darker corner and she kissed him. The man responded enthusiastically.

When the music stopped and the lighting became brighter, everyone drifted back to their own partners; some, having sobered up, looked a bit sheepish. They felt surprised at their own behaviour.

Verity and Dulcie went off to their bedroom. Both realised that as much as they liked, or even loved, each other, it was Dulcie, only, who had desires for women, Verity being traditionally heterosexual. Without saying a word, both women went off to their single beds, with thoughts that the whole evening had been unreal – not believing that they'd both openly kissed other people.

Chapter 34

Aldeburgh Suffolk England

1992

Ronald Henrow, had headed for Aldeburgh the day following the departure of his wife, Dulcie, to Inglewood Health Hydro with her best friend and maybe, future lover, Verity Elden. He'd originally planned just to go for the Britten weekend, which programmed a series of concerts from the Friday to the Sunday, but with the autumn weather being so pleasant, he decided to spend the full week on the coast at Aldeburgh.

The Aldeburgh festival, which had been created by the composer, Benjamin Britten and his life partner, the tenor, Peter Pears, in 1948, held its annual festival every June, lasting just over a fortnight. During the rest of the year, as well as a Prom season during the month of August, other mini-series took place, including the Britten weekend in October. The main concert hall was located six miles from Aldeburgh, at the village of Snape. The venue, known as Snape Maltings, with its converted Victorian buildings, sat on the bank of the river Alde, surrounded by an area of outstanding natural beauty. The concert hall was established by Benjamin Britten in 1967, and was considered one of the finest concert halls in the world. Other smaller events were performed at the various churches in the area, as well as at the Jubilee Hall in Aldeburgh town, the venue that had started the whole festival off in 1948.

Ronald had booked every concert that was on offer for the Britten weekend. The Friday night opener was an orchestral concert of Britten's music that included a performance by the Irish mezzo soprano, Ann Murray, singing Britten's cantata 'Phaedra,' a late powerful work by the composer, written specifically for Janet Baker, and first performed at Snape Maltings during the 1976 Aldeburgh festival. On Saturday morning Ronald attended a chamber music concert at Aldeburgh church. The programme consisted of Britten's string quartets No's 1 and 2, as well as, Schubert's 'Death and the Maiden' string quartet: Schubert had been one of Britten's favourite composer's. At Orford church on the Saturday afternoon, the great English tenor, Anthony Rolfe Johnson sang several of the Britten's song cycles, with Graham Johnson (not related) at the piano, including a favourite song cycle of Ronald's, 'Winter Words,' based on poems by Thomas Hardy. Saturday night saw Ronald back at Snape Maltings, for a performance of one of the greatest choral masterpieces in all music: J S Bach's Mass in B minor. Ronald was in his element, having sung in the choir for a performance of the Mass at St Albans Cathedral, during 1990. Hearing the work performed in the fabulous acoustics of Snape Maltings was a revelation for Ronald. It was performed by the English Chamber Orchestra, choir and soloists, conducted by Charles Mackerras. The final concert of the weekend was on the Sunday afternoon and it was a star-studded event and a very hot ticket. The programme consisted of the three concertos of Britten, the early virtuoso piano concerto, the pre-war violin concerto and the late cello symphony. The Great Russian pianist Sviatoslav Richter was the soloist in the piano concerto, and the equally Great Russian cellist and conductor, Mstislav Rostropovich, was the soloist in the cello symphony.. The violin concertos soloist was a less starry name, but was entrusted to a young, up-and-coming violinist, Tasmin Little. She'd done herself proud in such august company, playing one of the great twentieth-century violin concertos. The English Chamber Orchestra was again on the platform, but this time conducted by Steuart Bedford. Ronald left Aldeburgh in raptures at the musical glories he'd experienced over the weekend.

When Ronald arrived in Aldeburgh on the previous Monday, he checked into a bed and breakfast guesthouse on the sea front. The guesthouse, one that Ronald had stayed at on a previous visit to Aldeburgh, was owned and run by a music-loving widow, and a choral singing soprano, who was a member of the Aldeburgh music club. The establishment was popular with visitors to the Aldeburgh festival, and to other musical events in Aldeburgh and Snape Maltings throughout the year. It would be a full house for the upcoming Britten weekend, but for the week leading up to the events it was only partially full.

Ronald's plan for the week was to walk the sea front in the morning and to spend the rest of the day studying for his PhD in musical history, which he'd neglected of late, due to staff shortages at his office with the Ministry of Defence; consequently, having to work overtime and as well as taking paperwork home to deal with in the evenings and weekend. He would finish off the day with dinner at one of the several friendly restaurants in the centre of Aldeburgh.

In fact, Ronald's plan for week hadn't quite turned out that way. He met up with an old friend from music college, who'd he'd lost touch with; his name was John Wallington, and he was staying at the same guesthouse, with his wife, Melanie, who Ronald had never previously met.

'Ronald, old man, how good to see you.'

'John, it's good to see you too. Are you here for the Britten weekend?'

'Yes, we are, please let me introduce my wife, Melanie.' Turning to his wife, he added. 'Darling, this is Ronald, an ex music buddy from college.'

A fresh-faced, bright-eyed blonde woman, seemingly aged forty something but looking more like aged thirty, gave Ronald big smile and a firm handshake, replied, 'Pleased to meet you, Ronald, John had mentioned you several times when discussing music, calling you, "the baroque guru." '

Melanie and John laughed but Ronald just felt a bit embarrassed, not being used to praise and never sure how to react to it.

John, noticing Ronald's awkwardness, quickly changed the subject. 'So, like us, you'd decided to make a week of it, having a mini holiday before the big concert weekend.'

'Well, sort of. I originally only booked for the weekend but when my wife, Dulcie, went off to a health hydro with her best friend for a week, I thought why not come down on the Monday and catch up with paperwork from the office, and some musical study, with a bit of sea air whilst anticipating the weekend's musical treasures.'

John gave Ronald a friendly pat on the shoulder, saying, 'Oh yes, I remember you from music college, always revising for exams, ha ha.' He concluded...'Once a swot – always a swot.'

Ronald thought that John was mocking him, and started to make excuses to move away from the couple.

Melanie, aware of John's friend's discomfort, addressed Ronald. 'Look, we're going to spend the next few days walking the coast and countryside. Why don't you join us?

'Oh, thanks, but I'm not into hiking. I'm happy to gently stroll along the sea front in the mornings and catch up with work in the afternoons.'

Melanie started to wax lyrical about the walking options from Aldeburgh. 'The great thing is that there are so many fantastic walks from here. Aldeburgh is situated exactly halfway into the sixty odd-mile coastal path from Lowestoft to Felixstowe – the whole path being waymarked. Then there is the surrounding beautiful countryside and forests, so one could have set circular walks, following the sandlings trail. Again they are waymarked all the way. Once you've got the taste for planned set walks, you'll be as obsessed with hiking as much as I believe you are with music.'

Ronald, impressed with Melanie's enthusiasm, said, 'Thanks, let me think about it.'

It was an extremely mild early October afternoon and Ronald, having skipped lunch, was starving. Not wishing to wait for restaurant opening time, he decided to head for the famous Aldeburgh fish and chip shop, located at the far end of the high street; they opened for the evening servings at 5 p.m. Even at that time there was a bit of a queue outside the shop. When his turn came, Ronald ordered a large cod and chips with a portion of gherkins and mushy peas. He walked to the nearest off-licence and bought a bottle of dry white wine, making sure the bottle was a screw-top one, and walked over the road, onto the beach, opposite the Brudenell hotel, and settled down by the beach wall, to shield from the wind. There still being some light in the day, he took his jacket off and laid it down on the stony beach to sit on, and tucked into the delicious meal, washing it down with the wine, drinking it straight from the bottle, and he felt deliriously happy, for the first time in ages.

By the time Ronald had finished his fish and chips and the bottle of wine, dusk was beginning to settle in, so he binned his food wrappings and wine bottle, walking back to the High Street and entering the White Hart pub, which was located next door the fish and chip shop. The pub, obtaining its first licence, as far back from as the year 1800, had become an Aldeburgh institution for the local population. It was a traditional no-frills spit-and-sawdust affair with its front doors kept open during the warmer months with bench seating lining each side of the doors. Regular Aldeburgh old timers commandeered the benches, with the younger crowd standing around on the pavement with pints of beer in their hands. As Ronald was waiting to be served at the bar, he felt a hand on his shoulder.

'Hello, Ronald, we meet again.' John Wallington was standing next to him, also waiting to be served.

'Oh, John, hi, I'm just getting myself a pint, can I get you something?'

'Thanks, Ronald – I'll have the same as you, a pint of the mouth-watering local Suffolk ale.'

Ronald looked around for Melanie, but couldn't see her.

'Melanie is outside in the queue for fish and chips, to take back to our room, so I'm going to very rude and take my pint back to rejoin the queue.

'No problem, John, you don't want to miss your slot. I had my fish and chips earlier, when it was still light enough to enjoy them on the beach.'

'That sounds like a much better plan than us having the meal in our bedroom.'

Just as John was walking away...Ronald said,

'If the walking invitation is still open, I would like to join you and Melanie'

'That's great, Ronald, I'll tell Melanie and I know that she'll be delighted!'

CHAPTER 35

The following morning, Ronald had a quick get-together with John and Melanie, before an early breakfast, Melanie going over their hiking itinerary for the next three days. The original plan was to aim for about fifteen miles a day. The Tuesday and the Thursday would be coastal path walks and the Wednesday would be a country walk following the sandlings trail. But the plan varied slightly as the week unfolded.

John advised Ronald to buy a good pair of walking boots at the High Street's shoe shop as soon as the shop opened at 9 a.m. John, having purchased items at the shop on a previous visit knew that the shop also stocked rucksacks, which would be needed to carry the packed lunch that the guest house would provide.

Once Ronald had been kitted out and collected his packed lunch from the guest house kitchen, the timings for the walk had been put out of kilter, but John and Melanie took it in good grace, readjusting the schedule to a shorter route for day one, aiming for longer ones on days two and three. So, instead of walking from Aldeburgh to the village of Walberswick, a total walk of fifteen miles, they settled for a shorter distance, mainly a shingle beach walk, taking in Dunwich Heath and their coastal cottages. The coastal path then passed through the ancient woodland of Greyfriars, arriving at the village of Dunwich, which had been in the Anglo-Saxon period, the capital of the Kingdom of the East Angles, but because of coastal erosion the town had disappeared. The decline began in 1286.

Walking in such beautiful surroundings such as the Suffolk coast, the Wallingtons liked to keep a steady medium pace, so as not to miss the fascinating wildlife. Additionally, the coastal walk passed within the vicinity of one of the country's most famous nature's reserves, Minsmere, home to thousands of rare birds.

They booked a taxi back to Aldeburgh.

Ronald was somewhat relieved that they'd decided on a shorter walk, as even a nine-mile plus hike seemed a challenge enough, let alone attempting a fifteen-mile marathon.

However, Ronald surprised himself by enjoying the walk more than he'd ever imagined he would. The fresh sea breezes, the surrounding nature, the unusual birds, which the Wallingtons had seemed extremely knowledgeable about, and especially, the physical exercise, made him realise that although he'd never previously indulged in walking as a leisure pursuit, it could be an activity he could continue to pursue when back home in Hertfordshire; maybe with his wife, Dulcie.

The following day, Wednesday, they commenced the walk much earlier in the morning, heading in the other direction from the previous day. The well signposted path to Snape was known as the 'Sailors Path', used in past centuries by smugglers. It was a beautiful woodland walk, until several miles on, one reached the river Alde's estuary, where the narrow dark woodland path opened up to a vista of the wide, huge Suffolk sky with a magnificent view of Snape Maltings in the distance. The walk continued on via the twists and turns towards Snape bridge – taking in wildlife habitat, combining marsh and reed bed. The freshwater dykes were home to otters, plus many kinds of insects and plants. The marshes were grazed by cattle that created the right conditions for wildlife.

Once they'd crossed over Snape Bridge it was time to break for their picnic at the Snape Maltings complex. The three of them sat together on a long wrought-iron bench in front of the concert hall, looking out towards the estuary and the reed beds. The picnic consisted of flasks of mushroom soup, chicken sandwiches, cakes and bottled water.

Fed and watered, the trio continued on.

The route chosen was going off the coastal path and onto the sandlings one. Following a short walk through Snape village they arrived at Blaxhall Common, which was a heartland full of birds, butterflies, reptiles and flowers specific to the area. Several miles on, the sandlings path took them to the village of Chillesford. There, they rested again on another wrought-iron bench, situated in the middle of the very quite village. The last of the provisions were consumed, flasks of coffee and biscuits.

The village of Chillisford was where the two paths, the coastal and the sandlings, met. Coming off the sandlings path via Blaxhall common, they walked a short distance up the road of the village and turned left into Tunstall Forest, rejoining the coastal path. Tunstall forest consisted of coniferous plantations which were great for ground-nesting birds such as the Nightjar and Woodlark. From the forest they crossed over the Snape/Orford main road to climb a fairly steep path to large farming area which eventually led down to near the village of Iken, home to St Botolph's Church, which could be seen from Snape Maltings. Turning left the path continued along the side of the river Alde, over boardwalks through the reeds and coming to a little beach. The path eventually led back to almost the same spot they'd had their picnic lunch – outside the Snape Maltings concert hall.

So that what was Melanie meant when she'd first explained to Ronald that a round walk could be planned with a combination of the coastal and sandlings paths.

Ronald, who hadn't realised that they'd end up back at Snape, the Wallington's not divulging the end destination, was so impressed that he asked if they could do a similar round walk, for their final one on Thursday.

A taxi took the three of them back to Aldeburgh.

The chat between the three of them during the two days of walking was mainly of a light-hearted banter approach, and they caught up on each other's lives, since the time John and Ronald were fellow adult music students. Ronald had realised, whilst exploring the Suffolk area of natural beauty, that despite him being a country boy from Gloucestershire, he was quite ignorant about nature and wildlife, so was grateful to John and Melanie for their impressive knowledge of the area and what to look out for as they progressed along the various paths. He felt that the fresh air and the exercise were doing him the world of good, and he regretted that having been a swot since early life – he'd missed out on an important aspect of healthy leisure activity

On the Thursday morning, they drove, in John's car, back to Dunwich, parking in the large, free beach car park. Walking through the village they had a choice of two paths, both leading to the village and seaside resort of Walberswick. They could take the path to the left of the village, which was the much longer sandlings path – the walk would take over three hours. If they chose to take the path to the right of the village, which was the much shorter coastal path, it would take about half that time. They decided to walk the longer sandlings path and switch to the coastal path for the return to Dunwich.

The walk was through Dunwich forest, eventually arriving at a clearing where they came across a crowd of men, wearing brown check suits and peak caps, with shot guns on their shoulders. Later on they saw and heard shooting in the air with pheasants falling to the ground. Moving away as fast as they could, the trio marched on to their destination, the path finishing right on the Walberswick beach.

Again, the picnic lunch was taken on one of the wrought-iron benches that were dotted around that part of the beach.

Walking the beach in the direction of Dunwich, they turned inland, crossing a small wooden bridge that led them onto the coastal path, passing a series of little River Blyth tributaries, full of ducks and swans. The next part of the walk was onto a grassy track that climbs slightly among the bracken to give fine views of the sea and the marshes. At a T-junction the path turned right, passing a World War Two air raid shelter and an 1800s wind pump, that was used to drain the salt marshes and grind feed for horses. It was burnt out in the 1960s, but the ruin remained a great landmark for walkers in an area that could be a bit confusing looking for the waymarks. They came out of the woods onto a lengthy stretch of boardwalk crossing that eventually led onto a gravel path onto the downhill stretch back to the village of Dunwich.

It had been a fabulous circular walk, five hours of walking plus an hour for the picnic.

By the third day of walking, a real camaraderie had come about between the three of them. They caught up with their individual career trajectories. John was a successful dentist whilst Melanie owned and ran a small florist shop in Rickmansworth, Hertfordshire, where they lived. They would have liked to have started a family, but they'd been unable to conceive, the problem seemed to be on John's side. Even though they were in their forties, they hadn't entirely given up on having children, naturally, or if not, by adopting.

Ronald opened up about his marriage to Dulcie, and how she had been instrumental in up scaling-up his career prospects, by changing from a manager of a local record shop, to a good job in London at the Ministry of Defence.

Ronald then explained to the Wallington's that the reason he had come to Aldeburgh on his own, was because his marriage was going through some turbulence. Dulcie seemed to think that she was in love with her best friend, Verity, and the two of them were spending the week at a health hydro in Berkshire.

Melanie said, 'Do you think that Verity feels the same about Dulcie?'

'Well, Verity's marriage was also in trouble. Her husband, Tobias, was having an affair with a woman from our gramophone club.' Ronald had told Melanie and John, all about the club during one of the walks. He continued. 'The four of us,

Tobias and Verity, me and Dulcie, were founder members of the club but since all the relationship upheavals, we've stopped attending, and so had Tobias's lady friend, which had meant that the club were five members short, which could mean that the club might dissolve.'

'Oh, that would be such a shame,' interjected John. 'I thought the gramophone club was a brilliant concept when you told us about it. I was even thinking about seeing if we could start something similar in Rickmansworth.'

'Hmmm, you could join ours, but I suppose the thirty-odd miles between Rickmansworth and St Albans would be too far to drive.'

'Yes, just a bit too far, I'm afraid, Ronald.'

'Let's hope that both marriages are repairable,' said Melanie, having got to like Ronald over the past few days, in spite of his awkwardness.

The three of them, went out to one of Aldeburgh's restaurants on the Thursday night to celebrate their three days of walking. They enjoyed a slap-up dinner with a good bottle of expensive claret that Ronald insisted would be his treat. But when the final bill arrived, Ronald; feeling generous towards Melanie and John, and so grateful that they'd introduced him to the joys of country hiking, paid the whole bill for the three of them.

They rested up on Friday, before the evening's first concert of the Britten weekend.

When Ronald arrived home in St Albans, he was greeted by Dulcie, and both exclaimed how well both of them looked, Dulcie from the week at Inglewood health hydro, and Ronald from his hiking days in Aldeburgh. Little more was said by either of them, both falling into each other's arms and heading off to the bedroom together.

Chapter 36

London 1992

'Have you seen this opera before?'

'No, I haven't, it's not done that often, is it?'

'Well, it was one of Verdi's neglected operas but in recent years it's returned to the repertoire of many opera companies. For me, what's exciting about attending tonight is to have the old maestro back in the orchestra pit of the Royal Opera House.'

'Oh, Toby, you're like a kid with crush on a pop star, ha ha ha.'

Toby, not quite realising that Hannah was having a little sport with him, responded defensively. 'Don't be silly, it's not the same at all. I just think that Georg Solti is one of the great conductors of our time, and he's now over eighty, when conductors, even the most fiery ones, such as Solti, reach a mellowness that goes to the heart of the music they're conducting.'

'You're very easy to tease.' Hannah had a big smile on her face as she squeezed Toby's hand.

'Anyway,' continued Hannah, 'one doesn't go to the opera for the conductor. It's the singers, surely?'

'Well, I won't bore you with explaining how important the conductor is to the success or otherwise of an opera performance.'

'I forget, Toby, that you're not the opera enthusiast in your marriage – it's Verity, and your passion is for orchestral and chamber music, and of course, worshiping conductor's, ha ha ha!'

'You're wicked, Hannah, but please, don't let's talk about my marriage; I feel guilty enough anyway about Verity.'

The couple were having a pre-opera meal at a small French bistro, near the opera house, Mon Plaisir, London's oldest French restaurant. They ordered onion soup, then sharing a coq au vin and a bottle of Beaujolais.

The opera was Verdi's *Simon Boccanegra*, the revised version from 1881. Toby and Verity had seen the opera at Glyndehurst, during the 1980s, and loved it – thinking then that the opera had been one of the composers greatest. An interesting aspect of the performance they were attending, apart from the return of Sir Georg Solti, who had been the music director of the Royal Opera during the 1960s, was the unscheduled debut, during the run of performances, of the Israeli baritone, Dov Katz, who'd stepped in when the original Italian artist suffered serious injury in a car crash, when travelling back home during the rehearsal period for a family event. Katz received rave reviews from the press following the first nights performance.

Tobias Elden was temporarily living with Hannah Longsmith in her corporate flat based within the Barbican complex, situated in the City of London. Hannah was at the pinnacle of her career with a leading New York financial institution, working from their London office. Hannah's main residence was in Hertfordshire, near St. Albans, but as part of her very generous remuneration, she was given a free flat in London, so if working late, she wouldn't have to commute back to Hertfordshire late at night. The flat, which came fully furnished, was a small one-bedroom affair, with all the mod cons one needed for busy executive lifestyles.

How did the affair start?

Without letting Toby know, Hannah had been sexually attracted to him from the time she'd chaired the panel that she'd been judging Toby, regarding the sexual harassment case against him. Although she had the casting vote and found in Toby's favour, she'd examined her conscience many times since then, but was convinced, or in any case, had convinced herself, that her decision at the time was a totally unbiased one.

Hannah wasn't a woman that gave out obvious sexual vibes. She was a serious professional who didn't suffer fools gladly. Her subordinates at work, both men and women, were a little afraid of her. But underneath that slightly frosty exterior, there was a very passionate woman. She'd been a lover of the arts, especially classical music and opera, since her teenage years, and had always been sexually liberal, having had many lovers over the years. Hannah never wanted to get married, having had no intention of tying herself down to one man, and certainly, did not wish to have children. She'd had an ongoing relationship with a colleague from the New York office for some years, which suited her lifestyle. They only saw each other a few times a year. When in New York, Hannah stayed with him, and vice versa; when he was in London, he'd stay with her, not in the small city flat, but in Hannah's substantial house in Hertfordshire.

What had attracted Hannah to Toby? Unlike her, Toby wore his passion on his sleeve. His Welsh background gave him an articulation of artistic rhetoric that was quite different from the average Englishman. His love of life made him sexy in her eyes, and he wasn't too bad looking either. The fact that he was married didn't bother her too much; men would do what men wanted to do, despite the obstacles.

Once Toby realised that Hannah was the woman he desired, not knowing, of course, how she'd respond, he'd started to pay her special attention whenever they were in close proximity. It was at the dinner party at his house that he'd played frottage with her. She responded doing the same to him, rubbing up her leg with his. He rang her soon after that evening and Hannah invited him to her house. There were no drinks, food or any other preliminaries, Hannah grabbing him as soon she closed the front door and started to kiss Toby. He was ecstatic, as he'd imagined spending a long evening trying to seduce Hannah, but such blatant sexual forwardness aroused him massively. Whist they were still in Hannah's hallway, she'd started to undo his shirt buttons, taking the garment off him completely. This was a thrill for him – Hannah's sheer shamelessness. There he'd stood, having his shirt removed, whilst Hannah had remained fully clothed. She'd then grabbed Toby's hand and led him upstairs to the bedroom. The sex was amazing and Toby was totally smitten.

The next day, he'd announced to Verity, that he was leaving the house and going to stay with Hannah at her London flat.

The performance of the opera, *Simon Boccanegra* was hugely enjoyed and very moving. Dov Katz was terrific in the title role and received an enthusiastic ovation at curtain call. But it was when the conductor Solti came onto the stage for his bow, the whole house rose to acclaim the maestro who'd, during his ten years in the 1960s as music director, had raised the standards of the company to one of the great opera houses of the world.

After two weeks of living in the small flat with Hannah, who'd worked late most nights, Toby decided to go back home. He was smitten with Hannah and determined to carry on seeing her, but he had to make his peace with Verity.

How did you enjoy your week with Dulcie at the health hydro? 'I must say, you look a picture of good health.'

'Thank you, Toby. I'm pleased you remembered that you still have a house and a wife.' Verity was trying hard, not always successfully, not to sound too cynical.

'It was a wonderful week actually. We'd stuck to a fruit diet until Friday – then indulged ourselves for the last couple of days. And all the treatments were great. But, to cut to the chase, nothing romantic or sexual occurred between me and Dulcie. Our great friendship remained intact as it always has been and always will be. However, what I discovered was I just couldn't do lesbianism. I'm totally heterosexual, although, I believe that

Dulcie has lesbian tendencies. But, the good news is that Dulcie and Ronald have reconciled since both coming home from their respective trips. Evidently, don't laugh now, but Ronald took up hiking whist in Aldeburgh, having met an old pal of his from their music college. This chap and his wife introduced Ronald to the delights of walking the coastal and other paths during the week they were there, before the concerts started up on the Friday.'

'So, said Toby, What about you?'

Toby replied, 'We've known each other for a long time; we've shared so much together and I still love you very much. But I must be nothing but totally honest with you.'

'OK, said Verity, what on your mind?'

'I would like to move back into our house – but I can't give up Hannah...'

'What's that woman got that I haven't? '

'Oh, Verity, it's not like that. You've got everything, but Hannah has, for me anyway, an erotic allure that's like a drug for me. There's no point making comparisons. Sex, for us, is like a comfort blanket; we're familiar with our every move, and it's lovely. But, with Hannah – Oh no, I just can't talk about it, and, anyway, it's unfair to you.'

'Well, lover boy, I became entangled with a young man whilst at Inglewood, and a passionate kiss ensued. So at least someone thought that I was more than just a comfort blanket.'

'Verity, please don't get bitter, it's not like you. I would have no objection if you had a discreet affair.

'I might just do that! The one thing I insist on though is that Hannah ceases to attend the gramophone events.'

'Yes, of course, I totally understand. Perhaps, we and the Henrows could start attending again.'

'Let's leave it until the new year and see how we and the Henrows are shaping up.'

'Fair enough, Verity. We'll pencil in January 1993 to return to the gramophone club.'

The two of them hugged, but there was an uneasy vibe in the air.

Chapter 37

Bettina Emberton.

I was born during the Second World War – 1944, in Manchester. I was brought up there by an average Jewish middle-class family. I say, average middle-class, but my family background was hardly average. My grandparents had come to Manchester from Poland, as a young married couple, in the first decade of the twentieth century, to escape the pogroms that had been rife in their village, which was populated almost entirely by orthodox Jews. They settled in Manchester, remaining religiously orthodox, my grandfather starting a business in the garment trade, my grandmother bearing, initially, two children, both boys, and much later a baby girl, who had been my mother, born in 1919. Unfortunately, my mother never knew her two brothers, as both had tragically died in a fire accident at home before she was born. My grandparents had gone to the local synagogue on a Friday night for prayers, leaving the two boys at home, with the Sabbath candles remaining lit. We never knew what had actually occurred and how the two boys lost their lives, but my grandparents never spoke about the details of the accident to my mother, trying to shield her from the horror, I, in turn, knew even less about the tragedy, other than the sorrow my grandmother suffered caused her to have a stroke, dying young.

My father, an only child, was Austrian from Vienna, who'd managed, as a nineteen-year old, to get smuggled out of the Nazi-occupied country in 1938, having been sponsored by a family in Manchester. He'd learned English at school in Vienna, and was reasonably proficient in the language when arriving in England. My grandmother on my father's side of the family was French. She had an illustrious family history, being a direct descendant of the opera composer Fromental Halevy.

Unfortunately, both my father's parents and their extended family, perished during the Holocaust. My father's family had been non-orthodox Jewish, very much involved in the cultured life of Vienna. My parents had met at a Jewish youth club in Manchester, my mother being two years older than my father. Following a short courtship, they got married, just before my father left to serve in the British Army for the duration of the Second World War. When home on leave he managed to get my mother pregnant, first with my brother in 1942, and then me in 1944.

When he was demobbed from the army at the end of the war, my father went into the jewellery business, initially as an employee and then forming his own company, which became very successful over the years.

My mother had been brought up in a strict Jewish orthodox household, whilst my father's background was completely secular, with only cultural references to Judaism. As a happily married couple, with each wanting to please the other, they both adjusted their beliefs to create married harmony. My mother adopted more interest in world history, instead of predominantly Jewish, and with my father's help and encouragement, they started to attend the theatre and to classical music concerts. Manchester was the home to the excellent Halle orchestra, with a great conductor at its helm during the post-war period, John Barbirolli. Meanwhile, my father, respecting the Jewish religious tradition that my mother had grown up with, agreed to keep a kosher home and at least, pay lip service to the Sabbath, by always having dinner at home on a Friday evening, and occasionally going to the synagogue on a Saturday morning. The fly in the ointment was that my grandfather, who lived with us. He hadn't moved one inch in modernising his way of life, causing my parents a certain amount of stress and friction at home, as my mother segued from religious rigour to my father's more secular outlook

So, yes, my childhood and teenage years, were typically middle class. My brother and I were spoilt with certain privileges, that we'd never acknowledged them to be anything different to our peers' and friends' lifestyles. There were piano and ballet classes for me, and, football coaching for my brother. When my brother was thirteen, he went through the Barmitzvah religious ritual, my parents hosting a dinner-dance event at the upmarket Midland Hotel, where all my parents' friends and business colleagues had been invited to, along with our relatives. I thought, to my young mind at the time, that the event had less to do with my brother and his friends, but more to do with impressing my parents' social circle, known as keeping up with the Joneses.

As I developed into young teenager, I started to question lots of things, especially religious belief, and specifically the rules and restrictions pertaining to Jewish life. When I began to be interested in the opposite sex, my parents made it very clear to me, that the only boyfriend that would be suitable would be a Jewish one. I found this attitude very narrow minded, as being involved in music, I was mixing with fellow budding musicians from many different backgrounds and religions, all of us loving the great composers sacred Christian masses and requiems, composed by Bach, Mozart and Beethoven, whether we were Christian, Muslim or Jewish.

At the age of sixteen I went on holiday with my parents, to Brighton, staying at the Grand Hotel, which was an institution in the famous seaside resort. My brother, being aged eighteen, was allowed to go on holiday with friends. So it was just the three of us in Brighton. My best friend, Denise Conway, had holidayed in Brighton the previous summer, and had boasted to me about what a great place Brighton was. Denise had also mentioned a night club in Hove, called Downtown, telling me, conspiratorially at school break, that the club was a great place to meet boys. I persuaded my parents to let me go to Downtown, but at first they flatly refused. But when I argued that they'd let my brother go to disco clubs at my age, they tried to suggest that it was different for boys, but I was having none of it, putting my foot down, telling my parents in no uncertain terms what's good for the goose was good for the gander, and they caved in

Feeling confident at having won the argument with my parents, my nerves got the better of me when I joined the queue at the club. The man checking for age verification, hardly looked at my document, and he ushered me into the club as I'd felt his eyes trained on my back.

Standing by the side of the dance floor, I became aware of a good-looking boy staring at me.

Not wanting to appear too forward, I half smiled at him, hoping he'd come over and start a conversation. He must have, by osmosis, read my mind, as the boy sauntered over to me, and we started to chat. I became bold, grabbing his hand and leading him to the dance floor.

His name was Dominic, the name being as attractive as the boy; we stayed together for the whole evening, enjoying ourselves enormously.

Dominic walked me back to the hotel along the sea front and he kissed me several times. Being inexperienced in kissing boys, I remembered being self-conscious, wondering whether I was doing it sexily enough to please Dominic. He tried to put his tongue in my mouth but I kept my mouth closed, not wanting to appear morally loose, having just met each other.

We arranged to meet the following day, but whilst having breakfast with my parents at the hotel, I'd heard the reception's Tannoy announcing, 'Would Miss Gerstein please go to the reception.' The other dining room guests stared at me as I made my way there, blushing profusely. My first thoughts, when Dominic made the excuse that his mate had agreed to visit an old friend, and, expected Dominic to accompany him, sounded a bit feeble, but he'd sounded so genuinely upset that they couldn't meet, that I'd given him the benefit of the doubt.

Having agreed to meet the following day, I'd been counting the hours till I got to see Dominic again. My parents then received the news that my grandfather had suddenly died. They immediately packed their bags for the three of us to head back to Manchester. I just had time to write a note to Dominic, with my telephone number, and leave it at the reception. I then realised that I'd never asked Dominic what his surname was. So, I addressed the note to Mr Dominic and informed reception that when the chap called, they should ask him to drop by the hotel to collect the note.

My mother answered the telephone when Dominic rang. Much to my embarrassment, she was extremely rude to the poor boy and let him know that the fact he wasn't Jewish made him unsuitable to date her daughter, and that he mustn't call again.

I was furious with my mother. I had an enormous row with her, stormed out of the room, and vowed to marry a non-Jewish man, when I was old enough to make my own decisions.

It was from that moment onwards that I started to drift away from keeping up certain Jewish rules and customs, just to please my parents. I decided that I would live a purely secular life, not based on any religious creed, and if I was going to worship anything, it would be music and music only.

Two years later, when I was aged eighteen, my parents moved to London. Manchester had become too limited for my father's growing business, and he decided to open a branch in Hatton Garden, the London home to the jewellery trade. My brother was at university in Dublin and I was going off to a teachers training college in central London, but decided that I didn't want to live with Mum and Dad at their new home, which was located in Edgware, north London. I shared a flat in Mornington Crescent with three other girls from college.

At college I'd decided that I didn't like my name of Rosalind, and started to call myself, Bettina, the name of a of a character in a novel I was then reading, and as I loved that particular character in the book, I adopted the name for myself.

My father eventually sold his business; Mum and Dad decided to move to Israel to start a new life there. My brother had become involved in the then fledgling computer business, and got a job in the US. I was teaching English and music at a school in Hampstead and decided to stay put in London.

As the years went on, my life settled into a predictable pattern. I loved living in London, having bought my own flat in Belsize Park, close to the school where I taught. I became part of a large circle of friends of both genders and was known by all as Bettina. I'd almost forgotten that my birth name had been Rosalind. My leisure time was taken up mostly with music, attending concerts and opera, as well as keeping up my piano playing, in which I would never become more than an enthusiastic amateur. I also loved the theatre and going to art galleries. I visited my parents in Israel once a year and they occasionally took a trip to London, staying with me whilst there. They also liked to return to Manchester to catch up with old friends. To be honest, my parents and I never became close again, after I'd rejected the Jewish religion completely. My brother settled in the US having married a Jewish girl from New York, and they had three children, two boys and a girl. They also lived a traditional Jewish life. In the circumstances, it was no wonder that my parents visited their son, daughter-in-law and grandchildren, far more often than see me in London.

So far, I hadn't met the man of my dreams, certainly no one that I'd consider marrying. I'd also decided quite early on that I didn't want children, so as I was getting older I hadn't felt the pressure of any body-clock deadline to conceive. I was aware that men were attracted to me and I spent a lot of time fending off unsuitable men. I'd been involved with several men over the years but no relationship had lasted for more than six months or so.

Then I met Peter Emberton. If it wasn't love at first sight, it was definitely love at second sight. Peter and I met in the stalls circle of the Royal Opera House, Covent Garden, during a performance of Richard Strauss's most famous opera, *Der Rosenkavalier*. I had two tickets to attend with my old friend from Manchester, Denise, who'd recently moved to London, to take up a job as editor of a well-know woman's magazine. Unfortunately, Denise had come down with a virus and was confined to bed. I went along to the sold-out performance and saw the queue for returns. In the front of the queue, stood a very handsome man, who was tall and beautifully dressed. I approached him and said that I had a spare ticket in the stalls circle, and would he care to purchase it from me. He virtually grabbed the ticket in case I changed my mind, blurting out that the stalls circle was his favourite seating area at the opera house.

The year was 1983 and the month was January, always a difficult month to get through after the festive period and before any signs of spring. I was aged thirty nine the big 4-0 was on the horizon and I'd been thinking about my life and what I'd been doing with it. I had been in a comfort bubble – single, with a steady job, lots of friends, with many interests, but I still felt, in my quieter moments, that life had more to offer and I had more to contribute to that life. I'd been feeling that it was time to move on from teaching, but to do what? My friend, Denise, who had many contacts in the media world, was telling me, one night when we'd been out drinking, that every second feature in the magazines that she was involved with was about dating, romance and relationships. Denise had been aware that I'd been successful, albeit, in an amateur way, of matching people together and thought I'd a gift for it. Why didn't I set up a matchmaking consultancy? My initial response was that Denise had had too many glasses of wine! After all, I'd not been too successful, so far, with my own love life. But later, I started to think seriously about what Denise had suggested.

The gentleman, who I sold my ticket to and was sitting next to me in the stalls circle of the opera house, seemed to be a knowledgeable opera enthusiast. Although the opera was very wordy he mimed the text throughout the evening, and he couldn't keep his hands still, discreetly conducting the music around his knees. The production on the stage was a famous one from 1966, by Luchino Visconti, and the current run of performances were the final ones of that production. The cast was stellar. Yvonne Minton, Gwyneth Jones, Hans Sotin and Yvonne Kenny, headed the cast, with the English conductor, Andrew Davis, who'd been gaining a reputation conducting Strauss, was in the pit.

Der Rosenkavalier was a long opera in three acts, part comedy, part romance, which created a whole world of historical Vienna on the stage, the music, in part, being a nod to the other Strauss, Johann, the waltz king.

At the first interval, we'd both made our separate ways to the bar losing ourselves amongst the huge throng of people gathered in the Paul Hamlyn Hall.

When the second act concluded, the gentleman introduced himself as we both gushed how much we were enjoying the performance. He asked me if I would care to join him for a drink, but I politely declined. I went off to the ladies to freshen up, returning to my seat to catch up with the programme book.

Just before the opera reached its conclusion, there's a gorgeous trio for the three sopranos, one playing the part of a young man, which makes for one of the most moving and subtlety emotional moments of any opera in the entire repertoire. A wise, thoughtful and mature woman was prepared to give up her adolescent lover, to a young girl who the adolescent had only recently met, realising that as she aged, she'd be unable to hold onto her young man. I noticed that my seating neighbour was trying, without much success, to hold back the tears during the singing of the trio. It was at that moment that I fell in love with Peter Emberton.

On his second request to join him for a drink, as we were leaving our seats, I accepted, and we went to a popular cocktail lounge, a few doors away from the opera house and sat on bar stools, as we drank several gin martinis. Peter told me that he'd been an opera lover all his adult life, travelling to many of the opera houses in Europe and the US, to hear favourite singers and to see particular productions. He'd also been keen to experience operas that had fallen out of the repertoire, that weren't being done in any of UK opera houses or summer festivals.

Peter had said without embarrassment, that he'd been married and divorced twice. He had two children, a boy and a girl, with his first wife, but was unfortunately estranged from them, and didn't wish to talk about it. His career was in business, import and export, without elaborating on what sector he was involved with. Peter was ten years older than me. When inquiring about my life, I felt that my life had been rather boring with inertia of sameness with my routine of activities, but I mentioned my idea to start a matchmaking agency. Peter had perked up at that ambition of mine, and said he'd like to finance such an adventurous enterprise.

We kissed at the end of the evening, and for some reason, I remembered the only other time I kissed someone on the first evening of meeting, and that was when I was sixteen, on holiday in Brighton with my parents, when the lovely young man that I met at a club, kissed me on the sea front. His name was Dominic.

Peter and I had sex on our second date, and I was hooked. I'd experienced sex with several men that I'd dated over the years, but I felt that it had been all part of the package. Having dated a particular man over a period of time, they'd earned the right to sleep with me. It had all been about their needs, but for me, although not being awful in any way, the sex had always lacked passion or any feelings of lust from my part. I'd come to the conclusion that I just wasn't a sexy woman. But with Peter, it had been completely different. He just had to look at me longingly, and I wanted to tear his clothes off. I just couldn't get enough sex with Peter; I'd become insatiable. It was the sort of sex I should have been having in my twenties, but I'd mistook friendship and things in common, such as musical taste or political views. With Peter, it had nothing to do with any of that. Although we were be both enthusiastic opera lovers, our political views were poles apart. He was a right-wing Tory whilst I was a Labour left winger. Whilst we were together, neither of us changed our beliefs, but as far as I was concerned it didn't matter a hoot. I was besotted with him.

Even though I didn't really know that much about Peter, we'd, on a whim, got married at Hampstead's registry office, with the only guests being my friend, Denise Conway, and a business colleague of Peter, acting as the best man. We honeymooned in Venice and Paris, taking in the opera in both cities. and bought a house on Hampstead Heath.

Peter generously financed my business venture, setting up a matchmaking organisation, with offices in Central London, and not wanting anything in return. The business, from day one, would belong 100 per cent to me.

I broke the news to my parents in Israel and to my brother in New York. When I told my parents that Peter wasn't Jewish, they made it clear to me that I should not even think about visiting them in Israel, and that they wouldn't be coming to London any time soon. My brother, though living a Jewish orthodox life, was more understanding and wished me a happy marriage.

Having been so cautious with men during my twenties and thirties, I'd thrown all caution to the wind with Peter. I married without knowing much about him and he hadn't divulged much, either about his ex-wives and children, or about his business activities.

We'd been married for just four years, when a scandal emerged with Peter's business life hitting the buffers. He'd evidently become heavily involved, commercially, with some rather dubious Russian characters in the Soviet Union, just when the Union itself was tottering, and many shady people were out to make a financial killing, by fair means or foul. The fraud squad in London began sniffing around Peter's business, as he liquidated his company hastily. He made sure that he transferred enough cash to accounts around several jurisdictions, but mostly in Switzerland. He said that he'd have to move out of the UK to somewhere as far away as possible; he was thinking of the U S or even to Australia.

As quickly as I'd agreed to marry Peter four years earlier, I knew instantly that our marriage was now over. I felt very uncomfortable being married to someone who'd had questionable business dealing and dodgy associates. Besides, I had no intention of leaving London, as my business was going well. I still loved Peter but I knew it was now hopeless. To be fair to him, he was financially generous to me. He didn't want anything from my business, despite having financed it. We sold the house for a hefty profit, Peter depositing half the sale price into my bank account, certainly enough to buy my own house, albeit, a smaller one. He also added a substantial sum over and above half the house sale profit. We'd separated for the statuary two years and then arranged a no-fault divorce. He didn't divulge where he'd emigrated to. The whole relationship with Peter had been like a dream to me. I decided to move out of London, buying a small house in a lovely Hertfordshire village, commuting daily to my London offices.

The irony of it all was that I'd established myself as a professional expert in dating and relationships but I'd made a complete hash of my own love life. I never saw or heard from Peter again, but I kept my married name of Emberton.

CHAPTER 38

Hertfordshire

January 1994

Alex Sutton

The new year started positively for me, with my novel, *The Variations on Love*, being published. The reviews for the book had been mainly positive, with a few dissenters.

I sent a copy of my book to all of the members of gramophone club, suggesting that at the next event that I'd be hosting, some time would be set aside for a discussion about the novel, but only if everyone would be in agreement at my suggestion. I gave it a couple of weeks before telephoning the members, the response being 100 percent positive. Unfortunately, Bettina Emberton was away in the French Riviera for the whole month of January, and had left the UK before she'd received her copy of the book, and wouldn't be back in time for my hosting evening.

All the regular members, except Hannah Longsmith and Bettina Emberton, showed up, each with a copy of my book in their hands. Hannah, who seemed to have ceased attending our events, with an *omertà* amongst members on the reasons why she'd left the group.

Three friends of mine, who'd never before attended a gramophone event, were already sitting and relaxing in my living room, when the others began to arrive. The old foursome, Toby, Verity, Ronald and Dulcie, were all in great form, their previous personal difficulties long forgotten. Hildegard and Benjamin Tiller were their usual friendly selves, Hildegard giving me a kiss and a hug, saying how much she'd enjoyed my book. Greg Witton came with his wife, Florence, who'd rarely attended an event. She mentioned to me that she was more of a book lover than a musical one and had been curious to hear what I had to say about my novel, which she admitted she hadn't read, but Greg had. Violet Smithson and Dorothy Bateman were also in attendance. I introduced my three friends to everyone in the room, Roger Garland, Marcus Elliot and Charles Farley. Everyone seemed curious about the men, but immediately, I turned to the music I'd chosen for the first half of the programme, and put, on my turntable, a recording of Mozart's piano concerto No. 21, known as 'Elvira Madigan.'

'Elvira Madigan' was a famous romantic 1967 Swedish film that used the concerto's gorgeous slow movement as the soundtrack to the film. The recording I put on was by the pianist who'd played on the original soundtrack, the late Gèza Anda. As the second part of the evening, was being devoted to discussions about my newly published novel, which was based on aspects of the three Mozart/Da Ponte operas. I thought to stick with Mozart in the first part of the evening. Following on from the concerto, I put on one of Mozart's greatest chamber music works, the String Quintet No. 4 in G minor – played by the Amadeus Quartet, with Cecil Aronowitz, on second viola.

I arranged for my three friends to leave the room during the interval, sending them off to my bedroom, told them to lock the door and keep quiet. I'd set up a table of drinks and snacks for them in the room.

Meanwhile, back in the living room, the group were looking around for the men. The assumption was that they'd left at the interval, having found the Mozart music not to their liking. The chit chat around the room as refreshments were consumed was about the recordings I'd just played. The talk centred on the film, 'Elvira Madigan.' and who'd seen it during the 60s. Toby mentioned the Amadeus Quartet and how many times he and

Verity had heard them in concert during the 60s and 70s, and how sad it was when they'd disbanded in 1987.

The three men were back in the living room for the start of the second half of the evening's proceedings. With all the others present in the room looking puzzled as to where they'd gone to during the interval. I addressed the room, thanking everyone for attending the event, and for agreeing to spend part two of evening talking about my newly published novel, *The Variations on Love*. I'd explained that the format would be as follows: 'my dear friend, Tobias Elden, whom I believe has read the book twice, will chair the discussion, by asking me questions, with anyone else free to chip in with any questions of their own.'

Toby stood up, came over to me, and gave me a hug.

'Alex had asked me whether I would chair the question and answer session, I'm delighted to do so, and yes, I'm happy to confirm that I've read the book twice. In my opinion, it's a fabulous novel, and I'm full of admiration for Alex. I didn't think he had it in him.' Toby chuckled and there were smiles all around the room.

'But, joking aside, why did you want to write a novel? Also, why did you decide to link the narrative around opera; in particular, Mozart's three Da Ponte operas?'

'Well, thank you for your question, Toby. We've all heard the well-known cliché, "Everyone has a novel in them." But, as we know, it's easier said than done, as most people don't ever get around to writing one. I was determined to do so, and because I'm a single man, without family responsibilities, and let me add in a whispered voice, the Labour Party, God bless them, don't work me too hard. I was able to spend a certain amount cf time in my office editing the text that I'd drafted at home the previous night.'

There was laughter in the room at my comments about work.

'As my friends here know, I'm a dedicated opera lover and have been for all my adult life. I've been intrigued in recent years on the way directors of opera productions have updated eighteenth and nineteenth century opera settings to modern times. The idea was to make opera more relevant to contemporary life, and, to bring younger audiences into the opera house. Some updating productions worked, others hadn't, and the whole process was very controversial with audiences. Of course, the musical score would always remain sacrosanct in performance and no conductor would dare mess with it. So I thought – why not do the same with a novel, which wouldn't have a musical score attached? After all, some people who never understood opera, had the notion that traditional opera plots were ridiculous and that opera lovers were euphemistically known as 'canary fanciers.' But I believed just the opposite – that most opera plots are great stories, independent of the music, and could stand up as the basis of a novel, especially if the story was transported to the twentieth century.'

Toby was nodding his head in approval at my remarks, but Ronald was shaking his head, as we all knew Ronald's negative view of most operas.

'Why did I choose Mozart? First and foremost, in my opinion, Mozart was one of the greatest of all opera composers and with the librettist, Lorenzo Da Ponte, created music drama masterpieces, namely, *Le Nozze di Figaro* and *Don Giovanni*. For the more problematic, dramatically speaking, *Cosi Fan Tutte*, Mozart wrote music of a most sublime nature.

'I wished to explore operas with an established librettist/composer partnership. After narrowing it down to three great operatic partnerships; Mozart/Da Ponte, Verdi/Boito and Strauss/Hofmannsthal, my inclination had been to choose Mozart/Da Ponte, for the sheer human quality of the characters they'd created, and, for me to be able to carve a narrative from all of the three works from their joint efforts.'

'Thank you, Alex. Next, I'd like to ask you, why you'd used, mainly, the same characters in all three operas, which was not the case with Da Ponte's librettos?'

'Good question. You're absolutely right, the three operas each contained totally different characters, but I was keen to develop four individuals throughout the book, namely Dominic Rivers, Ricky Wenger, Finley Reason and Sebastian Moran for aims which I'll make clear shortly. But funnily enough, I recently read about a production, somewhere in France, of all three operas performed as a trilogy, with a similar idea to mine. The French production, had the page, Cherubino, in *Figaro*, turn into the Don himself in *Don Giovanni*, and then morph into the older cynic, *Don Alfonso* in Cosi. I, of course, mixed and matched my four protagonists in a different way for the novel'

'Hmmm, said Toby, I'm sure I speak for everyone here. We're all curious about what revelation you're about to spring upon us, but meanwhile, a couple of more questions for you. Why the title, 'The Variation on Love' and which of the three operas caused you the most difficulty?'

'OK, I will explain everything, but first your two questions Toby. The title is a phrase Finley used whilst explaining his philosophy of "love" in a sequence from the *Cosi Fan Tutte* section. As far as the most difficult, it was definitely *Cosi*. I was unhappy with the misogynist aspect of the plot. Not knowing exactly which way to go with it, I ended up with all four lovers being unfaithful to their partners, but in different non-conventional ways, and went for a happy ending. It would be up to the readers to decide whether it was a convincing interpretation, or not. The *Figaro* chapters had been fairly straightforward for me, setting it in a country estate and concentring on Acts Two and Four only. The *Don Giovanni* sector was fun to write about, but aspects of events in the latter part of the plot had troubling personal memories for me.'

The audience was becoming restless, sensing that I had personal things to reveal. They didn't wish to hear any more about the writing process of my novel, as I'd dropped too many hints that I had things to divulge, so I'd better get on with it. I had a quiet word with Toby, who went back to his seat.

'I'm Sorry, friends – that I've been rather cryptic in some of my answers to Toby's questions, and I wish to thank him for leading the session. When I conclude what I've to say, please feel free to ask me anything you wish me to clarify.

'On several occasions when Toby and I had been chatting together, he'd been inquisitive about my past life and asked as to whether my book was in any way autobiographical. I vehemently denied that it was, as my life had been too boring to be of any interest to anyone. Well, I must apologise publicly to Toby, as I'd been somewhat economical with the truth. '

Toby, smiling, shouted out, 'I didn't believe you anyway, ha ha ha.'

There was general laughter around the room.

I continued, 'the truth is, that part of the novel was indeed autobiographical. Let me tell you about my three friends that have joined us here tonight. My friend, Marcus Elliot, had actually been a boyhood friend of mine, and, everything in the text about our respective boyhood experiences had been completely factual. Marcus is Ricky Wenger in the book. The opening chapters of the novel are, near enough, completely true'

Marcus was nodding his head and smiling.

We did go on holiday to Brighton together when I was aged seventeen. I'm sure that you've realised by now, that I'm the Dominic Rivers character. When Marcus and I went on that trip, I wanted to give myself a sexier name than Alex and I came up with Dominic. So, many years later when I'd started on my book, the name stuck. The surname of "Rivers" was completely fictitious. My friend, Roger Garland, was Finley Reason in the book. Roger, an old friend of Marcus had been a gentleman's hairdresser in Brighton, all those years ago, and true to his characteristics in the text, had a philosophical bent about him.'

Roger was blushing, but also laughing.

'And last but not least, my friend, Charles Farley, who was Sebastian Moran in the novel; he was the character that developed the most, in a positive way, throughout the three sections of the story. I hope Charles doesn't mind me divulging that he was a wealthy young man, and the son of a hereditary peer.'

Charles waved to everyone with a warm smile on his face.

'The four of us did, over the years, form a close bond, and they all kindly had given me permission to base my fictional characters on them. When I first met Roger and Charles in Brighton, Roger was indeed indebted to Charles for business loans. Marcus and I helped Roger out by working for Charles's father, who was a bit of a martinet, on his country estate, located just outside Brighton, as odd job men and gardeners.

Naturally, the opera's dramatic narratives in the novel were mainly fiction, except for certain incidents that were partly factual. Marcus and I did work for a while in a life assurance company doing sales. Marcus had been an excellent salesman but I was rubbish, a born non-sales person. And all four of us worked for a while in a restaurant in Ireland, which Charles owned, courtesy of his father.

'Now, here comes the hard bit and the reason why I've been so reticent to talk about my past life, when Toby tried, on several times to draw me out. You remember that in the *Don Giovanni* section, towards the end, Ricky, and later, Dominic, are arrested for sexual misconduct. I'm sorry to say that the arrests actually did occur in real life. Both Marcus, and I both spent time in prison.'

Marcus had his head in his hands.

'The hero during that terrible period was Charles. He paid for the finest lawyers to get us reduced sentences and he looked after us after we were released, when it was so difficult to obtain employment. Marcus, did indeed learn to cook whilst in prison, and became, over time, a Michelin-star chef, which he still is. I, with Charles's help, gained employment with the Labour Party, who generously overlooked my criminal record, and I've been working at their London headquarters ever since.'

Ronald put his hand up.

'Yes, Ronald'

Would you like to tell us what crime you'd committed to warrant a prison sentence?'

Typical Ronald, I thought.

Marcus and I looked at each other shaking our heads.

'Sorry, old chap, I've told you all we wish to say on the matter. It was a long time ago and we've paid our price to society. We've both lived exemplary lives since that time.

'Are there any more questions?'

Verity stood up and I nodded for her to go ahead,

'I'm just curious, Alex. Was the bit at the beginning of the book, where you met a young girl at a disco club in Brighton – did that actually happen? I think her name was Rosalind.'

I laughed, thinking that it had to be a woman who'd be interested in sweet young love.

'Yes, Verity, the episode was totally true. I've often wondered what had become of the girl.

'I rounded things off by a having a group hug with my three old friends. Everyone in the room stood and applauded, and tears came to my eyes.

269

CHAPTER 39

Hertfordshire – February 1994

I was at home on a Sunday, enjoying a lazy morning. I'd been thinking about the recent gramophone event that I'd hosted when I made my confession about my past, introducing my three great old friends who'd been the inspiration for the characters in my novel. Above all, I'd risked alienating my newer friends by admitting that I'd spent time in prison. But I didn't regret it, because if the group rejected me because of my youthful misdemeanour, they wouldn't be worth having as friends. So far, I'd had no adverse reaction from anyone, except Ronald, who'd been a bit peeved that I refused to offer details of the actual crime. The case against me was pretty much as I described it in the book.

Marcus, aka Ricky, had become out of control, women wise, and one night he overstepped the mark by forcing himself on a young woman. I, as in the opera, *Don Giovanni*, was playing his sidekick, Leporello, to his Don Giovanni. I amused the young woman's, (Zerlina, in the opera) boyfriend (Masetto, in the opera) as Marcus went about the seduction. So, yes, I was guilty of aiding and abetting the sexual abuse. My friends and I saw no reason to divulge any more details about the incident than I did at the event. To be fair to Marcus, he'd turned his life around completely after being released from prison.

Charles was never the villain. His alto ego, Sebastian, was in the book, as portrayed in the *Figaro* chapters. Charles's father was another matter; I'd based Sebastian on Charles's father. But Sebastian, as a character, did slowly segue into a decent human being as the narrative progressed. In the latter restaurant sections, Sebastian, did indeed show kindness and understanding, only occasionally, reverting to his earlier arrogant nature, becoming more like the Charles I'd known since my time in Brighton during 1960. The character of Lydia, Lady Moran, was a fictional invention.

Roger, aka, Finley, was the good guy, both in real life and in the novel. I'd met him at the same time I'd met Charles.

What I hadn't divulged to the gramophone group, was that my three friends had all been living in the US for many years. The three had flown to England, especially to support me at the event, having fully briefed them by letters and telephone calls, to exactly how much they'd been instrumental to me in constructing the characters that were to impersonate Da-Ponte's dramatic inventions for the three Mozart operas. I'd booked them into our town's excellent hotel, the four of us spending two weeks together before the event, enjoying an incredible reunion. They'd now returned to the US, and I'd promised faithfully to visit them there the following year. The publication of my book had solidified our friendships to a greater degree than ever; we considered ourselves blood brothers.

The one thing I regretted was that Bettina had missed the event. I wondered what she would have made of the personal revelations, especially about me having served time in prison.

I was in deep thoughts about recent events when I was shaken out of my reverie, by the ringing of the telephone.

'Hello, Alex, its Bettina here.'

'Ah, Bettina, you're back from France!'

I was conscious of my voice reaching an unnaturally higher pitch, silently telling myself, *calm down, man.*

'Yes, I spent the whole month of January with friends in Nice, and believe me, the weather was much better there than I gather it's been here, ha ha.'

'Well, yes, you're right about that, the weather was of a typical January ilk, cold and wet, with very little sunshine. You're lucky to be able to take a whole month off from work.'

'That's the advantage of being one's own boss. January is traditionally a quiet month for matchmaking, following a busy Christmas period, and before the desperation for a partner in time for Valentine's Day.'

Bettina's voice seemed to take on a more tremulous tone.

'Listen, Alex, I was sorry to have missed your gramophone event, and the first thing I did when I arrived back home was to read your book, which you'd kindly posted to me before Christmas. Unfortunately, I hadn't a chance to read it before going away.'

'Did you enjoy the book, Bettina?'

'Oh, yes, yes. I thought it was terrific. It was so clever of you to dissect the Mozart's operas into the trajectory of several contemporary characters navigating modern life.'

I could feel myself blushing. 'Thank you. It's very kind of you to say so'

'Alex...could we meet? There's something I'd like to talk to you about.'

I thought...*Oh, here we go, once a business person, always a business person*. Bettina had been the same the first time we'd met at my first gramophone hosting evening, when she'd handed me her business card. Bettina was unable to speak to anyone who's unencumbered without prospecting them to join her matchmaking scheme.

My voice tone changed from being bashfully grateful for the praise of my book, to the slightly sharper tone I'd adopt when receiving telephone sales cold calls.

'Yes, of course, Bettina, I'd be happy to meet when convenient for both of us.'

'Actually, it's more urgent than that, Alex.'

There was definitely a nervous tick in her voice.

'Could you pop over this afternoon for tea? How about at 4 ...?'

Her urgency to meet today shocked me. Perhaps I was doing her an injustice and something important had cropped up.

In a quiet tremulous voice, I replied. 'Yes, Bettina, I'm free this afternoon and will pop over to your place at four.'

Putting down the phone, I felt puzzled as to what this was all about.

Ringing Bettina's front door bell at the agreed time, I was worried and a bit alarmed. Bettina's welcome was warm and friendly, but she gazed oddly at my face, certainly, in a different way she'd previously looked at me. I was somewhat discombobulated.

Tea and cakes were served with Bettina telling me all about her month in the South of France, and, how much she'd enjoyed her time there. She again stressed how sorry she was to have missed my gramophone event.

I realised for sure that whatever it was that Bettina wanted to see me about, it was something more troubling to her than just trying to recruit me as a client for her matchmaking scheme.

'Alex, I always understood that your novel was pure fiction.'

I just nodded, not replying.

'I may be going mad, suffering from a flawed memory, or maybe I'm just a delusional middle-aged woman, with a hangover from the menopause.'

I wondered exactly what Bettina was going to tell me.

'When I was aged sixteen, in 1960, I went on holiday with my parents, travelling from our home in Manchester to Brighton, staying at the Grand Hotel. Whilst there, my grandfather, who lived with us, died, and we had to return home just a couple of days into our holiday.'

It was my turn to look at Bettina in utmost shock!

Bettina, noticing my change of expression, continued...

'I know there's a truism that sometimes, truth is stranger than fiction, but this is all too much of a coincidence. I visited a disco along the coast in Hove on our first night of the holiday. I met a young man at the club, about the same age as me, or maybe slightly older. Having spent the whole evening together, he escorted me back to my hotel; we'd walked along the sea front, stopping for a kiss. That was my first kiss and I thought that I was in love. I remember his name, as it was a favourite name of mine. The boys name was Dominic.'

I was thinking... *I must be asleep enjoying a pleasant dream.* No, I was definitely awake.

'Yes, I remember it well, and I did call myself Dominic, the name being a pseudonym. As it was the first time I'd been away from home just with a friend, I wanted a sexier name than plain Alex. But if my memory was correct, the beautiful girl I met that night was called Rosalind. I even remember that her surname was "Gerstein." Years later, when I decided to start to write my book, I thought to stick with the name, Dominic, especially as the early part of the book that described aspects of my childhood and teenage years were virtually identical to the real life of Alex Sutton.

Bettina, stared at me open mouthed and said, 'I can't remember the surname Sutton, but your name in the book was "Rivers." '

'I must have overlooked giving you my surname in Brighton, because, I remembered going to the hotel to collect your note about your grandfather and having to abandon the holiday, and the note was addressed to Mr Dominic.

'The surname, "Rivers" was purely fictitious.'

'So, what do I call you, Alex or Dominic?'

'Oh, I'm definitely Alex, but I don't want readers of the book to know that it was partly autobiographical. That's if I'll have any readers except my dear friends, ha ha.'

'Alex is definitely not as sexy as Dominic.' Bettina laughed. 'What other parts of the book are you describing yourself?'

'Not much really, except that the characters of Ricky, Finley and Sebastian were based on real friends of mine, whom you'd have met if you'd attended my gramophone event. During my adult life I've been involved in industries that formed part of the books narrative, namely life assurance and hospitality in Ireland.

'But,' I continued, 'why are both your names changed?'

'My current surname of Emberton was the name of my ex-husband, and Bettina, as with you, I thought that the name Bettina had a sexier ring to it than Rosalind, ha ha. I took the name from a favourite character of mine in a film when I'd set-up home on my own in London in the 1970s.

'I owe you an apology for the way my mother spoke to you on the telephone, when you tried to call me in Manchester. My relationship with her was never quite the same after that.'

'No no, you've no need to apologise, it was a long time ago; we were both very young and speaking for myself I felt that I was in love, despite the fact that I'd only known you for a few short hours. Ah ah, young love, but I was devastated at the time. The strange thing was that when I met you again at my first gramophone event, I'd thought that I knew you from somewhere, but couldn't for the life of me think where.'

'To be honest, I didn't think the same when I'd met you again, but did think that you seemed a very nice man.'

I blushed.

'You see, Dominic, sorry, I mean, Alex, when you left me back at the hotel that night, I thought that I was in love too, and couldn't sleep, anticipating our planned meeting for the following day. So, when you called to say you had to visit your friend's friend, I thought it was an excuse and that you'd just had a bit of fun with me and weren't bothered. The other thing that was going through my mind was that my kissing on the sea front wasn't sexy enough for you.'

I blushed again.

'So, when you tried to call me in Manchester. I realised that you were genuinely interested in me, but unfortunately, my mother's rudeness stopped any further meeting between us, and that was that. I continued to think about you for a good few years, then life moved on, as it always would do.'

Bettina said that she'd kept a bottle of champagne in the fridge for a special occasion and as she stood up to go and get the bottle, I leaped up from my chair and went over to her and we hugged each other. We stayed motionless for what seemed an age, but was probably only for long enough for both of us to burst into tears. We were crying for our lost innocent youth.

Sipping champagne, we felt a sense of unreality about our incredible reunion. What were the odds that we'd ever meet again, especially since we'd known each other as Bettina and Alex through the gramophone club for the last couple of years, not for a moment suspecting we were actually Rosalind and Dominic, prospective boy and girlfriend during 1960? If not for my book, we would never have known.

We polished off the champagne.

I stayed at Bettina's house for the rest of the evening. Bettina rustled up some supper and opened a bottle of wine. We talked, talked and talked about our respective lives from 1960 onwards, with me filling in all the gaps that weren't in the novel, even owning up to my criminal record and time in prison, which didn't faze Bettina at all, and she told me all about her teaching career, her estrangement from her parents, the marriage and divorce from Peter Emberton, who'd financed her current business, Love Me Do.

I phoned for a taxi when it was time to go home, at about midnight, as I'd had too much to drink to even think about getting into my car, despite the short distance between our two homes. I could cycle over in the morning to collect the car. My bike would fit into my hatchback car.

Back at home, my head was swimming with a hundred million thoughts going through my mind. I couldn't think of going to bed, so I poured myself a brandy and port, always a good settler, following an evening of wine and champagne.

I was still finding it hard to acknowledge that Bettina Emberton, a late-forties, sophisticated, extremely attractive businesswoman, was once Rosalind Gerstein, the lovely sixteen-year-old girl that I'd been smitten with briefly in Brighton, thirty-two years ago.

I hadn't meant to put my own young life into the book, but to write a modern narrative, using the plots of the Mozart operas as the core base of the drama. But, when I sat down to start writing the book I was stuck on how to actually start. Without realising it, incidents from my own early life, almost wrote themselves on the paper. And then, I remembered about the seventeen-year old me, who'd taken the plunge to go on holiday without my parents, travelling to Brighton with the older Marcus, who'd only become a friend, because of the tragic death of his younger brother, Felix, (Melvyn in the book), who'd been my best friend. Meeting Rosalind at the club, thinking that she'd be my first girlfriend, was scuppered by her mother because I wasn't Jewish. Marcus Elliot had introduced me to Charles Farley and Roger Garland, in Brighton. The fact that the four of us became lifetime friends inspired me to use us four as the main characters of the book. But I had to get their permission to do so and they were all by then living in the US. I telephoned each one briefly, and then wrote letters to them regularly during the writing process to keep them updated of where the narrative was going. When I finished writing the book, before offering it to a publisher, I posted the first complete draft to my three friends for approval. Marcus was initially concerned about using our prison episode in the *Don Giovanni* section, but came round to understanding that it was needed for the plot, as I hadn't felt it credible to write that the Don would be dragged down to hell by a statue in the twentieth century!

When the book had been published, I invited the three friends to visit me and attend the gramophone event, where my plan was to introduce the men, and come clean on how much they'd been the inspiration for my book. When they initially expressed their reluctance for me to expose to the group that they were the alto egos of the plot, I promised that all the attendees at the event would be sworn to secrecy, and wouldn't divulge any of the information to the outside world. I added that I could completely trust the members in that regard.

Permission was granted, but of course, Bettina, aka Rosalind, hadn't attended the event and therefore was not included in the guarantees I received from all the other members at the conclusion of the evening. I would have to have a word with her, requesting confidentially with all the revelations of last night. I had no reason to believe that Bettina wouldn't comply with my wishes. But, as it turned out, over the next few weeks, when I had several evenings out with Bettina, I completely forgot to mention it.

CHAPTER 40

March 1994

I lived a solitary bachelor life in later years and that probably accounted for my staid appearance in terms of clothes that I chose to wear; dark three piece suits, white shirts and plain ties, with rather clunky black leather shoes. The only variation was that at weekends it was a blazer with slacks, sporting a cravat around my neck instead of a tie. I kept to the same style of shoe, but dark brown instead of black. I still had a full head of hair, the local barber regularly giving it a short back and sides cut. I remained hatless and didn't smoke; in fact, had never done so.

So I decided to smarten myself up. I bought a couple of expensive Italian suits, which were cut in a contemporary, but elegant style – colours of light navy and medium grey. Instead of standard white, I bought wide-collar blue shirts, and several brightly coloured patterned ties. I visited the St James's area of London and bought a couple of pairs of stylish leather monk shoes, from a well-known shoe shop in upmarket Jermyn Street. Finally, taking a leaf out of the character in my novel, Ricky Wenger, when he decided to change his appearance into a more eye-catching style, I visited the same hatters, Lock & Co., based in St James Street, and bought, for the first time in my life, a top-of-the-range trilby hat – the sales assistant assuring me that I was tall enough to look good with the hat on my head. For casual wear, I bought several pairs of jeans that I'd never worn before – a range of T-shirts, and loafer shoes. I abandoned my local barber shop and booked an appointment with Molton Brown hairdressers in London's New Bond Street, where a pretentious young man, decided to re-style my hair, keeping it at a longer length covering the back of my neck, and bulking up the hair high in front of my forehead. I was thinking, as the hair transformation was fussily being created, that as soon as I'd put my trilby hat on, my hair would flatten down to what it had always been!

When I arrived at the home of Benjamin, and Hildegard Tiller, for the next gramophone event that the couple were hosting, everyone congratulated me on my new appearance, the general consensus being that I was looking ten years younger, and that the different style of clothing were all excellently chosen. Bettina was there, and, without saying anything to me, gave me a big smile and thumbs up. Both Bettina and I had decided not to reveal our discovery of being, in real life, the Dominic and the Rosalind of the novel. In fact, no more was spoken throughout the evening, of all the revealing dramatic information of the previous event, because several new people to the club were attending, and, everyone was conscious of their promise not to disclose any of what had dramatically unfolded on that evening. Arriving late, Hannah Longsmith turned up for the first time in ages. I noticed that she kept very much to herself all through the event.

With all the excitement of the book publication, the personal revelations at my hosting event and my, still secret reunion with Bettina, I neglected my friendship with Toby Elden and our regular get-togethers in London or at Sopwell House in St Albans. Also, I never reciprocated the invitation to his home dinner party from back in 1992.

Bettina and I had dinner together in London a couple of times following our marathon afternoon and evening at her house, when our lives were turned upside down confronting our respective past. Once we'd come to terms that we were actually both the youngsters who had met in Brighton way back in time, we began to explore the alternative narrative on how our lives would have gone in a total different direction if we'd had the opportunity to date each other and develop a relationship over time.

'Sorry, Alex, it wouldn't have worked out because of the geographical distance between us. In any event, we were too young and naive to have been able to sustain a long-term relationship.'

'Hmmm – I don't agree. I know several couples, who, either met at school, or as teenagers, like us at the time, and have been happily married for many years.'

'Well, it's a nice thought. It seems that you're more a romantic than me, ha-ha! Maybe being a matchmaker has hardened me in the whole love business.'

We were dining at an old established restaurant in London's Soho. L'Escargot, was a French restaurant that specialised in seafood. We were acting as if we were on a first or second date, perhaps a couple who'd been introduced by Bettina's matchmaking scheme. But, every now and again, we looked at each other in wonderment, not quite believing that this was our second life chance. But the truth was that there was no overwhelming physical attraction between us as there had been in our first life. My own love life history had been somewhat underwhelming with only a few short-term relationships over the years, that had never amounted to much. However, writing the book had given me a renewed interest in exploring the possibilities of finding a new fully physical relationship with a suitable woman.

There was no wonder that Bettina had not shown a current dating interest in me.

I decided to also invite Ronald and Dulcie to my proposed dinner party, although I'd had my issues with Ronald in the past and I'd thought that his recent questioning of me, requesting details of my criminal conviction, was lacking in sensitivity, to say the least. On the other hand, I liked Dulcie, and the couple had seemed more in tune with each other recently, certainly, more so, than when I'd been at Toby and Verity's dinner party, when their relationship seemed to be heading for the rocks. Besides, the foursome had a history of joint dinner parties, and I thought they appreciated me respecting their long standing tradition. Bettina would be joining me as my partner for the evening.

As I lived on my own, I cooked myself simple easy meals, but, if I'd wanted more haute-cuisine food I'd indulge myself by eating at a foodie restaurant in London. However, I'd worked in a restaurant during my time in Ireland, under my friend Marcus Elliot, who was the head chef, and I picked up a lot of cooking tips from him.

My plan was to serve roast duck as the main course. I would do a cold vichyssoise for starters, which I could prepare in advance. Bettina had generously offered to make the bread and the dessert, which would be trifle. I would buy three whole ducks, heavily salt them overnight leaving them in the fridge. In the morning of the dinner party, I would take the ducks out of the fridge, wipe all the salt off the birds and wrap lots of kitchen roll around and in the ducks to dry them out. Before cooking them I'd prick the skins of the breasts and the legs with a sharp knife.

I would cook them in the oven, each duck separately on the three oven shelves' on a very low temperature for slow roasting. The duck would sit on a rack of an oven tin, where the natural oils from the bird drips into the oven tin. One did not need to sprinkle any separate oil or spread any butter on the ducks. Once the ducks were in the oven I would peel some potatoes, rinse them and gently bring them to the boil. Then I'd drain and cut them into small squares, and like for the ducks, completely dry them out. Once dried and by that time, plenty of duck oil would have lined the oven tins, so I would equally divide the squared potatoes, slipping them into the separate tins. I'd cut the ducks in half, keep them warm and serve each guest one half of a duck. The ducks' giblets would be used to make the stock for the sauce, which would be a fresh orange and port wine one. When the ducks were cooked the skins should be nice and crispy. The potatoes may need a bit more cooking once the ducks had been taken out of the oven, and one could raise the oven temperature a little. When ready the potatoes should be crispy on top and soft inside, with a duck oil flavour, which hopefully would be absolutely delicious. The accompanying vegetable would be a cooked red cabbage, and like the vichyssoise, prepared in advance. Bettina would bring the bread and the dessert to my place late afternoon, well before the other guests arrived. I would also serve a small cheese selection, after the main course and before the dessert. I was thinking of a *taleggio* and a few soft cheeses.

Drinks wise, the obligatory champagne to kick things off. I wouldn't serve wine with the soup but had full bodied claret for the main course. I'd serve a good Burgundy white with the cheese and a dessert wine sauterne to accompany Bettina's fantastic trifle. And for a liqueur, I'd offer either a cognac or a port, or perhaps a mix of the two together.

Bettina arrived with her bread and dessert and she helped me with laying the table, which was a perfect size for a dinner seating six people. Once I'd done as much as I possibly could as prep, Bettina and I sat down and relaxed with a cup of tea. I suggested that amongst friends tonight, we should divulge who we were in the novel, however weird it was that we'd both been living close by to each other, with different names from our youthful lives. Bettina, nodded. She hadn't disagreed with what I had suggested but said that we didn't want the evening to be focused on us; after all, they'd spent the whole of the recent gramophone event on learning about who was who in the novel.

The four guests had all arrived, travelling in one car. Dulcie, who wasn't drinking, except for the odd glass, was doing the driving. As the guests were settling down comfortably in the living room, I opened the first bottle of champagne. Clinking glasses, the four were at their most affable selves, concentrating their interest on Bettina, who'd been rather quiet during Hildegard and Benjamin's hosting evening.

Bettina and I went into the kitchen to do the final touches for the meal.

Meanwhile, back in the living room, Dulcie quietly asked Toby. 'Are those two now a couple?'

'I haven't a clue,' said Toby. 'Alex and I haven't met up for any jaunts since his big event, which was more like a book launch than a gramophone evening, ha ha ha.'

They all shut up when I came back into the room with a second bottle of champagne.

'You're all very quiet in here.' I topped up everyone's glass, except Dulcie's, handing around small bowls of crisps, nuts and olives, excusing myself again.

'Maybe they are together,' said Verity, 'after all, Alex has smartened himself up big time, and his whole demeanour is screaming self-confidence.'

'I'll say one thing though,' chipped in Toby, 'our Alex is a dark horse, ha ha.'

Ronald hadn't engaged with the chat at all.

Bettina had that female touch that I lacked. She set the table beautifully with candles and flowers that she'd arrived with earlier. I escorted my friends into the dining room, asking them to bring their glasses of champagne with them, as I wasn't serving a wine with the starter.

The conversation was muted during the starter course, as everyone was hungry having drunk several glasses of champagne. The vichyssoise was complimented and I made a point of saying that it was Bettina who made the bread.

I set down the decanter of the claret, before Bettina and I headed back into the kitchen to prepare to serve the main course.

Ronald, who'd been quiet so far, commented to the others, 'Well, they look like a couple to me which would really be a turn up for the book.'

Verity added, 'Perhaps Bettina has advised Alex on his new wardrobe, or even chose the clothes for him.'

The conversation ceased when Bettina and I bought in the main course. The half duck, surrounded by orange slices, dominated the large plates that I'd chosen to use. The sauce, roast potatoes and red cabbage, were all served separately. Spontaneous applause broke out when the guests saw the duck, all pronouncing that roast duck was a favourite dish of theirs, and asked if it had been a joint effort. Bettina said that, no. the starter and main course was all Alex. I quickly jumped in to say that the dessert was Bettina's, and besides, she'd been a great help in getting everything ready.

Everyone tucked in with Ronald, who was generally parsimonious with compliments, stated that it was the best roast duck he'd ever tasted and that he loved the crispness of the skin. The others nodded in agreement.

The conversation was muted whilst we were all tucking into the food. I made sure wine glasses were topped up, except for Dulcie, who was sticking to drinking water. During a break between the main course and the cheese, the chat picked up with talk about all my recent disclosures, and especially, the meeting my of old friends who'd been the inspiration for the main characters in my novel. I put my hand up and said, 'stop! I didn't invite you for dinner to continue on from where we left off here some weeks ago. Let's hear about you guys about whatever went on in your lives in late 1992 has all been resolved.'

The foursome looked at each other, thinking that I was a bit bold to bring up the matter of their relationship hiccups of the recent past. Ronald, holding Dulcie's hand pompously, said, 'Well, Dulcie and I have never been happier than we are now.' Dulcie nodded but was looking somewhat embarrassed.

Bettina, who wasn't saying very much, got up from the table to serve the cheese, whilst I poured the white Burgundy wine.

Ronald piped up, 'Alex, if you're asking personal questions, let me ask you one, 'Are you and Bettina now an item?'

I chuckled, with the thought that Ronald, even though being fully justified with his question, had an awkward way of communicating.

It was Bettina, who looked straight at Ronald, said, 'No, we're not, as you call it "an item." I'm just helping Alex out tonight, and if I can say, hopefully for all of us, that he's a fantastic cook!'

'Hear, hear,' was the spontaneous response.

It was time for dessert. I brought the large bowl of trifle to the table and pointed the palm of my hand towards Bettina, miming a 'thank you' for her efforts. The others nodded in ascent.

A general murmuring of 'delicious' as we all got stuck into the trifle. I served the dessert wine.

Coffee and liqueurs followed.

Animated conversation resumed, with Toby dominating the table, describing some recent concerts that he and Verity had recently attended. Perhaps it was all the alcohol that Toby had consumed, but he suddenly changed tack and announced...

'Like our friends, Ronald and Dulcie, Verity and I are also happy together, but unlike them, our lifestyle that we've both agreed to pursue, is a non-conventional one.'

Eyebrows shot up as we all looked at Toby in anticipation of what he was going to say.

'Hannah Longsmith and I were having an affair, and that's why Hannah had stopped attending the gramophone events.'

Verity interjected. 'That was part of my agreement with Toby, when he confessed about the affair, that I didn't want to have to see her there.'

'But, Verity,' said Bettina, 'Hannah was at the recent event hosted by Hildegard and Benjamin.'

'Yes,' replied Verity, That was back then, when everything came to head between Toby and me, but things had moved on, and I was OK to see Hannah again.'

'You mean,' I butted in, 'that the affair is over?'

Toby immediately responded. 'Oh no, the affair continued and we're still seeing each other. You see, Verity sees other men, generally younger men who she meets at a certain private members' club that discreetly caters for attached people who wish to meet other attached people.'

I thought, How strange that fact and fiction are coalescing here. My fictional character, Lydia, in my novel, had a penchant for younger men, and my friend, Verity, has a similar taste.

Bettina, thought, Verity could have come to see me professionally, when I was still matching people for affairs. But, I gave up on that side of things, as I never had enough women coming forward. And the fact that Toby came for a consultation, I would never disclose to anyone, as the first rule of my profession is that all clients had total confidentiality.

We all looked at Verity who, although was showing embarrassment at Toby's forthrightness, decided not to let herself be judged.

'Look, I was happy and contented with all aspects of our life together. Although I may have had secret desires, I would never have acted on them if Toby hadn't had his affair with Hannah. But, wait, I wasn't going to be the wronged woman who'd either suffered in silence or sued for a divorce. No. No, that's throwing the baby out with the bathwater. I loved Toby and I'd wanted us to continue the life together that we'd carved out for ourselves over many years. So I agreed that Toby could go on seeing Hannah, but I didn't want to meet with her at the gramophone club. But over time, I changed my mind. Hannah is a long-standing member of the club, and she is not only a committed music lover, but is very knowledgeable on the recorded repertoire. So Hannah's back at the club and I'm actually pleased about that. Regarding my own tastes, I thought that maybe I secretly desired women, but no. That wasn't the case.'

Dulcie was looking a bit uncomfortable at the mention of desiring women. Nevertheless, she wanted to have her say. 'Verity and I enjoyed a week together at Inglewood Health Hydro in the lovely village of Kintbury in Berkshire. On the Friday night, after being on a fruit diet all week, we indulged in a slap-up meal with several bottles of wine. Following dinner, a disco night was on offer in their cellar bar. Verity and I joined the throng and had more drinks. Everyone down in that cellar was on a high and much flirtation was going on. Anyway, to cut to the chase, Verity enjoyed a flirtation with a handsome younger man, and I did the same with an attractive woman who was of a similar age to me. Verity and I had shared a bedroom at the Hydro, just as friends, and on that Friday night, we both knew that our sexual tastes were not aligned. So, moving on, Verity and I attend the adult club together. I would seek a woman partner of any age group, with Verity being always on the lookout for a younger man.'

Dulcie smiled at Verity, who gave her friend thumbs up, as if to say, 'Well done, Dulcie, for being so open about your predilection for women, and about our joint jaunts to the adult club.

My thoughts were what a couple of plucky women Verity and Dulcie were. They weren't prepared to settle for how middle-class women of a certain vintage were expected to behave.

Toby was happy, because he was smitten with Hannah, sexually, but wanted to live his life with Verity. But – what about Ronald?

Reading our minds, Ronald said. 'I'm not only OK with what Dulcie gets up to, but I actually encouraged her, as it makes her happy and that makes me happy too. By the way, I'm not interested in pursuing either another woman, or a man, for that matter. I'm just not that way inclined. Dulcie and I now have a better understanding of each other than we'd ever had in the past.

Phew. We all looked at Ronald in admiration. He didn't have a jealous bone in his body; his awkward and often annoying way of expressing himself was balanced by his attitude to Dulcie. Once again, as on several previous occasions, I had to revise my opinion of Ronald. He was definitely a total one off!

CHAPTER 41

Toby, for once, hadn't been dominating the conversation whilst the women had had their say, and we listened to Ronald's acquiescence. But Toby suddenly piped up, 'Enough about our sexual tastes and desires, I've got something else to announce.'

We all looked to Toby, and I was pleased for his intervention, as I was concerned that the evening that I envisaged being all about entertaining friends, who were *bon vivant* enthusiasts, morph into a Freudian confession session on sexual desire.

I said, 'Let's move back into the living room, which is more comfortable. Take your glass with you and I'll bring in the cognac and port decanters, so please help yourself whilst I clear the tables. Does anyone want more coffee?'

There were no takers for coffee but I could see that both Toby and Ronald were pleased that the decanters were following them into the living room.

Bettina – who'd been very quiet whilst the other ladies were in confession mode, said, 'I'll help you clear the table, Alex.'

'No, no, Bettina, you've done enough, please go in with the others.' I gently pushed her in that direction before she protested.

I was pleased to have a few minutes in the kitchen. I'd enjoyed the sociability of the evening, but as I was so used to living on my own here, I needed a few minutes without other people around me.

Meanwhile, Toby, who topped up his glass with a good measure of cognac, was back to his usual avuncular self. 'I'm glad you're here, Bettina, because I've something interesting to tell you.'

Bettina was all ears.

'Well, you know that since my retirement from TNB, I freelance with various media organisations. Knowing my enthusiasm for classical music, a new media outlet, specialising in promoting the arts, was arranging interviews with leaders of arts organisations, from art gallery curators to publishers of literary fiction to music festival leaders, has commissioned me to interview a chap called Stephen Zandors, who is the chief executive of a new opera festival in the west of Ireland, known as The Lough Corrib Opera Festival.

Bettina was listening to Toby with interest, but wondered at what it had to do with her.

Toby continued, 'This chap, Zandors, is a rather convivial figure who used to be the artistic director of the famous Glyndehurst opera festival in Sussex, which Verity and I attend every year. He became involved in setting up an opera festival in the beautiful remote area of Connemara, County Galway. The festival launched last year in September 1993 with performances of the original 1857 version of Giuseppe Verdi's *Simon Boccanegra*. They also produced performances of Michael Tippett's opera, *The Knot Garden*. Evidently, Zandors took a huge risk in giving up Glyndehurst for a project that could have fallen flat on its face. After all, other than the Wexford opera festival, in Ireland's southeast, the small country hadn't a reputation for high-end opera.

I had quietly re-entered the room, whilst Toby was in full flow.

'However, against all odds, the festival was a roaring success. The international critics came in droves to review both operas, which were rarities around Europe's opera houses. The standard of the performances were, evidently, superb, and that, together with typical Irish hospitality, was a winning combination.'

As music lovers all were interested in what Toby was saying, but sometimes one felt that he just liked the sound of his own voice. But where was this leading?

'Zandor's then told me about their plans for this year, taking place in September. They be following up on last year's success with yet another version of *Simon Boccanegra*, but this time, a brand new score, composed by Timothy Seda, a young up-and-coming composer, based on a lost libretto by Arrigo Boito, Verdi's collaborator on his late operas. They are also staying loyal to Michael Tippett by producing his most recent opera, titled *New Year*. The original plan was to stage three operas by Giacomo Meyerbeer over three successive festivals, starting in 1994, but, for various reasons, it was decided to postpone Meyerbeer's operas, only to commence the cycle as from the1995 festival.

'Now, here comes the bit that might be of special interest to you, Bettina. As well as those two operas, they'll be doing a third, by special request of their artistic director, the conductor, Simon Negrini, taking on Fromental Halevy's, one time famous opera, *La Juive*. It would be a big undertaking for any opera company, but for a newish tight-budgeted remote festival, to quote Stephen Zardors, "its complete madness".'

I looked at Bettina, who was flush with excitement; I wondered why this had anything to do with her. But the others, who were staring at Bettina, obviously knew something that I didn't. I was about to find out.

'Bettina, I didn't want to give him your name without your permission, but I did tell Zandors that I had a good friend who is a direct descendant of the composer Halevy. He said he would be delighted if you could make contact with him, and I said that I would pass his request on to you.

I was just finding out something about Bettina that I hadn't known, but obviously the others did, and wondered how that had come about.

Bettina said to Toby. 'Why didn't you contact me sooner about this news?'

Toby, who'd been feeling pleased with himself at his having obtained this information, straight from the horse's mouth of the Irish festival, now felt that he was being chastised by Bettina.

Putting his hand up, Toby replied that the interview had only happened last week, and knowing he was seeing Bettina at dinner the following week, thought he'd wait until they'd be all together at Alex's place.

Bettina apologised to Toby and thanked him profusely for the information, saying that she would definitely contact the gentleman if Toby would give her his contact details.

Ronald yawned. He'd never had much interest in Verdi or French nineteenth-century opera, although he was a keen fan of the music of Michael Tippett. 'I think it's time to head home,' said Ronald.

It was my turn to finish the party with an announcement that would totally surprise my friends. Bettina and I had discussed it before the guests arrived, and we'd agreed that it would be best to wait until the end of the evening to make the revelation to our friends. Our reasoning was that we didn't wish for our news to dominate the whole evening.

From feeling tired, there was a new alertness in the room, with Bettina looking a bit anxious.

'I have something to share with you. At my recent gramophone event, there were a lot of disclosures about autobiographical aspects of my novel, and you all met my three friends that were my inspiration for three characters that dominated the novel. But, what I didn't know that evening, and of course, Bettina was away so unable to attend, I know now. On the evening itself, during questions, Verity had asked me about my youthful meeting in Brighton with a young girl named Rosalind who, for different reasons, failed to go further than the one evening with me. That episode was in an early chapter of the book, and Verity wanted to know if the episode was factual, and did I ever find out what had happened to Rosalind. Well, it was indeed factual, and I now know not only what had happened to Rosalind but where she is at this very moment.'

I turned to face Bettina. 'Ladies and gentlemen, may I present Bettina Emberton, who at the age of sixteen in Brighton was then named, Rosalind Gerstein!'

There was stunned silence in the room.

Bettina thought she'd better break the spell. 'I'd been disappointed to miss Alex's hosting evening, as you know, I was away in the south of France for the whole month of January, so I didn't get a chance to read Alex's book. But when I returned home early in February, the first thing I did was get stuck into the novel. I hadn't got very far in, when I read about Dominic and Rosalind. Other than having a different first name, and by the way, he'd never did disclose his surname, the way it was described in the book, was exactly as I remembered it all those years ago. I stayed up all that night reading the book to completion, contacting Alex the next morning asking him to come around on that very day, which luckily, was a Sunday. Together, we quickly came to the conclusion that we were the very same couple who had enjoyed a fleeting teenage romantic escapade in \Brighton. As you know from the text, it went no further, as my mother stamped on any thoughts that I could have entertained the idea of a non-Jewish boyfriend.'

Ronald was the first to break the quietness in the room. So you're Jewish then?'

Bettina looked at Ronald, oddly, thinking, *'What's wrong with that guy?'*

'I think I'd made that fairy obvious, Ronald, when I was discussing Halèvy with Toby, at my house, and you were sitting right besides us, listening to our conversation.

Ronald said, 'I must have missed that bit, Bettina.'

'But the name Rosalind Gerstein?' asked Dulcie.

Bettina explained to the four what she'd previously told me. How she'd changed her name to Bettina and that she'd been briefly married to a man named Emberton.

The four looked at both Bettina and me in amazement and thought that it was time to leave the two of us on our own. Thanking us profusely for a wonderful evening on so many different levels, they departed for home.

'Phew'... what an evening!' I remarked.

Bettina and I plonked down on the sofa in sheer exhaustion, not daring to look at the time.

'I better clear up the kitchen.'

'Don't bother now, Alex, leave it all until the morning, although it is nearly morning, ha ha ha.

They seemed shell-shocked when they left.

'Yes, they did, but you took away Toby's thunder when you revealed who we have been for real.'

'About that, Bettina, I didn't know about your family connection to the composer of the opera, *La Juive.*'

'Well, 'said Bettina. 'You're obviously not as observant as Toby was when he inquired about the portrait of a Victorian gentleman on the wall of my living room.'

'Oh,' I said. 'I hadn't noticed it.'

'To be fair, Alex, you were rather distracted when you were over at my place. Some time ago, when things were bad between the two couples, I invited the four over to see if I could be of any help with their problems. Whilst there, Toby noticed the portrait.'

'And were you of any help?'

Bettina shrugged, 'I don't know, to be honest, but in any case, they seem to have sorted things out between them.'

'Were you a bit shocked at the way Verity and Dulcie spoke about their sexual appetites?'

'Are you joking, Alex? Have you forgotten what I do for a living? Believe me, I've heard much more explicit than that. I'm not the sixteen-year-old Rosalind Gerstein anymore!'

The thought crossed my mind that Bettina was probably much more sexually experienced than I was. She'd mentioned over one of our dinner dates that her husband had been a fantastic lover, and she'd been besotted with him. But she added that he was also very secretive about his family and about his business affairs, which, from what she'd gleaned he was operating only borderline legal. On the credit side, she'd told me that his divorce settlement was financially generous.

'Shall I phone for a taxi?'

On the spur of the moment, I said, 'Why don't you stay the night or what's left of it.'

'Mmm...I'm not sure I should.'

'I'm not suggesting anything sexual.'

'Oh,' Bettina chuckled. 'That's a shame, ha ha ha.'

'I'll just go and make up the bed in the spare room.'

As I stood up to leave the room, Bettina said in a quiet, throaty voice, 'Come back here, you innocent man. Having written explicit sex scenes in the novel – you obviously have an erotic imagination, even if you present yourself as rather timid.'

'I don't see myself as a timid person, Bettina. I've experienced passion in several relationships over the years, but I don't shout from the rooftops about what I've experienced, unlike my friend, Marcus, who was Ricky in the novel, who'd always show off about his conquests.'

'I think you protest too much, Alex, you don't have to explain yourself. I imagine that besides our little escapade together, early in the book, some of the latter hair-raising adventures also contain a fair amount of actuality in your real life. You've admitted that the prison narrative did indeed happen to you, so I wonder what else was factual, not fiction.

'It was a mixture of both, but I was the least naughty of the naughty boys.

'You know, when I first met you again as Alex, at my initiation evening to the gramophone club a couple of years ago, I thought you were a bit of a dull old stick and I would have been amazed that you were that lad that I'd hankered after, long after our one evening meeting in Brighton. But, now I can see what had attracted me to you back then. You project an image of yourself in a way that's not really the real you, otherwise you just couldn't have written that book, even if it had been 100 per cent fiction.'

'To be honest, I was a bit miffed that you handed me a business card at the end of the evening. I thought that was out of order, and you'd only attended to prospect for clients.'

'Ha ha-ha, there you go, Alex. There was nothing timid about you just now chastising me, and you'd be right – it was remiss of me to do so.

'To be honest, Alex, I'm not sure we'd work as a couple in a relationship. You've now retired from your career at a ridiculous early age, but I'm full on in my business and I've got plans to expand into other areas of the dating world, which has huge growth potential.'

'I wasn't seeking a relationship, Bettina. I'm happy and contended to be living on my own. What with my writing and my musical interests, I don't need anything else at this stage of my life.'

'Are you thinking of writing another book?'

'Yes, I am. My book, it seems, had caught the current zeitgeist of the popularity of opera, especially, the three Mozart/Da Ponte ones. The Joseph Losey 1979 film of *Don Giovanni* was hugely popular with the general public. It got a lot people into opera houses, who'd previously thought that opera was not for them.

'I remember once when I was in Paris, *Don Giovanni* was on the bill at the Palais Garnier, and I was minded to head for the opera house and get myself a ticket. When I arrived I immediately saw a large queue outside the box office. Realising that the performance was sold out, I joined the queue. Asking someone next to me, what was drawing the crowds to that particular performance, I was told that it was because the bass baritone, Ruggero Raimondi, was singing the title role of *Don Giovanni*, and he'd been the Don in the popular Joseph Losey film. I wasn't concerned, and was sure that I'd get a seat, or even a standing place. After all, in the 60s I queued at Covent Garden for returns, for both Maria Callas, and Joan Sutherland performances, and, had always managed to buy a ticket. But that night in Paris was only time in my opera and concert-going life that I failed to get into a performance after having joined a queue for returns.'

'So, will you be choosing another opera themed book, and if so, which composer/librettist partnership will you be thinking of?'

'Well, it's only a distant thought so far, but I'm certainly attracted to the partnership of librettist, Hugo von Hofmannsthal and composer, Richard Strauss. The partnership of Arrigo Boito and Giuseppe Verdi would have also been of interest, especially regarding the two versions of *Simon Boccanegra*, which the librettist and composer worked on together, mostly by hundreds of letters between the pair. But somebody got there before me, a chap by the name of D B Minter, whose book was recently published.'

'Oh, I see, Alex, I must look out for D B Minter's book, as I'm a great admirer of the opera, *Simon Boccanegra,* but I've only ever heard the revised version.'

'I'd just come into the room when Toby was talking about the launch of the opera festival in the west of Ireland last year ... opening with the original version of *Simon Boccanegra*.'

'Hmmm.' Bettina was furrowing her brow. 'I wonder what this man Stephen something or other, wants to talk to me about. Mind you, I would seriously consider making a trip to Ireland to get the chance to hear a fully staged production of my ancestor's opera, *La Juive*.'

'Incidentally, Bettina, on a different issue, I thought that you and Toby were flirting together at one of the gramophone events, before the two couples stopped attending, and I'm curious, as to whether the two of you have ever got together? You don't need to answer as it's really none of my business.'

'No, Alex, it would be none of your business, but since you've brought this up, let me clarify. Don't get me wrong, Toby is an attractive man, with a winning way of expressing himself, and I really like him. But you'd be wrong to think that we were ever lovers, or even contemplating going there. I know that at that particular event we were deep in conversation and some there were coming to the wrong conclusion. The fact of the matter was that Toby was consulting me on a professional basis, and as I take the notion of client confidentiality Seriously, I will say no more on the subject.

I was impressed with Bettina's refusal to gossip about our mutual friend, owing to professional etiquette. Changing tack, I asked what she thought of the relationship between Toby and Hannah.

'Well, Alex, who are we to judge as to whether the pair are a natural match? Believe me – doing what I do professionally, you'd be surprised how some unlikely couplings click with each other, whilst others, who one would assume would make a perfect couple, fail at the first hurdle.'

'Hmmm... "There's nowt as queer as folk."'

'Talking about queer folks, Alex, are you going to take me to bed...?'

I went very quiet.

'I think we owe each other that, at least, after all these years.'

I was hesitant, but replied that I didn't think it was a good idea, especially not tonight.

'Not only is it very late, but we've both had loads to drink and chatted too much. I want you to want to make love to the living and breathing "Alex" and not to the fictional character of "Dominic." '

'But it was "Dominic" that I fell for all those years ago.'

'No, Bettina, it was "Alex", posing as "Dominic." '

'I'll tell you what. You can sleep in my bed, and I'll make myself comfy on the settee down here.'

I took Bettina to my bedroom and gave her a chaste kiss on the cheek.

'Goodnight, Bettina, for what's left of it.'

Bettina did not reply, as I closed the bedroom door, taking myself a blanket from the airing cupboard and settled down on the settee for a few short hours of shut eye.

CHAPTER 42

Bettina telephoned Stephen Zandors in Ireland, having got all his details from Toby.

Stephen was friendly and charming – thrilled to be talking to an actual descendant of one of the Lough Corrib opera's featured composers for their 1994 festival. He asked her lots of questions about the family tree, Bettina replying as best as she could, explaining that the line was from her father's side, whose mother, Bettina's grandmother, was a Halèvy from France, who'd married into an Austrian family and had lived her adult life in Vienna. Without going into too much detail, she indicated that her Austrian side of the family did not survive the Nazi period, but that her father managed to get to Britain where he'd met her mother in Manchester. Stephen had listened carefully to Bettina, making the expected sympathetic words of condolences regarding her grandparents.

Stephen continued with telling Bettina how excited they all were at the festival, following an early run through of *La Juive*. The conductor, the artistic director, Simon Negrini, told the cast and the production team, that it had been a career ambition to conduct the greatest opera with a Jewish theme, as he was himself, of Jewish heritage. Negrini said that their ambition was nothing less for the festival than to be pioneers in re-establishing *La Juive* back into the world's opera houses.

'Mrs Emberton, I would like to invite you, on behalf of the festival's management, with Mr Emberton, to the festival, as our special guest. We would arrange travel and accommodation for you, plus, of course, two tickets for the opera and for any other events you may wish to attend during your stay. We would also be delighted, whilst you're with us, to give our audience a short talk on the Halèvy family. You don't have to give me an answer now, but if you let me have your address, I'll put everything in writing to you.'

'Phew... Mr Zandors, that's hugely generous of you.'

'Please call me Stephen.'

'Likewise, I'm Bettina. I would love to attend the festival and believe it or not, I've never heard the opera in a live performance, only on a recording. But Stephen, firstly, Mr Emberton and I are divorced and we're not in contact with each other. Secondly, I am more than happy to pay for my travel and accommodation, and as far as doing a talk, I'd like to have a think about that.'

The call ended with Bettina giving Stephen her address and him adding that the invitation was for two people; she could bring whoever she wanted to.

Stephen was as good as his word, A few days later a letter arrived, together with a brochure of the festivals complete programme, confirming everything that they'd discussed on the telephone. He requested that Bettina to get back to him with the dates of her arrival and her departure, and what events she wished to attend. The letter finished with asking to name the person who was accompanying her and to let him know if she was happy to give a short talk.

She thought that Stephen Zandors offer was extremely magnanimous, and she was highly excited about visiting Ireland for the first time, as well as, of course, attending at last, a full production of her an ancestor's masterpiece. But she was determined to pay for her travel and accommodation.

But who was she to invite with her? The obvious candidate would be Alex, an opera lover, who'd just published a book loosely based around Mozart's operas. The two of them had unfinished business, going back to a lifetime ago, but she was humiliated when Alex turned her offer down of them going to bed together at the end of his recent dinner party. The other candidate would be Toby, who'd interviewed Zandors about his festival, and had told him about her connection with the composer Halévy. So, yes, she would ask Toby and Verity to accompany her to the festival.

What made her decision not to invite Alex to the festival the only course of action she could have made – was due to an incident that occurred soon after she received Zandors invitation.

It had been a unusually quiet day at Bettina's office in London, with no new client consultations in her diary and no existing clients contacting her with feedback about their current dating introductions, either positive or negative.

Then, out of the blue, a journalist from the bestselling newspaper, The Sunday News, telephoned Bettina. The journalists, a well spoken, charming man by the name of Hector Bolling, explained that his newspaper was running a series on the dating industry in their Sunday magazine, and they had a spare slot in the following week's edition; the paper would love to include a feature on the matchmaking scheme Love Me Dc.

Bettina, having been caught by surprise, wasn't sure how to respond. In general, she was sceptical of journalists, keeping them at bay, but still conscious of the old adage that 'there's no such thing as bad publicity. '

In her mind, Bettina had lots of interesting stories to tell about her matchmaking scheme and how different clients react to dating introductions. But her mind had gone blank, and nothing in particular came to mind. So without really thinking of the consequences of confidentiality, she blurted out the story of Alex's novel, and how she discovered to her amazement that a boy-meets-girl teenage infatuation written about in the early part of a novel that an acquaintance of hers had recently published, and was supposedly total fiction, but it transpired that it was partly autobiographical, and the real-life young couple were her and the author.

The journalist was ecstatic, realising he'd got a juicy scoop. Hector Bolling tried to get the name of the author or, even more valuable to him, the title of the book. Bettina had the sense not to reveal either of the requests.

When the journalist hung up, Bettina had felt very uneasy at what she'd revealed to Bolling, but the damage had been done.

I'd spilt my morning coffee when I saw the article in the Sunday Press, which Bolling had expanded to make the article sensational. Knowing the reputation of the particular newspaper, they were more than likely to be able to track me down, embarrass me for stating on the book's preface that the characters were pure fiction, when in fact I'd been writing about my own life, therefore, harming future sales of the book.

I was livid and telephoned Bettina, letting rip, accusing her of being dishonest and disloyal. Bettina, shocked at my anger, tried to explain that she hadn't disclosed my name or the title of his book, and besides, I had never expressed to her anything about confidentiality, so I had no right to call her dishonest.

I slammed down the phone.

When I'd calmed down I'd realised that I'd totally forgotten to include Bettina in the confidentiality clause that all the others privy to the books genesis had given their word to honour my request. Still, Bettina being a woman of the world, should have known how journalists and popular newspapers treat stories. She never should have gone there with the scurrilous Hector Bolling.

Bettina contacted Toby, thanking him again for introducing her to Stephen Zandors, telling him how pleased she at the way the phone call had panned out. When she asked Toby as to whether he and Verity would like to join her at the festival in September, he seemed surprised that she was inviting them and not Alex.

'I thought Alex would be your obvious choice, Bettina.'

'The less said about Alex the better,' was her sharp response.

Toby was thinking that some serious falling out must have occurred between them. That would be such as shame as they'd seemed such a good team together, at Alex's dinner party.

'Well. Yes. Bettina, the festival is something I would love to attend, but I would have to consult Verity, to check what her plans are for September.'

Toby did check with Verity and she told him that she and Dulcie were going back to Inglewood Health Hydro together again for two weeks in September. When Toby checked back with Bettina as to the exact dates of the festival, it transpired that the dates clashed with the fortnight the women had booked to go to Inglewood.

Bettina wondered if it was a good idea to invite Toby without Verity. People there would think they were a couple, and the last thing she wanted was to get tangled up in Toby's complicated domestic life. But in the end she decided that Toby had earned the right to be her guest as he'd engineered the contact with Zandors in the first place.

When she spoke to Zandors again she explained the situation to him, namely, that Toby was just a friend and they'd need two separate rooms for the accommodation. Zandors was delighted that Bettina had invited the man who'd interviewed him about the festival, whom he considered a decent and interesting chap. Bettina had concluded the call saying that she'd get back to him about his suggestion of her giving a talk on Halèvy at the festival.

Bettina realised that although she was proud of being a descendant from such a renowned figure, she knew less about him and his family tree than she perhaps let others think that she did. In truth, as a youngster she hadn't shown much interest in her father's ancestry, other than **sympathy for the Nazi tragedy** that engulfed the family. In any case the name, Halèvy meant little to most people these days, even those who had an interest in opera. After all, Halèvy wasn't a Mozart, or a Puccini. In the twentieth century, Halèvy fame was more to do with him being the father-in-law of Georges Bizet, the composer of the opera, *Carmen*, than for his own works.

Perhaps, she'd contact her father in Israel, who'd be able to give her further information about the family heritage. But she'd lost touch with her parents since her marriage to the non-Jewish Peter, and she didn't wish to bring up old personal wounds with her now elderly parents. All she really knew was what her father had told her at the time she started to show an interest in opera. He'd said it to her in an off-hand manner, as it was nothing special to have a once-famous composer as a family ancestor. Her father was extremely reluctant to talk about his family that he'd left behind in Vienna whilst he managed to escape the Nazi claw. Perhaps he felt guilty and didn't wish to be reminded of those times. Besides, although growing up in the cultural hot house of Vienna, Bettina's father had never shown any interest in opera. When Bettina first left home to set up on my own, her father gave her the portrait of Halèvy as a gift; that was what Toby had spotted when he was in her house, and that observation had indirectly led to Bettina receiving the festival invite.

Bettina telephone Stephen, with her decision not to give a talk at the festival and thanking him for offering her the opportunity. She explained that she didn't feel her skill set included public speaking. She added that it would be understandable if his kind invitation was rescinded. Stephen was having none of it and doubled down on the invitation, saying he'd be waiting for her travel dates and her choice of events she wished to attend.

Over coffee in a St Albans cafe, Bettina and Toby had a good long perusal at the festival brochure. Although, Toby had outlined some of the programme at Alex's recent dinner party, they weren't concentrating, as they were curious as to where his story was leading.

They obviously wanted tickets for the main event, a fully staged production of Fromental Halévy's grand opera, *La Juive*. As neither of them were dedicated lovers of contemporary opera, the two of them considered requesting tickets for just one of the two productions on offer. The choice was between, Michael Tippett's 1989 opera, *New Year*, following up on the festival's 1993 production of the composer's 1970 opera, *The Knot Garden,* or a brand new work, commissioned by the festival, the music written by a young up-and-coming composer, Timothy Seda. Seda had been given an Italian libretto that had been handed down to the festival's artistic director, Simon Negrini, through family connections. The libretto, supposedly written by the Italian poet and librettist, Arrigo Boito, who offered it to Verdi as an alternative take on the composer's great opera *Simon Boccanegra* that the two artists were then revising. As the libretto contained a gay element to the narrative, Verdi rejected it outright and the libretto languished with Negrini family members for generations. The festival had also commissioned a translator, as Seda had insisted, that the operas' text should be in the English language. So, the whole project was like putting old wine into a brand new bottle.

'Perhaps it looks a bit greedy,' said Toby, but I quite fancy both of the contemporary operas. I suggest that you ask Zandors for tickets for the three operas, and any other events we wish to attend, we book and pay for whilst there. What do you think?

'Well, I see that Stephen Zandors wife, the famous cellist Helena Mentones, is giving a solo recital, playing all six of Bach's cello suites, and I wouldn't like to miss that.'

'OK then, let's go for all three operas plus the Mentones recital. I'm sure that Zandors will be pleased that we'll be attending four events, even though he's paying for the seats. Ha ha ha.'

'That means, though, that we'll have to attend the whole fortnight of the festival, as the two contemporary operas are being performed on separate weeks. I thought originally of one week there.'

'Would that be a problem, Bettina?'

'Not really, as it would give us a chance to take in a bit of sightseeing, having never visited Ireland before.'

Stephen was as good as his word. His post included airline tickets, hotel vouchers and two tickets for their choice of events. Bettina let Toby know all the details and they both expressed their excitement about the visit to the Lough Corrib Opera Festival, in early autumn.

Roll on September!

CHAPTER 43

Ireland,
County Galway,
September 1994.

The 1994 Lough Corrib Opera festival opened with a bang, with fireworks on the lake after the mayor of Galway officially got the two-week jamboree under way. It was only the second year of its existence, following the 1993 festival that had got the whole madcap initial idea to a triumphant conclusion. The challenge was to not only maintain the excellence of the previous year but to even exceed that success.

Building on the previous year, when the festival offered two opera productions, 1994 was presenting three operas, including a world premiere, with the composer conducting his own opera. Besides, the eighty-nine-year-old composer of the opera, *New Year*, Sir Michael Tippett, who was unable to be at the festival for the previous year's production of his opera, *The Knot Garden*, because of ill health, would be the festival's highly esteemed guest speaker. There would be a reunion with the artistic director, as Negrini and Tippett went back a long way. Negrini had been the composer's assistant at Schoffs, Tippett's music publisher in London, during 1959, when Negrini was a young man of age twenty-four. They'd even been on holiday together in Cornwall, with Negrini helping the composer with ideas for his second opera, *King Priam*.

The schedule of events over the festivals two weeks had been tweaked slightly since the publication of the festival brochure at the beginning of the year. Week one would present three performance of Halèvy's *La Juive* and three of performances Seda's new opera on the *Simon Boccanegra's* story, now titled, *Boccanegra, the Doge of Genoa*, so as not to be confused with Verdi's opera. On the first Sunday of the festival, Simon Negrini, would again, as in 1993, conduct a youth orchestra from the Galway music college in an orchestral concert. The programme would be: Samuel Barber's cello concerto, with Negrini's daughter, Helena Mentones, as the cello soloist. The second half of the programme would kick-off with *Vitava*, also known as The Mouldau, the second and most popular movement of Smetana's most important work. The six movements are titled *Ma Vlast* (My Homeland). To round things off, Negrini decided to add Respighi's third tone-poem, 'Feste Romane' ('Roman Festivals') to the first two of the cycle, 'The Fountains of Rome' and the 'Pines of Rome' that they'd programmed the previous year. Negrini had chosen a real international programme to stress that the new festival was international in its outlook. An American concerto, a Czech tone poem, in celebration of the newly (1992) created country of the Czech Republic, and a colourful description of Rome, to honour Italy, which was such an important country for opera.

Sir Michael Tippett would give a talk on the Wednesday morning, a much anticipated event.

Week two would present further three performances of *La Juive* and three performances of Tippett's *New Year*. Helena Mentones would perform the six Bach cello suites over two morning concerts. The three first suites were to be played on the Wednesday, and, the final three suites on the Thursday. The final day of the festival would be a repeat of the 1993 programme format. It would be another gala concert to raise funds for future festivals which had been incredibly successful the previous year.

When Bettina and Toby arrived at the festival on the opening day of the festival, having flown to Knock, west of Ireland airport in the neighbouring County Mayo, and driven in a hired car to the festival through stunning scenery, Stephen Zandors greeting them warmly, being as friendly and charming as he'd been on the various telephone calls with Bettina. He made sure that all the main players of the festival were on hand to meet and greet their special guests. They were introduced to Simon Negrini and to his daughter, who was also Zandor's wife, Helena Mentones. Bettina had heard Mentones perform several times in London, both in chamber music at the Wigmore Hall, and at with a concerto at the Barbican concert hall. She was definitely a fan of the American cellist. The well-known Israeli baritone, Dov Katz, was not performing during the current festival, but as he was Negrini's life partner, was there at Negrini's side. When introduced to him, his wide smile and friendly demeanour made Bettina take to him immediately. Last but certainly not least, they were introduced to May and Harvey Donnell, the owners of the country house estate and founders of the festival. They came across as a totally down-to-earth couple, a long way from corporate big wigs that both Bettina and Toby had come across in their professional life.

They'd all been thrilled to learn that Bettina's family tree led directly to the composer of the festival's most anticipated opera presentation, Halévy's *La Juive,* and thanked her profusely for attending the festival.

Stephen had explained to Bettina and Toby that it wasn't possible to accommodate them in the main house, as the limited amount of rooms there had been allocated to cast members and production team only.

They were given two separate double rooms at Renvyle House Hotel, about an hour's drive away from the festival's location, and a shuttle bus was on hand to transport guests between the two sites.

Initially, Bettina and Toby were disappointed that they weren't being accommodated closer to the performing venue, but once they arrived at the handsome looking hotel, having been driven through glorious Connemara, they were warmly greeted by the hotel's manager, the irrepressible Ken Moyes, who'd just received an award from the Good Hotel Guide of Great Britain and Ireland. The award was for exceptional hospitality.

Bettina and Toby hadn't booked the performance for the opening night of the festival. So they unwound at Renvyle, enjoying a good walk around the hotel grounds, which led down to the seashore. A few drinks in the bar were followed by dinner in the restaurant over a nice bottle of wine.

Relaxing over their meal, conversation, other than practical matters engaged with during the journey, started to flow.

'Don't get me wrong, Bettina, I'm delighted that you extended your invite to me, but I'm still curious as to why you didn't ask Alex to accompany you here?

'Hmmm, Alex and I had a fall out, which was actually my fault.'

Bettina explained to Toby what had happened with the journalist, Hector Bolling, and Alex's furious reaction when he read Bolling's article in *The Sunday News*, which had been sexed up.

'But, as you hadn't divulged anyone's name or book titles, what's the problem?'

'Alex was convinced that Bolling would find out that he was the man in the story, and that would have seriously harmed sales of his book, as making him seem dishonest, as he has a blurb on his book claiming that all the characters had been fictional, with no resemblance to any real person.'

'Hmmm, well, all authors of fiction have that disclaimer, but my understanding is that most novels contain a certain element of autobiography. But surely, Bettina, you'd agreed to the confidentially clause that all of us had sworn to?'

'Are you forgetting that I wasn't there the night Alex had revealed everything, introducing the friends he'd used as the main characters?

'I was unaware of the confidentially agreement. Alex had obviously meant to include me in the clause, but following the subsequent shock of revealing ourselves to each other, as the real Rosalind and Dominic, we'd both been all over the place and it got overlooked.'

'Well, yes, it must have come as a big shock to both of you when you rediscovered each other. I mean, what were the odds on that happening?'

'It would be a million to one!'

'So, in that case, it's such a shame that you've turned against each other.'

'Oh, yes, you're right, but there's more to it than that, Toby, I shouldn't really be telling you this, but...'

'Hold it there. Let's order another bottle of wine.'

The waiter bought over a bottle and poured into each glass, after Toby had waived away the waiters offer for one of them to taste the wine.

There was a short silence between them as they sipped the wine.

'OK, Toby, what happened the night of Alex's dinner party, after we'd told you and the others, just before you were leaving, that we actually were in real life, the young boy and girl that had met in Brighton, as set out in the book, Alex and I spent hours talking about all sort of things. But, to cut to the chase, very late into the night, I offered to go to bed with Alex, and to my surprise, he turned me down, which upset me. It was a blow to my confidence.'

'Bloody hell, Bettina, I certainly wouldn't turn you down!' Toby uttered with a wolfish grin on his face.

'There's no chance of that, Toby.'

'But seriously, Bettina, what reason did he give?'

'Well, I said that we owed it to each other and that we'd waited a long time. But he replied that he wanted me to desire Alex and not Dominic, and didn't feel that was the case.'

'Hmmm, I suppose I could see his point, said Toby, but in my book, a man should never turn down an offer from a beautiful woman. It may never come around again. Ha ha ha.'

Turning the tables on Toby, Bettina asked about him and Hannah.

'What do you want to know?'

'Well, not to be unkind, Hannah is quite austere in her looks, dress and manner, and it is hard to see her in a sexual role.'

Toby, not looking too pleased, responded. 'As someone who's in the dating business, I'm surprised at your comments. You of all people shouldn't judge a woman by her looks or on her general demeanour!'

Bettina, feeling chastised, made the excuse that she only wanted to open up the discussion about him, and move on from talking about her and Alex.

'Fair enough, Bettina, but there's something you should know about Hannah, but this is definitely confidential and I don't want all of the gramophone members to have something else to gossip about.'

'Despite evidence to the contrary I can be trusted to keep my mouth shut. After all, no one knows about you having consulted me professionally, about seeking an affair.'

'By the way, are you still running a scheme for "affairs"?'

'No, it wasn't a practical scheme. Not enough women were coming forward.

'Funnily enough, after I'd abandoned the scheme and went back to introductions for singles only, the problem I'd encountered previously, that not enough men were coming forward, totally disappeared, and from that day onwards, I've never been short of male clients.'

'Good to hear it, Bettina, that's great. Anyway, back to Hannah. The gramophone members always thought that Hannah joined the gramophone club the same way as everyone else – that's moving to the area and seeing the notice in the local library. But it wasn't the case at all.'

'A situation had occurred at work some years past, me being accused of sexual misconduct with a junior staff member. I was entirely innocent as the young woman had attached herself to me and I rejected her. As the saying goes, "there's nothing like a woman scorned." I was put on gardening leave and there was a tribunal, three men and three women with a woman chairperson. The woman in question was Hannah Longsmith, then, as now, head of an important city financial institution. When it was put to the vote for a decision on my fate, the three women members of the panel found in favour of my accuser and the three men on the panel found in favour of me. Hannah, as the chair, had the deciding vote. She'd chewed over all the evidence of the case overnight and came down in my favour. If it had gone the other way, I would have lost the job that I loved and lost my pension. Hannah had always insisted that she'd been completely inscrutable in her role at the time and judged the case purely by the evidence in front of her. Even if I'd tried to charm her she would have been immune to the tactic.

Anyway, we kept in touch and when she bought a house in their area, and I found out that she was a serious music lover, I recommenced the gramophone club.'

'Hmmm... How interesting, Toby, but did Verity know any of this?'

'Yes, Bettina, Verity was with me all the way and I had her total support. But other than Verity, you're the only other person that knows about my travails at the time, and Hannah's role in my reprieve.'

'So, did you feel that you owed her and eventually ask her out on a date?'

'Absolutely not, the two things were totally separate. I'd never thought of her in dating terms, I just respected her for being so knowledgeable about finance and economics, an area that I, like most people in the arts or in the media, know very little about and care for even less. But the thing about Hannah was that she straddled both disciplines. She's not a superficial music lover; she has a knowledge and understanding of a wide variety of composers from the medieval to the modern period. But even more impressive was that she kept her light under a bushel, never showing off her superior knowledge to any of the gramophone members, not like my dear friend Ronald, who could not miss an opportunity to tell everyone how much he knows about his favoured composers.'

'Well, yes, Ronald, let's not bring him in to our discussion. So, you fell for Hannah intellectually, not physically?'

'Both, actually; I'm sure you remember that abortive consultation we had. I'm sure that I mentioned my attraction to masculine looking women, and you seemed a bit surprised at that. Well, it was only after that consultation that it came to me in a flash that what I was looking for was actually staring me in the face; that was Hannah. It all happened quite quickly after that, and the rest is history.'

'Does Hannah mind about you being here with me?'

Toby laughed. 'She doesn't mind at all. As far as Hannah is concerned, she wouldn't care if we had sex together. She's not like that. She's the most liberal person I've ever known. Sex for Hannah is like eating a delicious meal. Great while it lasts but instantly forgettable. That's what I love about her, but she's always discreet. I'm a lucky man to have both Hannah and Verity.'

'And are things still good between you and Verity?'

'There absolutely capital. I imagine that both she and Dulcie are having a great time at their health hydro.'

'You mean, Dulcie will be flirting with women, whilst Verity is eying up the young men.'

'Ha ha, yes exactly, it all makes perfect sense, Bettina. Both women will arrive home glowing with good health and happiness from anything else they may have got up to, and who benefits from that – Ronald and my good self, of course.

'But I would admit that if I hadn't started my relationship with Hannah, Verity would never had considered doing what's she's doing. With Dulcie, it's slightly different. I always suspected that she was a closet lesbian; she's always had eyes on Verity. Her marriage with Ronald was never a romantic affair, but they rubbed along together, until they didn't. Again, it was only when Verity broke away from living a conventional sexual life that it encouraged Dulcie to do the same.'

Bettina was fascinated listening to Toby, confirming in her mind that her original idea to offer an 'affairs' programme at Love Me Do wasn't such a stupid idea after all, It had just needed a different type of marketing; a more subtle approach to attract the women.

Coming out of her reverie, Bettina said, 'So all's well that ends well, with the Elden's and the Henrow's.'

'Well, Mary Whitehouse wouldn't approve, ha ha ha, but it works for us and I believe it works for our friends, Dulcie and Ronald.'

'I make no moral judgement Toby, after all, who am I to talk, having experimented with an "affairs" programme in my business. But personally I couldn't be in that sort of set up. If I ever embarked on another relationship, and I doubt I ever will, it would have to be a 100 per-cent monogamous one.'

'I'm sure you're being sincere in what you're saying, Bettina; no disrespect, but it's easy to make that sort of pronouncement when being single and feeling idealistic. Believe me, Verity and I were the most romantic and idealistic couple of all times in our early years together, but over a long-term relationship, things can change, and different needs sometimes emerge.

'Anyway, for what it's worth and from everything I've heard and seen, you and Alex were made for each other, and you should try and repair the breakdown of your friendship.'

'Hmmm, you must have drunk too much wine, Toby. Yes, I would over time like to renew our friendship; after all, we go back a long way. But – a full on relationship with Alex? I don't think so... we're not suited at all.'

'But, Bettina, you recently asked Alex to take you to bed.'

'Mmm, I must have drunk too much wine on that night!'

'Bettina, I've been thinking back to your rupture with Alex. It could be that he's being overprotective about his novel. I've been reading about new and future trends in fiction writing, and it seems that autobiographical novels are being predicted to be the next coming thing. Obviously, we know that Alex's book was, accidentally, partly based on his early life and the life of his friends. However, Alex's ambition was to write about opera, and in particular, Mozart's Da Ponte operas, but in a contemporary guise. That, you must admit, he did admirably. But, at the start of writing, it seemed that he was stuck for characterisations and nearly gave up before he got going. So, it was only when he thought about using who and what he knew, that he was able to continue. I don't think it should be anything to be embarrassed about. Furthermore, if that knowledge was made public, it wouldn't affect the sales of the book; it just may enhance them.'

Bettina was thinking seriously about what Toby was saying and said, 'But that decision would be for Alex and Alex only.'

'Of course, and the timing wouldn't be right at the moment. But maybe, once the dust has settled, he might appreciate the point I've just made. I managed to obtain contact details of his boyhood friend, Marcus, Ricky in the novel, who lives in the US, as does Alex's other two friends. It was Ricky of course, in the book, who insisted that Dominic had to visit his friend, Finley, on the day the two of you had planned to spend together. Would the outcome at the time, between the two of you, be any different, if you'd had that extra day together in Brighton?'

'Who knows,' responded Bettina trying to hold back a yawn. 'I'm getting really tired, Toby, I think we'd better call it a night. I'm sure the staff would like to close up the restaurant.'

'Yes, of course, Bettina, it's been a great evening and I've so much enjoyed our chat.'

'So have I, Toby.' Bettina stood up, having decided to head up to her room; she gave Toby a big hug as she made her way out of the dining room. Toby sat for a few minutes until a waiter arrived with a bill for him to sign. He duly did, apologising for keeping the table for so long, handing the waiter a tip. The waiter thanked him and wished him goodnight. Toby left the room, heading towards reception and the front doors, having decided to get a breath of fresh air. He wanted to chew over in

his head the fascinating exchange with Bettina before retiring to
his room for the night.

322

CHAPTER 44

The following few days saw Bettina and Toby fully engaged in the festival events. Hearing remarks around the festival bars and lounges, it seemed that the first performance on the previous evening of the opera, *La Juive* was an absolute sensation. For the majority of the audience, it would have been their first encounter with the opera. As *La Juive* was a rarity in the world's opera houses a consensus had built up that the opera was perhaps not of the highest quality. But the word around the festival was puzzlement as to why one is not hearing this work on a regular basis, at Covent Garden and elsewhere. The truth was that *La Juive* was once considered not only an absolute banker of an opera but truly a great masterpiece. The opera was placed at the heart of nineteenth-century French grand opera, which besides, Halèvy, also included Giacomo Meyerbeer, another Jewish composer, not French as Halèvy was, but a German who'd conquered Paris with his grand operas. The following few years, would see the Lough Corrib Opera Festival staging an ongoing series of Meyerbeer's most famous operas. The problem with the operas by Halèvy, Meyerbeer and others, was that after the Second World War, with the age of musical modernism at its height, extravagant French grand operas, in five acts, opulent scenery and an obligatory ballet included had gone out of fashion, and those operas vanished from the opera houses' repertory. The festival's artistic director, and chief conductor of the festival, Simon Negrini, having persuaded his friend and son-in-law, Stephen Zandors, to stage *La Juive* at the current festival, would subsequently be on a mission around Europe, where he regularly conducted at the leading opera houses, to take on Halèvy's masterwork and bring it back to life. Opera lovers deserved nothing less.

The evening's opera was the world premiere of *Boccanegra, the Doge of Genoa*, composed and conducted by Timothy Seda, with a newly discovered libretto by Arrigo Boito. The world's leading opera critics were in attendance, even some who'd been a bit snooty about reviewing *La Juive*, were eager to write about the opera premiere with such a fascinating backstory. In the end the backstory was possibly the most interesting thing about the opera.

Musically, Verdi's great score, for both the 1857 and 1881 versions of *Simon Boccanegra*, was hugely missed, and although Seda's rather anaemic music had its moments, especially the evocative orchestral interludes, overall it was small beer from a young composer who was just finding his feet. Some commentators didn't really believe that the libretto had been written by Boito, and there'd been no proof that in fact it had been. The Negrini Italian family relatives had handed it to Simon Negrini, during a run of the 1857 version of *Simon Boccanegra* in Venice. It was during that stay in Venice that Negrini discovered that he was related to the tenor, Carlo Negrini, who'd sang the role of Gabrielle Adorno at the premiere of the 1857 version of *Simon Boccanegra* in Venice. It had also been rumoured that some critics took against the new opera due to it having a gay element, which would be surprising in the late twentieth century. It was no wonder, the libretto didn't pass muster with Verdi back in 1880. In any event, it was a great coup for a brand new festival, only in the second year of its existence, to stage a controversial world premiere, with an old libretto, which might, or might not, have been written by Boito.

Bettina and Toby were kinder to the work than some of the critics. They thought that away from the hothouse of an international opera festival, maybe with student performances at music colleges, or at small touring companies, the opera might just fare better. At least the opera was short in duration – one act only lasting ninety minutes. It allowed Bettina and Toby to enjoy a dinner after the performance at a still reasonable hour!

On the following night, Bettina and Toby were sitting in the festival theatre in eager anticipation of finally experiencing a performance of *La Juive*. Negrini entered the pit, turned to the audience, bowed to great applause, lifted his baton and the orchestra started to play the overture. Knowing the music from a recording, Bettina was looking forward to hearing the arias, ensembles and choruses, she'd become familiar with, having played the records over and over again. But listening to a recording was not the same as experiencing a staged performance. Bettina had known that the plot of the opera was a tragedy with a horrific ending, but a lot of nineteenth-century operas, with catchy tunes and famous beautiful arias, were in the context of a gruesome drama. One of Verdi's most popular operas, *Il Trovatore*, contained many memorable tuneful numbers, but its ghastly tragic conclusion was sometimes overlooked, whilst audiences wallowed in the music. Uncannily, the final scene of *Il Trovatore*, was, dramatically, similar to the denouement of *La Juive*.

The performance of *La Juive* was sung in the original French, but with subtitles, so that one could follow the drama word for word. What Bettina was seeing acting out on the stage was personal for her. The opera, set in the early fifteenth century, had been updated in the festivals production, to the fascist period of the 1930s. Watching pure antisemitism being portrayed on the stage was painful for her. During the first interval whilst Toby went to order drinks from the bar, Bettina locked herself in the ladies loo and cried her eyes out. Her emotions were mixed. Hearing the music, which was being performed fantastically well, gave her happy memories of childhood and adolescence; however, watching the action on the stage brought back family history that she'd buried away deep in her psyche. The breakdown of her relationship with her parents saddened her. Her father's family, murdered by the Nazi's, was rarely spoken about at home, as was his family tree that led, through his French mother, to the composer of the very opera that she was watching. She wondered how much antisemitism her ancestor, Halèvy, had suffered from, despite the overwhelming success of his opera. She wasn't sure whether she could continue watching the rest of the performance, and had she been on her own, she would have left the theatre. But as she was with Toby, it would have been rude to do so. She wiped away her tears, refreshed her makeup, put a mask of a smile on her face and made her way back into the auditorium.

The finale to the opera was every bit of gruesome as had been expected. The production hadn't shied away from the absolute horror of the ending. Dramatically, it was pure theatre, brilliantly done by the director, but for Bettina, it had been a representation of real life, specifically her own family's life history. As soon as the performance was over, the audience exploding into wild applause, Bettina felt that she had to get away and couldn't bring herself to join in the clapping and stamping. She made an excuse to Toby and headed for the exit. She walked around the lake – the evening was still showing a fading natural light – trying to pull herself together, as she had to get the shuttle bus, with Toby, back to their hotel in Renvyle.

Back at Renvyle...Bettina apologised to Toby for having been a wet blanket throughout the evening, but Toby had understood how much the opera must have affected her emotionally, and he reacted as the perfect gentleman towards his friend. Bettina had felt unable to join Toby for a late supper in the restaurant, excusing herself to go off to her bed. Toby didn't fancy eating on his own, so he went off to the bar, where the manager and entertainer, Ken Moyle, was singing an Irish ditty, accompanying himself on a guitar. The bar was packed, mostly with men, with a few women scattered around the room. The men, including Moyle, were all drinking pints with the women on shorts. The atmosphere was noisy and lively but good humoured nevertheless. Toby got himself a pint and soaked up the vibe in the room. It was just what he needed following an intense evening of opera, together with Bettina's high voltage reaction, at having finally experienced a live performance of her ancestors greatest, most popular, but harrowing work.

The following morning Bettina had been back to her old cheerful self. She apologised again for having been such poor company the previous evening. She decided, that having got the angst of the work out of her system, the opera needed another visit to just wallow in the fabulous music and great singing from a star cast. Toby was happy enough to see *La Juive* again, making the point that, despite Negrini's determination to champion the opera, who knew if they'd ever get a chance to hear it again in an opera house...

That evening they attended the orchestral concert they hadn't originally booked to hear. Buying tickets at the box office as well as tickets for the next performance of *La Juive*, they enjoyed hearing a young orchestra play their hearts out for maestro Negrini, in works by Smetana and Respighi. But the real sensation of the concert, was hearing the cellist, Helena Mentones, as soloist in Samuel Barber's lyrical and virtuosic cello concerto, composed in 1945. A great performance lovingly accompanied by her father, Negrini, conducting his youthful band.

They enjoyed a couple of days sightseeing around Connemara and even took a ferry out to the Island, Inishbofin, a beautiful scenic spot with a small residential community but without motor vehicles of any kind. They ate a lobster lunch on the sea front and strolled down to the beach. It was a gloriously sunny day and quite warm for September. Relaxing on the white sandy beach they imagined being in the Caribbean, not in rainy old Ireland!

The second time they'd attended a performance of *La Juive*, Bettina took the drama in her stride and gloried in the hit numbers of the score and the overall musical performance was even more assured than at the previous show, everyone singing and playing with absolute confidence. Having seats near the orchestra pit, Bettina and Toby couldn't keep their eyes off the conductor, Simon Negrini, who'd coaxed the singers and orchestral players, mouthing every syllable of the text with the singers and looking at his players with love in his eyes, conveying his absolute belief in Halèvy's creation. Unlike previously, this time, Bettina and Toby, stayed for all clapping and standing ovations for the cast and especially for maestro Negrini.

CHAPTER 45

Hertfordshire,

England.

I was at home on my own listening to a new recording that I'd recently purchased. The recording was of *The Alpine Symphony*, by Richard Strauss, the composer's largest orchestral work, depicting climbing a mountain from dawn to dusk. The huge orchestra required, including a wind machine, cowbells, two sets of timpani, an organ, and up to twenty horns. I had been thinking that the piece would be a great one to programme at a future gramophone event that I'd be hosting. Perhaps it could be a whole R Strauss evening, including *The Alpine Symphony*, some opera excerpts and a selection of his songs, which were many and varied. With my mind full of Strauss programme planning, annoyingly, the telephone rang. I turned the music off and answered the phone, wondering who was calling.

'Hello Alex, Ronald here, Ronald Henrow.' I chuckled to myself. What other man, named Ronald, did I know? Besides, I'd recognise his odd-sounding voice straight away without announcing his full name.

'Hi Ronald, how are you?'

'Yes, yes, all's good.'

Wondering what Ronald was phoning me about, I prolonged the introduction by asking him about Dulcie.

'Dulcie's at her health hydro in Berkshire with Verity and from I hear, they're having a whale of a time there.'

'Oh right, that's good to hear.'

'Listen, Alex, did you know that Toby was in Ireland for.... that? What's the festival called? Was it something to do with Lake Corrib?

'Do you mean, Ronald, The Lough Corrib Opera Festival? I didn't know about Toby's whereabouts, actually. But what's that got to do with me?'

'Alex, it's got everything to do with you. Bettina is there with Toby!'

'Hmmm... so what?'

Ronald was beginning to become exasperated with Alex's casual response. Trying to keep calm, he continued.

'Look Alex, please be serious and listen to me. I'm calling you as a friend to mark your cards. I've known Toby for a long time. He's a dear friend, but he can't resist an attractive woman, which you must agree, Bettina would definitely fit that description. Don't get me wrong, Toby is a gentleman and would abide by Bettina's wishes, if she made them clear to Toby from the off. But they will be together for two whole weeks in a hot-house atmosphere, away from friends and colleagues, attending opera, concerts, enjoying meals and sightseeing in beautiful Connemara. Besides all that, Bettina would surely be emotionally affected by hearing her ancestor's opera, in a live performance, and as Toby would be by her side, well, who knows how her emotions would express themselves.'

Alex thought that Ronald was being surprisingly articulate but wasn't sure what any of what he said had anything to do with him.

'Ronald, am I missing something here?'

'Oh, you fool, don't you see? Toby had no need for Bettina, but you have. He has a wife that he loves and a mistress who he's besotted over. If the two of them got together in Ireland, for Toby, it would be just ships in the night, but in my observation, Bettina, besides giving the appearance of being a tough business operator, is in fact, a vulnerable woman, and Toby is an easy man to fall in love with. But if that happens, it will be disastrous for them both.'

Alex didn't understand Ronald's concern. He had no romantic intentions towards Bettina, especially following the journalist episode and previously turning down her offer to go to bed with him.

'Look, Ronald, I really appreciate your worry on the matter, but I've no claim on Bettina, and I'm not responsible for Toby, however much \I'm fond of him as a dear friend.'

'You just don't get it, do you, Alex? It's obvious to your friends that you and Bettina are meant to be with each other. Fate has conspired for the two of you to meet again by chance after thirty-four years. If that's not an omen that you're meant for each other then I don't know what is!'

I thought that Ronald was lots of things but one thing I hadn't considered about him... that he was a 'romantic.'

'Ronald, with regard to my love life, Bettina and I aren't the Rosalind and Dominic from 1960. Besides, as you know from the book, we only knew each other for a few short hours. As well as that, Bettina and I had serious fallout recently.'

As if he hadn't heard what I'd just said – Ronald ploughed on. 'I think you should get over to that opera festival. It's on for another week; Bettina and Toby would be there the whole of the second week. I'll tell you what, we'll go together.'

'But you don't like opera, especially of the nineteenth-century variety.'

'You're right about that, Alex. I doubt that I could sit through Halevy's *La Juive*, with all due respects to Bettina, but I believe they're performing a Michael Tippett opera during week two of the festival, and as you know, I'm a great fan of Tippett.'

'So, you have it all worked out, Ronald. Let me sleep on it and I'll ring you in the morning and let you know one way or another.'

'OK... but if you let this opportunity pass you by, you'll regret it for the rest of your life. Goodnight Alex.' Ronald put down the receiver.

Despite my initial scepticism of Ronald's suggestion, which I thought was a ridiculous idea, some little acorn in the back of mind, prompted me not to reject it out of hand. Ronald was such a strange fellow, but yet again, he surprised me with what was a pure act of friendship. After all, why would he have bothered to phone me with what seemed to me to be a hair brained proposal, if he hadn't been thinking of my welfare?

The call had unsettled me and I couldn't continue to listen to large scale, Richard Strauss. I switched the music to Bach's *Goldberg Variations*, played on the piano by Glenn Gould. I always relaxed to that disc. I poured myself a whisky and water and sat in contemplation.

I reviewed everything that had gone on between Bettina and I since the shock of our incredible discovery, that we were who'd we'd once been. We've spent hours each describing our life's journey since the innocent times of adolescents, but it was hard to put ourselves back into the youngsters of 1960. Memories become hazy after such a long time gap, but my mature analysis of what I'd felt on that auspicious night in Brighton, when I was a lad of seventeen, was that I'd fallen in love with love. I'd been on holiday with Marcus Elliot, who'd been older and more experienced than me. My influences of 'love' hadn't come from girlfriends, as I'd not had a girlfriend before Brighton, but from

Hollywood romantic films, which I'd been addicted to as a teenager. Meeting Rosalind that night at the club, I'd thought that I'd been a lead character in a film, and as in the films, once we'd had our first kiss on the beach, we would have been in love, and the start of being together for the rest of our lives.

The problem with meeting Rosalind, aka Bettina, again, was that trying to recapture that Hollywood romantic film ideal had been a futile exercise, which coloured my thinking that although I'd desired Rosalind, I didn't desire Bettina.

What I needed to do was to imagine that I'd never met Bettina before, and forget about Rosalind and Dominic. I needed to recapture, not how I'd felt when I'd met Rosalind, but when I first saw Bettina at my first gramophone hosting evening. I thought that she was beautiful and self-assured, but actually out of my league. And, to think that beautiful Bettina, had asked me to take her to bed, but I'd turned her down. I could be described as…'Once a fool always a fool'– to have spurned her that night. Then, to be so angry with her over the interview with that scumbag journalist, Bolling, which had been perfectly understandable, to a certain degree, was completely over the top. Yes, I'd been an idiot and no wonder friends could see things that I'd been unable to see myself.

I telephoned Ronald first thing the following morning and said yes, I would travel with him to Ireland. I would take my chances with Bettina, and if she rejected me, I at least would have experienced the festival and heard a couple of operas that would have been new to me. Besides, although having lived and worked in Ireland's south-east, I'd never visited the beautiful west coast, which I'd heard so much about when I lived there.

Ronald was delighted that he managed to convince me that my interests would best be served by turning up unexpectedly at the festival to try to woo Bettina. Ronald had taken-on a smug, I-know-best tone of voice, when after I thanked him for having nudged me in the right direction, he replied, 'Yes, Alex, I knew you'd come around to my suggestion!'

'Look, Ronald, I'll pay for the airline tickets for us both, and also book the accommodation.'

'No, no, Alex, we'll share the costs between us. But once we're there I suggest we do our own thing, as I won't be interested in attending Halèvy's *La Juive*, but would probably book for more than one performance of Michael Tippett's '*New Year*.'

'OK, Ronald, I won't argue with you, but at least let me arrange the bookings?'

'I think we should get there soonest, Alex. How about travelling tomorrow?'

'I could do that, Ronald. I'll get on it as soon as we're off the phone. Please let me have your passport number so I can get us on a plane, tomorrow, if possible.'

Alex managed to get a flight to 'Knock' airport in County Mayo for the next day. They'd arrange a hired car on arrival at Knock. Accommodation, hopefully, could be sorted out once they arrived at the festival's campus.

The two friends set out for the west of Ireland the following morning.

CHAPTER 46

Lough Corrib Opera Festival

1994.

Bettina and Toby were sitting at a table in the festival bar, situated by the lake, and enjoying a drink, when two men walked up to the bar counter, ordering two pints of beer.

Toby nudged Bettina.

'Did you see the two men sitting with their backs to us at the bar counter enter the bar area?'

'No, I didn't.'

'Nor did I, but their backs look awfully familiar, or is it my imagination?'

Just then, one of the men turned around and caught Toby's eye. 'Bettina, look... the man at the bar is the spitting image of Ronald Henrow. Hang on, it is Ronald... what the hell is he doing here?'

The other man, having heard a familiar voice, turned around and saw them both – Toby and Bettina, sitting at the table with drinks in their hands.

'There they are, Ronald' – I was pointing to the pair – Bettina and Toby.'

Recognition of the others hit them all at the same time, and as Ronald and I jumped off the bar counter, Toby and Bettina came rushing towards us.

Hugs all round. Ronald and I were too excited to utter a word...
whilst Toby and Bettina were in complete shock.

Eventually, we all sat down together, and Ronald, for once in his life, was diplomatic,

'With Dulcie away with Verity, I thought I'd get over here to join you two, and get to attend the Michael Tippett opera. And then I thought I'd ask Alex to join me, him being such a keen opera lover... so here we are!'

I was impressed that Ronald hadn't embarrassed him by announcing the real reason they'd come.

Ronald said that they had managed to secure two single rooms at Renvyle House Hotel, as anything more local to the festival was unavailable.

'Oh,' piped-up Toby, 'both Bettina and I are staying there and it was more than fine, it is a terrific establishment in a most beautiful scenic location. I'll tell you what, though, I've got a large double room that I'm swimming around in, so if you fancy, you could bunk in with me, and save paying for two rooms, and book just one single room for Alex.

Ronald and I looked at each other and shrugged. 'I'd be happy to share with you, Toby, if you'd be happy with the single room, Alex.'

'Yes, of course. A single room is absolutely fine for me.'

There was method in Ronald's madness in agreeing to share a room with Toby. He'd thought it prudent to keep an eye on Toby, leaving the coast clear for me to stay close to Bettina. Although, he'd put the idea into my head that Toby would make a play for Bettina, whilst the two of them were here on their own, he'd never really believed that Toby would disrespect the terms of his invite, which had been as friends only. So why did he alert me to that possibility and why agree to share a room with Toby, when he would have preferred a room of his own?

Firstly, back in England, he'd needed a reason to persuade me to make the trip, and secondly, he couldn't be absolutely sure that at some stage during the festival, Toby wouldn't make a move on Bettina. Sometimes, the sexual urge was stronger than any moral resolve previously undertaken.

As it had been a musical event-free evening, the four of us had dinner together in the main restaurant of the festival, which was located in the original hotel building, overseen by the hosts and owners of the whole estate, May and Harvey Donnell. May was in charge of the kitchen and served fabulous food that was a combination of haute cuisine French and traditional Irish. Harvey looked after the bar and served the wine during dinner.

The conversation during dinner was on the first week of the festival and how much Bettina and Toby had enjoyed the operas, an orchestral concert and the general fun and friendly atmosphere around the whole enterprise, for which the Irish were past masters. Bettina didn't mention her distressing reaction to the initial performance of *La Juive* but talked about the second performance attended and how great the music was. Both were hugely enthusiastic about the concert the young student musicians gave, and raved about the cello playing of Helena Mentones performance of the Samuel Barber concerto. They were less gushing about the new opera by Timothy Seda, only saying that it had been interesting.

For the second week, they were looking forward to Tippett's opera and were especially excited about hearing Helena Mentones, perform the six cello suites of J S Bach over two daytime concerts.

The newcomers had been curious about the group of people who seemed to be the core team running the festival. Bettina explained that Stephen Zandors, the chief executive, was married to Helena Mentones, who also happened to be the daughter of the artistic director, the conductor, Simon Negrini. Simon's partner was the baritone, Dov Katz, who'd been the star singer at last year's inaugural festival, but was here this year just to support his partner.

Ronald announced that he'd booked two of the three performances of the Tippett, but would skip *La Juive*. He regretted missing Tippett's personal appearance at the festival and his morning lecture. Bettina and Toby looked a bit shamefaced as they hadn't attended the composer's lecture, but had seen the great man shuffling around the festival campus. However, they'd booked to attend a performance of the Tippett opera. I asked Bettina if she'd accompany me to a performance of *La Juive;* Bettina responded that she'd be more than happy to attend a further performance of the opera. We all agreed to attend the two Bach recitals of everyone's favourite cellist... Helena Mentones.

We all loved the Tippett opera, a youthful work from a man in his eighties, with a libretto that he'd written himself, as he'd done with his previous four operas. The drama had the strap-line, 'somewhere and today, nowhere and tomorrow.' It was about two worlds coming together, which included a space ship arriving on earth, the spaceman becoming involved with problematic characters in a difficult urban town. The eclectic score contained a mix of jazz, blues and dance music, all within a traditional classical orchestra that had Tippett's hallmark of lyrical ecstasy and rhythmic vitality.

The performance was brilliantly conducted by Simon Negrini, with love and care. Negrini and Tippett had known each other for many years, the conductor being determined to show his friend and mentor's opera in the best possible light.

Ronald had been so enthusiastic about the Tippett opera that besides the two performances he'd booked for, he'd also attended the final third one, in which the enthusiastic reception from the audience, at the operas conclusion, was particularly heart-warming. Although Tippett was on-hand for the final rehearsals of *New Year*, including the dress rehearsal, and was able to give Negrini as much help as he could deciphering his complicated score, he was unable to stay on at the festival for the actual three public performances.

I accompanied Bettina to her third, and to my first performance of the opera, *La Juive*. At last, Bettina and I were on our own, without one, or two, of the men with us. It had been several days of fun with the four of us together, attending festival events, enjoying excellent dinners and touring around the Connemara coast and countryside. This evening, though, I felt that I was actually on a date with Bettina for the first time since arriving at the festival. I was really looking forward to hearing *La Juive*, not having heard the opera before, even on a recording. Obviously, for Bettina, the opera was personal, and the odd hint I gauged from her was that the first performance in particular had been an emotional roller coaster for her. For me, it had always been an opera that I'd been curious about, and if it had had performances in London in recent years, I would have made an effort to hear it. Some European opera companies occasionally produced the opera, but regretfully, I'd let the opera pass me by.

From the off, I felt that the music was fabulous, up there with the finest French grand operas. The tenor singing the lead character of Eleazar was the artist famous world-wide in the role, Ned Schigott, who sang his famous Act Four aria *Rachel! Quand du Seigneur* with distinction. The role of Eleazar's daughter, Rachel, was sung by the English soprano, Jessica Fosters, who was excellent both in her singing and in her acting. The story of the opera about religious persecution in the late middle ages, and updated to the Nazi period in the current production, was certainly hard hitting, with a gruesome ending, but no more so than other popular operas in the repertory. In operatic terms *La Juive*, to my mind, was a neglected masterpiece,

Bettina, of course, being a descendant of the composer, was unable to judge the piece purely in a rational sense, especially with the Nazi period update, I knew little about Bettina's background, but I was aware that her grandparents and extended family members had been Holocaust victims.

I looked at Bettina in the darkened auditorium and saw the pained expression on her face, and my heart went out to her. I took hold of her hand and that seemed to calm her demeanour.

We took the early shuttle back to Renvyle, immediately following the end of the opera. Bettina was quiet on the bus, whilst I held her hand for most of the journey.

Back at Renvyle, we managed to get a table at the restaurant, and immediately ordered a couple of gin and tonics, and a bottle of red wine. We ate seafood cocktails and sirloin steaks.

Once we'd downed our gin and tonics and got stuck into the wine, we both started to unwind.

'So, Alex... what persuaded you to travel here for the festival?'

'Well, it was Ronald who put the idea into my head. He said that he was concerned that Toby would make a play for you whilst here together.'

Bettina looked bemused. 'I'm quite capable of saying "no" to Toby, or to anyone else, for that matter.'

'Well, to be fair to Ronald, he was thinking of me...'

'You...?'

I started to shift around on my seat. 'Ronald's raison d'être was that he thought that you and I were fated to be together, and he'd hate to see me mess up the opportunity.'

'Hmmm... I just don't get it. First of all, what did Ronald know about us two, other than we'd briefly known each other as youngsters? Secondly, whatever Ronald thought, and incidentally, Toby had said something similar to me last week, but you and I are basically ground zero, relationship wise.'

'Ah, yes, hmmm... I owe you an apology on two counts. I was a bloody fool the night of our dinner party, when I'd stupidly turned you down.'

Bettina retorted sharply, 'Well – you won't get another chance!'

Ignoring that remark, I continued in apology mode. I also completely overreacted to the journalist incident, as it was my fault that I forgot to mention the confidential clause to you.'

'Nevertheless, Alex I was wrong to tell the journalist, Bolling, what I did.'

'Could I make a suggestion, Bettina?'

Bettina nodded in assent.

'Let's join the reprobates in the main bar, where the singing manager of the hotel, Ken Moyle, holds court, and, entertains his followers, with singing, guitar and piano playing, as well reciting poetry. Some of the residents, once they've drunk enough alcohol will strut their stuff.'

'How do you know all that?'

'The other night, Toby dragged me in there when both you and Ronald went off to your respective rooms for an early night – we had the time of our lives, Toby even singing some Welsh folk tunes, to Ken Moyle's delight.'

Bettina gave me big smile. 'Well, Alex, we started off at a disco club in Brighton, let's move on from "ground zero" and join the... what you call "reprobates" and let our hair down, by joining in the Irish craic!'

I bought a bottle of champagne from the bar and they settled down to soak up the atmosphere of people gathered for a night of pure enjoyment.

Sipping the champagne and listening to Moyle singing a selection of Irish folk songs, accompanying himself on his guitar, Bettina and Alex started to let go of any misunderstandings that had come between them... the years fell away.

The bar began to get more raucous. Moyle's was upping the ante and encouraging participation from individuals around the room.

Maybe it was the champagne, on top of the wine and the gin, consumed earlier in the restaurant, I got Dutch courage, excusing myself from Bettina, walking towards Moyle, who'd just changed from playing the guitar to tickling the ivories, waiting for requests from guests who were looking for an opportunity to show off their vocal chords. When writing my novel, I'd got writer's block when I 'd come to converting Mozart's *Don Giovanni* into a believable contemporary narrative, so I'd amused myself by learning the famous comic aria, that the Don's servant, Leporello, sings to one of his master's conquests. The aria was known as the Catalogue Aria, *Madamina il catalogo e questo*. It lists the multiple conquests of the Don from one end of Europe to the other. I have a reasonable baritone voice; the aria's difficulties were not in the pitch, which was fairly straightforward, but rather the huge amount of words to memorise. As a patter aria, one was meant to almost swallow the words for comic effect. I learned the aria and then I got my mojo back to continue my writing, and never had a chance to perform the aria that I'd painstakingly learned.

I introduced myself to Ken Moyle and mentioned the opera *Don Giovanni.*

'Ah, yes, my favourite opera, I know all the arias.'

'What about the Catalogue aria, Ken?'

'I know it well. It's not difficult to accompany on the piano, but so many words.'

I briefly explained about my book and of learning the aria, which, until now, I'd never sang in public, but the words were fixed in my head.

Moyle looked at me with scepticism. 'Are you sure it's not just the drink talking, ha ha ha!'

I laughed with Moyle but said to him, 'Let's do it.'

I was amazed that Moyle, without fishing around for sheet music, knew the piano accompaniment straight off, whilst I launched into the aria. The noisy chatter around the room ceased immediately, as the crowd wondered if I'd anything to do with the opera festival over at Lough Corrib. I stumbled on a few words in the second part of the long aria, but overall it was decent rendition. The reception to my performance was warm and friendly, including a few cheers. Moyle shook my hand strongly and wouldn't let it go.

'Are you an opera singer as well as an author?'

I chuckled at the question. 'No. No, I'm definitely not a singer of any sort, except in my bathroom to myself!'

'What's the title of your book?'

'The book is titled *The Variations on Love*.'

'I must buy a copy, Alex.'

Walking back to where Bettina and I had been sitting, I was getting pats on my back from various people with remarks such as 'well done' and 'great performance.'

Bettina gave me a hug, saying, 'you do keep your light under a bushel.'

Well, that was the beginning and the end of my singing career, an absolute one off!'

'Let's get out of here,' Bettina whispered in my ear.

I took Bettina's hand, leaving the bar and going outdoors for a breath of fresh air.

It was a clear night sky with a slight breeze, making it a bit chilly. Bettina shivered, which prompted me to hug her tight.

I was feeling extremely lustful towards Bettina, but I wasn't sure how to approach it. I'd turned her down last time, so in no way would she risk being rejected for a second time. I would have to make the move, but it would be poetic justice for Bettina to get her own back and send me packing.

We'd come to a stalemate situation – the conversation had stalled.

'I think we should turn in.' Bettina breaking the silence, whilst freeing herself from my arms.

I nodded in assent as we moved back indoors and made our way slowly upstairs to our respective rooms.

Once in my room that I realised that I'd screwed things up. I sensed that we both wanted the same outcome for the night but neither of us wanted to make the initial move, fearing being spurned.

I sat for a few minutes thinking what to do about the impasse. There was only one solution – go to her room and if I was rejected, so be it, but at least I'd have tried. I knew her room number, as I'd escorted Bettina to it, before scuttling back to my own room with my tail between my legs.

 I took a deep breath, marching quickly out of the door before I could change my mind. I gave two sharp knocks on the Bettina's door. She came to open the door immediately and was, like me, fully clothed.

With a grin on her face, she said, 'What kept you? I knew you'd come...'

Falling into each other's arms, we continued the kiss that started thirty-four years earlier on Brighton beach.

But this wasn't the innocent sixteen-year old, Rosalind. Her sexual confidence was of a mature woman who knew all about the sex act in all their many varieties of bodily manoeuvres that would enhance feelings of desire and lust, leading to multiple orgasms.

Bettina took the lead and I happily went along with that dynamic, as I realised that my role would be the submissive to Bettina's dominant role.

As our sex together became passionate, and then even more passionate, I was astonished at how much we naturally made love, with no awkward corners to negotiate, as often happens when new lovers embark on a sexual relationship. Her instructions with descriptions in fruity language just built my desire for Bettina to greater heights.

Finally, after several false alarms, as we didn't want to stop being like Tristan and Isolde, as if we'd taken a potion that took us into a sphere that hovered between life and death, where nothing else mattered in the world except the two of us being lost in heightened ecstasy. We'd joined together to become one body, and then we let go, re-entering the world in a massive physical release.

We lay there, completely still, feeling deflated for a moment or two. Deflation had morphed into happiness when we realised what had just occurred.

I couldn't stop kissing and hugging Bettina, but we'd yet to utter a word to each other since awakening from our reverie.

I broke the silence. 'I just wanted it to go on forever.

'Bettina smiled. 'It could do, if that's what we both wanted.'

'I don't want anything else from life, except for us to make love together.'

'Yes, my darling Alex, I feel exactly the same.'

Following another long silence between us, both with our thoughts, was broken with my soliloquy...

'We share a similar story to the legend of Tristan and Isolde. They had had a past life together, having met again in completely different circumstances, with Isolde being full of recriminations towards someone who she'd once had strong feelings for, but then felt betrayed by Tristan. They took a potion that they thought was a suicide drink, but which had been switched to a love potion by Isolde's faithful companion Brangane, who'd understood that it hadn't been a betrayal at all, but a misunderstanding. Instead of dying together they'd become the most passionate lovers in the world, and only death would eventually separate the pair.'

'You're a real romantic... Alex. I never want to be with another man. You satisfy me like I've never been satisfied before.

When hearing those words it made me want to make love to Bettina again, immediately.

But I couldn't resist asking her what had changed her previous coolness towards me.

'Hmmm... You seemed a contradiction in so many ways that I couldn't decide about my feelings towards you. Before I knew about our past, when I first met you as Alex, I thought you a bit of a dull dog – a nice man but with little sex appeal. Later, when I read your book, I began to see you in a different light. Your novel was very sexy in parts, written with huge imagination and knowledge of Mozart's operas. Once we'd revealed ourselves to each other, everything became blurred and I couldn't work out my feelings towards you. It was like your Tristan and Isolde misunderstandings and recriminations. But when earlier last evening, when you had the courage to stand up in front of a room full of strangers to perform a very wordy aria from *Don Giovanni* in such an expressive way, I knew then that you'd hidden your true passionate nature behind a smokescreen of a Mr Ordinary.

'I matured as a sexual being when I met my husband, Peter. Before Peter, I'd thought of myself as someone who wasn't into sex as a major force in my life. Not exactly feeling asexual, and quite enjoying it when opportunities arose with different boyfriends. But it only played a minor part in my life and I never wanted to have children. Getting together with Peter changed all that. I'd become a passionate lover and that passion for sex with Peter remained throughout our time together. But – and this is a big but – Peter was a very dominant lover, which fitted his personality in life. To make sex work, as well as it did, between us, I had to negate my own sexual dominant natural role to accommodate Peter, and that I did willingly. But, immediately with you, Alex, I instinctively knew that your natural role would be submissive, and that released in me to be what I always knew I was ... in sexual terms anyway, which was a dominant.'

I listened to Bettina's 'stream of conscious' sexual narrative with absolute love and awe, at the way she expressed herself in sexual terms, without any embarrassment. I responded by admitting that I'd always known that my role in the sex act would be as a submissive. I never would have been a Don

Giovanni, or a lecherous Count in *Le Nozze de Figaro,* or even a young Cherubino, from the same opera, despite that my alter ego, Dominic, in the novel, who I'd cast as Cherubino. No, I knew from the time just after you and I met in Brighton that, unlike my friend Marcus, who was a born Don Giovanni replica, I'd always be the Leporello of the opera, singing of my master's conquests, but not copying them.'

'Alex, my love, every dominant must find their submissive, and I've found you, and I never want to lose you.'

Moving closer to me, Bettina, without saying a word, was telepathic in knowing that I was ready to make love again...

CHAPTER 47

'Let's get married, Bettina.'

'Is that a proposal, Alex?'

'Why, yes of course it's a proposal. Did you want me to go on my hands and knees?'

'Mmm, that would nice in the privacy of our bedroom... ha ha ha'

'We could get married here in Galway. I'm sure they have a registry office in the city.'

'Not so fast, lover boy. Whilst you were sleeping in late this morning, I've been ahead of the game. I already made up my mind that we'll get married here. I wasn't going to wait for you to ask, so I made some inquiries. I'm afraid it's not possible, as we'd need to give three months' notice at the registry office, and besides, we'd need our birth certificates which I'm sure you don't carry around with you and nor do I.

'Ha, well, it was a lovely idea Bettina.'

Later in the day, we bumped into Stephen Zandors in the festival bar. I hadn't at that stage been introduced to Zandors, so the usual formalities took place. Stephen had recognised the name, asking me, if, by any chance, I was the author of the recently published novel, *The Variations on Love*, that he was currently reading. When I responded in the affirmative, Stephen became hugely complimentary. Indicating his fascination with my ideas on updating Mozart operas, he considered inviting me to direct a production of one of the three Mozart/Da Ponte operas, if the festival ever got around to mimicking Glyndehurst Opera, and embarking on a Mozart opera series.

I was hugely flattered with Stephen's suggestion, which was something I'd never have considered. I assumed that directing an opera would be totally out of my league.

Holding hands with me, Bettina told Stephen about the pair's snap decision to marry. They thought that whilst staying in such beautiful surroundings, it would be fabulous to have the marriage ceremony, followed by a small celebration, whilst they were still in the west of Ireland. However, we'd be made to understand, that practically, it wouldn't be possible to arrange a snap marriage at Galway's registry office.

Stephen's reaction was heart-warming. Having never met me before, and only knowing Bettina mainly via telephone calls to invite her to the festival, he hugged us both as if we were family or close friends. He was genuinely really happy for us, remembering his own on and off relationship with his darling wife, Helena. He'd almost messed things up, but it all came together for them at last year's festival, when they'd decided to marry, making him the happiest man alive. He reckoned that it was a lucky omen, hearing about this lovely couple who'd wished to follow on from Helena's and his example, deciding to marry whilst attending the festival.

With a big smile on his face, Stephen said that he would do everything he could to help us in our beautiful quest.

'Do you mind if I ask, if either of you have any religious requirements?'

'Well, Stephen, said Bettina, you know, of course, that I have a Jewish background. But I'm now totally non-religious, although I'm still a proud Jew, both in historical and cultural terms. Unfortunately, I've been estranged from my parents, who live in Israel, since I married my first husband, who wasn't Jewish.'

I added, 'My background was typically middle-class English. My parents were regular churchgoers at our local parish church.'

'Which denomination was that?'

'Oh, it was the Church of England. Sadly, both my parents died, and I'm an only child. Anyway, like Bettina, I'm personally non-religious.'

'Thanks, both of you, for being so open about personal matters. Give me twenty-four hours and I will let you know what I can do.'

Once Stephen had left the bar, Bettina and I still holding hands, looked at each other. 'Phew, said Bettina, we hadn't expected that.'

Suddenly, the two missing friends, Toby and Ronald, sauntered into the bar, both looking chirpy. The first thing they noticed was that Bettina and I were holding hands. There was a knowing look between the two men.

'We haven't seen the two of you in the last couple of days. Had you deserted the festival?' I asked,

Toby replied, 'As we'd decided not to attend any events on the previous two days, we thought to do a bit of sightseeing. We drove down to Ennis, staying overnight there at a local hotel and explored the Burren, which was absolutely amazing. Its beguiling landscape is beautiful and majestic, with limestone pavements and curious rock formations in a unique ecosystem of native flowers and plants.'

'That sounds wonderful, Toby, but I thought you had tickets for the two morning recitals of Bach cello suites, being performed by Helena Mentones.'

Toby, looking a bit shamefaced, responded.

'You're right, we did have tickets for Mentones, but we both got cabin fever and wanted to escape the hothouse of the festival environment and see a bit more of this fascinating country. In any case, we gave the tickets back to the box office who were delighted to receive them as there was a waiting list for returns.'

Ronald, chipped in,' but we didn't take the money back that they offered as a refund, so the festival could sell them twice.'

'Fair enough, but you missed two fantastic recitals, Bettina exclaimed, getting her pence worth in the exchange.

'We realised that,' replied Toby. 'But to be honest, Mentones performs regularly at London's Wigmore Hall and we could hear her there, but I'm unsure as to whether we'd get another opportunity to see the unique Burren,'

Ronald was smirking, staring at us, as we had our arms around each other, and said in Ronald's non-diplomatic way...

'Let's not beat around the bush. Toby and I had decided to give you two a bit of space and by the looks of it we made the right decision... Ha ha ha.'

I thought, *trust Ronald to say it like it is*, but to be fair to him, it helped us that the two guys hadn't been around last night.

Stephen Zandors was back in the bar, coming directly over to Bettina and me. He seemed over excited, not the cool Englishman, his default pose.

'I've great news for you, and it has only taken an hour, not the twenty-four I said it would be. I spoke to the mayor of Galway, whom I've got to know well, since my time here. The same mayor who officially opened the festival, ten days ago. I put your dilemma to him and he's agreed for you to get married in Galway next Monday, the day after the finale of the festival. He'll need you to sign an agreement form that as soon as you get home to England, you'll both send a copy of your birth certificates to the mayor's office.'

Bettina and I looked at each other in astonishment, not uttering a word.

Stephen said, 'You haven't changed your minds, have you?'

We both spoke at the same time, almost shouting, 'Of course not.' And in a quieter voice Bettina added, 'We're overwhelmed by your kindness to us and can't thank you enough.'

Stephen waived his hands, saying, 'It was my pleasure and your wedding would be a fitting finale, following the gala night official conclusion, to this year's festival.

Bettina kissed Stephen on his cheek, saying, we'll be forever grateful to you, Stephen.'

Toby and Ronald were standing there in amazement watching and listening to the exchange between their friends and the chief executive of the festival. Their decision to leave the festival temporarily, to give Bettina and me a chance to repair our previous estranged relationship, without them being under our feet, had been more successful than they could ever had imagined.

CHAPTER 48

Everything moved swiftly from the moment Stephen Zandors had given them the green light to go ahead with their marriage plans. At first we thought that it would be just the two of us, with Toby and Ronald, present, if of course, they'd be happy to change their travel plans, to stay on, for at least another couple of days, after the end of the festival.

Toby and Ronald had other ideas. Ronald, in particular, felt really pleased with himself, as without his somewhat awkward telephone call to me, the exciting development between us would not have occurred.

Toby took charge of the telephone calls. His plan was to get as many friends as possible to travel to Ireland for the celebrations, but realising, that everyone would have to change their immediate plans, to get over there in time.

The obvious first call was to his wife, Verity, who'd returned, with Dulcie, from their stay at the health hydro. Verity was very excited to hear the news, confirming that of course she'd come, and would get on to Dulcie straight after the call. Toby wanted as many gramophone club members as possible to be there, but wondered whether Verity would be okay if he included Hannah in the invites. Verity, good egg as she was, was fine about Hannah.

When Verity telephoned Dulcie, she already knew about the wedding, as Ronald had called. Dulcie added that she'd suggested to Ronald, that except for Hannah, the two of them would contact the gramophone members to save the men phoning them from Ireland.

When Ronald told Toby that the wives would take care of the gramophone members, Toby, wondered who else they could invite. He remembered that he had the contact details of Marcus Elliot, in America, and knowing it was a long shot, made the long-distance call.

I was on cloud nine, feeling a happiness I thought would never happen to me. The one sad thing was that as both my parents were dead, with no siblings, and only a few cousins who I had never been close to, I didn't have family to share the good news with.

I wanted Toby as my best man, but realised that I owed Ronald big time, for his unlikely initiative in setting me on this romantic journey. I decided that I'd ask them both to be joint best men. I'd need a ring, and would take Bettina to the local town of Clifden where I believed there was a jewellery shop, and hoped that they'd have something suitable.

Bettina had been thinking about her parents, her mother, in particular, who'd given young Dominic short shrift all those years ago. What would she say, if she told her that the same young man and her were about to get married. But she just couldn't do it; the Jewish question would arise again and she'd get upset. Bettina didn't want anything to impede her deliriously happy state of mind. But she did pluck up courage to make the call to New York to tell her brother the good news, and about the man she was marrying.

Bettina also telephoned her office in London to let them know that her return to work had been delayed, mentioning casually that the reason she was staying on in Ireland was to get married. She could hear the excitement her news had generated amongst her colleagues.

Her two closest assistants inquired as to whether they could fly over to Ireland to attend the wedding. Bettina was at first reluctant, wondering as to whether to business could cope with the three of them being away at the same time. Her colleague convinced her that the newer staff recruits, were now up to speed, and could handle anything that was thrown at them.

The numbers were building, and when Zandors had become aware that the guest list was going to be more than one or two, and they'd also have to include the Galway Mayor, and his wife, amongst the guests, he realised that it wouldn't be possible to hold the party at the Donnells small establishment. Besides the public areas not being big enough, the guests would require accommodation, and the Donnell's wouldn't have enough rooms. The party would have to take place at the Renvyle House Hotel. He'd have a word with his good friend, Ken Moyle, the manager at Renvyle, and hopefully, Ken would be able to accommodate the guests and organise the party. Stephen knew that Ken was the host par excellence, and that sort of spontaneous event was right up his street.

When everything had been arranged, Stephen called a meeting with us updating the situation.. The registry office formalities had to be a private affair, with a maximum of two guests. He checked that a ring had been purchased. The wedding party would be held at Renvyle and Ken Moyle would be 'master of ceremonies.' He had enough available rooms to accommodate about twenty people, but if the numbers were more than that, he'd be able to arrange extra accommodation in the nearby village of Tully Cross. Stephen suggested that they should extend an invitation to May and Harvey Donnell, who obviously wouldn't require accommodation; nor would Mr and Mrs Mayor, for that matter...

Stephen continued, 'Helena and I have a house in Tully Cross, and we'd be happy to stay on an extra night in the house, to attend the wedding party. But we'd be off to London early the following morning, and both Helena and I would be happy for the two of you to stay at our house for a few days after the wedding, if you'd like the idea of a bit of peace and quiet, following the festivities. Unfortunately, Helena father, Simon Negrini, and his partner, Dov Katz, had engagements in London, following the festival's final day, so they wouldn't be able to attend. Alas, as Negrini, was Helena's piano accompanist, she'd only be able to play solo cello, which would be unsuitable repertory for a party. However, Moyle's had arranged for a local band to play, folk and pop music. Finally, Moyle had said that you didn't have to pay anything upfront. He'd post out to your English address, a fully itemised invoice following the event.

Bettina and I were stunned that Zandors had gone to so much trouble on their behalf, and had even offered them his house to stay in. The feeling was that they'd made a friend for life, and as long as Lough Corrib Festival survived, they'd be there every September.

The first to arrive at Lough Corrib were Verity and Dulcie, followed by Greg and Florence Witton. Not far behind were Hildegard and Benjamin Tiller. Violet Smithson and Dorothy Bateman came together and would be happy to share a room. Hannah Longsmith arrived with her American male friend, who no one had ever met before. She introduced him as Franklin Houseman. Toby was relieved that Hannah had the wit to bring Franklin with her, so Verity wouldn't feel uncomfortable. It showed a bit of class on Hannah's behalf.

Bettina's oldest friend, Denise Conway, who Bettina wouldn't have even considered not inviting, arrived and the two friends couldn't stop hugging each other. Bettina's two colleagues from work were next to turn up. They also would share a room.

Everyone had been seriously instructed not to buy or bring any presents. They'd all agreed, but secretly, the gramophone members had their own ideas about presenting the couple with a group gift when back in Hertfordshire.

As a total surprise, Bettina's brother, Cedric, had flown into Shannon, hiring a car to drive up to Connemara. Brother and sister hardly recognised each other, as it had been so many years since they'd been together. They spend time catching up with all the missing years. Bettina explained who the groom was, that he was the same person our mother had given marching orders to, the young man she'd met in Brighton all those years before. Cedric admitted that he was separated from his wife, but still saw his children regularly. He also explained that he had lost his religious beliefs, but hadn't the courage to tell mum and dad, or that he was separated from his wife. He admitted that he was a coward, but countered the self-criticism to say that their parents were both in poor health, and that Bettina should make her peace with them before it was too late.

Bettina thought that she'd have to ask Zandors as to whether they could bring one more person to the registry office, as she had to have her brother beside her. She didn't want to choose, either, between Toby and Ronald. Both men deserved to be there.

Just as Bettina was feeling a bit sad for me, who, besides the gramophone crew, I hadn't any long-term friends, or family, attending... the three musketeers, friends that I had known for a very long time, arrived from the US.

I was absolutely gobsmacked, but totally delighted, to meet them so soon again, Marcus Elliot, Roger Garland and Charles Farley. They explained that Toby, who somehow got Marcus's telephone number, when they'd been recently at Alex's revelatory gramophone event, gave Marcus the great news, and when Marcus shared the news with the others, they made a snap decision to fly over and join in the celebrations.

Marcus asked me,' So, Alex, who's the bride?'

 I'd momentarily forgotten that Bettina wasn't at the event and the friends knew nothing about Bettina's connection to the Brighton days.

'Well, what I'm about to reveal will surprise you all, but especially Marcus.'

The men were all ears, and I had come to the conclusion that all my previous concerns about not revealing the autobiographical aspects of my novel, was nonsense. I couldn't believe that I'd badly fallen out with my beloved, because of that concern. The self-imposed ban on revealing the second coming of Bettina and me was well and truly over.

'Do you remember, Marcus, when we first travelled to Brighton during 1960, and we went our separate ways on the first night there? I went to a disco club and met a girl I was keen on, and we'd planned to meet again the following day. But, when I arrived back at our bed and breakfast that night full of excitement at having met the girl of my dreams, you poured cold water on my romantic nature, telling me, that at my age I should be playing the field, not setting my sights on having a regular girlfriend. Anyway, you said, quite aggressively, that I couldn't spend the next day with the girl, because you'd promised to visit your friend Roger Garland, aka Finley, who'd needed your help, and I had to go with you.

'That sounds like an early chapter in your novel, Alex, except the names are different.'

'Yes, of course they are. The early chapters in my book are pure autofiction. In real life what I just said actually happened.'

'Okay, so did you ever see the girl again?'

'No, I did not in the novel, but in real life, I did. The girl turned out to be a current member of the gramophone club, under a different name. That's the woman I'm marrying, the very same person I'd originally met at that disco club, when she was aged sixteen, and I was aged seventeen.

Just then, Bettina sauntered up to us, with me making the introductions.

The three men just stood there, opened mouth, not believing that such a thing was possible in real life. Coincidences like that just didn't happen, except in fantasy stories, but of course, it had happened and in a couple of days we'd be husband and wife.

Zandors had checked with the mayor, and he gave the all clear for one extra person to attend the registry office.

Although we hadn't intended to attend the festivals final concert, the gala night, Stephen said that he'd like to introduce us to the audience at the end of the evening. We weren't that keen, but felt that we couldn't say no to Stephen, as he'd given up his precious time to arrange the whole wedding for us. To spice things up, I related the story of our meeting that had been a replica of an early part of the novel, and the coincidence of us meeting again. Stephen, being an opera man through and through, which was full of outlandish plots, had thought that nothing could surprise him, but our story really did, and he was speechless.

On the gala night, we didn't sit through the concert, having dinner instead. But not to disappoint Stephen we slipped into the back of the stalls at the end of the concert, during the various thank you speeches. When the time came, he asked us up onto the stage, and introduced us to the audience. He then spoke about Bettina being a descendant of Halèvy, the composer of the festivals great success, the opera *La Juive*. He turned to me and spoke in glowing terms about my book, recommending it highly to the audience. Finally, with our permission, he related the events of our initial meeting, as set out in the novel, which was in fact, the real-life story, and our subsequent meeting again, by pure chance, in later life. The audience had seemed fascinated by our story and that fascination turned to cheering and foot stamping when Stephen finished, by announcing, that we were getting married the next day... here in beautiful Connemara.

We both came away feeling very flattered that Stephen had used his platform to highlight our story; it was a perfect eve of wedding night.

CHAPTER 49

THE WEDDING

The five of us arranged for a car to take us to the registry office the next morning. The short non-religious ceremony was conducted by a young friendly official, with the mayor standing in the background. We signed various documents including the agreement to send them a copy of our birth certificates. Ronald did the honours of handing the ring to me, and I put it on Bettina's finger at the appropriate moment. It was the perfect fit. Following a few homilies by the official about love and marriage, he pronounced us man and wife, and I kissed the bride. With congratulations, kisses and hugs, thanking the official and the mayor, we made our way back to Renvyle House Hotel, where the celebrations were awaiting us.

The party was high octane from the off. Although, it some ways, we'd preferred to have had the party at the main house of the festival, with its quirky elegance, Renvyle House was actually the venue which should have had the tag-line, 'the fun palace' attached to it. Ken Moyle, the manager, was a born host. His whole raison d'etre in life was to make people happy. Moyle was overseeing everything with an eye for even the smallest detail.

We'd decided not to have a sit-down meal, being too formal for the type of party we wanted. The finger food that Renvyle's kitchen served was outstanding and there was plenty of it. We'd ditched the idea of fancy over-sweet cocktails and stuck with vintage champagne and top-quality wines.

Moyle couldn't resist being part of the entertainment, moving his piano from the bar to the party room, playing popular Irish tunes mixed with well-known show number. Later on, the local band took to the stage to get the guests dancing. The music was disco oriented, the usual suspects for the occasion, encouraging a sing along. The band kept the volume at a level, where it didn't kill conversation. or blast ear drums.

We'd banned speeches, even the traditional best man and groom response ones.

However, I took to the floor to the thank everybody for making the effort, at such short notice, to attend the celebrations and share in Bettina's and my happiness. I thanked the mayor for being extremely helpful in arranging the Galway wedding; I made special mention of thanking the transatlantic visitors, Cedric Gerstein, Bettina's brother and my own long-time friends, Marcus Elliot, Roger Garland and Charles Farley. I made a special mention of Ronald Henrow, that was responsible for pushing me in Bettina's direction at the crucial moment. I finished by reiterating our no-present policy, and said that Bettina and I had decided that we'd take care of all our guests' hotel bills up until tomorrow, (knowing that some of our friends would be staying on for a few more days to explore glorious Connemara.) Last but not least, I said how grateful we'd always be to Stephen Zandors, who, without his incredible help, the wedding would not have been able to take place in Galway and Connemara.

Bettina and I had decided to take up Stephen and Helena's very generous offer to stay on in the area for a week in their house in nearby Tully Cross, which was set in a scenic outlook of outstanding natural beauty.

As the party started to wind down, the mayor and his wife, the Donnell's and the Zandors having already said their goodbyes and had departed, we thought to let our friends carry on partying as we quietly slipped away. I took hold of Bettina's hand as we climbed the stairs to our bedroom, to make love for the first time as man and wife.

D B Minter
Aldeburgh, Suffolk. 09 04 2025
The book is published by HAMDEN LTD

Anthony Holden's book "The Man Who Wrote Mozart" (2006) was a great source of information about the extraordinary life of Lorenzo Da Ponte.

The Royal Opera House, English National Opera and Glyndebourne Festival Opera programme notes were helpful in setting the texts for the three Mozart opera plot summaries.

All the characters in the novel are fictional, except for passing references to various musicians and artists, past and present. The book also contains references to certain institutions, hotels, clubs, restaurants, retailers and historical events.

About the author

The Little Red Book is the second of the trilogy of novels by D B Minter. The novels have links to famous operas from the past, where the updated dramatic narrative of mystery, romance and fantasy that D B creates – uncannily correspond with the opera plot.
The first novel, The Incidental Legacy of Carlo Negrini, published in 2024, referenced the Verdi opera, *Simon Boccanegra* from 1857, revised in 1881 with a text by Arrigo Boito. Following on from The Little Red Book, the third and final novel of the trilogy will feature the opera partnership of the composer Richard Strauss, and the poet/librettist Hugo von Hofmannsthal.

D B Minter was born in the county of Hertfordshire, England, and is currently a resident of Aldeburgh, Suffolk. During the 1970s and the 1980s D B lived and worked in Dublin, Ireland, where he met his wife, Deirdre.
A proud father and grandfather, D B and Deirdre enjoy exploring the beautiful coast and countryside of Suffolk together, as well as attending concert and opera performances. At home, listening to music, reading books and creating delicious meals, are their preferred leisure activities.